a sweet celebrity romance

Awestruck

DANA LECHEMINANT

ISBN: 978-1-965106-14-3
First Print Edition: October 2025
Bow and Arrow Press

To the girls who make the world a better place:
you'll always be a princess at heart

Awestruck:
filled with amazement and respect

Hollywood Hot Scoop

Bad Bodyguard Bounces Yet Again: Freya's Protection Problem

SCOOPERS, I KNOW YOU, like me, have been anxiously awaiting Princess Freya Alverra's ascension to the crown, but it looks like our favorite royal has bigger problems than choosing her coronation gown: her game of real-life bodyguard musical chairs.

After yet another exit from Candora's most important post, we're starting to wonder if the problem is the hires...or the hiree herself. I'm not one to criticize, but it's looking like there's a common denominator here, and it's not the string of hunky men coming in and out of the palace. Is Her Royal Highness too picky, or is it that no one can actually stand to spend longer than a few hours with her?

Sure, Freya has Derek Riley in her corner, but let's be real here. The guy's too good to ghost anyone. Even a princess. Could it be that our hometown hero is trapped in his friendship with the high and mighty Freya Alverra? Derek, if you're reading this, blink twice if you need an easy out! I'll gladly come to your rescue!

None of the rest of the Glam Gang (Freya's celeb besties, for our new followers) are talking, which isn't surprising. I, for one, wouldn't know how to explain someone failing eight times to find a glorified babysitter! We can only hope that once she's crowned queen—*if* she's crowned—Freya keeps to her own country and sets her collection of Americans free, letting them live their lives in peace for once.

Word on the street is Freya's newest bodyguard is set to take on the daunting task in the next week or two, only weeks before Candora's upcoming royal election, so make sure you subscribe if you want a front row seat to the train wreck that is surely on its way! XO

CHAPTER ONE

FREYA

IN ALL MY YEARS of preparing to become a queen, I never thought it would be an American to stand in my way. Literally.

"Mr. Reid." My voice is laced with irritation, and it is far too early in the day for that. "Is there any particular reason you are blocking the doorway?"

Reid's expression does not shift a millimeter. As I have quickly come to learn is his way, he keeps his gaze just over my head so he looks *over* me rather than *at* me. "My apologies, Your Highness, but I am following orders."

"Whose orders?" They certainly were not mine.

"Her Majesty has directed me to—"

"Mum," I grumble under my breath. What is she up to? Standing on my toes, I try to bring myself higher so Reid is forced to look me in the eye, but his gaze simply rises along with me. "Have you forgotten that you work for me now, Mr. Reid?"

There. The slightest twitch of his mouth, though I could hardly call it a smile. This man has been training under my old bodyguard for the last

month, and I have yet to see him smile once. If I did not trust my friend
Derek with all my heart, I would not have agreed to give Reid a chance as
my personal protection officer based on the little I know about him. His
American nationality, rather than being a native Candoran, is difficult
enough to stomach—such a break from tradition will not sit well with
the people—but if I am to endure his aloof stoicism for the unforeseeable
future, I will be seeking out an alternative within the month.

Eight bodyguards in the last year. Eight failures. Eight reasons to
wonder if having protection is as necessary as the Royal Council seems
to think. It is not as if I leave the palace to begin with.

"With all due respect, Your Highness," Reid says to the air above my
head, "my position as your protection agent doesn't go into effect until
after the Council Meeting this afternoon."

I wonder how he manages to show no emotion like that. I am practiced in keeping my expressions muted, but I have never been able to hide
everything I feel. It is a sore subject for my mother, who has spent the last
fifteen years as Candora's reigning monarch and is all things royal and
respectable.

She blames my inability to fully school my features on my attachment
to Derek Riley and the other American friends I have grown close to over
the last few years. She is as attached to Derek as I am, but her argument
remains. Because of them, I am not entirely the proper princess I should
be.

Folding my arms, I drop back to my sensible heels, noting the way
Reid's gaze dips with me. He is disciplined, I will give him that, but I
require far more than discipline in a bodyguard. "You are aware that you
are currently *preventing* me from attending that Council meeting, yes?"

He nods. "Yes, Your Highness."

Behind him stand the large wooden doors to the conference room,
where I am certain the entire Council is already gathered, along with the
king and queen.

"Why am I not allowed inside?" I ask Reid.

He tightens his jaw and says nothing.

My irritation only rises. "You have only been in my country for five weeks and are already loyal to the queen? I thought you Americans were generally more willful than this."

"Oi, best not insult the man's pride and joy," a voice says behind me. "Elliot gets touchy about his patriotism."

Rolling my eyes, I turn to greet my younger brother, unsure which one he is until I see him. "Hex." He and Sander, his twin, sound eerily alike, and most people cannot distinguish between the two. Even I sometimes have trouble. I suspect my brothers make it difficult on purpose; though twenty-seven years old, they have yet to mature into sensible adults.

To my surprise, Hex throws an arm around Reid's shoulder and faces me. The bodyguard hardly reacts, but there is a new light in his eyes. "My darling sister," Hex says with a condescending tone he has perfected solely for me, "surely you know better than to speak poorly of the land of the free. The home of the brave."

Reid clears his throat and ducks away from Hex's arm. He tugs on his suit to straighten it, then returns to his stiff stance, a hand locked on the other wrist in front of him and eyes on the corridor behind me. "You are supposed to be in your fencing lesson, Prince Hendrik."

Hex scoffs and leans against the wall, arms folded and one leg crossed over the other. He looks very much like me, blond hair and blue eyes, but his bearing is entirely different from mine. Sometimes I envy his ability to be casual, but I would never give up my chance to be queen and lead my people. Hex and Sander have no aims for the throne, and their carefree natures reflect that. I do not have the same luxury.

"It's no fun sparring with anyone but you," Hex says. He looks at me. "Did you know Elliot is a fencing master, Fringe?"

I narrow my eyes at the nickname, but I am more concerned with the familiarity between the man who is supposed to be my bodyguard—not for another hour, apparently—and a prince of Candora. "I was not aware," I say slowly, studying Reid carefully. There is a tightness around his eyes, and I would guess he knows he is out of line by sparring with my brother when, as my bodyguard, he is about to become one of the most important people in the country.

As it seems I am not permitted to attend the Council today, perhaps I could use Hex's presence to learn a little more about the man before me. I have not had the opportunity since his arrival last month, which has frustrated me to no end. "You were a soldier prior to your appointment, were you not, Mr. Reid?"

He stands a little taller. "Yes, Your Highness. Sergeant First Class in the 10th SFG Second Battalion. Special Forces."

I do not know what that means—Candora has been fortunate in avoiding wartimes for the past two generations—but I nod as if I understand. "Is fencing a common practice among the Special Forces in America?"

Another ghost of a smile twitches at the corner of his lips. "No, ma'am."

"Then where is it you learned to—"

"*Vitte*, Freya," Hex says. He flinches when I glare at him for using the Candoran curse. "Do you need to interrogate the man? Gregor has already spent the last month questioning him. I think you can trust he's not here to take down the monarchy."

I had not considered such a thing, but now that thought is in my head. *Thank you for that, Hex.* "I am not interrogating him," I argue. "I was only curious. Considering his upcoming position, I am allowed curiosity."

For the first time since my arrival outside the conference room, Reid's eyes slip down to mine. The shock of his sudden focus hits me like the zap of a static charge, but the eye contact lasts only a moment, then he is back to watching the corridor. This is the first time I have been close to the man, and I am surprised by the color of his eyes. Dark amber, like the sap of the evergreen trees that grow in the mountains on the north end of our island. It is not a color I have seen in someone's eyes before, and the warmth of it is in direct contrast to the detached personality he has.

A personality he has except with my brother, it seems. Have both my brothers sparred with him? Sander is less enthusiastic about weaponry, but his skills nearly match those of Hex. And those of Sergeant Elliot Reid, apparently. Why have I not seen them fencing together?

Ah, yes. Because Mum has been extra diligent in my tutelage lately, which only makes my current predicament more frustrating. Confusing.

"Is there a reason you and Elliot are standing out in the corridor, Fringe?" Hex asks, finally realizing where we are. "I thought you had a fancy meeting."

"I do have a meeting," I reply, silently willing Reid to look at me again. I doubt he would be able to hold fast to his orders if he deigned to look me in the eyes when he told me I was not allowed inside the room behind him. "But *Elliot* will not let me in."

I hoped using his first name would draw on the camaraderie he shares with my brother. While it does gain the bodyguard's attention, pulling his eyes back to me, his stance only grows more imposing. I did not think that was possible, given his impressive size to begin with. Reid certainly has the build of a bodyguard, with shoulders broad enough to intimidate anyone who might cross him.

"I'm afraid I can't let you in, Your Highness," he says, eyes still locked on me.

Vitte, his gaze is strong. Perhaps his tendency to look above me is for the best, as I feel every second of his notice.

Swallowing, I dig deep into myself for the confidence that has been slipping for the last several minutes, ever since he first blocked my entry. "Mr. Reid, I demand that you allow me to pass."

He smiles.

No, that is the wrong word. Only one side of his mouth lifts, and there is no sense of kindness to the expression. It is a *smirk*. He is *smirking* at the crown princess! I am appalled by his audacity.

"My apologies, Princess," he says, as if reading my thoughts. "But I can't obey."

Hex snickers, glancing between the two of us. "Careful, El," he mutters. "You do not want to see Freya when she is angry."

"Oh, he is *El* now, is he?" I glare at my brother, though I cannot remember the last time I intimidated either him or Sander. Despite being six years my junior, they have seen too many of my blunders and teenage missteps to take me seriously. "Mr. Reid is not here to be your friend, Hex."

Hex doesn't flinch. "No, apparently he's here to keep you out of your meetings."

Reid clears his throat. "I don't mean to frustrate you, Your Highness."

I do not believe that for a second. Not when there is still a shadow of that smirk on his lips as he continues to watch me. Why is it now that he has looked at me he does not look away? The depth of his gaze is unnerving.

I am not the type of person to be unnerved.

"But really," Hex says, frowning now. "Why are you outside?"

"Her Majesty has decreed it," I grumble.

Glancing at the door, Hex lifts an eyebrow. "Mum's keeping you out?"

"She didn't tell me her reasons," Reid says.

I glare at *him* now. "Could you not have said as much earlier?"

Oh, that smirk is going to frustrate me to no end, and he seems to know it. I do not know whether it is Hex's influence or the fact that this is my first real conversation with my new bodyguard, but Elliot Reid is coming to life as he silently laughs at my growing anger. "I figured it wouldn't help the situation," he says lightly. "Again, my apologies."

"Being sorry does not justify a wrongful action," I warn him. "If you intend to keep your position—which you do not yet have, as you have said—then you should learn to keep your opinions to yourself, Mr. Reid."

He dips his head so slightly that it almost feels like an insult rather than a gesture of agreement. "I will take that into consideration, Your Highness." Then he grins at me. The expression only lasts long enough for me to make note of it before he is back to standing stalwart at his post, his eyes fixed over my head. "In my defense, none of my actions have been wrongful. I've followed orders, nothing more."

In all the failed candidates for the position of my bodyguard, I have not once encountered insubordination like this. Although, that is not quite what this is. He is faithfully following my mother's orders, and as she outranks me, I cannot be angry with him for that. But I *can* be angry for his disrespect. His amusement at my expense. His...*sass*. The last thing I need is a bodyguard who will talk back to me and treat me like a child when he is several years my junior.

How old is he? I learned the information when he first arrived, but the last month has kept me too busy to remember. Twenty-six? That sounds right. When Derek first recommended the soldier to me, I nearly laughed when I discovered his age. Surely he is too young, both to have so many accolades and to be responsible for my life. But résumé assured me Sergeant Reid was the best of the best, and I trusted my friend. Reid's résumé is, in a word, impressive, assuming it is all accurate, but I would have thought Derek recognized my need for a personality that would match mine. That has been ninety percent of the battle in finding a bodyguard who fits.

Whoever becomes my protection agent in a more permanent capacity will be with me at all hours of the day. He will be privy to my every moment, good and bad. A snarky ex-soldier who is younger than my immature brothers and finds amusement in my frustration is likely to drive me mad before I ever ascend to the throne.

"So," Hex says, once again glancing between the two of us. "Does this mean you're stuck here and therefore not available for a quick match, El?"

Reid's eyes narrow. "As long as your sister wants to get into the conference room, yes. I'll be here."

An unladylike groan slips out of me, and I take several steps back as embarrassment fills my face with heat. I turn before I can see Reid's reaction to the sound, pulling my phone from the pocket of my slacks. Hex happily starts chatting with Reid, so I hope my conversation is relatively private. Just in case, I take a few more steps down the hall as I pull up Derek's number and hit the dial button. If I go too far, I worry Reid will follow.

"Hey, Peach." To my relief, Derek answers. It is always a gamble with him. As one of the most sought-after actors in Hollywood, he has a lot of people eager to take his time, and it is early in California. "What's up?"

"'What's up?'" I repeat. "What is up is you are clearly determined to drive me to insanity."

He chuckles. "Elliot started today, didn't he?"

The fact that he so easily guesses the source of my frustration does not bode well for Reid's future career in Candora. "You knew he would get on my nerves?"

"I knew he would keep you on your toes, but that's not the same thing. Aren't you supposed to be in a meeting right now?" Leave it to Derek to know my schedule as well as he knows his own.

I grip my phone tighter, glancing behind me to make sure Reid and Hex are still occupied. Reid's impressive resume included the ability to speak several languages, as well as read lips. I wish I could remember which languages he speaks, as that would make this conversation easier to hide.

Turning so my back is once again facing Reid, I switch from English to Russian. I would speak Candoran, as Derek is fluent in the language as well as others, but I would not be surprised if Reid has picked up on enough over the last month to get by. "He has not even started as my bodyguard, and I already want to dismiss him."

After a pause, Derek responds with near perfect Russian. "It's that bad, huh?"

"I do not think your *friend* has the right temperament for a protection officer, Derek Riley, and I fear I may need to begin questioning your judgment."

"You should do that anyway, Peach."

He says that, but in the seven years I have known this man, he has never once been wrong. Remembering that, I sigh and tell myself to take a calming breath. I switch back to English; Derek's Russian is better than mine, and hopefully I am done complaining. "Do you really think Reid is a viable candidate?"

"Yeah, I do. But it's also not my decision on whether he stays or goes. That's on you, and he knows this is a trial run."

That is comforting, and I am sure Gregor told Reid as much when he first arrived. It has been the same with all of them.

As if sensing my thoughts, Derek asks, "What does Gregor think of him?"

I sigh. "This is the only man he has spent more than a couple of weeks with. I think Gregor practically views him as a second son."

That gets Derek laughing, which I should have expected. Gregor likes no one, but I spoke true. My old bodyguard has had nothing but praise for the ex-soldier. "Give Elliot some time, Freya. Like you said, he hasn't even started."

"Started as my bodyguard, no, but he has certainly begun getting on my nerves."

"He's good at that."

"How, exactly, do you know a Sergeant First Class in the Special Forces?" I ask. Derek has a habit of collecting friends and contacts all over the world, from all walks of life and levels of fame and influence, but from what I know about Reid, he has spent the last half a decade overseas. It seems unlikely that an actor and a soldier would become close friends or even meet.

Derek hums, as if thinking about how he wants to answer that question. "I don't remember," he says after a moment.

"Lies," I reply without hesitation. He does not generally keep secrets from his friends, and I am curious why he would try now. "The truth, Riley."

"He's my cousin."

"Oh." Those words hit me with more force than I expect. Derek rarely speaks of his family. I have only heard him mention his parents once or twice over the years I have known him, and I did not realize he had any relatives beyond them. "Derek, why did you not say in the beginning?"

I turn to look at Reid once more, and suddenly the similarities are obvious. Perhaps that is because Reid is actually smiling. Not smirking, like he did with me, but smiling wide as Hex talks with wild hand gestures. The way Reid's smile twists up at an angle is very much like Derek's smile. Though Reid's face has softer edges, there is something in the shape of his eyes that reminds me of Derek's as well. Most likely Reid comes from Derek's mother's side, but as there is no quicker way to convince Derek he needs to end a conversation than to bring up his parents, I cannot know for sure.

"I don't like nepotism," Derek says after a long moment of silence. "You know how it is."

I do. While I have a birthright to the throne, Candora will hold monarchical elections in September, only a few weeks from now. If the people decide I am not suitable to be their queen, they will choose someone else to wear the crown. In the history of Candora, the Alverra family—my family—has always held the monarchy seat, but that could change. If my people do not want me as their leader, I will accept their decision because one's parentage should not qualify them for power.

While unlikely, that chance is always there.

I firmly believe I am the best choice for my country, but deep down I have always harbored a fear that I am not enough. That I have not proven myself worthy of the people's support.

"I wish I had known about your relation to Mr. Reid," I tell Derek. "If he is your family, then I am certain he is a good man."

"I hope that was never in question. But if he steps out of line, you're more than welcome to send him packing."

I snicker, allowing a smile despite this revelation complicating matters going forward if Reid *cannot* learn to fall in line. Derek may say the choice of keeping Reid is up to me, but now I will be worried about disappointing one of my dearest friends. "If he possesses even half of your stubbornness, Derek Riley, then we are going to have a problem."

A throat clears behind me, and I startle, spinning around to find Reid standing mere inches away from me. This is the closest I have ever been to the man, and he is tall enough that my eyes are suddenly fixed on the way his arms fill the sleeves of his suit. The way the buttons on his white shirt strain with every breath he takes. Yes, he indeed has the muscular build of a competent protector.

"Sorry to interrupt," he says, nodding to the phone in my hand. "You're needed in the conference room."

I blink. After the way he kept me out, I did not expect to set foot in that room today. "Oh. Really?"

He nods once. "Tell Derek I say hi."

Derek laughs. "Good luck, Peach." He hangs up before I can say anything.

Reid steps to the side, holding out an arm toward the now-open door of the conference room. Several pairs of eyes are looking out at me, waiting for me to join them. Hex has disappeared, which does not surprise me. He and Sander avoid politics whenever possible.

I take a deep breath and stand a little taller. "Thank you," I tell Reid, not certain he deserves it. But I am Princess Freya Alverra, heir to the Candoran throne, and I am nothing if not polite. Though he bestows me with another amused smile, I hold my head high and practically march into the conference room.

My eyes land first on Dad and the way he looks uncomfortable, which does not bode well for me, but then I look at Mum and feel the weight of her gaze.

"Freya," she says in her authoritative way she uses when in her role as queen rather than my mother. "We need to talk."

I gulp. That is never a good sentence coming from a queen.

Chapter two

Elliot

I HAVE NO IDEA why I'm here.

That's not true. I'm here because my obnoxiously famous cousin has a strange sense of humor and a hodgepodge of friends whose collective net worth and influence could probably be used to run the world if they weren't decent people. I'm here because I need a job to keep my mind occupied, and my skill set makes me overqualified for pretty much anything except what I was already doing.

I don't know why I'm *here*. Standing at the back of a room filled with stuffy politicians and three very uptight royals.

"What is this about?" Princess Freya asks. She has her gaze fixed on the queen, which makes sense. Queen Ingrid is by far the most intimidating person in the room, though some of these lords are a close second. I've only spoken to a couple of them, but neither man was shy about telling me how little he liked the idea of an American soldier being granted such a high level of security clearance.

I don't like it either, but here I am.

"Will you sit, darling?" the king says, gesturing to the chair at the foot of the table. Stellan—as he has frequently told me to call him—is probably the only person in this room who seems to sense Princess Freya's nerves. At least, he's the only one who is openly acknowledging them.

I wasn't lying when I told the princess that I didn't know why her mother wanted her to wait outside, but I doubt it's anything good. I'm pretty sure that's why the queen told me that I was going to be part of this meeting.

I'd be a lot more comfortable waiting outside. Whatever this is, the tension in the room is only going to get worse.

Princess Freya doesn't move, still standing behind her chair. "Why was I not allowed inside, Mum?"

The queen clears her throat, her expression disapproving at the informal address, though with her that isn't saying much. In the weeks that I've been here, learning everything I need to know about the Alverra family and the government structure of Candora, Queen Ingrid has impressed me with her ability to keep a straight face. I've even tried to provoke more of a reaction out of her and gotten nothing but a sharpness in her eyes.

Derek would probably punch me if he knew I've done that multiple times, but my fearlessness has only made Ingrid like me more. My job may be to protect the princess, but ultimately I report to the queen, and she appreciates my strength of will. According to her, I'll need it when I start shadowing Freya.

Ingrid meets my gaze just long enough to indicate I should pay attention. I stand straighter, gripping my wrist behind my back.

"Are you sure you will not sit, Freya?" Stellan asks, though he already seems to know the answer before his daughter throws him a sharp look.

"Lord Ostervik," the queen says, "if you will."

The lord clears his throat and touches a piece of paper in front of him. "Your Highness," he says to the princess, "as you know, Queen Ingrid and King Stellan have decided to step down from the throne, which means the elections are coming next month."

Freya clenches her jaw as a fire starts burning in her eyes, but her expression is overall calm now as she settles in her chair.

My mentor, Gregor, has had plenty to say about the Candoran heir and says she is intelligent, kind, and resilient, but there's obviously more to her than what she presents. There has to be if she thinks she can run a country on her own. Today is the first time I've gotten close to her, and if I hadn't heard otherwise, I would think she was more of a metaphorical princess—pampered, spoiled, superficial—rather than a political figure. She literally looks like the queen in that kids' movie my friend's girls love so much, the one with the two sisters and the snow. Or the one with the princess in the tower with all the hair?

Regardless, Freya may look delicate and fragile, but there's a power lurking inside her. I can't decide if it's dangerous or useful, and I don't like not knowing. Is she going to be a problem, or is she going to be strong enough to hold her own in the difficult position of queen?

"Yes," the princess says eventually, her eyes sweeping the room. "I am aware of the elections, as that is how the monarchy has been governed for generations."

I pinch my lips together before I laugh. She definitely has some spunk in her. Hex and Sander like to say their sister is as much a heavyweight champ as she is a fairy. They're equally terrified and protective of her.

Lord Ostervik clears his throat. "Yes, well, there have arisen some...shall we say *complications* in the matter of—"

"What sort of complications?"

"Well, it is..." He looks to his fellow Council members, his eyes widening ever so slightly as he silently pleads for help. That can't be good.

"You have an opponent," the queen says with no attempts at sugar-coating. "And he is quickly gaining popularity."

From my understanding, any Candoran can run in opposition to whichever member of the royal family is vying for the throne after a monarch steps down, but I don't think it's ever happened. Gregor mentioned once that the Alverra family has been in power as long as Candora has been a country. It's impressive, though I've yet to decide if it's because of the Alverras' competency or if it's complacency on the people's part. Electing someone other than the ruling family affects the entire government structure, but I haven't had a chance to dig deep into what that means.

I can see Candorans sticking with the status quo to keep things simple. So far, the political structure seems to be working. The country is partially controlled by two houses, the House of Lords and the House of Commons, but the ruling king or queen—and to a point their spouse if they have one—still has the bulk of power and is more than just a figurehead, particularly when it comes to foreign affairs. Changing that could put Candora in a vulnerable position.

"An opponent?" Freya asks, curling her fingers into fists on her lap. I've got a view of her hands where I stand, but no one else does. If not for that, I would think she was calm about this new revelation because nothing else about her shows distress. "Who wants the throne?"

"Markham Grimstad," Ingrid says at the same time one of the Council members hands Freya a tablet.

I get one too, for which I'm grateful. I read through the dossier quickly, noting the fact that Grimstad is only thirty-five and has a strong background in business and politics. His career started when he was an assistant to a member of Parliament after getting his degree in political science and law, followed by him beating out an established member of the House of Commons by a record number of votes when he was only twenty-seven. He has been Speaker of the House for the last three years despite his young age and isn't afraid to push change in favor of the lower classes, which make up the majority of the kingdom. Several laws have been amended or changed entirely since his entrance into Parliament.

He looks like a good candidate for a king. Too good.

"Your thoughts, Mr. Reid?" Ingrid says, surprising me with the question. Because of my background, we've talked politics a few times since I was hired, but nothing this immediately relevant. Still, I definitely have thoughts.

I keep my eyes on the tablet, now scrolling through the accolades the guy earned while at Oxford. The school has a reputation that adds to his qualifications. "I think, Your Majesty, there are going to be strong arguments in his favor, and his rising popularity isn't something to take lightly."

"Thank you for your opinion," Freya says sharply, "but I disagree. Markham Grimstad is charismatic, yes, but his policy leaves much to be desired."

"It's not always a matter of policy," I argue, though I probably shouldn't. Yeah, the queen asked for my opinion, but the princess clearly doesn't want it. "Everyone can say Hitler's ideas weren't great, but look what he managed to do."

She scoffs. "Of course you would turn to Hitler. You are aware there are many charismatic dictators in history, not just the one, yes?"

Shrugging, I tuck the tablet under my arm and stand tall. "Mussolini, Stalin, Hussein, Caesar... Any of them could make my point. From experience, elections are as much a popularity contest as they are about politics, and I wouldn't underestimate Grimstad's platform. He's running 'for the people.'" I quote the last article I looked at a moment ago. "Arguing that the Alverra family has lost touch with their own countrymen. His ideas may be radical, but they're going to be appealing compared to the way things have been for a lot of people."

Catching the king's raised eyebrows, I bow my head. "Forgive me, Your Majesties. I'm speaking out of turn."

"Yes," Freya agrees at the same time Ingrid says, "I asked for your opinion, Mr. Reid. An outside perspective can be valuable."

"Should we be listening to a foreigner?" Freya asks. Her voice carries clear exasperation, but now she won't look at me. "Surely those of us in this room, the American excluded, have thoughts enough to—"

"What would you suggest in this situation, Mr. Reid?" Ingrid asks over her daughter.

I can't stop my eyebrows from lifting. This really isn't my place, and if I'm going to be working with Freya, I'd rather she didn't hate me. "With respect, Your Majesty, I agree with the princess. I'm here to protect, not to be a diplomat."

"Thank you," Freya says.

"Be that as it may," Ingrid replies, "I know my daughter, and your position may require more diplomacy than you were told."

"*Your daughter* is sitting directly across from you," Freya hisses, losing some of her control as her irritation comes to the forefront. "She can speak for herself." She turns to me, her expression hard. "I need a protection agent, not a politician. As you are certainly not the latter, I will kindly request that you focus on the former while the position is yours. You will wait out in the corridor, Mr. Reid."

I look to Queen Ingrid, wondering if my orders still come from her or if my responsibility has officially shifted to the princess. Ingrid nods subtly, and I can practically feel the shift in tension in the room when Freya sees the nod as well.

I wanted excitement—I definitely have it now.

"Outside," Freya commands, her expression growing harder.

Nodding my acknowledgement, I return the tablet to the Council member and slip out to the hallway to take up my post at the door. Rather than continuing in English, Freya begins speaking in rapid Candoran before the door closes, and while I only pick up pieces, it's clear she isn't happy about any of the day's topics.

"Derek," I mutter, grabbing my phone and dialing his number. "What have you gotten me into?"

The line connects after two rings, and Derek speaks without greeting. "You are aware that it's four thirty in the morning here, right?"

"I distinctly remember you telling me this job would be easy," I reply, just as bluntly.

He laughs lightly. "I never said that. I said this job would be the perfect thing to help you unwind and settle into something new."

"I cannot stress how tightly wound I am right now. She hates me, and some pretty-boy politician thinks he can be king."

"Which part of that do you think you can't handle?"

That question stuns me into silence. I can't really say that I know Derek well—his dad and mine never interacted—but ever since we first connected about a year ago, he has constantly surprised me. Whenever we talk, he seems to understand more about me than I've ever understood about anyone. Now is no exception.

"I didn't say I couldn't handle it," I mutter.

"So what's the problem?"

"The problem is your princess friend is more likely to give up her claim on the throne than she is to keep me on, and I'll be unemployed."

Derek laughs again. "I think you're overestimating Freya's willingness to hire yet another bodyguard."

"Comforting." I sweep my eyes over both ends of the hallway to make sure this part of the palace is empty, though it's unnecessary. The palace has exceptional security measures, to the point where I don't know why Freya needs a bodyguard in the first place since she rarely ventures outside the walls.

Gregor, the man who trained me, said she has become increasingly more noticed around the world since becoming friends with Derek, and most of my protection duties will come into play during her frequent visits to California.

But what about the rest of the time?

I *need* to stay busy. If I don't, my thoughts inevitably stray to the past and the mistakes that still haunt me when I'm not on my guard.

"I have a meeting with a producer in a few hours," Derek says, pulling my attention back to my phone. "So I'm going back to bed. Give things with Freya some time to settle, and you'll work things out between the two of you."

"Are you always this confident?" My question is genuine, though my grumbled tone suggests otherwise. I've seen some of his movies and watched interviews, and he is always unfailingly sure of himself. Even on those rare occasions we've hung out, I've never seen him anything *but* confident, and it's eerie. Having come from a position where hesitation could lead to deadly consequences, I get it, but Derek's not a soldier. He doesn't need the level of control he has over his life.

Chuckling, he takes longer to answer that question than I expect. "When it comes to my friends? Usually."

Which means he *does* have moments of doubt. It's nice to know he's human.

"You're always welcome to reach out, Elliot."

"Yeah. Thanks." It's not that I don't believe him, but I'm not one who seeks out conversation. Today was uncharacteristic, and only because I hoped Derek would have some insider knowledge of the princess. '*You'll work things out*' isn't all that helpful, and the stuff I really need help with—the stuff that led to me being here—isn't the kind of stuff a guy like him can fix.

That's all on me.

"You good?" Derek asks, his words hesitant.

"Yeah. Sorry to bother you."

"I'm not bothered."

I don't believe that for a second, but I say my goodbyes and hang up without responding to that comment.

I can handle this. My shoulder twinges, enough that I have to roll out the discomfort left from an old injury. It doesn't get too bad when I have the chance to work it out, like sparring with Hex and Sander, but I won't get as much opportunity to do that as I have the last month.

Now that I'm the princess's official protection agent, my focus has to be her. Assuming she allows it.

After ten minutes of me waiting in the empty hallway, Freya storms through the doors and passes me without a word. I glance into the room, making eye contact with the queen, and she gives me a look that seems to be wishing me luck.

Guess my job has officially started.

Though I stay hot on her heels, Freya doesn't acknowledge me until we've rounded the corner, but even then she speaks back to me without turning her head. "I will make this as clear as I am able, Mr. Reid. Your job is to protect me. Not to criticize or judge or offer your opinion. Am I understood?"

"Yes, ma'am."

"You will address me as 'Your Highness' and nothing else."

I hold back a snicker. I have it on good authority—AKA her brothers—that she hates being called by her title, so this order is strictly to put me in my place. "Got it."

"You will be privy to the most vulnerable parts of my life," Freya continues, "but that does not make you my friend."

"I'm not looking for a friend, anyway."

She stops, whirling around to gaze up at me. As before, I hold my gaze just over her head, partially because it seems to annoy her but mostly to keep an eye on our surroundings. "Why are you here, Mr. Reid?"

For reasons she doesn't need to know. "To ensure your safety, Your Highness."

She huffs. "You cannot evade me forever. If you wish to keep this position, I need to know I can trust you."

"What about my response felt untrue?"

"Your sass will not help you stay," she warns.

I can't help but meet her eyes, which blaze with irritation and what looks an awful lot like curiosity. She thinks I'm sassy? My old ODA would get a kick out of that one. I was always the serious one in my Special Forces detachment. The man with the plan. The guy so focused on the mission ahead that I never deviated.

The one time I did, it ended in disaster.

As a weight settles on my shoulders, I force a smirk and tell myself I can't get lost in memories. It won't do me or the princess any good. "No sass," I say, as if repeating an order. "Anything else I should know?"

Freya lifts her nose high. "I do not need you always a step behind me. Especially not here in my home." She makes a little shooing motion with her hands.

I hold my ground. "With all due respect, Your Highness, there are enough people with access to the palace that I will have to disagree."

"All of them have been vetted and have the proper clearance," she argues with a frown.

"Markham Grimstad has access to the lower court, along with the rest of the House of Commons."

"The lower court, yes, but not the upper levels." Freya folds her arms as she continues to study me. "Do you expect me to be the first casualty of the Candoran royal family?"

She makes a good point. In the history of modern Candora, the royal family has never been in any true danger, though Gregor would argue that is because of security heads like him. Still... I fold my arms to match her. "I expect trouble as the election gets closer, and so should you."

"My safety is the least of my concerns at the moment."

Is she serious? "It should be at the top."

"I see you have already forgotten my first order."

I roll my eyes, making her scoff. "To protect you? That's all I'm doing, Princess."

"I was referring to your opinion, Mr. Reid."

"You asked for my opinion," I counter.

"I..." Her eyes narrow, and she points a finger at my chin. "Keep your distance. Know your place. Be silent." She continues down the hall but stops when I follow close behind, her exasperation clear in her voice as she turns to me again. "Mr. Reid, please."

That's not a word I expected from her, especially when I've ruffled her feathers. But if she thinks I'll back off and pretend my protection is nothing but a formality, she's in for disappointment. "My only job is to keep you safe, Princess. I'm going to do that to the best of my ability, and you may not like my methods. That's fine, but it won't change my plans. If I think there's a threat, I expect you to do what I tell you."

"I am to take orders from you, am I?" Her frustration settles deeper, leaving her seething. But I also sense a bit of appreciation in her eyes, though I'm going to guess she doesn't want me to know she respects that I won't be pushed around. She seems like the kind of person who needs to be in control and will not relinquish it easily.

I've dealt with enough soldiers who didn't like to follow orders, and they all eventually fall in line. A princess shouldn't be any different.

"Only when necessary," I tell her, offering a smile. "Your Highness."

She huffs and spins on her heel, marching down the hallway. I'm right behind her, my mind running over ways I can convince her to trust me. Derek's right, and Freya and I need time to settle into things. But what he doesn't know is that we don't *have* time, not with the election looming closer and an unexpected opponent on the rise. If Freya is going to trust me to keep her safe, she's going to have to lower her walls and let me in.

Maybe, if I push her hard enough, she'll do that sooner than later.

CHAPTER THREE

FREYA

"We have talked this topic to death and recommend we move forward with more pressing matters."

"I agree. A few rallies in the streets do not mean the government is under attack."

"They are looking for attention. This younger generation is too influenced by the internet."

"Precisely. Now, we need to discuss this year's Celestial Ball..."

When the endless conversation moves to the annual ball, my focus shifts from the notes I have been taking on my tablet to the amphitheater in front of me, where the members of the House of Lords have convened for the weekly Parliament meeting. The tiered semi-circle of blue velvet-gilt chairs rises from my seat next to my mother at the base, and this position has always made me feel as if I am on display.

Today, however, the conversation has proceeded with little input from the queen, and I have gone mostly ignored. Apparently, political unrest in the weeks before I take my mother's place is far too trivial a thing to bother the royal family, but the more I have heard, the more nervous I have become.

I am, to put it lightly, shocked by the abrupt shift in topic as the lords and ladies discuss the Celestial Ball. I have sat through more of these meetings than I can count, and somehow I have never noticed how thoroughly these men and women have distanced themselves from the rest of the country. I can admit I came into this meeting with a similar opinion to most of the assembly, namely that Markham Grimstad's platform is not something we need to worry about, but now...

Looking back at my notes, taken from today's short discussion as well as my own research, it is clear that more and more people are giving Grimstad their support, claiming that my family has lost sight of our people. They want change, even if that change means a shift in the way our government has been run for centuries. Candorans are out in the streets, rallying for Grimstad and demanding a reformation.

What I hoped would be an election easily won is quickly turning into an uncertainty I am not prepared for.

I sense Reid behind me, as he has been for the last several days, and I am certain he has grown more tense as the meeting has gone on. This is his first session, and every few minutes, he lets out a soft scoff or mutters something under his breath. He has, surprisingly, kept his opinions to himself this week, though he has yet to display any adherence to my wish for space. He is always right there, looming.

"What is your opinion, Your Highness?" someone asks.

I stopped paying enough attention and therefore have no idea who addressed me just now. But of the sixty people in the room, there are few who ever choose to address me specifically when my mother is next to me. Lady Branthorn is deep in whispered conversation with her mother, and Lord Velbrant, the executive lawyer of the House of Lords, is reading something on his tablet. That leaves the Duke of Rensvik, who is gazing at me fixedly.

Why could it not have been one of the other two? The duke has never been afraid to voice his opinions on my inability to lead a country and is one of the primary causes of the insecurity that I have never been able to overcome.

Sitting up straighter, I offer a nod of acknowledgment and berate myself for not remaining focused. My lack of attention will not soften his opinion of me. "Forgive me, but I do not—"

"He wants to know your thoughts on the ball," Reid says, his voice low.

Heat washes over my face, but gratitude keeps full embarrassment at bay. "I do not think my opinion of a party would be an important use of our time," I say coolly. "However, if you would like my thoughts on the growing unrest of our people, I would be happy to—"

"That is a topic better discussed in the Commons," Rensvik says with a scoff. "We have already dismissed—"

"I was not finished speaking, Your Grace." I narrow my eyes at the duke. "What I would have said before you interrupted was a remark on my desire to investigate how unhappy the people are and how much potential Markham Grimstad has to change the political climate of our country. As his platform directly opposes mine, you can see why that might take more of my attention than an annual ball."

Mum clears her throat, disapproving, but several members of the House of Lords have turned their attention to me in surprise. I usually remain quiet, as I technically do not have any power until I take my mother's place, and it seems most of the assembly cannot decide what to make of my sharp response.

"As such," I say, when no one offers up a reply, "I suggest we discuss how Grimstad poses a threat to some of *your* positions if he manages to win the coming election, however unlikely. Again, more pressing of a topic than table arrangements, would you not agree?"

As the assembly dissolves into a buzz of murmurs, Reid coughs behind me, and I have my suspicions that he is covering a laugh. I shouldn't smile, but I allow the smallest twitch of my lips. The soldier so rarely breaks that I feel a strange triumph for eliciting a reaction out of him, even if I still dislike his presence. He has, for the most part, followed my orders this week, so I cannot be fully angry with him.

"I think," Mum says, silencing the room, "we should adjourn for the day, and I will see to it that we have a more thorough agenda for next week's session. Thank you, Lords and Ladies of the House." She stands, and the assembly stands with her. "Freya."

Reluctantly, I follow her through the side door reserved for the monarch and into a private antechamber, anticipating her lecture.

"Freya," she says with a sigh and takes the paracetamol her protection agent, Margo, has waiting for her. "If you are going to antagonize Rensvik, at least do it in private. You know the sway he holds over Lords."

I wait until she is drinking water to roll my eyes, as she would not appreciate the gesture if she saw it. "Yes, well, I would not antagonize him if he would stop treating me like a child."

"Rensvik is stuck in his ways. I fear he will always see you as the girl you were when you began attending these meetings with me." At least I am not the only one who dislikes the duke's strict adherence to tradition. Even my mother has not been able to sway some of his opinions, and I suspect it is because he believes a king should always have more power than a queen.

Unfortunately for the duke, no titles in Candora fall strictly to one gender or the other. Mum, as the daughter of the last king, is the ruling monarch. Despite being a king in title, Dad will always have less influence than she does.

"I wish you had not ended the meeting when you did," I admit. "I have been watching some of Grimstad's videos, and—"

"Mr. Reid," Mum says, cutting me off. "Do you have any opinions from today's session?"

I scoff, knowing my guard will speak freely now that he has been given permission. For some reason, my mother seems to think he has a useful perspective to give, though I cannot understand why. "Yes, do tell us."

Reid, who kept himself back by the door, steps forward and nods to my mother without acknowledging my comment. "I can't say I'm familiar with a lot of the politics yet, but I'd be curious to see what they talk about in the House of Commons."

"We do not typically attend Commons," Mum replies, offering a brief smile. "The people need a voice without sovereign influence, and anything of consequence is sent up to Lords in a quarterly memo."

Reid's jaw tightens as he briefly glances at me. "I wonder if you should let Grimstad, as Speaker of the House of Commons, attend Lords each week to balance things out more. Maybe he wouldn't be so set on running for power if he felt he had a voice."

"Says the man who admits to not understanding our politics," I grumble. "I cannot wait to hear more of your thoughts."

"Freya," Mum says sharply. "If you cannot contain yourself, you are more than welcome to leave." She gestures to the door, which means it is not an invitation. It is an order. The only reason I comply is because this could be my only moment to get a break from Reid's constant hovering.

As I slip through the door, I meet Reid's gaze long enough to see the worry in his eyes, which only fuels my desire to put some distance between us. I would have preferred he did not witness my mother treating me as a child rather than her successor, but I will accept this respite with my head held high.

I do not know where to go—Reid will inevitably find me, as he always does—but my feet take me outside to the courtyard and into the weak sunshine. A thin layer of clouds blankets the sky after the morning's rain, leaving the world in a soft haze. But there is fresh air out here, and I have spent too much time in the castle of late.

I make it as far as the doors to the stable and garage before a palace guard blocks my path, his expression apologetic. "Forgive me, Your Highness," he says, "but I can't let you go beyond this point on your own."

His orders could have come from anyone—Mum, Gregor, Reid—which makes it difficult to know where to place my ire. Obviously I know better than to venture out of the castle on my own, but I would have liked the choice.

Feeling trapped, I alter my course to the training grounds where several of the guards do their workouts and weapon training. I used to come here more often when I was younger, learning self-defense and archery, but my life has become a nonstop calendar of social events and political meetings. For the most part, I enjoy those things, but the last week has been stifling.

I blame Reid for the suffocating sensation that constantly follows me. Even if I wanted to take a trip into the city, I doubt he would allow it. He would say it is too dangerous until we know more about Grimstad's supporters, but if I could talk to some of my people and understand their needs, I would have a better knowledge of what I need to do going forward into this election. I cannot get that from inside these walls.

Spotting my brothers among the palace guards, I find a seat on a wrought-iron bench to watch the sparring. Hex, as always, makes fighting look easy and has barely broken a sweat as he boxes with a fellow guard. His footsteps light and his body quick to move, he seems to float over the dirt as he dodges, punches, and kicks. Neither he nor his opponent are hitting hard enough to injure, but their skill is evident. Particularly Hex's. I do not think I have seen him lose a fight in years.

Sander is much the same, though he has always had a quieter style, keeping to defense until he finds the right moment to strike. Most often, he manages to take his opponents down in only a few offensive moves. Where Hex's skills and confidence are immediately obvious, people tend to underestimate Sander when they first meet him.

In truth, I have no idea which of them is the better fighter because they made a pact years ago to never go up against each other. Heaven help anyone who chooses to take them both on.

A thought sparks to life as I watch my brothers defeat their opponents almost at the same time, eliciting applause from their observers. Reid would never approve of a trip into town, and I would be foolish to go on my own. But I happen to know two incredibly skilled fighters who could keep me safe and would likely agree to my reasoning.

I need to know what the people want from me, and that is not something I can learn from inside a castle.

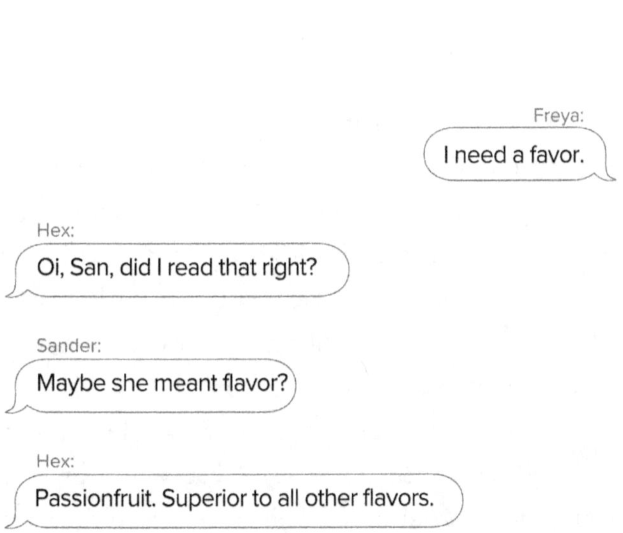

Sander:
Depends on the context. Lemon is more versatile.

Hex:
She didn't ask for versatile.

Sander:
She didn't ask for the best, either.

Freya:
You are both imbeciles. Will you help me or not?

Neither of my brothers answers the question, but I do not have to wait long before there is a knock at the secret door behind the bookshelf in my room. At least they are not so dimwitted as to ignore my request.

I purposefully waited until Reid was replaced by the night guard before texting my brothers, but I am still cautious when I open the bookcase to let Hex and Sander into my room from one of the secret passages connecting the rooms in the family wing.

"Keep your voices down," I warn them.

"Why?" Hex asks in a dramatically loud whisper.

Because I am certain Reid has managed to befriend the entire palace guard and many of the other staff as well, which means I cannot trust the night guard to be discreet if he hears anything we say. I would say I am surprised everyone likes Reid as well as they do, but he is closely related to Derek Riley. Universal likeability must be a family trait.

"It is late," I say, instead of the real reason.

Hex and Sander glance at each other, their matching faces suddenly masked as they have a silent conversation between them. In general, they are far more expressive than I allow myself, so these moments when they hide their thoughts from anyone but themselves always unnerve me.

"So, what is this once-in-a-lifetime favor?" Sander asks, folding his arms as his features soften into his usual warm smile.

Hex flops onto my couch. "I am all too eager to hear what you think counts as a favor, Fringe."

"Will you take your feet off the cushion?" I sit on the couch as soon as he does as I ask. "You do not have to turn this into something bigger than it is."

Chuckling, Sander sits in the armchair across from us. "You never ask for help," he argues. "Which makes this a big deal."

I suppose he has a point. "First, you must promise not to tell anyone about this."

Hex frowns. "Sure, but—"

"Not even your friend, *El*. Mr. Reid cannot know about this."

That intrigues them, and they both sit up.

"This is getting more and more interesting," Hex says, his smile growing. "Is our perfect sister finally breaking a rule?"

"I never thought I'd see the day," Sander says and lifts his eyebrows high. "I think we need to commemorate this somehow."

"Turn it into a national holiday?" Hex suggests. "Though I'm not sure Mum would approve, unless we get her drunk like she was at Mormor's eightieth birthday."

"We could commission a monument to honor the day."

"A statue! It can have all three of us and—"

"Will you shut up?" I say with a sigh. "I have changed my mind."

The twins groan, and Hex grabs my hand as he says, "No, we're sorry. We'll be serious."

"Is that even possible?" I ask.

Sander chuckles. "Only when we try really hard. What is this favor, Freya?"

Now I feel foolish, and I wish I had not gotten so excited about the possibility. "I..." I might as well tell them, or they will never leave it alone. "I want to go into Invem."

The silence that follows my admission sits thick and heavy in the air, and I hold my breath as I wait for their reactions.

"Oh, that was the end?" Hex says, lifting an eyebrow. "I thought there would be more...well, more."

Rolling my eyes, I slouch in my seat and hug one of the many throw pillows. "I am not allowed out of the castle without an escort."

"So take Elliot with you," Sander says with a shrug. "That's his job."

"His job is to keep me safe," I grumble. "Mum and Gregor believe the city is too dangerous for me, and there is little chance he will go against orders."

Sander meets Hex's gaze, his eyes narrowing slightly. "Have you asked him to take you?"

"Of course," I say, covering the lie with a scoff. "I am not so foolish as to go behind his back when he is so dedicated to his position."

Hex snickers and tosses a pillow at me, hitting me in the face. "You didn't ask him," he guesses. "If you had, he would not have let us any-where near you because he would have known you would do this. The man's smarter than you think, Fringe. Smarter than you, I'd wager." Before I can feel the sting of his opinion, he continues speaking. "Okay, so you want to go into Invem. And do what?"

I had not gotten that far in my thinking, particularly because it took all my courage to ask my brothers to come hear my plan. "I suppose I want to talk to people," I say, though my uncertainty will not help my brothers think I am more intelligent than Elliot. "Without them knowing who I am."

"Why?" both twins ask at the same time.

I sigh. "Because I need to know how the Candoran people really feel about the monarchy and my upcoming rule, and they would never tell the crown princess the truth, now would they? They have been rally-ing in the streets, but their grievances are unclear."

"They definitely wouldn't talk to you," Sander agrees, scratching his chin. "But how are you supposed to blend in?" He waves a hand at me, gesturing from my head to my toe. "You have only ever looked and acted like a princess."

"Unlike the two of you," I grumble back.

"It's a good thing Sander and I don't act like princesses," Hex says.

I throw the pillow back at him, and he catches it with ease. "You know what I mean."

"Just pretend to be one of your American friends."

I consider that, though I am uncertain if that would work. My male friends would be impossible to emulate, but the women would be no easier. Bonnie is too glamorous and constantly in the public eye, so her life is not much different from mine. She even has a bodyguard.

Kasey is…the opposite of me. She wears her husband's clothes and rarely puts on makeup and does not care what anyone thinks of her. And Carissa has only been my friend for a couple of months, so I have not had the chance to spend much time with her.

I have not spent much time with any of my friends of late. This election has made it impossible.

"I will have to put on a disguise," I decide, hoping that will be enough.

"What do you expect us to do?" Sander asks. His expression is wary, and I am certain he will take the most to convince. Hex is usually up for anything that makes his life more interesting, but I will not be able to make this plan work if one of them is skeptical.

"I was hoping one of you would take Mr. Reid's place while the other ensures he does not find out what we are doing," I say and wince.

Hex laughs, shaking his head, and Sander's frown deepens. "You want us to lie to Elliot?" Sander asks. He sounds almost hurt.

"You want us to turn into bodyguards?" Hex adds, still full of amusement. "Seems like a lot of faith to put into a couple of imbeciles."

I sigh and rub my temples. If I did not love these two with all my heart, they would drive me crazy. I can only hope they mature sooner than later. "You are the best fighters *and* the best shots this country has ever seen."

"Well," Hex says, tilting his head and smiling proudly. "We're not as good as—"

"If you try to tell me you are not as good as Elliot Reid, I will know you are lying," I snap. "There is no way he is both more intelligent than me and stronger than the two of you. He can be a lot of things, but perfect is not one of them."

To my irritation, my brothers share a smirk as if my comment was something to laugh at. "You really hate him, don't you?" Sander asks. "Why?"

Because he is bold, confident, and does not fear crossing me. Because he has thus far proven himself to be skilled at his job and therefore has not given me any good reasons to dismiss him. I say none of this aloud—my brothers would have ready arguments for why those traits should be praised rather than condemned.

"Will you help me understand the Candoran people or not?" I ask, folding my arms as I stare them down.

Sharing one last look, the twins nod.

"Thank you."

"I'll go into the city with you," Sander decides. "Hex is probably better at distracting Elliot, if the need comes up."

I am grateful he made the decision instead of leaving it up to me. Either of my brothers would be a good choice to protect me, but I would insult one by choosing the other. Even if no insult was taken, they would pretend otherwise because as much as they support me, they delight in tormenting me.

"If you really plan to be in disguise," Hex says, hopping up and moving to my closet, "this is going to take some time. So we should probably get started."

CHAPTER FOUR

FREYA

I WISH I COULD say I have been to the capital city many times. I suppose I have, if one counts traveling through the streets in a vehicle. (Sander does not count that.) It has been many years since my last journey to the city, so I feel completely out of place as Sander parks our motorbike next to several bicycles along one of the busier streets.

Busy by Candoran standards means a bus takes this route every twenty minutes, fifteen when it rains.

As I slip from the motorbike and steady myself after an exhilarating ride, a sense of freedom washes over me and leaves me almost teary-eyed. I have not done something like this in so long, and I can only imagine what my mother would say if she knew. By some miracle, we passed no one on our way out to the garage, though I heard Hex's voice in the main hall of the palace as we took one of the side doors. I assume he was distracting a guard to clear our path. Thanks to my helmet, the guards at the gate were oblivious to my identity as Sander chatted with them for a moment before they let him drive through under the pretext of returning a date to the city.

I suppose I should be worried about how easily I escaped, but I choose to focus on taking advantage of my time while I have it.

Sander checks something on his phone as I remove my helmet and rest it on the motorbike's seat. His brow is furrowed, expression tight, and I am certain he still thinks this is a bad idea. But then he says, "There's a popular pub down this way," and offers me his arm.

"Thank you for joining me," I tell him, doing my best to hold him loosely despite the nerves that begin growing as soon as we start walking. Invem is a safe city, more so than most capitals around the country, so I hardly expect anything to go wrong. But if things do take a turn, I will have to rely on Sander and my own feet to get me to safety.

I am conscious of my health, but there are not many reasons for a princess like me to build up stamina in running.

Sander grumbles something, his eyes still darting around us even though the street is quiet. It is late, so perhaps most of the residents of Invem have already returned home and gone to bed. "Here we are," he says, stopping outside a well-lit establishment and pulling a baseball cap from his pocket. It is something I once stole from my friend Bonnie—who originally received it from an old boyfriend—because I found it charming and very American, but I have never worn it. Hex thinks it will help me blend in despite the style not being popular among Candoran adults.

I wrinkle my nose at the cap. "Is this necessary?"

Stuffing it onto my head, he nods. "You aren't exactly unknown, Fringe. If people get a good look at you, they'll know you're the future queen."

Personally, I prefer to think I will experience the same effect that preserves Clark Kent's identity as Superman. No one will expect me to be in a pub on a Friday evening, so they will not even consider the connection.

Sander narrows his eyes at me, proving he knows my thoughts when he says, "You know Superman is a comic book character, yeah?"

I roll my eyes, wishing I hadn't brought up my theory when I was changing into my least opulent clothes. "Yes, I am aware. But Derek—"

"Maybe don't take the word of an actor either," he mutters.

Of my family, Sander is the only one who did not take an immediate liking to Derek and thinks there is more to my friend than the confident actor Derek portrays. Yes, Derek has his secrets, but they are things from his past. Not from his current life. Our friend Liam is convinced Derek is secretly a spy, but I have known Derek long enough to know that he does not hide his occupation. He hides who he really is.

There is a difference.

"Come on," Sander says with a grimace. "Let's get this over with."

As we enter the pub, I am hit with a wall of sound and smells. The air has an edge of alcohol, beneath which hangs the cloying scent of fried food and something distinctly human. A rugby game plays on a screen, loud enough to be heard over the buzz of conversation and upbeat music coming from somewhere. It is overwhelming and beautiful all at once.

"Grab us a seat, will you?" Sander says, nodding to the only empty table in the place before pushing his way through the crowded space to get to the bar. Presumably to order some drinks, which will be a welcome addition to the night's adventure. I drink very little, as it is not proper for a political figure to dull her senses with alcohol, but tonight, I am not a princess. Tonight, I am simply a citizen of Candora.

This could be the best idea I have had in a long time.

Sander returns within minutes with a white wine and something carbonated. When I raise an eyebrow at him, he shrugs and hands me the wine. "Soda," he explains with a nod to his glass. "I'm not taking any chances tonight, Fringe. I need to stay alert."

"If I were not with you, you would drink something else?"

He chuckles and settles into his chair with a more relaxed stance than I would have expected, given his claim to be on his guard. Perhaps he only wishes to *appear* relaxed to avoid suspicion, and I do my best to mimic him. "You think I'd come to a pub and drink soda?" he replies.

I have never seen my brothers when they go out at night, but maybe they often come into the city and drink themselves into a stupor. Surely our parents would not allow such a thing, but I do not know much about my brothers' habits and behaviors beyond what I see at the palace. They could have whole lives I know nothing about, and I am reminded of how the gate guard believed Sander when he said he had a date with him.

Are my innocent baby brothers gone?

Sander's chuckle shifts to a heartier laugh. "Do you think so little of us, Fringe? On the rare occasions we go out, it's usually with other guards, and none of us like getting knackered. Makes the job harder."

I frown. "How do you always know what I am thinking?"

He pokes me in the forehead. "Because you make it easy."

I wonder if Mr. Reid can read my expressions as well. I am not always the best at hiding my emotions, but surely I do not give *everything* away. As my bodyguard has made it clear that he has no plans to give me physical space, I am determined to create distance however I can. Keeping him from my inner thoughts is paramount to that determination.

I will have to try harder.

Sander and I grow quiet, both of us turning our attention to the people around us and the conversations that are clear enough to understand. I do not expect many people to spend their Friday evening talking of the election or their princess, but I still hope to gain a better understanding of the political climate. Where do their frustrations primarily lie? Anything about what the average person hopes for in their life could be beneficial as I figure out my course of action leading to the election.

One of the rugby teams scores, and the pub breaks into cheers. While my friend Cole plays rugby in the States, I know very little about the sport in my own corner of the world. A shame, considering Candora has a national team.

One of these days I should invite Cole to visit so I can get to know his girlfriend, Carissa, better. Cole is almost like a brother to me, and I hate how little time I have been able to spend with him and my other friends lately. If he were here, he could explain the rules of the game to me.

"Samoa is beating England," Sander says, taking a sip of his soda.

My confusion must have been on my face, which means I am already failing at my goal to keep my emotions to myself. "Do we dislike England?" I ask.

A few people look my way, giving me disgruntled looks before turning back to the game.

Chuckling, Sander shakes his head at me. "You need to get out more. Or at least remember your history."

Interesting. We were once caught in British colonialism like much of the world, but our small island—equidistant from England, Denmark, and Norway—is remote enough that the old Candoran people held the English off and retained independence. Our political relationship with the British has been good in recent years, so I am surprised this sort of disagreement still exists even centuries later. I tuck this information away in case it becomes useful, but I doubt it relates to the people's unrest. Just as learning the rules of rugby will not help me as a leader, even if it would help me be a better friend.

"At least Grimstad is trying to do something about it."

I perk up as the conversation behind me shifts to something relevant, and I do my best to listen over the noise of the pub.

"So he says," a second man replies to the first. "I'll believe it when I see it, but his ideas are good."

"As if he would ever win an election."

"He might. Lotta people are fed up, and it's not like the Alverras have ever paid attention."

I meet Sander's gaze, wondering if he is hearing what I am. Though he still looks relaxed, there is a tension in his eyes as he sips his drink and discreetly watches whoever sits behind me. One of his fingers taps on the table, a rhythmic movement that makes me wonder what my brother might be thinking as the conversation continues. I can hardly believe we are hearing exactly the sort of thing I came for.

"The election can't come soon enough," the first man grumbles. "Then we can stop listening to all that nonsense about how the princess will bring a fresh perspective. She's nothing but a copy of her mum."

"Maybe she'll try to turn our politics American," the other says with a chuckle. "We'll become a new state, and she can finally be like her precious Hollywood celebrities."

"She might as well give Candora to Grimstad and leave the country, if she loves the Americans so much. Why bother becoming queen when she can't be bothered to spend time in her own country?"

I cannot hold back my frown as the men start making jokes about my friends. Or rather my friendship with them. I rarely get to spend time with my American friends as it is, no matter how much I adore them, but the thought of my countrymen disliking my association with them... It is too painful to even consider cutting ties. Aside from my family, they are the only people in the world who truly know me, and I have not been able to visit them for *months* because my focus has been so fixed on preparing for the crown.

Can my people not see how thoroughly I have dedicated my life to serving them? The sacrifices I have made to become what they need?

Sander catches my eye and shakes his head subtly, though I am uncertain what he means by that, as his expression has turned into nothing but muted disinterest.

The men behind me are still talking, but I regret this decision to come and listen. I have learned nothing that I did not already assume. Grimstad is a real threat, and my people do not have faith in my loyalty to my homeland. How can I possibly change their minds in a few weeks, even if I learn what they are looking for in a monarch?

I stand and head for the door, stifled and heavy. There are too many people. Too much noise. Too many thoughts and doubts in my mind. Something happens in the rugby match, causing people to cheer once more, and I am jostled by the crowd. I nearly lose my balance, bumping into a woman and losing my cap in the process.

"Alright?" the woman says as she steadies me with her hands, but then our eyes meet, and she gasps, dropping her hold just as Sander comes up beside me. "Princess Freya!"

All conversation stops, leaving the air thick with discomfort as dozens of gazes fix upon me. Only seconds later, the whispers begin. Nothing about the growing buzz sounds friendly.

"Go," Sander says, nudging me toward the door.

I gape at him. "What?"

Someone steps closer, and Sander's entire demeanor shifts, turning him from casual pub goer to palace guard as he makes himself bigger to shield me. "Freya, go outside. *Now.*"

Two more people move forward, and fear grips me tight, urging my feet to the door even though I do not wish to leave my brother on his own. Will they attack him for bringing me here? I stumble outside as half of me is desperate to go back in and drag Sander with me. The other half of me is a coward and stands on the dark and silent walkway. Waiting.

No one follows me, but I cannot decide if that is because they are more interested in Sander or because he is holding them back. But no matter what is happening inside, I know better than to go back into the pub.

"What do I do?" I whisper, wrapping an arm around my waist as I start to pace. I have never been alone like this outside the palace, and it seems my bravery exists only when I have someone bigger and stronger to look after me.

The pub door opens, and I hold my breath, praying it is Sander safe and sound and ready to take me home. But the man who comes out is unfamiliar, his eyes narrowed as he takes me in. "What's a princess doing in a place like this?" he asks slowly.

The disgust in his voice turns my blood to ice. This man is not my friend. I take a breath, calling on my years of feigning confidence. "Can I not join my fellow—"

"You're not one of us," he growls, taking a step closer. Nothing about his haggard face or wrinkled clothing suggests any sympathy when we clearly come from different worlds. I should run, but my feet refuse to move as he tilts his head to study me. "You royals sit up there in your ivory tower, pretending to care while the rich get richer and the rest of us are left with nothing."

That is not true. "We care," I whisper.

He chuckles, and in a flash his fingers clamp around my arm and tug me toward him. "You don't, but someone else will."

"Please." He will not hurt me. Will he? I try to pull my arm free, but he holds too tight. Surely he is not stupid enough to attack a member of the royal family.

"Come and see what life here is really like, Princess."

My fear spikes as he pulls harder. "Let me—"

Something slams into the man, jarring me out of his hold as someone shoves my attacker into the wall of the pub. Sander!

"Hands off the princess unless you want to lose them."

Oh. Not Sander.

My breath escapes my lungs in a shaky exhale that leaves me dizzy. *Elliot.*

CHAPTER FIVE

ELLIOT

I DON'T KNOW WHO I'm more angry with—Hex and Sander, for letting the princess wander the city at night; Freya, for being stupid enough to sneak out; or whoever this guy is, for tempting me to do more than rough him up a bit. The man beneath me only struggles for a second before he realizes there's no getting out of my chokehold without this turning into a dangerous situation.

Dangerous for him.

"I'm going to count to three," I say, keeping my voice calm as I loosen the pressure on his throat so he can breathe. "If you're not out of sight by the time I finish, I'll—"

He bolts, slipping away from my hold and disappearing around the corner. *Coward.*

Freya scoffs, and the sound hits me like a punch to the gut.

"Are you out of your mind?" I snarl, turning on her so quickly that she backs up a step. "You could have gotten yourself killed."

Lifting her chin, she tries to look brave but can't hide the lingering fear in her eyes. "No one would be foolish enough to harm a member of the royal family."

"You've got to be kidding me." I run a hand through my hair, scanning the street to make sure the skirmish hasn't caught anyone's attention yet. I shouldn't have let the guy go, but I'm more concerned about getting the princess back where she belongs.

Anger flashes across her face. "What do you mean by that, Mr. Reid?"

She does *not* want me to answer that question. "You need to get back to the palace. Now."

"But Sander—"

"Sander can take care of himself." A thread of guilt and worry works its way through me, and I glance at the pub. No one else has come outside, which hopefully means Sander is de-escalating whatever was happening inside and not in trouble. I can't help him *and* protect the princess. He was stupid enough to agree to Freya's idea, so he had better be smart enough to fix what came of it. "We're leaving."

Freya tugs her arm out of my reach before I can touch her. "I am not going anywhere with you. Not without my brother."

She's going to keep resisting, and sooner or later someone *will* come after us. I don't care if it's one of Grimstad's loyalists or a peaceful citizen; Freya needs to disappear before tonight's adventure turns into something more.

I point in the direction of the palace and drop my voice to a growl. "Go."

She folds her arms, lifting her chin high. "No."

"Then my apologies in advance." With one last glance at the pub door, I bend down and scoop the princess over my shoulders in a fireman's carry.

She shrieks and resists, but the princess hasn't lived the same life as her brothers and has next to no strength, which makes it easy to start heading up the street despite her protests. Were this any other major city, we would have hundreds of witnesses, but Invem is remarkably quiet. Anyone who isn't at home is likely inside one of the many pubs, leaving me free to carry the princess back to safety without notice.

Physically free, anyway. She's doing her best to verbally fight me.

"Unhand me, you barbarian!" she shouts as light rain starts to drizzle over us. "I will have you court martialed! I will see that you are returned to your country and never leave again!"

"Sounds great," I mutter, looking for the motorcycle that Sander said would be waiting up the road because mine is parked in the other direction. His text was too vague for my liking, so we'll be working on clear communication in the future.

"I could have you thrown in the dungeon for the rest of your miserable life!" Freya snarls, followed by several grumblings in Candoran.

Finally finding the bike, I pause and adjust my grip on the princess's limbs as she tries to free herself once more. It won't be easy getting her on the vehicle, but we need to get back to the palace as quickly as possible, and this is our best option. "Is that what you would have done to your friend back there after he had his way with you?" I ask.

Her struggling stops. "He would not have done anything to me, no matter what he said."

Goodness, how naive can she be? Shifting her weight, I roll her over my head and into my arms so I can glare at her. She yelps, clinging to my neck, but freezes when she meets my gaze. "Stupidity like that will get you killed," I say, my voice heavy and rough so she will hopefully understand the severity of the situation she was just in. "A man who grabs your arm like that will have no qualms about doing worse. Get on the bike."

I set her on her feet, keeping a firm hold on her arm, and though she seems to debate trying to break free, she eventually sighs and straddles the motorcycle. I stuff a helmet onto her head, and as she reaches up to buckle it beneath her chin, I take her by the hips and move her to the very back of the seat despite her indignant gasp.

"You are too bold, Mr. Reid."

"So I've been told." I swing my leg over the seat and settle in front of her, starting up the bike and turning to glare at her again. "You're going to have to hold on, Princess."

Rolling her eyes, she tucks her arms around my waist, barely touching me.

I grab her hands and pull her forward until she's pressed into my back, and then I kick the bike into gear before she can complain about my manhandling. Freya gasps and tightens her grip as we lurch forward and zoom toward the palace. Not fast enough for my taste, but with the rain I won't further risk her safety, especially when I'm frustrated like this.

The drive from Invem isn't far, but it's long enough that Freya's anger builds until she's practically burning with it in every inch of her. The guards at the main gate let us in without question, and based on the tension that fills Freya's body, she has started to figure out how I ended up rescuing her.

The king and queen, Hex at their side along with Gregor and half a dozen palace guards, wait for us outside the massive garage, and the greeting party likely confirms Freya's suspicions.

"I will kill him," she mutters as I slow the bike to a stop.

Hex winces and slinks behind his father, the first sign of fear I've ever seen in him.

Ignoring my offered hand, Freya climbs off the motorcycle and walks with surprising meekness toward her parents. She may be a grown woman, but even the bravest soul would wither under those disapproving expressions. The queen is holding nothing back tonight as she scowls in the misty rain. "Mum," Freya says, her voice thin. "Dad. *Traitor*."

Hex snickers as he steps from his hiding place. "Hey, I gave you a head start. You're alive, yeah? You should be thanking me."

"Hendrik," Queen Ingrid says in a warning tone, and then her attention is back on Freya. "What were you thinking, going out in the middle of the night? And on your own?"

Freya squares her shoulders. "I need to understand our people if I am to serve them."

"That answers neither of my questions."

"Was it you who told the palace guard not to let me out of the palace?"

"Freya."

"You?" She looks at her father, who lifts the corner of his lips in an empathetic smile. Turning back to the queen, Freya straightens to her full height, hands in fists at her side. "If I am to be queen, you cannot be an obstacle in every direction I try to go!"

"I agree with the queen," I say, still sitting on the bike. I'd rather keep a physical distance from the family feud, and I'm a lot more comfortable with a quick escape route if I need it. After the way I handled Freya in the city, I don't see this evening going in my favor. "Her decision was clearly for a good reason."

Freya's eyes are fiery, reflecting the lights of the courtyard when she turns to me. "You forget your place, Mr. Reid."

The sound of a second motorcycle cuts over the top of her anger, growing louder until Sander drives into the courtyard on the bike I took and comes to a stop a few feet from where I'm sitting. He tugs the helmet from his head, reading the situation quickly as he looks at his family and the gathered guards.

"Sorry, mate," he mutters to me.

I nod to acknowledge him. I'm glad he was with the princess, but he never should have let her go in the first place.

"Aleksander," the queen says, her tone measured. "You and I need to discuss the night's events, along with Mr. Reid, so we might determine whether—"

"He needs to go." Freya folds her arms and fixes a glare on me. "Reid. I want him out of this country immediately."

Well, I had a good run.

"Freya, be reasonable," Stellan says, resting a hand on his daughter's shoulder.

She jerks away from his touch. "*Reasonable* would be arresting the American for putting his hands on me," she snarls.

All eyes turn to me, and my stomach tightens as I lift my hands in the air. "I was only trying to get her back here safely."

"I saw it through the window," Sander says. He's fighting a smile and losing the battle. "He did what I would have done in that situation."

"Other witnesses?" At the sound of Gregor's rough voice, I meet the security head's hard gaze.

"No," Sander says.

"None that I saw," I add carefully, "but I didn't have time to do a thorough sweep." I can only hope there weren't any cameras. Witnesses are one thing, but photographic proof of my less-than-proper methods would likely injure not just me but the royal family as a whole. If I had had more of a warning, I would have been better prepared.

"He was entirely out of line," Freya snaps, then turns to me. "You are dismissed."

"No," the queen and Gregor say in unison.

Honestly, I can't decide if it would be better if I did go. Derek was wrong, and the princess and I clearly don't work well together. But I'm not usually one to quit, so as long as Gregor wants me in his employ, I'll be here.

"It is evident Mr. Reid is exactly the protection you need," the queen says, and Gregor agrees with a sharp nod. "More so if you are going to act the childish fool."

I wince at the same time as the princess. That was too harsh, and Freya looks like she's been slapped. I don't blame her. She's thirty-three, and while she may be naive about some things, she's not a child.

Lifting her chin in a show of confidence that does nothing to hide her hurt, Freya looks me right in the eyes. "I will not be leaving my room tomorrow," she says, her tone firm. "Therefore, your services will not be needed, though I am certain you will place guards around my every exit as you see fit. Goodnight."

She doesn't stomp off like I think she might, instead keeping her head high as she gracefully heads inside, two guards trailing behind her at Gregor's signal.

The instant the princess is out of view, Queen Ingrid's shoulders drop in weariness. "Why?" she breathes.

I don't know who's supposed to answer that question, but Sander steps forward. "Her idea was a good one."

The queen presses two fingers to her temple. "Putting herself in danger?"

"She wasn't—"

"What happened?" I ask, cutting him off.

He shrugs. "Nothing a round of drinks couldn't fix." Looking at his mother, he offers her a sheepish smile. "You'll receive a bill tomorrow, Mum."

"And you will pay it," she replies coolly. "To bed, both of you."

Hex and Sander go inside without argument, though from the looks on their faces, I'm probably going to have them at my door as soon as I'm done here. That could be a while.

"Tell me everything," the queen says to me on a sigh. "And please tell me you have ideas for how to handle my daughter before she leads me to an early grave."

I do, but she's not going to like it.

Ingrid sees my hesitation, her eyes narrowing as she takes an umbrella from one of the guards. "You may speak openly, Mr. Reid."

Even though Princess Freya was incredibly foolish tonight, I can't help but admit there's a part of me that admires her tenacity. She doesn't need *handling*. She needs opportunity.

Preferably in a way that doesn't put her in danger and make my job harder than it already is.

Slowly getting off the bike, I approach the others with caution. The queen asked me to speak openly, so I do, even if a part of me knows this is likely to put my job in jeopardy. It's not like I'm on solid ground to begin with. "Freya's going to do what she thinks is right, whether you approve or not, and I think her heart was in the right place tonight."

Ingrid's jaw tightens. "Is that so?"

"I'm not saying I condone her methods." I cannot stress how much I hate what she did tonight and the spike of fear that hit me when Hex woke me and told me what was happening. "But she's right in that she won't know how to oppose Grimstad's popularity if she doesn't know what the people are looking for in a ruler. She needs to be out there like he is."

Whatever the queen expected me to say, it wasn't that, and all semblance of composure leaves her as she gapes at me. "You think my daughter should travel the country and *put herself in danger?*"

Don't smile, Elliot. I hold back a grin, but barely. This probably isn't the time to provoke my employer and accuse her of being dramatic. "I think she should *campaign*," I argue. "Show Candora who she really is. I'll be there to ensure there isn't any danger." My shoulder throbs, but I ignore the reminder of a past mission that didn't end how I'd planned. Candora isn't a war-torn country, and protecting a princess isn't strategizing for an entire twelve-man unit. I'll be fine.

"He has a point," Stellan says, speaking for only the second time tonight. The king tends to keep to himself and defer to his wife, which might be the only reason Ingrid doesn't shut me down immediately. He only speaks up when he truly believes something.

Taking Stellan's hand, the queen stares at me as she processes what I'm saying with worry marring her usually controlled features. She knows her daughter better than I do, and if I'm convinced that tonight won't be Freya's only attempt to go out among the people, surely she knows it as well. It'll be a lot easier to protect Freya if her adventures are sanctioned by the crown.

"Gregor?" Ingrid says softly.

The head of security steps forward, his gray head bowed. "I would arrange everything alongside Mr. Reid, Your Majesty."

"You approve?"

A small smile plays at the corner of his lips. "I know Princess Freya as well as you do, and Reid speaks true. I do not believe tonight will be an isolated event."

The queen turns back to me, her silence heavy in the humid night air until she asks, "So I have lost control of my daughter?" she asks wearily.

I stand tall, tucking my hands behind my back. "With all due respect, you taught her to be a queen, which means she is going to make decisions that she thinks are best and won't always follow your lead."

"I don't like this," she says, more to her husband than to me.

"But they're right," Stellan replies. "You know Freya. If this is what she has set her mind on, neither you nor I can stop her."

"But you could, Mr. Reid," the queen says, almost desperately.

I smile, unable to hold it back any longer. I can't believe I'm standing here in the rain, arguing with a queen and coming out the victor. "You hired me to protect your daughter, Your Majesty, not to make choices for her. If she chooses to leave this palace, I will be with her every step of the way. The choice *you* need to make is whether I have help."

With a sigh, Ingrid stands tall again and settles a calm expression on her face. "I can see why Derek recommended you, Mr. Reid. You are almost as willful as my daughter, and your boldness serves you well. I do not agree with the idea of Freya traversing the country, but I accept that I have little say in the matter. If you and Gregor can guarantee her safety, then I will allow it."

"You have my word, Your Majesty," Gregor says, giving me a look that tells me to join him in the office when I am able, then he bows to the king and queen and heads inside with the rest of the palace guard. Only the king and queen's bodyguards remain, standing at a far enough distance that they likely won't overhear the rest of the conversation.

I stay where I am, sensing further directions from the queen. She technically agreed to my campaign idea, but I doubt everything is settled yet.

Pinching her nose, Ingrid takes a few deep breaths. "I assume you will take Aleksander and Hendrik with you?"

"They're by far the best of the palace guard, and having your children all together for something like this will show a united front among the Alverra family." What I don't add is the notion that it isn't just Freya who's under scrutiny. The most vocal people rallying behind Grimstad have made it clear that they think the entire family is out of touch, hence the need for an overhaul. Besides, Hex and Sander are charismatic and have spent the most time among the working class while training for the palace guard. Even as princes, they're way more relatable than their uptight older sister and will be able to help prove Freya's opponents wrong.

The queen shudders. "All of them," she murmurs.

"It's better than Hex joining the RIA," Stellan points out.

The Royal Intelligence Agency, Candora's spy network, has apparently been trying to recruit Hex for years, but he remains adamant that he wants no part of it. He certainly has the skill and would be a huge asset to the agency, but I'd be happier having him at my side with Sander. If

Freya continues to be reckless like she was tonight, protecting her is going to take all three of us.

"I won't let anything happen to any of your children," I assure the queen, still standing at attention.

"No," she agrees. "You will not. You will protect them with your life, Mr. Reid."

Involuntarily, my mind flashes back to a rubbled city scorched by sun and heat. Gunshots echoing around me. My brother-in-arms pushing me out of the way, taking fire that should have been mine.

I swallow as my shoulder throbs again. I should have died that day, but Griff took my place.

If I have the chance to repay the favor for someone else, I will take it without hesitation, which makes it easy to promise, "I will."

Hollywood Hot Scoop

Her Royal Highness's New Guard Dog

WE ALL KNOW PRINCESS Freya Alverra has a habit of going through bodyguards like I go through boyfriends, but this latest one takes the cake. Why? HE'S AMERICAN. That's right, Scoopers! Her Highness has balked at centuries-old tradition and hired one of us Yanks to protect her, and from what we hear, he's more than suited to the job.

With the princess's upcoming election, we have boots on the ground in Candora, and one of our sources says Freya's new guard dog recently prevented what could have been a disaster, coming to Freya's rescue against a gang of thugs.

While we don't know much about the mysterious American who snagged the gig of a lifetime, there's no question that he's a hulking hunk of a man who managed to strike terror into his enemies.

Don't worry, Scoopers. We'll get you a picture soon enough, but until then, we'll have to imagine the man who is here to protect our favorite princess. (I'm going to imagine him looking like Derek Riley in *Man of the Embers*. Yummy!)

Speaking of Derek Riley, we asked our hometown hero what he thought about Freya's new bodacious bodyguard, and I don't know about you, but I'm sensing some jealousy on Derek's side. Maybe our leading man doesn't see Princess Freya as just a friend. Check out the video below and let us know if you agree in the comments! Make sure you subscribe so you can keep up with the upcoming Candoran election here on *Hollywood Hot Scoop*. XO

CHAPTER SIX

FREYA

AT SOME POINT, THE woman who brings the tea service every morning will admit to using the squeakiest cart when she comes into my room. She has denied it many times, but I am convinced there is a reason she has not bothered to get the cart repaired, and that reason is to annoy me.

"It is too early for tea," I grumble from my bed without opening my eyes.

"My apologies, Your Highness." But it sounds like she carries on with her work anyway, cups clinking and trays rattling.

If she would bring me something stronger than tea, I would be less annoyed, but my love for coffee has yet to make an impression on the kitchen staff. I have even purchased the necessary equipment, but they are adamant that a proper Candoran princess should only drink weak tea.

When the staff member finally leaves me alone in my room once more, I lie in my tangle of bedcovers in the hope of falling back asleep, but I already know it is pointless. I did not sleep during the night, so why would I sleep now when the sun peeks through the curtains?

Groaning, I slowly sit up and look around the room with bleary eyes. In the limited moments I managed to sleep last night, I dreamed I was walking the streets of Invem after my coronation. Someone shouted at me from the cheering crowd, telling me that I was not wanted, and Markham Grimstad was waiting for me a few steps ahead, his hand outstretched to steal the crown from my head.

Needless to say, it was not a pleasant dream, and I am exhausted.

Sighing, I untangle myself from my covers and cross the room to where the tea tray waits for me along with a tablet with the day's newspaper. As I pour a cup of tea, I scan the front page without taking in the meaning of any of the words. The headline says something about pretense and manipulation and—

I nearly drop the kettle when I see my name. Suddenly alert, I read the headline again.

Are Pretense and Manipulation the New Normal for
Freya Alverra?

Before I can read more than the first couple of paragraphs, which highlight my apparent deception in a pub in Invem, my phone lights up with a call where it waits next to the tea tray. I expect to see Derek's name, but it is Cole calling me.

"It is late," I say when I connect the call.

Cole chuckles. "For you it's early." With nine hours of difference between Candora and Los Angeles, our schedules do not easily allow for phone calls. "Have you looked at any of your texts?"

"As you said, it is early." Though, I would guess my friends have heard of my misadventure. With their lives so often in the public eye, they have learned to pay attention to the gossip. "I imagine you are not calling for a happy reason."

"*Hot Scoop* is in Candora."

I let out a curse and press my phone to my chest, my eyes shut tight. *Hollywood Hot Scoop*, an absolutely atrocious tabloid in the States, has done their very best to ruin the lives of my friends over the last few years. They have been particularly vicious in the past year, since the day they heavily targeted Liam after he had an altercation with someone at one of his concerts. I have been a topic of interest because of my relationships with so many high profile celebrities, but I had hoped I would be free from the gossip while here at home.

"What did they say?" I ask, almost too afraid to learn the answer.

Cole hums in clear debate with himself. "Ignorance can be bliss, Peach." His warning, combined with the nickname Liam gave me when we met a few years ago, reminds me how it was only a few months ago when Cole and his girlfriend, Carissa, were the website's primary targets. Before that it was Bonnie and her fiancé, Hank. The tabloid can be as cruel as they are fictitious in their claims.

"I will read it regardless," I tell Cole. "Give me a summary to prepare me."

"They found out your new bodyguard is American."

"Vitte." I had hoped to avoid that knowledge getting out.

"They claim you were attacked by a gang of thugs." He says this bit with a tone that suggests he is rolling his eyes.

I do the same. "It was only one man."

"What? You were really attacked? Freya!"

His concern brings some much-needed warmth to my chest, but I do not need him to worry about me from afar when his focus should be on his girlfriend. "It is my job to worry about you," I say. "Not the other way around."

"That's not how family works, Peach."

"I am fine. Elliot was there. He kept me safe."

I owe my bodyguard an apology. In the light of day and away from the moment, I can see why my plan was foolish. It is clear the people are more than simply frustrated. They were outraged when they realized I was in their space without their knowledge.

"Is Elliot going to last longer than the others?" Cole asks. There is hesitation in his question, and I wish this was a video call so I could see his face. Does he think me ridiculous for sending so many bodyguards away?

Perhaps the problem was not the bodyguards. Maybe *Hollywood Hot Scoop* was right, and I am the reason my protection agents did not stay long in their positions.

"I do not know," I say honestly. "I have a difficult time trusting, and he is frustrating."

"But he's a friend of Derek's, right? That has to count for something."

I wonder why Derek does not tell the others that Elliot is his cousin, but now is not the time to contemplate my friend's private life. Right now, I need to find Elliot and apologize for my conduct last night.

"Cole, you know I am always happy to talk to you."

He chuckles. "But you're busy. I know. Carissa says hi."

"Give her my greetings in return."

"She says hi back," Cole says, the words muffled as he speaks away from the phone.

"That is not what I said," I complain. "You make me sound as if I am one of you."

"Aren't you?"

No. I cannot be. Not if I wish to be a queen my people trust and respect. The thought of distancing myself from my friends further than I already have brings an ache to my chest, but it may be unavoidable. "Good night, Cole."

"Good morning, Freya."

After drinking a cup of abysmal tea, I dress slowly, trying to formulate the best way to apologize to Elliot. I accept that I was unfair to him, but I do not come by humility easily, and admitting my faults will be painful.

Painful but necessary. If not for my sake, for my brothers'. I put them in a difficult situation and asked them to betray their friend.

I still have not settled on what to say when I step outside my room once my attendant, Runa, has seen to my hair. The single guard posted beyond the door stands at attention. I expected more from Elliot, and the lack of extra supervision almost feels like an apology. Clearing my throat, I wait for the guard to meet my gaze. He does not.

"Where is Mr. Reid?" I ask, unable to hide my annoyance in my tone. I did not think I would miss the way Elliot is not afraid to look at me, but I do.

The guard stiffens, as if uncomfortable with my question. "I believe he is at the training grounds, Your Highness," he tells my shoes.

Intrigued, I thank the guard and begin my trek down the corridor with him a few steps behind. In the strangest way, he feels too far away, and I smile as I make my way through the palace. Only one day away from Elliot's diligence, and I miss his methods.

Or perhaps I simply miss knowing I am safe, even when I leave him behind. To think what may have happened if he had not come to my rescue... A shudder runs through me as I descend the stairs to the exterior doors. It is probably best not to think about what might have been.

The morning is warm, the skies unusually clear as I step into the sunny courtyard. Many of the palace guards are out training today, but it does not take me long to find Elliot amongst his peers as he spars hand-to-hand opposite Hex.

He is holding his own against my unbeatable brother.

"So it is true," I mutter as I come closer, standing near a few other guards who have taken to watching the fight. Like me, they have likely not seen anyone come this close to matching my brother's talents, and based on some of the muttered comments, a few of the guards have wagered money on the winner of this skirmish.

Normally, I would bet on Hex, but the longer I watch Elliot, the more I understand why Derek recommended him for the position as my protection agent. Particularly because Elliot has removed his shirt and is showing off the intimidating amount of muscle on his body, all of it straining and stretching as he jabs and dodges. He is...impressive.

He is also showing off several tattoos that span the length of his left arm. His right displays one as well, but most of the images are relegated to the one arm. I have only ever seen Elliot fully dressed, with long sleeves to hide the ink, and I wish he would stand still so I could make out some of the banded designs needled into his skin. Liam is the only one of my friends with a tattoo, but his is small, the lines thin. Elliot's tattoos are bold, broad, and seem to tell a story.

One of the spectating guards looks over at me and startles, dropping into a quick bow. "Your Highness," he says loudly, prompting the others to mirror him.

Elliot looks over, and Hex wallops him in the face, nearly knocking him off his feet.

"Oi!" Hex shouts, grabbing Elliot's arm before he loses his balance. "I thought you would dodge!"

Which means that hit was my fault. Wincing, I consider hurrying back inside because an apology after that distraction will not come across as genuine. But Elliot has turned his focus to me. With a tight jaw and a storm in his brown eyes, he shakes hands with Hex, then steps closer to me.

"Princess," he greets with a dip of his head.

"Elliot."

He tilts his head to the side, as if surprised that I would address him after last night. "You said my name."

Oh. I suppose I did. I have been thinking of him by his given name all morning, though I did not realize until now. "After experiencing you up close and personal," I say with a roll of my eyes, "it is more applicable, would you not agree?" Although, my time on his shoulders did not feel as intimate as this moment does, with his ridged torso on full display and his skin glistening with perspiration. His tattoos—I see now they are several Celtic knots twisting around his arm—are intriguing enough by themselves, but my stomach flutters each time my gaze accidentally drops to his bare skin and the way it stretches over taut muscles. He is entirely strong, more so than even Cole, and I have never seen a man like him.

"I thought you were going to stay in your room," he says, pulling my gaze back to his face.

Heat rises up my neck, leaving me overwarm in the sunshine. I feel out of place standing next to this man, my fair and delicate skin contrasting his tan and weathered body. "Oh. Er, yes, well, I thought I should..." I shake my head. "Could you please clothe yourself, Mr. Reid?"

He chuckles and folds his arms. There is a chain around his neck, a set of military tags hanging over his chest, but the name engraved on them is not his. *Joshua Griffin.* But I do not get a chance to wonder who that is because Elliot speaks with that same sassy tone he has used before. "Is my state of undress bothering you?"

No, it is not, which is the problem. I should not be admiring my protection agent, no matter how impressive his physique. "I wish to converse with you, and I find your current state..." Oh, why did I begin this sentence? What can I say that will not sound ridiculous? "Distracting."

Hex laughs and tosses a bit of black fabric to Elliot, who pulls the shirt over his head, unfortunately hiding his strength from view. "Methinks the lady doth protest too much."

I scowl at my brother. "If you are going to quote *Hamlet*, could you at least do it properly?" While I have less to look at now that Elliot has covered his torso, his arms are still on full display, each tattoo trying to grab my attention for study. "I...er..."

"Spit it out, Fringe."

Glancing at the palace guards watching our exchange with interest, I am suddenly too mortified to speak. I am not certain I can afford to show weakness in front of these men, even if Gregor trusts them implicitly.

Elliot frowns at me, then catches the attention of the other guards and mutters, "Give us some space, boys."

A few of them grumble, but to my surprise they all go back to their training even though Elliot has no authority over them. I would have thought they would consider the American below them, but it seems Elliot has managed to ingratiate himself to more than Gregor's and my family's favors.

I refuse to believe this man is perfect, but the more I learn about him…

Once I am alone with Elliot and Hex, who seems to think he is needed as a mediator between us, I take a deep breath, willing myself to speak, no matter how difficult. "I…" Goodness, I did not think apologizing would be *this* hard. "I am s…"

Elliot's lips twist into a smirk, his brown eyes dancing in the sunlight and looking almost golden. "Yes, Princess?"

"Sorry." The word ekes out of me, practically inaudible.

Hex snorts. "What was that?"

I grit my teeth. "I am sorry."

"I still can't hear—"

Elliot jabs his elbow into my brother's side, cutting him off. "Thank you," he says with a dip of his head. "I'm sorry for the way I handled you."

"I wish I could have seen that," Hex says with a wistful sigh, and I glare at him, tempted to pinch his side where he is the most ticklish.

Snickering, Elliot looks at him and lifts a single eyebrow. "Keep in mind I'm under no obligation to protect *you*, Hex."

To my complete surprise, a laugh escapes my throat, and I cover my mouth as I try to ignore the way Elliot's whole expression shifts at the sound. I do not have a flattering laugh, and I seem to have shocked him with it. "I have misjudged you, Mr. Reid," I say slowly, heat climbing my face. "And I owe you my gratitude for what you did last night. I was impulsive."

"Yeah, you were."

My good feelings toward the man vanish. "Must you say everything you are thinking?"

He grins. "With you, it seems the best plan of action."

"I am not fond of your plans of action." *Effective though they may be*, I silently add.

Elliot shrugs, his massive arms still folded over his chest. "I don't expect you to be, as long as you're alive and well."

"Did you at least learn something last night?" Hex asks, pushing himself into the conversation again.

"I did," I say and relay what I overheard from the table next to mine. "I learned that people are not idly hoping for change. Grimstad's chances are greater than I would like." My phone buzzes in my pocket, likely my mother summoning me to her office to discuss the article in the newspaper. She most certainly will not allow me outside the palace after this. "I fear I do not know how to change the people's opinions of me," I finish with a sigh.

"For starters," Elliot says, lips forming into a smirk once more, "you can try to talk like you're from this century."

"That is a battle that can't be won," Hex says with a heavy sigh. "Fringe came out of the womb sounding like royalty."

I reach out and pinch his arm, making him yelp. "You are insufferable!"

"I'm only speaking the truth!" he argues and lunges at me to retaliate.

Before Hex can even touch me, Elliot knocks him off his feet and steps between us. "Nice try," he growls at my brother, who bursts into laughter in the dirt.

While I would like to beg my brother to act his age for once in his life, all of the air has left my lungs, leaving me dizzy. "I…" I force a breath. "I hardly need protection from my own brother," I whisper, though I have never seen a man move so quickly. To say I am impressed would be a gross understatement, and I can only imagine what he would do if I were in real danger.

Elliot meets my gaze with stormy eyes. "I take my job very seriously," he says, his tone gravelly. "No one touches you without your permission."

Vitte. I resist the urge to press a hand to my racing heart as I stare up at him. "Does that include you?"

His lips tick up in a tiny smile. "Depends on the situation." He really does look so much like Derek. Not in coloring, but in the cut of his jaw and strength of his features. It almost makes him seem familiar. Perhaps Derek was right, and Elliot is the perfect man for the job.

I will not admit as much out loud. Not in a million years. Yet Elliot seems to hear my thoughts as his smile shifts into a smirk. Am I truly so easily read, or does he know exactly what he is?

"Shall I leave the two of you alone?" Hex asks, still laughing as he rises and brushes dirt from the seat of his trousers.

I do not realize how close Elliot is standing until he takes a step back, and suddenly I can breathe again. "I too take my job seriously," I say, ignoring my brother's insinuation. "And I need to fix things. I need to show my people they can trust me."

"Mum's never going to let you out again," Hex says.

But Elliot's smirk grows, leaving him looking almost mischievous.

When he says nothing, I ask, "What is it you are thinking, Mr. Reid?"

He snorts a laugh, far too amused for my liking. "I knew you'd come around."

I cannot help but smile as well. "In this instance only, I would like your opinion."

"You know you could have asked me, right?"

"For your opinion? I believe I just did."

Chuckling, he shakes his head. "No, I mean you could have asked me to go into the city. I would have taken you."

Warmth splashes across my face, mixed with an icy edge of regret that leaves me uncomfortable. *I could have asked him.* My humility can come with some trust as well. I have been wrong about Elliot in every instance thus far, so perhaps it would be better for me to stop assuming I know him and start letting him show me who he really is.

"You are right," I admit quietly. "I should have asked."

"I'm glad you agree, because the same is true for the queen."

Another guffaw of laughter escapes me. "You may have her trust, Mr. Reid, but that does not mean you have any sway over her. My mother rarely changes her mind."

"I changed *your* mind, didn't I?"

Yes, he did, and I have no idea how. I came down here to apologize, and somehow I have accepted him as my bodyguard and decided to trust him. "Yes, well, I am not my mother."

His gaze turns scrutinizing, but not in a bad way. He almost seems to be committing me to memory as his eyes trail over me. I cannot tell if he approves of what he sees, and it bothers me to no end that I want him to. "No, you're not your mother," he says. "That's a good thing. And fortunately for you, the queen has already agreed to let you campaign, so leaving the palace will be easier than you think."

My jaw drops, and Hex looks just as shocked as he stares at Elliot with wide eyes. "What?" I gasp.

With one final smirk, Elliot lets his arms fall and heads toward the palace doors. "We leave in four days," he calls back, "so you'd better start planning some speeches."

Ironically, this might be the first time in my life that I am completely speechless.

CHAPTER SEVEN

ELLIOT

IT'S A GOOD THING Gregor handled most of the logistics because there's no way I would have thought of everything required for a campaign trail like this. Cooks, stylists, an EMT, and several other palace employees are on the roster, people I wouldn't have considered. I can handle basic security, but I would have planned transport time around the speed of the cars. Not the speed of the horses we're bringing with us. *Horses*. One of the cities we're visiting doesn't have roads capable of accommodating vehicles, so everything will be brought into those locations by coach, and most of the guards are on horseback.

Which means instead of half an hour's drive to Breckenholt, our first stop, I'm stuck in this car with Freya for two hours because Gregor won't let me split up the caravan. *Two. Hours.* I'm not made for sitting still like this, and the princess is starting to notice.

She's sitting across from me in the extended town car the royal family uses, her focus on a tablet, but every minute or so she looks up, and her smile grows a little more, as if she knows how desperate I am to be out riding with the princes instead of in here.

An hour into the drive, she clicks her tablet off and sets it on the seat next to her. "You seem nervous, Mr. Reid."

I've been working on keeping my knee from bouncing, which wouldn't exactly give off the confident, put-together image I want to convey. "I'm fine," I mutter. I would be less anxious if I were facing forward and could see where we're going, but Freya took the forward-facing seat.

She presses her lips together, tilting her head as she watches me. "Breckenholt is much safer than Invem if one goes by the reported crime rate."

"Like I said, I'm fine." We have plenty of men to keep areas secure while the princess gives a speech to the townspeople everywhere we go, and I'm curious if any rallies for Grimstad will pop up outside Invem. I'm not anticipating trouble but will be ready for it.

Freya's smile grows. "I admit I do not believe you, Mr. Reid. You are allowed a modicum of anxiety, as this is your first foray into—"

"Okay, we need to work on that." I sit forward, eager to change the subject before Freya makes me focus more on my discomfort from being trapped in this car. "I know you were raised in a palace, but come on."

She frowns. "What?"

"You can't tell me you've been friends with a bunch of Americans for years but haven't picked up a more casual way of speaking." I kind of like the way she's so proper, but this whole campaign came about because she wants to get closer to the people of her country. I wrinkle my nose when she narrows her eyes at me. It's not like this is the first time I've brought this up. "This is the twenty-first century, Princess. Try to talk like it."

She scoffs, flipping her hair over her shoulder. This is the first time I've seen it down—half of it, anyway—and it's longer and thicker than I expected. I overheard her complaining to her attendant, Runa, that it would inevitably become a tangled mess before the end of the day, but

Runa insisted on a more casual hairstyle for her first campaign appearance.

I'm so glad Runa agreed with me when I suggested she try to help Freya loosen up a bit over the next two weeks, but I'm surprised she had the courage to stand up to the princess. I was out in the hall this morning, discussing some details with the two guards I have taking point so I can focus on the princess, but I could hear the argument happening inside Freya's chamber.

Freya was adamant that having her hair up is crucial to her appearance. Runa argued that Freya would be happier if she were comfortable. Freya insisted her comfort included her hair being up and out of the way. I get the feeling her hair is a sort of shield, and I wonder what she hides behind it.

Shifting her hair again, Freya lifts her chin high as she says, "I hardly think my manner of speech will—"

"If the people of Candora think you're elitist, talking like you're from the British aristocracy of 1830 is only going to prove them right." I grit my teeth when the car hits a bump in the road, and my anxiety spikes as I'm reminded once again that I can't see where we're going. There has to be a better way to travel while still maintaining proximity to the princess.

Freya huffs and folds her arms, as if my comment has no basis of truth. "Mr. Reid, I—"

"Elliot." I slip out of my jacket, hoping that will help me cool down. "Call me Elliot." She's done it before, and I much prefer that to my last name. Too many memories from my days as Sergeant Reid.

"Elliot." She sighs. "It is not easy to change my way of speaking when I have been doing it my entire life."

Laughing, I start rolling my sleeves up because it's still too warm. "It's just another language, Princess." I switch to speaking in French. "It takes practice." Then in Russian: "Your brothers don't have any problems with sounding normal."

Freya narrows her eyes and responds in Candoran. "My brothers excel in everything they do and could not care less what others think of them." At least, I think that's what she says. My Candoran isn't as fluent as I would like yet, but I have plans to practice with the twins while we're out here so I don't miss anything. Most people in this country speak English, but I'm going to guess the farther we get from the capital, the more people will gravitate toward their native tongue.

Shaking my head, I go back to speaking English. "From what I hear, you're as smart as they are. More so." Is that a blush on the ever-confident princess? I hold back a smirk. For all her outward confidence, she's too easily affected by a simple compliment. "Derek told me you've been his friend for more than half a decade. That's plenty of time to have picked up on some things. He also says you fit right in with his group of friends, so I know you have it in you."

She clenches her jaw, turning to look out the window for a moment. "Derek has told me almost nothing about *you*," she says coolly.

I can't decide if she means it as an insult, but it won't work regardless. "That's because Derek and I barely know each other. We didn't even meet until last October."

That pulls her gaze back to me. "Truly?"

I shrug. "We don't need to get into my family."

"What if I want to?"

Biting the inside of my lips, I debate if that would be a good idea. Getting familiar with my charge is necessary if I'm going to properly protect her, but I don't need her to know *me*. For a lot of reasons. "Not the best idea," I decide out loud.

But Freya leans forward, instantly putting me on edge with her sudden nearness. "If I am to practice sounding less royal, I will need to do so in a conversation. I will give you a choice. We can either discuss your family, or you can tell me about your tattoos."

Thrown by the two options she presented me with, I recognize too late that she's trying to turn the conversation away from herself. "My tattoos?" I look down as her gaze starts tracing one of the Celtic knots that loop around my left arm. I can understand her curiosity about my family, with the way I deflected, but what about my ink is so interesting that she considers it a worthy alternative?

"Well?" She looks up, meeting my eyes with her own. They are quite striking, a bold blue color that seems even brighter with the skies outside hanging heavy with gray clouds. "Which would you prefer, Elliot?"

Neither. My left shoulder throbs, directly beneath the owl wings tattooed there, and I instantly know which topic I would choose. If this campaign is going to go smoothly, I need Freya to trust me, and she won't be able to do that if I don't give her at least something.

"It was always just me and my dad," I say, squirming in my seat when we hit another rut in the road. "Never knew my mom. She took off when I was born."

With a satisfied glint in her eyes, Freya settles back in her seat and says, "Any siblings?"

"Nope."

"You are related to Derek on your father's side?"

It's strange to me that she doesn't already know this, considering how close she is to Derek. Hex and Sander have talked about how much time their sister spends in Los Angeles or on video calls with her friends. I can see Derek being a private kind of guy, with how famous he's become, but why wouldn't he trust Freya with his family dynamics?

"Yeah," I say, furrowing my brow as I study her. "His dad and mine are brothers."

She tilts her head. "But you have different surnames."

"He's not the first actor to use a stage name."

"Are you close with your father?"

Close is a relative term, but I'm guessing she's curious about my relationship compared to hers. The Alverra family are tight-knit for being royals, and I envy that. Particularly her closeness with her brothers. For all their teasing, the twins adore her, and it's clear to see how much she likes them in return. I was on my own as a kid, which is why I bonded so tightly with my detachment unit when I joined the Special Forces. They were my brothers, for all intents and purposes. It's been nice to have Hex and Sander to fill that gap left behind when I resigned, but it isn't quite the same.

My eyes drop to my exposed forearm again, scanning the dark lines that represent the soldiers I served with. It's been almost a year since I left my unit, and I still feel like I betrayed them by leaving. It doesn't help that they keep messaging me, begging me to come back.

"I guess you could say my dad and I were close," I say, keeping my voice even while my chest grows tight at the thought of my brothers-in-arms. "He and my uncle didn't get along, so it really was just the two of us."

"Was?"

I nod and hold out my right arm, where a date sits etched into the side of a mountain tattooed on my inner wrist. The day my father died. "He got sick. Passed last year, which is how I met Derek."

Her eyebrows rise. "At the funeral?" she guesses. When I nod, she pulls her eyebrows together. "He never said..."

"I'm getting the feeling there are a lot of things Derek's never said."

The car turns quiet, and I can't tell if Freya is hurt by the things I'm telling her or if she's just processing what she's learning about her friend. If any of this is stuff Derek doesn't want me to share, he probably should have said so, but I don't think he expected me to talk with Freya like this. I didn't expect it either, but this is the first time the princess and I have actually been alone. She's somehow figured out how to get under my skin, which I don't love.

"Tell me, Elliot Reid," Freya says after a long while. She meets my eyes again, and there's a new sort of determination in her gaze. Something tells me this isn't the last time she'll get me to talk, which is not good for my sanity when it comes to this job. "Are you alone in the world?"

For some reason, that question makes me smile. "Yeah, but it's not so bad." Technically, I chose a solitary life. I could stay in better touch with my old team, but it's easier to keep my distance after everything that went down. The less I interact with them, the less tempted I'll be to reenlist and hope they can pull enough strings to get me back on the team. Everyone's better off if I don't do that.

Her expression turns sad. "Elliot."

Clearing my throat, I sit up straight and tug my sleeves back down, as if hiding my tattoos will keep her from getting through my shields again. "You should be glad. It's the only reason I can be here to keep you safe."

She accepts my deflection with a soft smile. "Hex and Sander seem grateful for your friendship. One can only hope your example will teach them to be serious now and then."

The twins are plenty serious. When they need to be. It's obvious that she loves her brothers, but when she says things like that, I wonder if she really knows them and their struggles. She clearly doesn't know much about Derek either despite him being one of her closest friends. She asked if I'm alone, but I'm starting to think I'm not the lonely one in this car.

"I do not think the twins have had many people match their skills," Freya continues, "and as they refuse to fight each other, they have had no one to properly spar with."

I chuckle. "It's not like they need the practice." I'm not one to talk myself up, but it takes all my concentration to keep up with those two, and that's saying something. "Not like you," I add, narrowing my eyes at her. "I thought that conversation was supposed to be a way for you to practice sounding like the rest of us."

Her smile turns almost devious, which is a look I haven't seen on her before. I like it. "Ah, I see you have caught me."

"You've."

"What?"

I shake my head as I shift in my seat. "It's those contractions that will help you sound more relatable. 'I see *you've* caught me' is what you should have said."

Sighing, she rolls her eyes and returns her gaze to the window. "I see *you're* going to be a most irritating companion."

Companion. It's an interesting word choice, though she doesn't seem to notice what she said. I'm here to protect her. To make sure she lives the life she wants to live and let no one get in her way. I didn't come here to be her friend.

But as I sit across from her while we trundle through the countryside, I can't help but wonder if a friend is exactly what she needs.

CHAPTER EIGHT

FREYA

ALL IN ALL, MY first speech of the campaign went better than I expected. No one shouted insults, no one booed me off the temporary stage, and no one threw rotten fruit at me. But the applause when I finished was lackluster at best, and I am convinced most of the people of the town of Breckenholt only came out to the town square because they were curious. Yes, a few dozen of them have formed a line to greet me and welcome me to their town, but thus far everyone lingering in groups around the square have seemed more skeptical of my intentions than interested in meeting me.

Praise the heavens for Hex, who took to wandering the crowd while I spoke and has managed to befriend a group of young adults who have crowded around him like he is the most compelling person they have ever met. Maybe he is. Or maybe he simply does not have the weight of the crown looming over his head, so he is allowed to be fun and free.

"Your Highness." The middle-aged woman at the front of the line bows, her expression tight. "Welcome to Breckenholt. I'm Britta Nilson.

I own the inn where you'll be staying tonight, so please let me know if there is anything you need. Anything at all."

Goodness, she looks terrified. I smile wide, doing my best to make it look warm and relaxed. My friend Bonnie has, thankfully, taught me how to make a fake smile look natural, something she has mastered during her years as an actress. "I am certain everything will be lovely. I thank you for your hospitality."

A throat clears behind me.

Gritting my teeth, I take a breath and force my shoulders to relax. "You're very kind, and I'm looking forward to my stay." I refuse to look behind me to see if that satisfies Elliot.

Britta offers another short bow and steps aside to make space for the next person. Though I have a chair I might use, I remain on my feet, hoping it will make me look less superior. I only wish I had accepted Runa's suggestion that I wear more comfortable shoes, as these heels are not being kind to my feet.

"Princess Freya." The man who steps forward is already in a formal bow, his right hand pressed to his heart and his left arm tucked behind him, and he remains in that position while he speaks. "I was hoping we would run into each other sooner rather than later."

A spike of fear pierces me in the chest, though I am not sure why. "Is that so?" I glance behind me, breathing a little easier when I realize Elliot is only a few inches from me, his eyes fixed on the man.

Elliot growls out a name. "Grimstad."

The man rises, an amused smile on his face as he meets Elliot's hard gaze. "You've done your research, bodyguard."

This is Markham Grimstad? The man who is running against me? He looks nothing like his picture on the Candoran government website. That man is polished and stoic. This man looks at home among the other villagers, his jaw covered in a trim brown beard, his hair a bit too long, his clothes plain.

He chuckles when he looks at me. "It's strange we've never met, isn't it, Your Highness? I'm at the palace every week, so you would think we'd have run into each other before now."

My words stick in my throat. I was not prepared to come face-to-face with my opponent, especially not like this, when the whole reason I am here is because of him. What am I supposed to say? My entire life of training and preparing for diplomatic conversations has completely faded, leaving me with nothing but my own wits. Wits that have also abandoned me.

Grimstad does not seem to mind my silence, still smiling as he glances at the line behind him. "I don't want to interrupt your meet-and-greet, but I wondered if you and I could talk when you're done here. Candidate to candidate."

I look at Elliot again, as if he has the answers.

He shrugs. "Up to you, Princess. I can arrange a meeting with Grimstad's people if you accept."

"Oh, I don't have people." Grimstad chuckles again and folds his arms. "It's only me. I don't need all this pomp and circumstance to get my point across. I suspect that'll still be the case when I'm elected."

He will not be elected if I have any say in the matter, and yet he seems convinced that my position will be his. Of all the arrogant, conceited, ridiculous notions... "I believe I should be done for the day, Mr. Reid," I say and wave to those still in line. "Aleksander?" When my brother steps up to my side from the line of palace guards, I tell him, "If you could offer my apologies to those who have been waiting so patiently, I would be most grateful. Mr. Reid?"

With one final look at Grimstad, Elliot directs me past the guards standing at attention and to Britta's inn, where she and some of her staff are ready to receive me. I go straight to my room, though I have to wait until one of the guards sweeps the room and ensures everything is as it should be. That only adds to my irritation over Grimstad's arrogance, and though I wish to lie down and scream into a pillow, I move instead to the window and look out over the still-gathered crowd. Grimstad has joined the group surrounding Hex and seems to be charming them as easily as my brother did.

Does he think his victory is guaranteed?

"Princess?" Elliot stands in the doorway, hands behind his back as he watches me.

I sigh. "I wish you would not call me that." At least it is better than calling me 'Your Highness,' which is a surefire way to remind me of my station. Of my inability to connect with my own people. "I have a name, and you might as well use it."

"I could call you Fringe."

I wince and turn back to the window to watch the easy way Grimstad interacts with the townspeople. "I would rather you did not."

"Why do your brothers call you that, anyway?"

Memories of a terrible haircut from two decades ago flash through my head. I do not wish to revisit the way my fringe was cut far too high on my forehead and at a severe angle, but I know my brothers too well. If I do not tell Elliot the reason, one of them will.

Sighing, I pick up my phone from the desk and search for a picture. "In my defense," I say once I have found one, "I was only twelve, and I did not choose the cut." I wait until he comes closer, then hand him my phone.

To Elliot's credit, he does not laugh despite the humor dancing in his eyes and a smile threatening to break free. "Yeah, I don't think I can call you Fringe when it'll make me think of that."

"You could call me Freya."

"I could," he agrees, which does not sound promising. He is likely to concoct his own nickname for me, and I am not certain I trust anything he might come up with.

Besides, he shared some of his inner self with me during the drive this morning. I owe him part of me.

"My friends call me Peach."

"Why?"

I look out the window once more, smiling as I remember the first day I met Liam Connolly. He was the newest addition to Derek's carefully curated group of friends, joining us only a few years ago. Despite being quite famous himself at the time—Liam is a veritable music genius—he was nervous to meet me and called me Princess Peach instead of Freya. "My friend Liam says I resemble the princess in a popular video game," I explain with a small laugh.

"I can see it."

I turn to him in surprise. He does not seem the type to have played video games as a child. "Can you?"

"Appearance-wise, sure, but you don't strike me as a damsel in distress." Elliot's eyes trail over my hair, making me all too aware that it has been years since I left it down like this in public. Leaving even half of it loose this way makes me feel like I no longer have part of my armor, and I am vulnerable. After a moment, his gaze shifts over my shoulder, to the town square outside, and I can breathe again. "They're eating out of the palm of his hand, aren't they?"

Grimstad laughs at something, his gaggle of admirers joining in. I do not see Hex anymore, and it looks like most of the palace guards have taken up their posts around the inn, leaving Grimstad full control of the square. The people of Breckenholt look far more welcoming of my opponent than they were of me, which does not make for a promising start to my campaign.

"He is younger than I expected," I say, frowning as Grimstad does a playful and complicated handshake with a young man.

"He's only thirty-five. Just a couple of years older than you, which is part of his platform."

I turn my head in surprise. "How do you know that?"

Still gazing out the window, Elliot shrugs. "I got the same dossier you did."

"Yes, but knowing these things about Grimstad is not part of your job."

"Isn't it? Grimstad is in direct opposition to you and poses a threat."

"Politically, maybe, but not physically."

"Doesn't matter." Elliot's eyes drop to me, and we seem to realize at the same time that we are standing rather close to each other. Close enough that I catch a hint of his clean scent and notice a ring of honey at the edge of his brown eyes. He takes a step back, tucking his arms behind him as he murmurs, "A threat is a threat." His lips twist up. "I take my job very seriously." His echo from the courtyard the other day brings back the memory of how he overpowered my unbeatable brother.

That is something I would not mind witnessing again. Have I lost my mind if I almost hope for some sort of danger to befall me while I am away from Invem? Perhaps, but I would like to see what Elliot is capable of.

"I am well aware of your dedication, Elliot," I say, my voice breathier than I mean it to be.

His smile grows.

"You're going to have to change your strategy," Hex says as he steps through the open door. "They love him."

I groan. "Do not tell me that, Hex."

He shrugs as he joins us at the window to look out, an arm around each of our shoulders. "It's the truth. If I wasn't already convinced you need to be out here learning about the day-to-day life of an average Candoran, I would be now."

"Speeches aren't going to do you any good," Sander says from the doorway. It seems my room is the place to be right now.

"I agree," Hex says.

I look at both my brothers in turn, hating that they seem so confident about this when I have barely managed to stumble my way through so far. I have prepared my entire life to be queen, and yet it seems I am the least equipped to get there. "What does that mean?" I ask.

"It means Grimstad has been getting his hands dirty," Elliot mutters. His gaze is on the square again, fixed and focused. "He not only has a lifetime of experience to share with your people, but he also isn't afraid to put in the work."

I follow his gaze, wondering what he is seeing to make him say that. Grimstad is just talking with the gathered people, but he looks right at home with them. He *is* one of them, something I can never be. Not if I want to be their queen. Surely Grimstad would lose that connection if he were elected and could not keep every promise he must be making to the people.

I hate that I do not have an answer to this problem. No Alverra monarch has had to deal with opposition like this. "How do I combat that?" I ask the room in general, knowing they will not have the answer either.

All three of them give each other meaningful looks. I cannot decide if I love the way Elliot seems to be as connected to my brothers as they are to each other, or if that makes me nervous. He is more lighthearted with them than he is with me, and I worry their immaturity will influence him instead of the other way around.

But no, I cannot think that when I am already anxious. Elliot has given me no reason to think he will be anything but what he has promised. He told me some of his past today and has given me another reason to trust him, and that holds far more weight than unfounded fears. I only wish he would tell me more.

There is much more to this man than the stubborn soldier, and a large part of me wants to know him. *Really* know him. I want to know why he will not talk about his tattoos. I want to know why he chose the path of

Special Forces, and why he left when he has the skills to be great. I want to know why he looks at me so often with those searching eyes when the only thing required of him is to keep me safe. He has no reason to look deeper, and yet...

"This isn't my area of expertise," Elliot says, tucking his hands behind his back.

Sander rolls his eyes. "I thought you were the strategic genius on your detachment team." Is that what Elliot's position was? Strategy? I should have paid more attention to his résumé instead of blindly trusting Derek's recommendation.

Elliot huffs. "I'm no geni—"

"Most of your career has involved dealing with insurrection movements amid social and political issues."

My bodyguard grits his teeth, as if Sander's argument has irritated him. "Irrelevant."

Hex scoffs. "Hardly. You told us that one of your missions was based around influencing popular opinions to sway in favor of a new political leader. Is that not what we're doing now?"

While I am overwhelmed by the things my brothers are saying—this explains why my mother often asks for his opinion—I cannot help but notice something lurking in Elliot's eyes behind the irritation. It looks like pain. Guilt. Either he lied to Hex and Sander about his background, or Elliot Reid is hiding something else. He must feel me staring at him because he meets my gaze and masks the emotion I saw on his face.

For some reason, I wish to help him avoid the subject.

I clear my throat, pulling my brothers' attention to me as well. "I am tired from today's traveling, and I would like to rest before my dinner with Lady Volhorn." A shudder runs through me that I cannot hold back.

The countess was not pleased by my request to meet here at the town center, and she is not one who hides her disappointment. As this dinner was scheduled per my mother's instruction—she believes I must interact with the noble class as well as the working class—I need all the energy I can muster to endure her comments of distaste.

Sander and Hex share another silent conversation, but Elliot's eyes remain fixed on me until he ducks his head and excuses himself. "I'm going to take a look around town for a bit and see if I hear anything that might be useful. Princess, you'll have two guards at your door and three outside your window, should you need anything before your dinner." He bows his head slightly, then turns to my brothers. "I won't tell you what to do, but I suggest going to bed early tonight. Tomorrow will be a long day."

I cannot recall a time my brothers ever went to bed at a reasonable hour, and their matching smirks mirror my thoughts. "Sir, yes, sir!" Hex says with an American salute, his open palm perpendicular to his forehead.

Elliot sighs but says nothing else as he quits the room.

"He is right," I say, eyeing the twins.

Chuckling, Sander is the first to follow Elliot out as he says, "We'll get plenty of sleep, Fringe."

"Once we see what Breckenholt has to offer," Hex adds and follows him to the door, leaving me on my own.

My solitude will not last long—it never does. Runa will be here at any moment, and I suspect my mother will not be able to wait much longer before she calls for an update and an agenda for my dinner with Lady Volhorn. I use my free moments to watch Grimstad sit on the step of the small monument at the square's center, surrounded by people. Everything about his body language is calm and relaxed. Everything I was not. He has an advantage I cannot easily match, but surely there is a way to make up for my deficit when it comes to connecting to my people.

As I watch, Grimstad lifts his head and looks up in my direction. He must see me through the window because his smile grows, and he dips his head in a bow.

Before today, I knew winning this election would take some effort, but I can see I have underestimated my opponent. I can only hope he has underestimated me as well.

CHAPTER NINE

ELLIOT

"Elliot."

My gun's in my hand, the barrel pointed straight between the intruder's eyes before I recognize the voice of one of the twins. I exhale quickly and blink, telling my body to relax. *Lower the gun, El.* I do, but stiffly. It's hard enough to tell the twins apart in daylight and when I'm fully awake, but it's four in the morning and too dark out here to know which one of the princes thought it was a good idea to sneak up on me.

"What are you doing?" I hiss out, still on edge from the adrenaline spike that shot through me at his soft word.

He chuckles and leans against the wall of the building next to the inn. I found this alley during my earlier sweep of the town square—it offers a good vantage of the square while providing decent cover—and I didn't think there was access from the back. Apparently I was wrong.

I hate being wrong.

"I should ask you the same thing," he says, all nonchalance. Hex. He must be Hex.

I slip my Glock into my shoulder holster and turn my focus back to the square. "I thought I told you to go to bed early."

"You *suggested* it, if I recall. I'm not fond of taking orders."

"Are you fond of nearly getting yourself killed?" I grumble. "I could have shot you."

"I knew you wouldn't."

That makes one of us. I'm pretty sure I had started to doze off when he said my name, and I quickly rub the sleep from my eyes, wishing I had done more to prepare for this trip. The anxiety from the drive never fully dissipated, which means the car wasn't the problem. *I'm* the problem. That's the worst thing I could be dealing with right now.

Well, maybe the second worst thing.

"Do you see him?" I ask, my voice low.

Hex keeps his eyes on me, his expression serious. "Why do you think I came down here?"

"Where's Sander?"

"He's asleep. I got up to use the loo and noticed the lurker, and I thought maybe you'd be out here keeping an eye on him."

Someone has been standing in the shadows across the square for three hours now. I hoped he was a drunk waiting until the world stopped spinning before he walked home, but he's been too still. He's waiting for *something*. Or watching. I have never missed my tactical gear more than I do right now. Night vision would be especially helpful.

So would sleep.

"I would ask why you haven't sent one of the palace guards over to check it out," Hex says, shifting so he's standing next to my hiding place, "but I'm pretty sure I know the answer."

Swearing under my breath, I try to think of the best way to respond. "It's not that I don't trust the guards."

"But they're not you."

I sigh. I was used to having full confidence in my brothers-in-arms and knowing they would do the same thing I would in any given situation. We were so in tune with each other that sometimes it felt like we could read each other's minds. I don't have the same luxury with the Candoran guards, and I'm not sure I ever will.

"My job is to protect the heir to the throne," I say. "I won't leave her safety up to chance."

"Gregor trained them himself, just like he trained you."

"Gregor only trained me in Candoran customs," I mutter, narrowing my eyes as the man in the shadow shifts his position. There's a chance he saw Hex, but it doesn't seem to have bothered him. "I already knew everything else."

Hex snorts a laugh. "You say that, but you refuse to talk about your Green Beret days. You could be telling knobbies." When I glance back at him and raise an eyebrow in question, he laughs again. "Lying."

"Ah." It's not that I don't want to tell Hex and Sander about my Special Forces training, but the more I talk about it, the more they'll ask about the missions I went on. I've told them about a few to keep them satisfied, but if they ever ask for more... In theory, I could hold this position for a long time. If Freya becomes queen and decides I'm not terrible at my job, I could be here for years. The twins welcomed me right from the beginning, and at some point, I *should* trust them with the darker sides of my life.

But how does someone go about explaining how he got his best friend killed in action during an op gone wrong? That doesn't encourage continued friendship.

"Oi." Hex nudges my arm, making me tense up again, but then he gestures across the square, where the lurker's face is now illuminated by a phone screen.

He's too far to get a good read on his expression, but at least I can note some of his features. Thin nose, thick eyebrows, round chin. Distinct enough that I would recognize him if I saw him again. The screen goes dark, and the man melts into the shadows and disappears. He might come back, but my gut tells me his vigil is done for the night.

Doesn't mean mine will be.

As if reading my thoughts, Hex nudges me again. "You should get some sleep, El."

Probably, but I want to revisit what information the RIA has on dangerous people in Candora. The intelligence network sent me pictures last week, and I want to compare them to our friend across the square while the image of him is still fresh in my mind. He didn't seem dangerous, but I'm not willing to rule anything out until I know for sure. There was enough talk around town of support for Grimstad and reformation for me to be on alert. Electing Grimstad is one way to invoke change.

Removing his biggest obstacle is another.

"Yeah," I say, if only to get Hex to go back up to his room. I need him to be alert tomorrow, though a part of me likes the idea of shifting one of the twins' schedules to a night shift so there's someone competent on watch at all times.

But no, utilizing the princes as guards would defeat the purpose of having them here as part of the campaign, and they need to make appearances during the day. I have to remember that their lives are as important as Freya's. Protecting them is a lot less stressful than looking after the princess, but that doesn't mean I can lower my guard.

With the way Hex narrows his eyes at me in the dim moonlight filtering down between the buildings, it's clear he's not going to believe me if I tell him I'll be right behind him. Maybe I'll sleep for an hour or two, then come back down to the street. I'll make sure the outer guards know there was someone watching the inn. I didn't want to alert them before and have them accidentally scare off the lurker.

But as I follow Hex up the stairs to my room—the one next to Freya's—my body is telling me that my decision to stay on watch was a bad one. I can last longer than most on low to little sleep, but if I do this every night, it's going to start taking its toll and limit my ability to do my job. I need to be focused and take care of myself so I can be at top performance.

I don't have enough information telling me I have legitimate reasons to worry. Freya isn't in danger.

Yet.

My bed calls to me when I get to my room, but instead of collapsing onto it, I move to the window and look out through the darkness. I won't find the lurker there, but I'm still curious about his intentions. Looking for holes in security? Searching for openings in the princess's schedule? Hoping to make us nervous?

I grab my phone and move away from the window so the light won't be as obvious, intending to look for a match to the lurker in the RIA's database. Instead, I find an alert that brings me to a new article from the tabloid that seems suspiciously obsessed with my cousin, Derek. *Hollywood Hot Scoop*. I didn't even know the website existed until a few months ago, when Derek first reached out to me about coming to Candora, but now I've been dragged into their stupidity thanks to Freya's unsanctioned outing to Invem last week.

I haven't figured out how they found out about that night, but at least they didn't have many details.

Princess Freya's Frantic Fight to Find Followers, tonight's headline says, and I narrow my eyes as I skim through the article. It's all nonsense, talking about how Freya has taken to the campaign trail in a pathetic attempt to seem more friendly. The author has decided Freya thinks too highly of herself if she thinks making a few speeches will be enough to turn public opinion, stating that Freya's time would be better spent working retail if she really wants to know how regular people live. According to the article, Freya's interactions with Derek and his celebrity friends have tainted her view of the world and made her think she's better than she is.

Derek does not have this problem, or so the article says, and he manages to stay humble no matter how much his fame grows. Based on the comments, no one seems to recognize the sheer hypocrisy of everything this website posts.

"Sounds to me like someone is trying to get your attention, Derek," I mutter, closing the website and pulling up his number.

As always, he answers in only a couple of rings, but I barely hear what he says because the background is full of noise. "Hey, give me a second."

The line goes silent for about thirty seconds, during which I peek out the window again, as if something might have changed in the last five minutes. The square is still empty, though from up here I don't have as good a sight line of the corner where the man was standing. That could mean he didn't have a good view of the princess's window, but I'd have to check *her* view to be sure.

"Sorry," Derek says, and this time it's without the noise. "What's up?"

"Where are you?" That shouldn't be my first question. It doesn't matter where he is or what he does with his time, but my curiosity is too strong. My cousin's world is so completely different from mine, and I have no idea how a guy like him would spend his evenings.

"Uhhh." He draws the word out, like he's trying to come up with a believable lie. "Technically? I'm on a date."

"A date?" Again, none of my business, but for some reason that surprises me. According to the internet, Derek hasn't dated anyone since breaking things off with his still-a-friend ex-girlfriend, Bonnie, and he seems to keep to himself otherwise. It takes me way too long to realize the implications of what he said, and I wince. "Oh, uh, this can wait if you need to get back to—"

"She's fine. What's up? It's the middle of the night there."

Right. I feel weird about interrupting his date, but if he's willing to talk, I'll gladly get some answers. "Tell me about *Hollywood Hot Scoop*."

He lets out a heavy sigh that sounds so weary that I almost think it's the middle of the night for him too, even though it's around seven in California. "What did they do this time?" But his voice is distant, so I'm pretty sure he's already looking up the article. He swears under his breath, then says, "I guess it could be worse, and you weren't mentioned this time around, which probably means their source wasn't all that forthcoming. Has she seen this yet?"

I'm assuming he's talking about Freya. "Like you said, it's the middle of the night."

"Right. Outside of *Hot Scoop* being a pain in the butt, how are things going? I haven't heard from you for a couple weeks."

Did he expect to? He told me to figure it out, and that's what I've been doing. I'm pretty sure Freya trusts me now, if our most recent interactions are any indication, and that's really all I need from her. Instead of answering Derek's question, I ask, "Should I be worried about this tabloid causing problems?"

"Hmm, that depends on if they start following your campaign trail. They are generally pretty harmless, but when they want something, they're not afraid to play dirty."

"Freya told you about her plans," I guess, my voice shifting to more of a growl. I don't love that she's spreading information around, even if I trust Derek for the most part. It's easier to keep her safe if fewer people know where she'll be at any given point.

Derek chuckles. "Not in detail. She's smarter than that, Elliot."

"I wasn't implying she isn't. But I..." I need to sleep and stop being so paranoid. I need to trust in the men I have here with me because I certainly can't trust myself.

That last thought settles heavy in my gut, leaving me slightly nauseous. Gregor may have planned a lot of this trip, but he's trusting me with the minutia, and I'm no stranger to the adage that the devil is in the details. It's details that got Griff killed.

Swearing under my breath, I shake my head as if that might shake the thoughts away. My friend's death wasn't my fault. I couldn't have changed the outcome of that mission. I *know* that. But my heart doesn't always agree with my head.

"El." Derek's voice is soft. "You're good, right? Because I'm trusting you to look after my friend. If you're not okay, then—"

"I'm fine." I'm less fine knowing he somehow knows what's running through my head from more than five thousand miles away. He can't know me well enough to know my demons, even if he's one of the few people in the world who know why I left the Forces in the first place.

I never planned to tell him, but Derek has a way of convincing people to talk to him. When we met, I had just left my detachment, and since he's the only family I've got...

"You know it's okay to not be fine, right?" he says, though it's obvious in his wary tone that he thought about not asking that question.

I scoff. "Says the man who can do no wrong."

"The internet doesn't know everything."

Is he talking about himself? Or are we back to talking about the tabloid? I'm too tired to ask. "Any tips for combating this stupid website? I thought you of all people would have the right connections to get them shut down."

He sighs again. "You and me both."

Before I can respond, it sounds like a door opens on his end of the call, bringing the distant hum of the same noise I heard before. A sweet, feminine voice says, "There you are! I was worried I lost you."

"I should go," Derek says, his voice thin. "I'll try to keep an eye on *Hot Scoop* in case they flip a switch and start getting nasty."

"This isn't nasty?"

"You have no idea. Take care of—"

"Freya, I know. You've said."

"I was going to say take care of yourself. You don't have to overcomplicate things before you have reason to."

"Derek!" the same woman says, much closer to the phone this time. "They want to take some more pictures of the two of us together."

I can't help but chuckle. "Sounds like I interrupted something fun."

"Call or text whenever. Good luck, El."

"Who's El?" the woman asks indignantly right before the call ends.

Chuckling, I sit on my bed and let the darkness settle over me. Derek's life really is so different from mine, and I would be perfectly fine with keeping it that way. I'm going to do everything I can to avoid being in the spotlight like he is. Like Freya is. That's not a life I've ever wanted, and I don't know how they live with that constant scrutiny.

I need to protect Freya from that too before things get 'nasty,' as Derek put it.

With that thought, I stretch out on the bed and do my best to fall asleep quickly.

It doesn't work as well as I hope.

CHAPTER TEN

FREYA

Hank:

Do a children's book reading event.

Liam:

Oh I like Carissa's idea do a concert

Kasey:

My idea was similar to Hank's but with local storytellers sharing traditional stories from their area.

Bonnie:

You could also visit local businesses and see how their day-to-day lives go.

Liam:

Puppy parade with crowns to prove your adorable

Kasey:

*you're

Liam:

Whatever

Cole:

Go fishing with locals and let them talk freely.

Liam:

Drinking contest with the local fishermen!

Derek:

Liam, that isn't helping.

You need ways to sit down with the people and let them talk without your differences in station getting in the way. What about a Q&A meeting?

Freya:

I tried that, and it failed spectacularly, which is why I have come to all of you for help. Some of you are more helpful than others. Thank you for your ideas, but I should probably step away from my phone for a bit. Love you all!

Liam:

We have your back Peach even if you don't like my ideas

I sigh and lock my phone, setting it on the seat next to me in the town car as I close my eyes. I had hoped to find solutions to my thus far disastrous campaign, but my friends, well-meaning as they are, are not close enough to the situation to understand why I am struggling.

In the hope of learning more about public opinion, I turned my planned speech in the town of Kirkstead this afternoon into a sort of town hall, opening the floor to questions. The first woman who stood did not ask a question but instead complained about the disparity between the noble and the working classes, which led to each person afterward doing much the same. Their complaints, however valid, raised the tension in the room until the church where we set up erupted into chaos, and the palace guards had to shepherd me from the building as the people chanted Grimstad's name.

Elliot refused to remain in town longer than necessary, forgoing our stay in Kirkstead—and afternoon tea with a very put-out lord and lady—and making last-minute arrangements to spend an extra night in Windgaard where we are heading now. He has been on edge ever since, sitting stiff and silent across from me as the royal cavalcade makes its slow trek over the moors to the eastern coast.

Before I decided to reach out to my friends in California, I perused the many news stories that have popped up in the hours since the disastrous event, and I have come to realize that it might be better if I avoid the internet when I can. Not only has the tabloid site *Hollywood Hot Scoop* gotten wind of today's adventure—I refuse to read their article, for my sanity—but all of Candora is talking about my blunder. My attempts to fix my lack of knowledge have only put me further behind Grimstad's popularity, and my heart is heavy.

"Everything okay?" Elliot keeps his voice quiet, but tension is clear in the clipped way he speaks.

I open my eyes to find him watching me with those keen eyes of his. He has been quiet today, more of a soldier than usual, and I have missed his snark. Strange, when it irritated me so much at first.

I gesture to my phone. "I hoped my friends would have ideas for how to proceed, but I fear they are ill-equipped to properly find solutions to my predicament."

Elliot's lips twitch up, likely because of my choices of words. I must sound entirely pretentious, though I feel anything but important. I have clearly failed my people for the whole of my life.

"Yeah," he says, "well, we Americans aren't always the smartest when it comes to politics."

"This is less about politics and more about human connection," I argue. "I am certain the people of Kirkstead needed reassurance that they were being heard and their voices mattered, and I sat there in silence. I had no idea what to say." When Elliot offers no response to that, I groan and drop my face in my hands. "How can I be so terrible at something I have prepared for my entire life?"

"Campaigning? That's what you've been training for?" When I glare at him, he chuckles and shakes his head. "No one said ruling a country was easy, Princess."

"At this rate, I will rule nothing but my own life. If that."

He hums and shifts in his seat, stretching his legs out a bit. "Hypothetically speaking, what happens to your family if someone other than an Alverra is elected to rule?"

Historically, this has never happened, so I do not blame him for wondering. Even with my extensive knowledge of Candoran law, the hypothetical offers an unclear future. "The election process has not always been in place," I tell Elliot. "It was instated only two centuries ago, when the House of Commons concluded that birthright can become dangerous when left unchecked, and they managed to sway enough lords to their side to pass the vote.

"The change in law never would have happened if the members of Commons had not chosen to propose the idea during the reign of a particularly selfish king who came close to bringing Candora to ruin with his greed. The elections have never gotten in the way of an heir taking the throne, but they have kept my ancestors in check."

"Smart." Elliot folds his arms and waits for me to continue.

"This is the part of the law that becomes uncertain. Should someone other than the Alverra heir be chosen by the people to rule, the constitution will change, adapting to a purely electoral monarchy. Much like your government, I suppose, but with longer terms. There will be no line of succession."

"And your family?"

"We would remain among the nobility and have a seat in the House of Lords, maintaining our assets and some of our influence. But there is some question as to which assets belong to the crown and which belong to the Alverras. For example, my ancestors built the palace where I live, and yet half of the palace is dedicated to the government now. Does the building belong to those who have cared for it and made many cherished memories inside, or does it belong to the kingdom?"

And do we deserve to keep anything we have at all when we are simply the products of time and circumstance? That is a question I am afraid to ask out loud.

"So what you're saying is everything will be simpler if you beat Grimstad?" Elliot's eyebrows pull together as he studies me. "No pressure, then."

I let out a breathy laugh. "Yes, that would be simpler."

"But?"

I should not say what is on my mind, but I do anyway. "But maybe that is part of the problem. Maybe one of the reasons we are 'out of touch' with our people is because we have—" I pause when one of his eyebrows lifts ever so slightly. "*We've*—become too ingrained in the monarchy itself." More thoughts start building in my mind, enough to make my heart beat against my ribs. Thoughts I have never entertained. "What am I if not a princess?"

"I'm sure you're—"

"It is no wonder I cannot connect with people when I am barely connected to myself. The only time I ever feel like more than just a political figure is when I..." Stopping again, I take a moment to consider what I was about to say.

"When you what?" Elliot asks. I highly doubt this is a conversation he was hoping to have, but I am grateful that he is willing to listen.

"When I am with my friends," I finish with a frown.

Elliot purses his lips. "Your friends, the super famous celebrities and millionaires?"

I roll my eyes. "Yes, those friends. While it is true they are well known, and most of them are wealthy, the heart of our friendship is knowing we are as human as anyone else. We keep each other..." How did Cole put it once? "Grounded. Humble. Or, as humble as we can be, given our circumstances." I add that last part because Elliot looks like he might laugh.

"You feel normal around them because they're the only people who come close to your level of importance." Elliot shifts in his seat again, glancing out the window as his fingers curl into fists. "You're equals."

"Are you uncomfortable?" I ask him.

"I'm fine."

"You were equally restless this morning when we left Breckenholt, as well as during our travels yesterday."

He grunts. "I don't love facing backwards and not having an idea of where we're going," he admits in a mumble. "But I'm fine."

Picking up my phone and the blazer I draped across the seat next to me, I gesture to the space I cleared. "You are welcome to sit here."

He grimaces. "I don't want to crowd your space."

"I would not have offered it if I was not amenable to the idea."

He snorts a small laugh, shaking his head at me. "You're something else, Princess."

I am going to assume his remark is related to my manner of speech and not anything else about me. "Please," I say and gesture to the empty seat again. "If it would make you more comfortable, that would also put me at ease. If my bodyguard is nervous, how am I supposed to feel?"

He seems to debate for a moment, but then he slips over to the seat beside me and lets out a sigh as his gaze fixes out the window. "Thank you."

Though I did not expect it, my body relaxes as soon as his does, and I cannot decide if it is because he was truly making me nervous or if I am starting to like having him close. When things got out of hand at the church, he was right at my side, his arm wrapped around me in a way that made me certain nothing bad would happen to me. "Thank you for protecting me at the meeting today, Elliot."

His eyes drop to his knees, as if he is remembering the events of the afternoon. "I know today didn't go like you hoped, but you'll figure out what you're doing."

"How can you be sure?"

He offers a bright smile that warms the interior of the car. "Because you're a lot more than a pretty face, Princess. Anyone in their right mind can see that."

His smile may have warmed the car, but his words warm my heart. This man keeps surprising me, showing me facets of himself that I never would have guessed were there if I had stuck to my first impression of him. Not only is he strong, talented, and intelligent, but he is friendly, kind, and insightful. He is stubborn and clever and...goodness, he certainly takes up a lot of space. This town car has always felt spacious, but at the moment it feels small. I am more aware than ever of how big Elliot is when a bump in the road jostles me into his shoulder.

Now I see why he chose to sit on the opposite side before.

Not one to rescind an invitation, I fiddle my thumbs and try to focus on anything but his clean scent filling my nose. The warmth of his body seeping through the sleeve of his black jacket. The scars dotting his large hand resting on his thigh. What calamities have his hands seen?

"At least Grimstad was not there today," I say to break the silence.

He chuckles. "He was, actually."

"What?" My voice cracks as embarrassment washes over me. "Why did you not tell me?"

To my surprise, Elliot smirks as he watches the countryside go by. "I didn't realize you'd want to know."

"Of course I would want to know if my rival is watching me crash and burn!" Oh, what must that man think of me now? If he was arrogant before, he will be insufferable now.

"I figured he would make you nervous, and I was paying attention to other things. But don't worry. Hex kept close to him to make sure he didn't cause any trouble."

There is that, I suppose. But there is something in the way Elliot is avoiding my gaze that makes me think there is more to today's disaster than what I am aware of. "Elliot," I say with warning in my tone.

He glances at me. "What?"

I narrow my eyes at him. "'Other things'?"

To my surprise, that is enough to make him sigh and shift to better look at me. "Someone was watching the hotel in Breckenholt, and I saw him again in the audience at Kirkstead."

I should probably feel some fear after a declaration like that, but the connection is too vague and Elliot's demeanor is relatively calm. "And? Who is he?"

"I don't know," he grumbles.

"A reporter? Or he could be someone eager to hear what I have to say and was not satisfied in Breckenholt."

Elliot rolls his eyes. "He was watching the hotel for most of the night, and his appearance doesn't match any of the known journalists in Candora."

Two appearances do not make a pattern, so I am having a difficult time finding a reason to be worried. "Perhaps he is working for *Hollywood Hot Scoop.*"

"He's Candoran," Elliot counters. "Sander is sure of it."

So, Elliot had Hex watch Grimstad and Sander watch whoever this man is. I am glad my brothers are proving useful for once, but I think Elliot might be paranoid. "Should this worry me?"

"No."

"Then why tell me?"

"Because you asked." His lips tick up. "But no matter who he is, I won't let him or anyone else get anywhere close to you."

I lift an eyebrow. "So certain?"

"I don't do things halfway."

Of that I am well aware, and my mind flashes back to when he came to my rescue in Invem. The man was so determined to get me back home that he ignored all rules of etiquette. Thank goodness he did not have to resort to such methods today. I can only imagine the field day the press would have if my bodyguard was seen carrying me over his shoulders.

Face heating, I smooth my hair and look out the window. "Windgaard is one of the bigger cities in Candora, so it may be more difficult to determine if this man has followed us again."

"Well aware," Elliot mutters, clearly not thrilled by this thought. "Are you planning to do a speech again, or change it up like you did in Kirkstead?"

I have yet to decide. I do think the question and answer today was the wrong move, but so was the speech. I frown as I consider the ideas my friends gave me, my anxiety rising. "I do not know my best option," I say out loud, though I hate admitting weakness. I am always the one to give my friends advice, but I cannot seem to find the same wisdom for myself. "What do you think I should do?"

He turns to me at the same time I turn to him, his eyebrows pulled low. He looks the same way Derek does when he is particularly thoughtful. "You're asking for my opinion? Again?"

I let out a short, breathy laugh. "I suppose I am. But do not get used to it."

"Wouldn't dream of it."

"I thought, with your experience, you might have some ideas."

He shifts in his seat, shoulder brushing mine. "Honestly, I'm not sure I have enough information yet to give you any helpful suggestions, but it's always a good idea to be authentic to who you are."

"Says the man who wants me to change my manner of speech."

He chuckles. "Fair point, but I still think you'd be better off cutting out some of your formalities. They aren't who you are at the core."

He has a point, and I can't help but wonder who *Elliot* is at his core. I have seen him be lighthearted with my brothers, but he is serious and determined when he needs to be. There are so many other parts to him I have yet to see; I am certain of it. Who is Elliot Reid?

It may be a long time before I find out. I need all of my focus to forge a path forward on this campaign.

"Authentic," I say, testing the word. It only reminds me that I have been a princess, the future queen, for so long that I have almost forgotten the woman behind that role. If I meant it when I said I am most myself when I am with my friends, then it would stand to reason that I should use that to my advantage. To be authentic, how I act with them is how I should act with the Candoran people.

Could that work?

I have never been shy about interfering in my friends' lives. Sometimes, they do not know what they need or are too afraid to do what is necessary to get it. I once threatened to ban Cole from coming to my coronation if he did not face his trauma head on, and I constantly push Liam to write his music when he lets himself get distracted from what he loves.

I may be pushy, but my friends know better than to think I do not have their best interests at heart. Perhaps that is the direction I need to go with the Candoran people. Somehow. Rather than struggle to figure out what they want, I need to do things my own way. Stand strong and show them what they *need*, which I can only learn through observation.

I knew this from the start, but my poor attempt in Invem broke my confidence. Will I let one mistake stop me from doing what is best? No. I am Freya Alverra, and I will always rise to the challenges placed before me. I have to.

Unable to hold back my smile, I bite my bottom lip and shake my head. With how he reacted the last time, Elliot is unlikely to appreciate what I am thinking.

"What is that look for?" Elliot asks, his tone wary and his brow furrowed again, proving my suspicions correct.

Shrugging, I pick up my phone again so I can begin to make a plan. "I do not think you wish to know."

"Now I definitely want to know. What are you planning?"

Nothing yet, but a spark of renewed confidence comes to life inside me as I watch his body grow tense, as if he already knows what is coming. I have come to trust him, and I hope he will learn to trust me in return because he is right. I need to be authentic, and I cannot do it without him.

My adventure in the capital last week proved that.

Besides, he could use a little excitement in his life, with how tense he has been on this trip thus far. He is paranoid, and that will help no one.

"Will you relax?" I tell him, instead of answering his question. "I will be sure to tell you my ideas before I implement them."

He narrows his eyes, saying nothing, but his worried thoughts are clear.

Yes, I think being myself is exactly what I need to do.

CHAPTER ELEVEN

ELLIOT

"I can't believe you talked me into this," I say through gritted teeth, scanning for threats as our open-air bus trundles through the streets of Windgaard. I don't think I have ever been this stressed in my life, and I once had to extract a high-value informant out of a halfway collapsed warehouse while under fire because our cover had been blown.

This is worse.

"And if you look to your right," a portly gentleman says, his Candoran accent thick through his microphone, "you will see the sea wall where the great Captain Dunholm fended off British invaders for eight straight days with nothing but a small band of fishermen."

"Fascinating," I grumble. If I were in any other circumstances, it might actually be an interesting story, but I'm too busy cataloguing all the ways this could go wrong to pay attention.

Freya nudges her elbow into my side, her smile faltering when she hits the gun holstered beneath my jacket, like she didn't realize it was there. "You are getting on my nerves, Mr. Reid," she hisses under her breath. "I am trying to listen to our wonderful tour guide."

Our "wonderful tour guide" has brought up The Great Fish Fry of '98 six times now, as if a city-wide seafood feast is the most exciting thing to happen in the history of Candora.

"We're getting off at the next stop," I say as my leg starts bouncing. We shouldn't have gotten on the bus in the first place, but I made the mistake of trusting the princess when she said she wanted to check on something around the corner from our hotel. Thinking it would be a quick stop, I left the rest of the palace guards to get the event center ready in case Freya decides to continue with the original plan of giving a campaign speech.

Now we're on a tour bus. In plain sight. Riding around the whole of the city where anyone can get to the princess. If she dies because of this, it'll be entirely her fault.

But I'll be the one to take the blame.

"Mr. Reid," she says again and touches a hand to my bouncing knee. "Please."

My eyes jump to her warm fingers, stuck there for a long moment because this might be the first time she's touched me. Elbowing me in the ribs doesn't count, and she hit my Glock anyway, so the fact that her pale hand *remains* on my knee is making it difficult to concentrate. Maybe it's the lack of sleep over the last few days jumbling my thoughts, but suddenly the words *'she's touching me'* are on repeat in my head.

Only when she moves her hand can I think straight again. "I'm never listening to you again," I mutter so only she can hear. "You know that, right?"

Despite my low tone, the young couple in front of us glance back like they have multiple times throughout this tour. I don't think they heard me, but they've clearly recognized Freya. They look more intrigued than suspicious, which is the only reason I haven't tucked my hand inside my jacket to be ready to pull my gun at a moment's notice.

"Elliot," Freya says, softer this time. "This is a good idea."

I scoff.

"I know you agree with me because you stepped on the bus to begin with."

She has me there, but I didn't count on this tour being *four hours.* Seriously, I don't think there's a city in the world with enough points of interest to justify a tour this long. We're only an hour in, and I can only imagine how much detail I'll know about the smoked Haddock our guide ate almost thirty years ago by the end of the tour. He's already talking about the fish fry again.

"Remind me again why this is necessary," I say and narrow my eyes at the couple in front of us when they turn around again. They quickly face forward and start whispering to each other. "There are going to be pictures of you everywhere."

"Yes."

"*Freya.*"

"This is necessary," she says forcefully, "because I have never spent any significant time in this part of Candora, and I wish to rectify that."

The urge to groan rises with every word she speaks. If she's going to start taking public outings like this everywhere we go, and I highly suspect she is, she really needs to work on her speech patterns. It's one thing to change the way she talks when she's giving a practiced speech, but it's another to do it naturally in conversation when around regular people like we are now.

"Okay, Rapunzel," I say, shifting in my seat so I'm sort of facing her. My knee bumps into hers, pulling her eyes down for a moment, but she's back to looking at me a second later.

"What did you call me?"

I eye the blonde hair streaming down her back. It was in a loose braid when she came to find me and asked me to accompany her out of the hotel, but the hairdo fell apart as soon as the bus started moving. It's windy in Windgaard—big surprise—and now her hair is a mess. No wonder she keeps it up all the time.

"You heard me," I say with a shake of my head. "Here's the deal."

She lifts an eyebrow.

"I still think this is a bad idea and that we should get off at the next stop and hightail it back to the hotel before you're swarmed by people hoping to get a glimpse of you or worse."

Her eyebrow rises a little higher, giving her a haughty look that stokes the irritation and anxiety burning in my gut. "But?"

"But if I'm going to let you be out like this, you have to try."

As her expression shifts into confusion, she glances at the tour guide, who is somehow *still* talking about fish. "Try?" she repeats.

"Try to talk in a way that will make people feel connected to you. In a way that will make people trust you." I think back to one of my missions in Eastern Europe, when Griff and I had to convince a whole community to trust a wannabe politician who was trying to beat out his tyrannical opponent. We had to teach him how to talk in a way that didn't put distance between him and his constituents, as he had grown up in a completely different walk of life from their poverty-stricken area. Until he learned to match the people he wanted to represent, he had no sway.

Freya's eyebrows pull low as she watches me. "You are serious about this," she murmurs.

As if I might have been joking all the other times I suggested it. I thought for sure she would have at least believed her brothers, but they tease her too much for her to realize when they have good ideas. They should work on that if they're ever going to be anything but 'The Princes.'

"I'm always serious," I say and smirk, which makes her chuckle, but I let my smile drop because I *am* serious and need her to know as much. "I can admit you've gotten better in the last two days, but do you really think Mr. Halevik up there thinks he's your equal when you talk about rectifying your insignificant time spent in his birthplace?"

"Here is the infamous Colgrave Square!" Halevik, our tour guide, says brightly. The last two words distort over the speakers in his enthusiasm. "It was here in 1803 that a local Windgaard legend once protested a royal edict by running through the square stark naked."

Honestly, I'm not sure he's even noticed Freya here at the back. That, or he doesn't care that there's a princess on his tour. From the way he's been talking, I'm guessing he has given this tour hundreds of times, and the nine people on this bus are just a few of thousands that he will forget as soon as we step off the bus.

But then Freya raises her hand.

Halevik is about to keep speaking, but he stumbles over his words when he catches sight of her hand in the air. "A question?" he asks in pure shock, as if no one has ever had a question for him. Maybe his constant talking has put off anyone who might have.

Six pairs of eyes turn back to us as the other members of the tour look back, and my muscles tense. We've been pretty lucky in terms of attention from our fellow tourists, except for the one couple, but now I'm clocking recognition from almost all of them. Even the bored-looking teen who was probably dragged along by his parents.

"Yes," Freya says loudly, to be heard over the wind. "What was the edict he was protesting?"

Halevik frowns. "Oh, well, it was the change in who is allowed to inherit titles."

At some point I should read up on Candoran history. I have the last century pretty solid, but anything before that? "What was the change?" I ask.

"Titles were once passed through only the male line," Freya answers before Halevik can, "but the change made it possible for women to inherit."

"Exactly that," Halevik confirms, and he sounds impressed. Does he really not know who Freya is?

"That sounds like a good thing," I say.

"Many would agree with you," Halevik replies.

"What's your opinion?" Freya asks.

The other tourists keep looking back and forth from the front to the back as we speak, and I wonder if Freya's question has completely derailed the tour. We're still driving, passing landmarks we might have heard about if Freya hadn't interrupted.

Halevik shrugs. "I am nowhere close to being noble, so it means nothing to me." For a second, I think that's all he's going to say on the subject, but then he adds, "It left things more chaotic, not knowing who would have power and influence, particularly when a single woman was to inherit a title."

Freya's shoulders grow tense. "What's wrong with a woman having influence?"

"Nothing," Halevik answers without hesitation. "But they are more likely to be seen as a means to an end, which was why Colgrave was protesting. He thought the change left women vulnerable if they were titled and unmarried."

"Progressive," I mutter as I start tapping my fingers on my knees.

It's been more than two hundred years since this law went into effect, but do any Candorans today share Colgrave's worries? Are they afraid to vote for Freya because they think she'll leave the throne vulnerable? As far as I know, the ruling monarch has more power than their spouse regardless of gender, but whoever marries the monarch still has influence. And as much as I hate it, most men still think they have power over their female counterparts. Anyone who courts Freya, assuming she even allows it, will likely be after the throne rather than truly interested in her.

"I see your thoughts," Freya murmurs, her eyes on my drumming fingers. "I suspect my marital status may be one of the issues with my popularity, yes."

"If you look at the white-stoned building up ahead..." Halevik says, continuing with the tour.

After doing a sweep of the street we turn onto, I shift some of my focus back to the princess. "It's a common problem with royalty. Did you ever..." I stop, knowing better than to ask about Freya's dating life.

She scoffs and sits up straighter. "While I have had many prospects, no one has ever caught my interest."

"No arranged marriages I should know about?"

"None that I agreed to."

"But there have been attempts?"

She smirks. "I am quite a catch, you know, the future queen of Candora. Luckily for me, as queen I will have the law on my side. Outside of someone with power in their own country equal to mine and with the intent of forming a political alliance, only a Candoran can wed a Candoran monarch."

That doesn't sound lucky to me. I can't imagine someone telling me who to marry, in part because dating has never been high on my list of pursuits. Not a lot of time for romance when I enlisted straight out of high school and was recruited to the Special Forces as early as I could be. My knack for languages and being a quick learner made me an ideal candidate, and I never hesitated.

My shoulder throbs, and I can't stop my thoughts from drifting to Griff and the way he always ribbed me for being single. He adored his wife and his two little girls, and his love for them pushed him to do everything he could to return to them after every mission. He was the only one in our ODA with a family, and yet he was the only one to lose his life.

Nora, his wife, told me more than once that his death wasn't my fault, just like she told me more than once after my dad died that I couldn't spend the rest of my life alone because it was easier to spare myself the pain of more loss.

Whether she's right, I managed to find a job where being on my own is pretty much guaranteed. Unless Freya doesn't get elected, in which case I'll...do something. I don't know what. This job was a lifeline when I needed it most, and if I end up being unnecessary, I'll have to find something else to keep me busy. Something to challenge me so I don't get lost again like I did after leaving my detachment.

"Elliot? What is wrong?"

When Freya flinches the moment my gaze turns to her, I realize I'm scowling and relax my features. "Nothing."

Amusement lights up her eyes. "I would have thought you would be a better liar." She turns her attention to Halevik once more, and I have a feeling we're going to do the whole tour whether I want to or not.

At least Freya is certainly presenting a challenge, but this isn't exactly what I had in mind.

Chapter Twelve

Freya

I HAVE LEARNED SOME important things on this tour. One, there is much more to learn about my country than what I can read in history books. Two, Windgaard has excellent seafood, and I absolutely need to return for the next Great Fish Fry. And three, I am far better at making friends than Elliot, something I take great pride in when it has always been a struggle for me.

Mr. Halevik ended the tour at a tiny café off one of the many piers along the coastline, where we enjoyed the most delicious fish and chips I have ever eaten. I sat at the same table as the others despite my certainty that they would have liked me elsewhere, but now they are all talking and laughing with me while we drink tea after our meal. I think Mr. Halevik would have joined us too if I had not worn him out with my many questions throughout the rest of the tour, and he bade us farewell before disappearing with the bus and its driver.

Elliot has not left the doorway once. Not even when Jason, one of my new friends, invites him to join us.

"Is he always so serious?" Jason asks as he comes back to sit with his wife again. He and his wife, Laura, came to Candora for their first anniversary, and I hoped Elliot would respond better to a fellow American after the way he tried to bore a hole into Mr. Halevik's head with his glare when we stopped in a place other than where we started. It seems I was wrong, and Jason looks like he nearly met his demise by talking to my bodyguard.

I let out a wistful sigh. "Not always," I admit. "But I think he's nervous with me out on my own like this."

"You are not alone," Orla says, reaching across the table to grasp my hand. A woman in her late forties, she is from the northern mountains of Candora and has come to Windgaard to enjoy the seaside before summer ends. "We are all friends here!"

The others at the table agree with enthusiasm that makes Elliot roll his eyes. The restaurant is too small for him not to hear the conversation we are having, though he has yet to add to it.

I thought Elliot wanted me to befriend people—it is why I have been focusing hard on my manners of speech throughout this lunch—but he seems to think I have made the wrong friends. I disagree. While Jason and Laura will not be able to vote for me, nor the teenaged Evert and his Swedish parents, the other two at the table can. With the rate Grimstad's popularity is growing, I will take every vote I can get.

Besides, I adore these new friends of mine. It took a few minutes for them to warm up to the idea of eating lunch with royalty, but I am almost convinced they have forgotten that I am a princess. I learned a good deal about life in Candora from Mr. Halevik's tour, but I have learned more from sitting with these friends who were strangers only a few hours before.

Grinning, I squeeze Orla's hand and pull mine from her grasp. "Yes, I'm so glad I have made so many friends today."

"We are better than Derek Riley, right?" Evert asks.

I snort out a laugh. Sometimes I forget how far Derek's fame reaches. "That is a wicked question," I complain. "Derek has been my friend for far longer."

"I still can't believe you're friends with Derek *Riley*," Laura says as she fans herself, while Jason raises an eyebrow next to her. "If I were still single..." She squeaks when her husband pinches her side playfully, and she pats his face with an affectionate grin before turning back to me. "Did you ever think about dating him, Freya?"

I notice Elliot's head turning slightly, like his attention is on me now instead of the walkway outside. I ignore him. "No," I answer truthfully. "While Derek is one of my dearest friends, my love for him has only ever been platonic, just as his affection for me has only been friendly. We are too stubborn to be anything more."

"It's a good thing you're stubborn," Orla says. "You'll need it for this election, with the way Markham Grimstad is charging along."

"Charging is an excellent way to describe his campaign," I agree. "I wasn't even aware he wished to run for office until a couple of weeks ago."

"No one was," Roarke says. He, like Orla, is here on vacation, though I do not know much about him other than his name. He seems nice enough, if quiet. "I think that is part of his appeal."

I sit forward. "What do you mean?"

Shrugging, he sips his tea and explains, "He obviously had the support of the House of Commons to begin with, but I think he purposefully waited as long as he could before making his intentions known so he can capitalize on the novelty of the idea. No one has ever gone up against an Alverra." He grimaces a bit and takes another sip of tea, nodding at me to signify an apology. At least, that is what I assume the nod means. "Whether people really think his platform is a good one, I would guess they're more interested in the *idea* of him. With things being as they have been for a long time, people are eager for change."

"But *I* would be a change," I argue. I would never speak against my mother, but there are many things she and I do not agree on. Things I planned to do differently when I took the throne.

Roarke shrugs again. "People probably don't know that."

"That is precisely why I am going around the country, to understand what the people need and want and to show that I am willing to listen." I deflate a bit as I remember yesterday's chaos. In my frustration, I forgot to shift my words, and I remind myself to talk less formally. "But so far I'm not accomplishing much."

"We're listening!" Evert says brightly.

I smile at the teenager. "I appreciate that."

"I think this was a good way to go about things, going out and about without all the pomp and circumstance" Orla says, and then her expression turns mischievous. "Even if your handsome bodyguard disagrees."

Elliot huffs out a breath without looking back. "This is dangerous," he grumbles.

"This is Candora," Roarke argues. "Nothing dangerous ever happens here."

Elliot scoffs again.

"I have very much enjoyed today," I tell my new friends with all the sincerity I can muster. "But two votes from new friends can only get me so far, and that is me being presumptuous. You are allowed to vote however you wish, and I will not take offense."

"You have my vote," Orla says kindly.

Roarke grunts, which could go either way.

"I'm afraid I know how to run a country but not win one over," I admit, even if I hate how insecure that makes me sound. "No matter how determined I have been to be a good queen, I never thought I would have to prove it so quickly."

"What has this Grimstad guy been doing to prove he can be a good king?" Jason asks.

Grabbing hold of my hair, which is a tangled mess that will likely make Runa cry when I return to the hotel, I pull it over my shoulder and start running my fingers through it, hoping to keep my nerves from showing. "That is an excellent question, one I don't have the answer to. I know his policies, but there is more to his platform than that."

"He talks to people," Roarke says in a measured tone. "Boots on the ground. I've heard he talks to people in the queue at the grocer and at the bank, that he joins cricket matches in the park. He's a regular person, but he knows his politics too."

I get the sense that Roarke is one of Grimstad's followers despite his assertion that Grimstad's popularity is more of a fad than anything. I am glad he is still willing to talk to me and share insights. A friend, indeed.

If I am to mirror Grimstad's strategy, I need to come up with specific ideas rather than choosing the first thing I come across, like I did today. Spontaneity does not suit me well, and I work better with a plan.

Thinking back to my friends' suggestions yesterday, perhaps they were more astute than I realized. Bonnie suggested cleaning up a park; if I did it without any fanfare or cameras, I could talk to people while also serving them. A children's story-reading event would introduce me to parents who want the best future for their children. Derek said I should do things that put me on an equal footing with my people—my reasoning for taking a tour bus—and Derek is usually right when he has an idea. It certainly worked today.

All of those things could accomplish both my goals—observation and interaction.

"I want to meet and speak to as many people as I can," I say, letting go of my hair and dropping my hands into my lap. I look at Orla across from me. "I am open to suggestions. If I had not forced myself into your lives by taking the tour with you, how would you have liked to meet me?"

She gives me a warm smile. "It would have been fun to see a princess walk into my antique shop."

An interesting idea. More importantly, it is a good one. I cannot step into every business in Candora, but I could choose a few in every city and town we stop in. That would not be too difficult.

As if he hears my thoughts, Elliot glances back and meets my gaze, his eyes narrowing slightly. Anything I do will require him to adjust security measures, though I agree with Roarke that nothing dangerous ever happens in Candora.

The man who grabbed me in Invem was a fluke. A lone issue in the biggest city in the country.

"I once saw the King of Sweden on a bicycle in Stockholm," Evert says. "It was strange."

The Swedish king does not have the same power as a Candoran monarch—he is only a figurehead—but I still value the boy's input. "Do you think it would be strange to see me riding a bicycle in Candora?" I ask him.

He shrugs. "Maybe? But it would make you seem more normal."

"Am I not normal now?"

Turning a bright red, he ducks his head and mumbles, "You're too pretty to be normal."

Laughter bursts out of me at full volume, something I have avoided until now because the sound tends to alarm people. But my friends around the table join in, thankfully masking the obnoxious sound of my inelegant laughter. Even Elliot cracks a smile in the doorway.

"You are sweet," I tell Evert. "Perhaps I will try a horse rather than a bicycle." I would much prefer that to being in one of the horse-drawn coaches we have brought with us for the parts of the country without modern developed roads.

"I recommend you don't go everywhere with the entire palace guard surrounding you," Roarke says into his tea. Almost like he did not want me to hear him.

But I did hear him, and so did Elliot, who stiffens in the doorway and looks back with a furrow in his brow.

"That one may be more difficult," I say, keeping my words light. "Though I agree with you."

"Your handsome American is frightening enough as it is," Orla says with a giggle.

Elliot's lips twitch, and I am almost certain he is trying not to smirk with pride.

She is right to call my bodyguard handsome, though I would not call him frightening. Intimidating, yes, but I have seen enough of Elliot's softer side to know there is a heart beneath all that muscle. After all, he is the one who fought for me to be out here in the first place instead of trapped in the palace, away from all these people who need to be heard.

"Your Highness," Elliot says, pulling everyone's attention to him. "We should be heading back for your meeting."

I do not even know what time it is. I left my phone at the hotel, choosing to take the day as it comes, and I forgot about my meeting with the local nobility. I do not think I will be able to miss this one like I did yesterday, as there are several seats in Lords from Windgaard and its surrounding towns, and all of the nearby title holders have come into the city to meet with me this afternoon.

As much as I wish I could avoid them, I will need their support. The contrast between lunch with friends at a quaint seaside restaurant and a stuffy roundtable meeting with half a dozen lords and ladies hoping for my favor is going to be stark, I fear.

Rising to my feet, I smile at each person in turn. "My friends, thank you so much for letting me join you today. I wish you all the best." As they all bid their farewells, I step past Elliot and take a deep breath of the fresh sea air. We are mere steps from the ocean, with a wall separating the walking path from the water, and I could stand here for hours if Elliot were to let me. It feels like Derek's back patio that looks out over the Pacific Ocean, except Windgaard is far colder and windier. Unlike in Los Angeles, Candora's weather leans toward cold and wet more often than not, but I do love our rolling green hills and seaside cliffs.

"Are you coming, Rapunzel?" Elliot's eyes are on my hair as it whips around behind me.

"One moment." I quickly wrangle my hair into a serviceable braid, knowing it is still a mess but unable to do more without Runa here to fix it for me. I never learned more than a simple braid, which is ridiculous considering how much hair I have. If I lose this election, that will be the first thing I learn.

Oh, I should not joke about losing, even to myself.

"Ready?" Elliot asks when I am done, though he seems not to like the state of my hair, as he is now frowning at it. "We really do need to get back before Sander sends Hex out to find us."

I exaggerate a shudder. "Heaven help the people of Windgaard if Hex gets loose."

Choking out a laugh, Elliot gestures for me to start walking back to the closest road. This part of the city can only be accessed by foot or bicycle, so it is rather quiet right now, and I am grateful for that. While I adore my new friends back at the cafe, I could use some time to myself so I can make some plans for the next several days.

Elliot is the first to break the silence between us, and it is with a question I did not expect in the slightest. "You really never wanted to date Derek?"

I turn to gape at him. "Why would I?"

He shrugs, keeping his eyes on our surroundings. "Because he's perfect, or so people say."

"You are very much like him, you know." I mean that in more ways than one. Not only do they both have skills with languages and are incredibly intelligent, but they look similar as well. Elliot's coloring may be lighter, but as I did not give him the chance to shave this morning before dragging him to the bus, he has the rough beginning of a brown beard that makes him look even more like my friend. It is remarkable that he and Derek could look this similar as merely cousins; their fathers must look alike as well.

Not that I would know—I have never seen pictures of Derek's parents. I do not even know their names. That never bothered me before, as Derek keeps most things close to the vest, but it bothers me now. Does he not think of me as one of his closest friends? I have known him for longer than almost anyone in our little group; only Cole has an advantage. Does Derek not trust me?

"You and Derek only met recently," I say carefully, "but did you know of him before that?"

Elliots shakes his head as we walk. "Only as an actor. Dad didn't like talking about his family."

"Did Derek know about you?"

"Don't think so."

"Then why did he go to your father's funeral?" These are things I should be asking Derek, but he would not answer my questions. Or if he did, he would not be straightforward with me. The man has not told any of us that his surname is Reid rather than Riley, though stage names in Hollywood are common. What else has he kept from his friends?

Elliot pauses at an intersection to look around. "He said something about hearing about it through the grapevine. No one knew he was there—not even me—until he cornered me after the service. Said he planned to leave immediately after, but then he found out I was Dad's son. Can I..." He purses his lips, then holds out his arm. "This is a busier street, so you can either take my arm, or I'm hailing us a cab."

At least he is offering me the choice, though it is clear by his disgusted expression that he does not like either of the options he has presented. If it were up to him, he would probably wait somewhere no one can see us until we have the whole palace guard to follow us to the hotel. As it is, we are starting to attract attention from people who recognize me. Several phones are pointed in our direction, and some people are inching closer.

I take Elliot's arm as my nerves start to build, though the feel of his muscle beneath my touch provides some courage. I am glad he is here, just as I am glad he allowed me today's adventure. "I do not think there are any cabs to hail," I tell him.

He groans, probably because I am right, and grabs his phone, pulling up my driver's number. He gives our location and urges the driver to hurry, and then he stands at attention. "My preference is to find a place to lie low until he gets here," he mutters as he watches people approach. Some of them look nervous, but others seem excited.

Ha! I was right about him. Squaring my shoulders, I put on a warm smile. "I prefer otherwise."

"I thought so. But if I say we need to go, then we need to go. Got it?"

Would he carry me over his shoulder again if I refused? He might, even if the photos and videos of that would lead to disaster. I should avoid that course of action. "I accept your terms."

His eyebrows shoot up, and he is temporarily distracted from the growing crowd as he looks down at me. "Really?"

Snickering, I pat his arm and pull free. "This time, yes." Then I wave at the nearest woman and beckon her forward. "Hello!" And when Elliot grumbles unintelligibly behind me, I cannot hold back my grin.

Hollywood Hot Scoop

Candoran Crown Candidate's Bodacious New Bodyguard

Yep, I knew we would get you with that one, and you won't be disappointed because we have PHOTOS. So many of them that we've set up a whole slideshow so you can get your fill. That's right, we finally have visual confirmation that Princess Freya's new American bodyguard is just as scrumptious as we imagined him to be, though I for one have no idea why he's trudging around after a wannabe queen when he could be soaking up the sun in Hollywood with yours truly. Why risk his life for a princess when I would happily be his queen? ;)

But I'm getting off track. Before you go drooling over these spectacular shots of the main man himself, can we address Freya's hair in that first shot? Talk about a rat's nest, am I right? She must be crumbling under the pressure of keeping up with her rival without getting booed off the stage, because that is not the princess we've come to know and love. That, or she badly needs a new stylist who knows how to combat the elements in Candora's Windy City.

I'm going with the former, because unlike her last two stops, Freya didn't bother with anything resembling a campaign speech today and chose instead to take a cheap tour bus to look down on everyone as she passed. I don't know about you, but that seems like a terrible way to show your people that you know what you're doing.

If I wasn't set on marrying Derek Riley, I would say he should hop across the pond and tie the knot with the panicking princess so he can show Freya how a real leader does things. King Derek has a nice ring to it, don't you think?

He'll have to get through the hubba hunk that is Freya's bodyguard first, and looking at the guy, I'm not sure who would win. This man is as ripped as he is beautiful, just like Derek, and I'm pretty sure we would all sell a kidney to see that showdown.

Check out the slideshow here and be sure to subscribe so you can be the first to know about everything leading up to the Candoran Election Day. We're working hard to get the bodyguard's name, but until then, stay tuned for your next hot scoop! XO

CHAPTER THIRTEEN

ELLIOT

North:

> You know it.

Bax:

> No wonder you won't come back to the team, bro.

Wade:

> Reid, I don't think this counts as lying low for a while, by the way.

Bax:

> He lived with Griff's family on base for almost a year. I think that counts as a while.

> By the way, if this princess thing doesn't work out, there's still a spot here for you.

Wade:

> No there isn't...

North:

> There will be when the rookie cracks and drops out.

Bax:

> That's happening sooner than later. Cap's about to lose his mind.

North:

> But seriously, when they inevitably kick us out I'm expecting you to get us all jobs with hot women because you clearly know what's up.

I CURSE AS I lock my phone and set it on the bed next to me. Then curse again because the first one wasn't strong enough. How did they find out? At least it's only three guys on the text, but I'm under no illusions they won't eventually tell the rest of the squad that my face is all over the internet.

I knew pictures of me with Freya were going to surface at some point, but holy hell. There's a slideshow. *A freaking slideshow.* Most of them are closeups of *me*, as if there's a universe where I am more interesting than the literal princess having casual conversations with people on the street.

My phone buzzes again, and I'm afraid to look. My old compatriots aren't going to leave me alone until I respond, but what am I supposed to say? They already have all the facts about my new job thanks to the most recent *Hollywood Hot Scoop* article, and this is only going to fuel their attempts to get me back on the team because they won't take my position seriously when this is what they see of it. Considering I haven't talked to any of them in months, I don't know why they're trying so hard.

Worse than that, I have no idea how to interact with them anymore.

I'm in a different world from them now, and jumping into conversation with them feels like a step backward. It took me long enough to get over the guilt I felt over Griff's death and abandoning the rest of the guys because of it, and I really need to focus on my current mission.

The current mission being convincing Freya that she's never going to wander the city like that again.

The woman spent over an hour talking to people in the street this afternoon before I could get her to climb into the car that was waiting for us, so she's not going to be easily persuaded. Not even a handful of irritated nobility dimmed her pride, even when they not so subtly suggested she might be forgetting her station. She held her head high throughout their criticisms, and I reluctantly have to admit that her conviction is admirable.

Even if it stresses me out.

After several more texts come in, I gingerly tap the screen and flinch when I see the previews of the texts from my old comrades. They are not holding back, now commenting on *Hot Scoop*'s high praise for my appearance. But there's another text below that thread, and that's the one I open.

If my old ODA knows about the *Hot Scoop* slideshow, it's no surprise that Derek knows about it too. But I *am* surprised that he's worried about me.

I should really be sleeping—today was exhausting even though it went as smoothly as an unplanned excursion could have gone—but sleep is going to elude me for a while. I prop up a pillow against the headboard and get comfortable as I type out a return text.

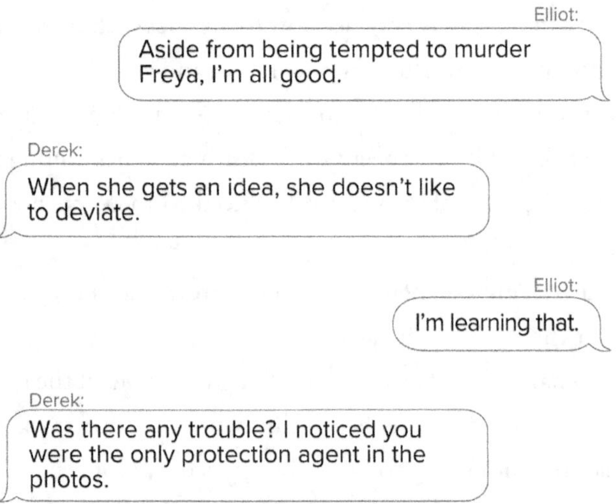

Of course he caught that. Thankfully, no one on the internet has mentioned that there weren't other guards around, and I would like to keep it that way. If someone decides to stir up trouble because they think

I won't be enough to keep Freya safe, they might actually have a chance to get to her. A slim chance, but a chance nonetheless.

Elliot:
No trouble, but I'm attributing that to luck. She got the drop on me, or I would have made better arrangements.

Derek:
She's good at that.

"Oh good," I mutter, not really needing confirmation that Freya is going to be more of a handful than I anticipated.

I wonder what someone like Wade would do in a job like mine, or North. Knowing North, he probably would have started flirting with Freya immediately and lasted less than a day as her bodyguard. Wade is more sensible, but he's not one to take charge unless he absolutely has to. Freya would walk all over him.

"What about you?" I ask my phone, as if my words might reach Derek. He played a bodyguard in a movie once, and he has the muscle mass to at least look intimidating. That's all the tabloids seem to care about, though the *Hot Scoop* article makes me itchy. I guess I should be flattered that whoever the author is, they think I'm attractive?

Yeah, I'm not flattered at all. There's something slimy about that website.

Elliot:
Is this Hot Scoop's nasty side coming out?

Derek:
Not in the slightest.

Elliot:
Did you read the part where they talked about Freya?

I swear again.

"You're worse than Hex," a voice says at the door.

Sander. Tempted to tell him to go away so I can try to get some sleep, I glance at the door that separates my suite from Freya's, then grab my gun and move to the main door to undo all the locks.

"Up late?" I mutter as I crack the door open, relaxing only when I see that it really is Sander and he's on his own.

He looks down at the gun in my fingers and fights a smile. "Paranoid?"

"I won't dignify that with an answer. What do you want?"

"Can I come in?"

I open the door wide, nodding to the two guards stationed in front of Freya's door as Sander slips inside, then lock the door behind him.

When my phone buzzes several times in succession, Sander lifts an eyebrow. "Do you need to get that?" Like I'm the one interrupting something.

Chuckling, I gesture for him to sit in one of the chairs while I fall onto my back on the bed. "It's either my old squad torturing me about those photos, or it's Derek giving me unhelpful advice."

Sander makes a noise in between a scoff and a grunt.

I lift my head. "Do you have something against Derek Riley?" The twins know Derek got me the job, but they don't know he's my cousin, and I am suddenly extremely interested in Sander's opinion of Derek. Queen Ingrid thinks Derek can do no wrong, and Hex seems indifferent. But I don't think I've ever heard Sander talk about the guy. Not specifically, anyway. He usually refers to Freya's friends as "the Americans."

Rolling his eyes, Sander shakes his head. "Not here to discuss Freya's weird friendship with the actor."

Interesting. "Then why are you here?"

"Because Markham Grimstad is down in the lobby and wants to talk to you."

That gets me to sit up, suddenly alert. "What?"

He nods. "The guards came to get me first, after you had me tail him yesterday, but he's pretty determined to have a conversation."

I run a hand through my hair, which has gotten long in the time I've been in Candora. I haven't cut it since leaving the States, and this is the first time in almost a decade that I haven't kept it regulation. I'm surprised none of my ODA mentioned it. Or maybe they have, but I'm still ignoring their texts.

"Why would Grimstad want to talk to me?" I ask, a bit distracted by my hair and the realization that I can do whatever I want with it for the first time in eight years. *Not important, El.*

"He's keeping that bit to himself," Sander says with a shrug. "I'm happy to tell him to bugger off if you want me to."

"No, I'll talk to him." I stand and grab a t-shirt, pulling it over my head as I think about what Grimstad might have to say. More than anything, I'm concerned that he's in the same place we are once again. He might have seen all the articles and posts about Freya's impromptu meet and greet and hurried to Windgaard from wherever he was, but my gut says he's following us.

Or he got his hands on our schedule, which would be a lot more complicated and force me to figure out who on the staff let things slip. Gregor trusts everyone we have with us, but the right motivation can make a desperate person go rogue.

I really don't want to have to start shaking down guards and cooks.

When I slip my holster on and slide my gun into it, Sander snorts a laugh. "Not going to hide it?"

"I'd rather he know what he's dealing with." Once I tug on my shoes, I unlock the door and head out, Sander behind me. I lock the door again right as the next door down opens and Freya steps out, and I curse.

Freya lifts an eyebrow. "That is some colorful language, Mr. Reid."

"Apologies." Even if it's warranted. "I thought you were asleep."

"It is hard to sleep with the two of you yammering next door."

It's a good thing I was texting Derek instead of talking to him. "You're not coming with me," I say with as much force as I can muster in my exhaustion.

She narrows her eyes. "If Grimstad is here, I would like to talk to him."

"He didn't ask to talk to *you*," I counter.

"Well..." Sander flinches when I turn my glare to him. "If you want to be technical, he first asked for Freya but said he would settle for you if she wouldn't come."

I am sorely tempted to punch him, but he would block me and dish it right back. "We need to work on your ability to keep things to yourself," I grumble before blocking Freya's way out the door. "You should have been asleep an hour ago, Rapunzel."

Her nose wrinkles at the name I started calling her earlier today. It isn't especially apt right now, with her hair twisted up and out of her way, but I like the way the name ruffles her. It's a small form of payback for the way she ruffled me when she put her hand on my knee on the bus. "As I said, you were keeping me up."

"Sander came in less than five minutes ago," I argue.

Freya steps forward and rises up on her toes, mere inches from me because I stand my ground. She looks both irritated and amused, which is an intriguing look for her. "In case it hasn't caught your notice, you are a giant of a man, Elliot Reid, and your steps are far from light. The next time you choose to pace, perhaps you could do it somewhere that isn't the room next to mine."

"Two contractions in one go," is the response that comes out of my mouth when it's one I should hold back. I purse my lips as her smug expression turns fiery, and then I shake my head. "Proud as I am that you're learning, I still won't let you go down and talk to Grimstad."

"Why not?"

"Because I need to figure out why he's following us, and I can't do that if you're distracting me."

She lifts a delicate eyebrow as her eyes trace my face. She looks...different. She's not wearing her usual makeup, so she looks younger than normal. Softer. But she's as beautiful as ever. "Distracting you?" she asks, her voice low and husky. "How am I a distraction when I am already the focus of your job?"

That's a good question and a clear sign that I can't do any more solo outings with the princess if I want to have the brain power to stay alert. I'm too tired for this nonsense. I should have Sander send Grimstad away. But the determination in the princess's gaze says she'll find a way to get down there with or without me, and I groan. "Fine."

Freya crows in triumph and shoves me out of her way, which works only because I wasn't expecting her warm hands on my chest. I stumble back but manage to grab her arm before she gets very far.

"Hold up," I growl.

She turns to me with wary eyes. "What now?"

I nod at her silk pajamas at the same time Sander snickers. "Maybe you should change first."

"Oh! Yes." With no sign of embarrassment—surprising—she hurries back into her room and shuts the door.

Groaning again, I run a hand down my face as Sander starts full-on laughing now. "She's going to be the death of me."

"It's nice to see her coming into her own again," Sander replies. "She was getting a little too subdued for a bit there." Is he trying to tell me that the stubborn, obstinate, and reckless woman I started working for was the *subdued* version of her? There must be horror on my face because Sander's laughter grows louder. "Oh, you're in for it now," he says, then heads for the lobby, ideally to prep a room for us to have this discussion with Grimstad that we shouldn't be having.

Freya appears back at her door in only a couple of minutes, now wearing a pair of jeans and a soft-looking navy sweater that makes her eyes look gray. "Is this more appropriate?" she asks, her words full of derision. She doesn't bother waiting for an answer, instead leading the way down the hall.

I glance at the two guards, both of whom have been trying not to laugh this whole time, and sigh. "Come on," I tell them, and the three of us follow the princess to what I am sure is going to be an interesting conversation.

Chapter Fourteen

Freya

THIS IS NOT HOW I intended to converse with Markham Grimstad, but I was not about to waste this opportunity. Still, as I stand with the other guards while Elliot makes sure the room where Grimstad is waiting is safe, I wonder if I made the wrong decision and should follow Sander upstairs to go to bed.

Elliot looks tired. He was with me most of the day, only leaving my side when I retired for the evening, and I did not make things easy for him today. When talking to people in the street, I let them crowd around me, which meant Elliot had to keep an eye on many people at once while watching the buildings around us as well, as if expecting threats from every angle. I was not worried—as I have told him before, Candora is incredibly safe—and he was remarkably professional, but I could see the strain I put on him.

I might have expected him to say something or force me to the car sooner, but I think he recognized the moment for what it was. People were *talking to me.* The circumstance was not planned or managed, and I said very little. Simply listened. That seemed to make an impact.

Unfortunately, it also brought Elliot to the forefront of the tabloids, which is its own beast.

Elliot steps out of the conference room and nods at me, which I assume means I can proceed, and he follows me inside. "You're going to keep this short, Grimstad."

Like the first time I saw him, Grimstad is not how I expect him to be as he stands upon my arrival and bows. He looks more like his government photo today, polished and trim, though his clothes are on the casual side. He seems to be straddling two worlds now.

"Your Highness." He takes a step toward me.

Elliot clears his throat. "Do I need to remind you of the rules?"

Rules? I scowl at the bodyguard behind me, but his focus is on the man on the other side of the room. "Elliot, you are not—"

"Don't blame your bodyguard," Grimstad says. "He has good reason not to trust me and is doing his job. It's late, so thank you for meeting with me."

"You are here." I wince at the inanity of that comment and try to clarify. "In Windgaard. And you were in Kirkstead and Breckenholt before that."

Grimacing, Grimstad nods. "I know it looks questionable."

"Hence the rules," Elliot grumbles.

"But I assure you I have my own travel plans. If they coincide with yours, it means whoever planned your campaign knew the ideal path across Candora."

That makes sense. Elliot will not like it, but I am choosing to trust Grimstad for now as I settle in the nearest chair, gesturing for Grimstad to do the same. "What is it you wanted to talk about so badly that you faced not only my brother but Mr. Reid as well?"

Grimstad smiles in a way that makes him look...nice. He is handsome in a way, yes, but mainly his countenance is an approachable one. "I like your brothers. I wish they would involve themselves more in the kingdom's affairs, but I understand why they don't. Government isn't for everyone."

"No, it is not," I agree.

His gaze shifts to Elliot, his smile unchanged. "I like your new bodyguard as well, even if some people have questioned your decision to bring in an outsider."

"Technically it was my mother's decision." I do not feel the need to tell him that I have come to approve of her choice. "Now, what is it you wanted to speak to me about?"

Clasping his hands on the table, Grimstad studies me for a moment. "I met up with an old friend tonight, and he said you were on his tour."

Elliot swears behind me, mirroring the word that crossed through my mind. "Who was this friend?" he asks.

"Sig Halevik. Before you go thinking he's causing trouble, he was delighted to have you along. But some of your questions stood out to him."

With the way Mr. Halevik treated me the same as he did the other tourists with us, I thought for sure he was unaware of who I was and simply did his job by answering questions. Apparently he was paying more attention to me than I realized.

"Which questions?" I ask.

"Anything that had to do with your suitability for the throne."

Heat blossoms on my cheeks. Throughout the tour, I told myself that I wanted to know more about Windgaard, and that was why I constantly interrupted Mr. Halevik's presentation. But I kept asking questions that would give me a better idea of the people's sentiments toward my situation rather than seeking historical facts. "I see I was not subtle."

"I'm sure you were brilliantly subtle," Grimstad argues with a shake of his head. "Halevik is simply more intelligent than people give him credit for."

Who else will I underestimate on this campaign? "I still do not see why this required a conversation in the middle of the night," I say somewhat brusquely. It is barely after ten, hardly the middle of the night, but this discussion has me on edge. I thought I had gained some ground, but perhaps my adventure today was merely another mistake.

Chuckling, Grimstad unclasps his hands and pulls them onto his lap, lowering his shoulders so he looks smaller. A calculated move on his part, I am sure, though I will not let him make me think anything but the truth when it comes to him. He is a dangerous opponent and currently threatens my entire way of life.

No, he is threatening the way of life for all of Candora.

"I know what you're doing, Freya," he says, his words soft.

"Her Highness," Elliot growls.

"Your Highness," Grimstad amends without any hint of irritation.

I narrow my eyes. "What am I doing?"

"Exactly the same as me. You're trying to understand what your people need and how you can help them." He does not say it as a flaw or an obstacle he must remove. He is simply stating fact.

"If I am?" I ask warily.

"Then I wish you all the best in your endeavors. This country needs change, and if you can bring it about, then..."

I barely dare to hope. "Then you will drop out of the running?"

He laughs, shoulders shaking as he gazes across the table at me. "I'm not letting you off that easily. I can also bring change, and if I'm what the people want, I think they should have that chance."

This man is...confusing. Everything he is saying reflects the truth, and yet he has not said anything negative against me despite being my opponent. He must have an ulterior motive behind his choice of words, though I cannot fathom what it is.

He sits forward. "I've been among the people far longer than you have, so I know well the concerns our people have about your rule, should you be crowned."

"So you know how to best me," I surmise.

"I know how to help you," he corrects.

"What?" It is Elliot who says that, and he stares at Grimstad like the man is talking nonsense. At least I am not the only one confused.

Grimstad shrugs. "Like I said, if the people choose you to be their queen, it should be because you are the best candidate for them. But there's one thing that worries them more than most, and I would imagine it is not something they'll tell you, even when you join them for lunch."

I can almost feel the tension rolling off Elliot's shoulders as he shifts closer to me, as if I might be in more danger from the calm and collected man sitting across from me than I was from the crowd on the street. "What is that?" I ask, not certain if I want to know.

"You are unmarried."

A humorless laugh escapes me. "I am aware."

"And that would leave the throne vulnerable."

That is what Halevik said.

"You are also unmarried," I counter.

Grimstad's smile grows, like he finds my comment amusing. "I'm aware."

"Does that not make you an equally vulnerable choice?"

"I have no interest in marriage unless it benefits more than myself, and as that outcome is unlikely, it would be a waste of time for anyone to try."

"No interest at all?" Why that is my question, I do not know. It surprises me, I suppose, to think a man as even-tempered and handsome as Markham Grimstad would deny himself a partner.

"I have little time for love and affection, and I imagine being king will not change that."

"I do not appreciate your presumption," I mutter. "You may not end up as king, no matter how popular you are."

Amusement flickers in his eyes. "Being king *would* not change that," he says, once again perfectly content to correct his mistake. "If you are elected queen, many people are worried that power-hungry men will do whatever it takes to become your husband regardless of the danger it poses to you and your family."

"Good thing she's got me," Elliot says in a growl.

Grimstad glances at him, a discerning look on his face before he turns his focus to me again. "Say you don't have that problem. Say you are safe from predatory suitors. You are thirty-three, Your Highness, and with no heir in sight, you—"

"You are two years older than me," I retort.

He acknowledges that with a nod. "But I also wouldn't be required to carry a royal line if I took the throne. You would. If something happens to you before you provide a line of succession, people are afraid it will leave Candora in a state of emergency, given your brothers' unwillingness to rule and your mother's inability to return to the throne once she relinquishes her right."

"That is why the people will not vote for me?"

"Among other reasons."

Uncomfortable, I sit rigid in my seat and consider what he is telling me. Sander and Hex still have claim to the throne, but they have made it clear on numerous occasions that they will never take the crown. There are laws against forcing someone of royal lineage to rule, just as there are laws against a monarch reclaiming their crown once they have given it up. With no willing candidate, the state of Candora's government would need to change, but it would not happen in a controlled way, such as through an election. If I were to suddenly lose my life, my country would more than likely suffer under a Parliament-appointed steward while the House of Lords implemented the new constitution and organized an election.

If Grimstad were to win *this* election now, the change would happen gradually over the course of his fifteen-year term rather than all at once.

The chances of me dying an untimely death are low, but if this is an obstacle in gaining the people's support, I will need to find a solution before the election.

I tap a finger on the table as I think. I know what Liam would say if he were here: "Time to get yourself a baby, ASAP!" He would say it in jest, but a part of him would be in earnest. It *would* solve the problem of succession. But I am neither prepared to become a mother, nor would that solution help me in the next two weeks. Bonnie and Cole would both tell me that I am the only person who can determine the course of my life, and I should not let someone like Grimstad put ideas in my head. I have no idea what Derek would say, and the urge to send him a text hits me hard.

He always knows what to do.

But I turn to Elliot instead. "What do you think of this, Mr. Reid?"

He was scowling at Grimstad, but he looks at me with his eyebrows high. "What?"

Despite the tense circumstances, I cannot hold back a smile at his bewilderment. "I am asking for your opinion."

"Again?" When I nod, he also seems to fight a grin before he says, "I think Grimstad is playing his worst cards and hoping you believe his bluff. He's nervous."

Grimstad's eyes narrow slightly, but his expression remains mostly calm. "I won't disagree, but these are legitimate fears of our countrymen."

"I think you were counting on Freya staying in the palace while you charm the Candoran people."

"It crossed my mind when this all began."

"I think you know she's the best person for the job but won't admit it, so you're looking for reasons to undermine her campaign," Elliot finishes, folding his arms.

Grimstad matches him, and I take a moment to study them both. They are similar in size, though Grimstad lacks much of Elliot's visible muscle, and each man is imposing in his own way. Elliot does not hide his strength like Grimstad does, but it is clear Grimstad is more than his silver tongue. If he chose to intimidate, he could probably do it well.

No matter their similarities, I am more drawn to Elliot. That could be because I trust him, and I do not know if I can trust Grimstad, even if the Candoran people do. There is more to what he is telling me.

"Thank you," I tell Elliot and put a hand on his arm, hoping he relaxes. Instead, his muscles tighten beneath my touch. This man is wound so tightly that I am beginning to worry what he might do if he does not let himself rest. I should end this conversation sooner than later. "Mr. Grimstad, I—"

"Markham, please." Grimstad's smile grows when he catches the look of surprise on my face. "Maybe we can become friends?"

"Not likely," Elliot growls under his breath.

Exhaling a soft laugh, I shake my head. "That is a bit of a stretch at the moment, Mr. Grimstad."

"Worth trying."

"I thank you for your insight tonight, but I am not concerned about my lack of a husband or child, and neither should the people be. Like you, my affection is only for Candora, and I would never leave it help-less."

Grimstad nods his head. "I am glad to hear it." His eyes flick to Elliot before resting on me again. "I wonder if you might allow me a moment alone with you, Your Highness."

"Absolutely not," Elliot says immediately.

Curious as I am to know what Grimstad might say without Elliot present, it is a bad idea. As much for my own safety as for Grimstad's, given Elliot's level of tension right now. "I think it best if we both retire," I say with a polite smile.

With another look at Elliot, Grimstad nods again. "As you wish. I'll let you get your rest so you can be fresh and vibrant for whatever you choose to do tomorrow."

I do not know for certain if that is a call to what *Hollywood Hot Scoop* said about me this evening, but I grit my teeth regardless. My appearance was not as pristine as it could have been, but not everyone has looked down on me today. Some posts on social media have suggested that my disheveled hair and clothing were a sign that I properly enjoyed my time in Windgaard.

On the other hand, one post from a Candoran newspaper guessed my ruffled appearance was courtesy of the handsome bodyguard behind me, which brought me to tears with laughter. It also pulled a blush onto my cheeks, but mostly I found it quite funny. To think Elliot would ever cross that professional boundary, when in reality he only touches me when absolutely necessary.

Before tonight, I have given little thought to my single status, but if I had, someone like Elliot would have never been an option for a future queen. Even with his many qualities... Did Elliot see the Candoran post, or has he been focused on *Hot Scoop*, which was particularly effusive toward him today? The tabloid is awful, but it is difficult to disagree with their assessment of my bodyguard's appearance.

"Time to be on your way, Mr. Grimstad," Elliot says and gestures to the door.

Knowing Grimstad is waiting on me, I stand and offer a nod when he rises to his feet and bows. "Goodnight, Mr. Grimstad."

"Good fortune on the rest of your campaign, Your Highness."

"Where are you going next?" Elliot asks.

Grimstad pauses at the door, looking back at my bodyguard. He seems to debate for a moment before he smiles in an amused way that makes me think his answer is going to be problematic. "Havenford."

Elliot and I *both* swear. That is where we are headed, which means I have not seen the last of Markham Grimstad. That should make me nervous, but more than anything I am curious. Will he continue to give me advice, or are we to be true rivals from here until the election?

Only time will tell.

"Well," I say, when Grimstad is gone and it is only the two of us left in the room. "What do you make of my opponent?"

"Asking my opinion twice in one night?" To my surprise, Elliot sinks into the chair on my right and runs a hand through his hair. I have not seen him this casual since we left the palace outside Invem, and it makes him look more tired than he did before. I must have really taken a lot out of him today, though I do not think Grimstad helped the matter. "You shouldn't underestimate him."

"Believe me, I had no plans to do so."

"Good, because he all but admitted he's nervous about the election, and there's no telling what he might do going forward."

"Do you think him dangerous?"

Elliot considers that question for a minute, his gaze distant, and then his expression hardens as he growls, "I don't know." The uncertainty seems to pain him to admit. "I'm no expert on people, but he seemed…"

"Sincere?" I offer. When he nods, I sigh. "I thought so too. But why would he choose to help me?"

"Either it's a strange play for leverage, or he's a decent guy." He wrinkles his nose. "It'll be harder to hate him if he's decent."

Snickering, I lean back in my chair and try to slouch like he does. My poor attempt is almost laughable after a lifetime of proper posture, and I sit up again. "I'm sorry."

His eyebrows rise. "For what?"

"For being the reason you are tired. I added a good deal of stress to your day, and then I did this."

He lifts his shoulders in a limp shrug. "I would have talked to Grimstad if you hadn't. But I probably wouldn't have been so polite. Your good manners have their uses after all." He grins at me, and something seems to shift between us. The moment feels much like whenever I am with Cole or Derek late at night, when the world is quiet and we have no reason to keep our shields up.

"We are friends, you and I," I murmur as I realize why the air between us is warm and calm.

Elliot's eyebrows rise again. "Are we?" He does not seem to be arguing. Simply asking.

"Well, by Grimstad's logic, we have been friends since the day I began calling you Elliot."

"I like that you call me that."

It is my turn to be surprised. I did not think he minded the familiarity, but I did not expect him to *like* it. "You do?"

Nodding, he rests his tattooed arm on the table and runs a finger along one of the Celtic knots weaving across his skin. "My old ODA always called me Reid."

"ODA?"

"Operational Detachment Alpha. My unit in the Forces. No matter our names, we found the shortest route to save time. Reid. Bax. Griff." His voice strains on that last one, right before he moves his hand to massage his shoulder above the tattoos. "Even in school, my few friends called me Reid, so only my dad called me Elliot until he…"

My heart aches; he must have had a lonely childhood with only his father as his family. "Do you miss him?"

"Sometimes. But we were apart for a long time, so I was already used to being on my own."

"Why did you join the military if it took you away from him?"

"Because I wanted to make a difference in the world. And I liked the rush." He smirks at me when he says that last bit. "Dad was always worried about me, but he understood my need to find my place in the world because I was never going to find it at home."

I did not expect him to answer any of these questions, and though I am tired from an adventurous day, I want him to keep talking. For some reason, I want to learn more about him almost as much as I want to learn about my people. "Your tattoos," I say and lean forward so I can see them better. "Are they related to your old team?"

"Yeah. One for each of them."

I can see ten banded knots, and I am guessing two more sit under the sleeve of his shirt with how evenly they are spaced. "You were close?"

"We had to be. In the Special Forces, you have to trust that the guy next to you has your back. We were brothers in everything but blood."

The urge to touch his skin and trace the ink that holds his comrades immortalized hits me with a force so strong that I almost do it, my fingers twitching in my lap. But it is a miracle he has spoken this much, and I will not break whatever spell he is under by shifting our dynamic away from how it should be.

"Why did you leave?" I ask, clasping my hands together to keep from making physical contact. I have touched him twice today, and each time left a strange, unsettled sensation in my chest.

He blinks, his eyebrows pulling low, and I know before he speaks that he is done telling me his secrets. I pushed too far. "You should go to bed, Princess."

"*You* should go to bed," I argue to mask my disappointment. "You look exhausted."

"Whose fault is that? Oh wait, you already admitted that it's yours." Standing, he offers his hand to me and helps me to my feet, and then he surprises me by tucking my arm through his like he did on the street earlier. Only, this time his bare skin is warm against mine, and something about the more intimate contact sits heavy in my stomach. As glad as I am to have a chance to see his tattoos again, it is better if he continues to wear his suits. This feels different from our limited physicality before today, almost like crossing a line we should never cross.

Do I let go? Of course not.

We are both quiet until we reach my door and Elliot slips his arm free, leaving me bereft of his warmth. But rather than leaving my side, he remains where he is, looking down at me with an unreadable emotion in his eyes. "I left the Forces because I needed something new," he says, so quietly that I have to lean closer to hear him, and we were already quite close as it was. "My dad died shortly after, so it felt like I'd made the right choice because I was in the States when it happened instead of some remote mountain village on a different continent."

"Were you home when he passed?"

He shakes his head, and my heart aches for him. "On base. I was a training officer in North Carolina, but it wasn't long before I realized I don't like dealing with willful soldiers."

He looks so miserable that I can't help but search for some way to lighten the mood. I want to go back to the moment when we decided we are friends. "You left willful soldiers to come deal with me," I say with a small laugh. "That does not sound like an upgrade."

That gets him laughing in return, and I love the way his whole face lights up with his amusement, like his worries wash away with his laughter. I cannot imagine what he has seen in his lifetime, but the way he has stood strong through it is admirable. "You're right," he says with a shake of his head. "You're way worse."

I grin up at him. "Yet you are still here."

"I am," he agrees, almost as a question. I understand his surprise, given how desperately I wanted him to go only a week ago.

Looking at him now, I cannot fathom how thoroughly I disliked him when he has been nothing but a support to me from the start. Without him, I would not be here in Windgaard, and I will never be able to thank him enough for making this campaign possible. Regardless of the election's outcome, these two weeks will change my life.

"Goodnight, Rapunzel," he murmurs, then bows his head and steps back.

I offer him a smile. "Goodnight, Elliot." When I close my door, I feel as if something has permanently changed between us. What that is, I do not know, but I spend a long time gazing at the door separating our suites and hoping he is getting the rest he needs.

He has spent all his energy looking after me the last few days.

But who is looking after him?

CHAPTER FIFTEEN

ELLIOT

HAVENFORD IS SMALLER THAN I expected, a tiny fishing village tucked away at the base of a sweeping cliff on the coast. Granted, I could only see so much when we arrived because a storm blew in this afternoon, leaving the whole countryside in a thick misty rain, but I haven't been able to figure out why Gregor added this town to the campaign trail. Or why Grimstad would come here as well.

I'm obviously missing something.

"How many people live here?" I grumble as I stare out the window of the inn we've commandeered, trying to see anything through the rain. All I can make out is an empty cobblestone street and a few thatch-roofed houses.

"Few hundred?" Hex tosses an almond in the air and catches it with his mouth. He and Sander were as eager to come here as Freya seemed to be, but no one has explained why. "It'll be better when the rain stops."

Even at the start of the campaign, there wasn't a planned speech for this stop, and all Freya told me in the car this morning was that she has everything under control and I don't need to worry. Which is exactly what she shouldn't have said if she doesn't want me to worry.

I can't keep her safe if I'm unprepared.

When we arrived, I tried to look up the town to get a better sense of what I'm facing, but I don't have enough cell service to get an internet signal, and the innkeeper gave me a funny look when I asked if there was Wi-Fi. While that hopefully means we'll also be safe from more *Hot Scoop* nonsense while we're here, I don't like being disconnected like this.

"What's wrong with you, El?" Hex asks, then tosses another nut into his mouth. With his legs stretched out on the chair across from him, he looks like he doesn't have a care in the world, and I envy his ability to relax.

I let my guard down last night after Grimstad left, and that was a bad move. Freya got more out of me than I would have liked, and a part of me still wanted to tell her my secrets when we were trapped in the car on the way here. It's better for everyone if I keep my shields up and stay focused on my job, but right now it feels like I'm the only one *not* taking it easy. Well, me and the guards I stationed outside, though they'll need to be relieved soon so they're not out in the elements for too long.

"Freya's napping," Hex says. "Sander's in her room with her. Not many people are dumb enough to be out in this storm, so you can relax a bit."

Shaking my head, I return my gaze to the window. He's right about everyone being inside—I haven't seen anyone in the village except for a few curious townspeople when we first arrived—but relax? That's not happening.

Sighing heavily, Hex drops his boots to the floor and gets to his feet like it's the most laborious movement in the world. He comes to join me at the window, throwing an arm around my shoulders, and then he presses a hand to my chest. "Seriously, Elliot. You're allowed to have down moments too. You're new to the bodyguard thing, but no one expects you to be *on* all the time, especially after what she put you through yesterday."

His hand over my heart has a strange effect, like I can suddenly breathe more easily. I knew I was tense, but my body practically crumbles under his touch, and I have to reach out and grip the window frame to keep upright.

"Mate..." Hex mutters before stepping back. His eyebrows are low as he looks at me with concern, and he seems ready to jump back in and catch me at a moment's notice.

It makes sense; I can only imagine how I look right now. My body feels heavy without Hex's touch, and I don't like it. I've come to see him and Sander as brothers like I did with my old ODA, but we haven't known each other for long. I shouldn't feel that much relief from a little bit of support.

I need to get a hold of myself.

Hex frowns. "Yeah, you definitely need some down time that isn't the few hours of sleep you get at night. You're wearing yourself thin."

I'm doing my job, and I might have slept better last night if Freya hadn't touched my arm while we talked to Grimstad. It was such a soothing gesture of familiarity that I haven't been able to stop thinking about it, or the way it spurred me to tuck her arm through mine as we walked back to her room. She called us friends, and even if I had hoped we would get to that point eventually, I didn't expect it to happen so quickly.

I didn't expect to feel the warmth of her friendship deep in my chest, like it's something I've been needing for a long time.

"How close was Freya to Gregor?" I ask, slowly releasing my grip on the window and standing straight. I'm fine. I've endured way more stress than this, and I need to pull myself together. *Concentrate.*

If Hex finds my question strange, he doesn't say so. "He was her protector from the day she was born," he says with a shrug. "He's family to all of us, but their dynamic was...different."

I raise an eyebrow. "What do you mean, different?"

"I mean my sister trusted Gregor with all of her secrets, good and bad, so he was probably the closest person to her. Closer than her friends or even us. She cried like a baby when he announced his retirement, even if she knew it was time."

I was afraid of that. I knew going into this job that I would be in close quarters with the princess for most of her day, but yesterday really knocked the truth of it into me. I go where she goes. I sleep when she sleeps. My whole life revolves around Freya Alverra, and that's...

Dangerous.

"You're not thinking of backing out of the job, are you?"

Hex looks so genuinely horrified that I laugh and shake my head. "And let you think you're the best fighter in Candora? Of course not." But I am surprised by how easy it is to say that I intend to stick to my position. No matter how unprepared I was for this job, I can't imagine leaving Freya's safety up to anyone but me. "She's stuck with me now, which means you are too."

"Good." Hex smiles. "In that case, I'm going to give you a choice."

I don't like the sound of that. "Okay?"

"You can either go upstairs and take a nap because you look like you've been to hell and back, or you and I are going out."

Glancing at the rain, I debate my options. I could refuse to do either, but Hex holds back when he fights me. Not sure I want to face him when I'm not at my best. So, I can try to get some sleep—not likely—or I can venture into the downpour that's showing no signs of stopping. I've been in worse conditions...

I swallow. Going out is a bad idea. "Freya needs—"

"Sander can look after Freya. Or I can stay with her, and you can go explore Havenford with San, but either way you're going out and taking a breather before you work yourself to death. If there's anywhere for you to relax, it's here." He folds his arms and lifts his eyebrows in a silent taunt, reminding me why he's so hard to beat in a fight. In terms of size, he's smaller than me, but I have never met a man with more grit and determination than Hex Alverra, except for his twin. Like Sander, he likes to let people underestimate him, and I know better than to fall into that trap.

I don't think I actually have a choice here.

"Fine," I say on a sigh. "We'll go out, and you can show me what's so special about this tiny town, but I'm only giving you an hour. One hour, and then we're back here. Got it?"

Hex already has an arm around my shoulders, guiding me to the door. "Yeah, sure. An hour. Let's go!"

"You're serious?"

The woman in front of me nods with all the seriousness that a seventy-year-old with a nonstop grin can muster. "A fish for a kiss," she says, which is what she said to me thirty seconds ago, so I *did* hear her right.

"A fish for a kiss," I repeat, as if that might make it make sense. I'm too tired for this.

A few feet to my left, Hex looks like he's having the time of his life as he sits with a man so weathered that I can barely see his eyes through his wrinkled skin, the two of them chatting and mending a fishing net.

What am I even doing? I spent the last *two hours* on a fishing boat hauling in teeming nets and wondering if we'd sink as the rain kept falling, but the instant the rain stopped, we were back on shore as the main street in Havenford burst to life. I'm tired, wet, and starving, but I just got told no one in Havenford accepts money, and if I want to eat some of the fish and chips that is making my stomach clench and my mouth water from its aroma, my payment will be a kiss.

A kiss.

What in the world is this place?

"Oi! Elliot!" That's Sander's voice, since Hex is still working on the net, and I turn to find him arm in arm with Freya and walking down the street with no other guards in sight. Is *he* serious?

"I'm going to kill you," I grumble even though he's too far away to hear me. He can read lips.

Sander merely grins and keeps heading in my direction.

At his side, Freya is beaming and taking in all the booths and shops that are popping up around us, like she's a little girl at a carnival. Is this what she was so excited about? A street market? We passed at least three of them in Windgaard while on our tour with Halevik, but she didn't ask to stop at any of them. Her hair is completely loose for only the second time since the tour started, and she looks...free. Like she has nothing to hide here.

"Well?" the old woman in front of me says, tilting her head as she continues to smile at me.

I feel like I crossed into the Twilight Zone at some point. It was probably while I was on the boat with Hex.

"Tova!" Sander slides his arm from Freya's when he reaches my side, and then he leans over the table and plants a kiss on the old woman's cheek. "It smells better than ever!"

She hands him a ceramic plate full of steaming fish and potato wedges. "You flatter me, Aleksander."

"A fish for a kiss," I mutter, rolling my eyes. "Got it." I still feel weird about kissing a woman I met two minutes ago, no matter how good her food smells.

Next to me, Freya giggles and nudges my arm. "Did Hex not explain things to you?" She leans forward and kisses the woman's other cheek. "I have missed you, Tova!"

When Freya gets her own plate of fish and chips, I glare at Hex until he looks up. He bites his lips to keep from laughing and returns to his work. "No," I say in a growl. "He didn't tell me anything."

Freya holds her plate toward me, and I gratefully take one of the chips to curb my hunger as she explains, "Havenford only deals in trades. They are a self-sufficient village with a firm policy that everyone has what they need."

I need food or I'm soon going to be in a worse mood than I already am, but I still don't want to kiss anyone for it. "Hmm." It looks like there are other booths offering food, and maybe one of them will take a different trade. But I'm almost afraid to ask.

"I don't like kisses either," Hex says, as if reading my thoughts. He shakes hands with the weathered old man, then comes over to me with something wrapped in cloth. He hands the cloth bundle to Tova, who takes it and offers a plate of food in return. "Bless you, Tova."

Tova pats his cheek. "And because I like Sven's butter so much, you can take this for your serious friend."

Hex accepts a second plate of food, and I'm ready to hug the man when he looks at me and says, "I need my kiss first, El."

I slap him instead, just forcefully enough that it catches him off guard and gives me a chance to snatch the plate from his hand. "Don't push your luck, Prince Hendrik." I stuff some of the fish into my mouth in case Hex tries to fight me and take it back, and the perfection of it hits me so hard that I almost moan. This definitely would have been worth a kiss.

With laughter in her eyes, Freya nudges my arm and nods in the direction of some picnic tables nearby. They're under the awnings of one of the shops, which means they're dry, so I gladly follow the three Alverra siblings and sit down between Freya and the street.

"What have you been doing this afternoon?" she asks when we're settled.

I glare at Hex again, and he laughs. "One of the fishermen needed some help," he explains.

"Oh, no wonder you are soaked to the bone!" Freya touches my arm again, her fingers hot against my chilled skin, even through my shirt. She needs to stop doing that. We can be friends, but clearly physical contact has a strong effect on me lately. "We should see if anyone has some dry clothes for you."

"I'd hate to find out what those would cost me," I mutter.

Her nose wrinkles with her smile, but my little quip didn't get a laugh out of her. I shouldn't be disappointed, but I am. I've only heard her full laugh a couple of times, and while it doesn't match her princessy exterior at all, her goose-like laughter fits her well. It makes her real.

The four of us dig in to our food, eating in silence for several minutes while the street continues to grow busier. It's coming alive now that the storm has passed, and for how small it is, I'm surprised by the energy of the place. It seems the entire town has come out with the sun.

"I always love visiting Havenford," Freya says. "It does not happen often, and I have not been back for many years, but it brings me so much joy when I am here."

"They really don't deal with money at all?" I ask. "How can that be sustainable?"

Sander snickers and tosses a chip at my face. "Tova must have liked you. Normally a trade has to be more substantial."

"Like butter?" I say to Hex, recalling the cloth bundle he gave Tova.

"Exactly," Freya answers for him. "Things people need. A cup of sugar for an egg. Helping a sheep birth a lamb in exchange for fixing roof slats."

"What about medicine? Electricity? Taxes?"

An all too familiar voice responds to my question. "I see the American is already confused."

Body tensing, I stand to face Grimstad and fold my arms. "I guess it's nice to see you weren't lying about your next stop." But it's certainly not nice to see him here. I really hoped he wouldn't show up so Freya could do her thing in peace. Whatever that thing is.

Grimstad chuckles and looks me up and down before bowing to the princess. "Your Highness. Prince Hendrik, Prince Aleksander, always nice to see you both."

To their credit, the twins barely acknowledge him and keep their focus on their food. Freya, on the other hand, smiles at Grimstad and gestures to the spot next to Hex. "Would you care to join us?"

Grimstad considers her offer for a moment, then nods. "If you don't mind waiting until I visit Tova for my own meal, then I would be happy to accept."

"Of course."

The instant he's out of earshot—or close enough to it—I turn to Freya and scowl. "I know we both decided he was being sincere last night, but did you really need to—"

"I would rather have him where I can see him," Freya says calmly. "If he is here for the same reason I am, then I would like to speak to him about it."

"What, exactly, is that reason?"

But I don't get an answer because Grimstad returns, a plate of fish in hand and a smudge of lipstick on his cheek. Apparently he was the recipient of the kiss *and* the fish, which is even less of an unfair trade than the deal I was presented with.

It takes a few seconds of awkwardness and a throat clearing from Freya before the twins scoot down the bench to make enough room for Grimstad to sit directly across from me, and the tension is thick at the table as he settles in. He must know none of us want him here, and yet he starts eating like this is a perfectly normal interaction.

It doesn't take long before he looks up and meets my glare with a politely confused smile. "Rough day?" he asks.

I narrow my eyes, letting my gaze fall to the lipstick on his cheek.

He coughs and grabs a napkin, rubbing the exact spot he was kissed. "Tova's fireplace was giving her trouble this morning when I got to town, and I happened to pass by as she was heading out to find someone to fix it."

"Sure you did," I growl.

Grimstad chuckles a little. "You know I grew up here, yeah?"

My mind quickly sorts through the information I internalized about him. "No, you were born in Lynholm." I'm sure of it. I may be tired, but I have my facts right.

"True," Grimstad acknowledges calmly. "But my parents' circumstances required me to come here and live with my grandparents for a few years, so I was raised by most of the village."

Cursing under my breath, I recall a brief line in the dossier about Grimstad that mentioned time spent with relatives during his secondary school years. It didn't feel important when I read it, and I was more focused on his adult years and political background.

Ignoring information is a mistake I can't afford to make, and I make a mental note to read through the dossier again as soon as we get back to the inn.

Until then… "So how did you pay for a school like Oxford?" I ask, hoping to fill in the pieces I'm missing. "Can't trade a few hours of manual labor for tuition."

Grimstad shrugs. "I was fortunate to receive a scholarship."

"Fortunate indeed."

Smile growing, he picks up a chip and points it at me as he says, "You really don't trust me, do you?"

"Should he?" Sander asks gruffly, looking around Hex to raise an eyebrow at the man.

"Have I given you any reasons not to?" Grimstad asks me.

My hands curl into fists. He's so calm that he makes me nervous, and I don't like it. "Aside from being a direct threat to my position?"

Grimstad smirks. "Aside from that."

"Easy, boys," Freya says, holding a hand between us. "Let us not besmirch Havenford with idiotic rivalries, yes? Mr. Grimstad, you—"

"I really wish you would call me Markham, Your Highness." Grimstad holds up a hand when she scowls at him, so at least he's smart enough to know he's going against the request she made last night. "We don't have to be friends, but I don't like the formality between us. Please."

Freya seems to debate for a moment before she sighs and nods. "Very well."

"You'll still address her as Your Highness unless she says otherwise," I throw in, though I really want to tell him that the likelihood of Freya being around him often enough to even use his name is slim to none. "Even then, I recommend you stick to her title."

Hex snorts into his food.

Am I aware that I rarely called Freya by her title even when she ordered me to? Yes. But we're past that now, so it's fine.

Grimstad, unflappable as ever, dips his head at me. "Of course. You were saying, Your Highness?"

Though I'm pretty sure Freya is resisting the urge to roll her eyes at me, mostly her expression is calm and confident. But even with her focus on Grimstad, her hand finds mine under the table and wraps around my clenched fist. It's only there for a moment before it returns to her lap. "Markham, aside from visiting old friends, I assume you are here to study the people of Havenford for your campaign."

"You have found me out. It gets harder to visit as life gets busier, so I thought it would be a good idea to refresh my memory on the way of life here. The rest of Candora could use some of their beliefs, as I'm sure you know."

Freya tilts her head to the side. "Does that make us united in this regard?"

"I suppose it does, but that's only one of many parts of my platform."

"Not a small part, I would imagine."

I want to pay attention to their conversation, even if I don't fully understand it, but my focus is stuck on my hand and the way my muscles relaxed at her touch. She only held my hand for a second or two, but my tension practically melted away when she did. It was like she was telling me with that touch that I can relax, and though my mind disagreed, my body immediately understood. The same thing happened with Hex earlier, and I'm not sure anyone has ever had such a visceral effect on me like these Alverras have.

"Obviously, it doesn't work on a country-wide scale," Grimstad says, pulling my attention back up. "Much as I wish we did, we don't have the natural resources to make sure every single citizen has everything they could ask for without money being involved."

"Nor can that many people change their way of life so thoroughly to be entirely selfless," Freya replies. "Not without some making signifi-cant sacrifices."

"Those with the most to give are unlikely to part with what they have."

Freya winces. "Unfortunately, I agree with you on that. But if we could implement even a portion of Havenford's ideals, Candora would thrive."

We? I glance at Sander, whose eyes are narrowed as he looks from his sister to her opponent as they go back and forth. Freya is more enthusiastic right now than I expected her to be, and Grimstad has a similar look of excitement in his eyes. I think they're talking about expanding this whole "trade what we have and take care of each other" mentality that the people of Havenford seem to have, but that's not how most people work. People are selfish. They look out for themselves and, if they're decent, use what extra they have to help their friends and family. They don't trade food for kisses because kisses don't buy shelter and clothing for their families.

In my experience, the most giving people are the ones who have the least, and Candora is full of wealthy, entitled nobility and a royal family who can pay me double what I made in the Special Forces. It's the rest of the country who can make the shift into a more selfless way of thinking, but that's why Grimstad is running in the first place. He's not part of the nobility or the wealthy, and his whole platform is about the common man.

I really hope Freya's engagement right now is because she's learning as much of Grimstad's plan as she can so she can counteract it. Not because he's starting to charm her into thinking he might be a good choice to rule.

Mostly because he *is* a good choice. That was obvious from the beginning.

"At least we can agree on something," Grimstad says and stands, his half-eaten plate of food in hand. "Your Highness, I don't want to monopolize your time while you're here, but it was nice to talk to you. Maybe we can speak again soon."

I'm on my feet in an instant, almost without thinking about what I'm doing. "Maybe not, Grim."

"Elliot," Freya says in warning.

As his lips quirk up in a smile, Grimstad glances at Freya before nodding at me. "Grim. Not super original, but I'll take it. Look after her, American. You never know what people might do."

I would grab his arm if Freya didn't grab mine first, holding me back. "Is that a threat?" I snarl, tempted to pull free and show Grimstad how I handle threats.

He looks down at the place Freya's fingers cling to my forearm, his eyebrows pulling together. "A request," he says calmly and meets my furious gaze again. "I don't want to see Princess Freya come to harm any more than I want to be king for my own gain. Not everyone is out for blood, Reid." He bows his head to Freya, who nods in return. "I believe the people are planning a party to celebrate all of their guests tonight. Your Highness, I would be honored to dance with you, if you choose to attend."

Not a chance.

"I would be delighted," Freya says.

I swear under my breath.

With a final nod, Grimstad turns and makes his way down the street, waving at people as he passes. All of them wave back.

"Wow," one of the twins says.

"Elliot." This time, when Freya says my name, she takes hold of my arm with both hands and pulls me down until I'm seated again. "I do not think he means me any harm. You can rela—"

"I can't relax," I argue, my eyes still on Grimstad's retreating frame. No matter what he says, his comment still felt like a threat. *You never know what people might do.*

Things were peaceful in Windgaard, but Breckenholt and Kirkstead were full of discontented people. The lurker at our first hotel followed us to the next town. The noblemen and women Freya has interacted with so far don't seem to care about anyone but themselves, something I noted in the House of Lords meeting last week. Tabloids and newspapers are keeping a close eye on Freya's progress, ready to attack her in writing at any moment.

Nothing about our circumstances makes me think I can let my guard down.

"El's not lying," Hex says to his siblings. "I got him out on a fishing boat and everything, and I'm pretty sure he's even more tense than before."

"This is Havenford," Sander says, reaching across the table and briefly putting his hand on my arm. It doesn't offer the same instant relief as Freya's and Hex's touches did, but I still feel the contact acutely. "Of all the places you can trust people to keep Freya safe, it's here."

"I wish I could believe you," I mutter. But if I don't treat everything as a threat unless proven otherwise, I might make a mistake like the one that led to Griff's death.

It wasn't your fault. Nora's voice echoes in my head, a reminder that she never blamed me for her husband's death. She's right. I'm not the one who shot him, and I didn't ask him to push me out of the way.

But it was my plan that went wrong.

"Elliot." Freya's fingers find my cheek, catching me by surprise, and she turns my head so I have to look at her.

Her blue eyes are so full of worry that I can't look away no matter how much I hate that she's seeing my weakness. It's been almost a year since that bad op, and I thought I had gotten over it. Why is all of this uncertainty and guilt coming up *now*? When I need to be at my absolute best?

With my attention fixed on her, Freya blushes and drops her hand. "Do you trust me, Elliot?"

I badly want to tell her no so I have no excuses not to stay focused and alert and lean into the frustration that builds every time I set eyes on Markham Grimstad. He's hiding something, and if I cared less about professionalism or had a valid reason to push, I could put my skills to better use and find out what Grimstad isn't saying.

But Freya's smile is soft and warm, and there's something about the way she looks at me sometimes that gets underneath my skin and won't leave. Especially after last night, when she declared us friends and something shifted between us. I've told her things I've barely told the people closest to me, and never once have I worried she would use my secrets against me.

"Of course I trust you," I murmur. "It's everyone else I have a problem with."

She smiles wider and sits up straighter, looking every bit the confident princess. The confident *queen* she could be. "I will give you every other day to be as paranoid as you would like, but give me this one. Okay?"

"I already gave you yesterday," I grumble, knowing I'll agree anyway because the longer I'm around this woman, the harder it is to say no to her. If the country could see this side of her, they'd have no choice but to vote for her.

She bites her lip as her smile turns into a full-blown grin that lights up her whole face. "Every day but this one, Elliot. I promise."

I'm really starting to wish I had taken that nap when Hex suggested it. "Fine."

CHAPTER SIXTEEN

FREYA

IF I THOUGHT IT would be simply difficult to convince Elliot to loosen up, I severely underestimated his dedication to his job. Or he is incapable of turning off his protective instincts, something I cannot fault him for. But if he does not unclench his jaw soon, it is going to remain stuck shut. He promised to let me spend the rest of the day how I choose, but the levels of stress he seems to be experiencing can in no way be good for him, so I am starting to think my request was a mistake.

I cannot fathom what he sees as a threat in this little town when everyone has been happy to enjoy our company, but Elliot seems certain something will go wrong if he lets his guard down and has a little fun. As Grimstad —Markham—said, the people of Havenford have turned our visit into a celebration, bringing out instruments and setting up a miniature festival in the village square. Markham is among them and has borrowed someone's violin to join the other musicians. Food, laughter, and drinks are plentiful, and the skies have cleared to bathe the streets in golden light as the afternoon makes way for evening.

And still Elliot looks like he will snap at anyone who gets too close to me, which is why I have slowly been moving farther away from him. He has been so focused on the people around us that he has yet to realize I am nearly on the other side of the square now. Some distance will be good for him, or at least that is what I tell myself. It will prove that I am perfectly safe, and maybe that way he will let himself breathe.

"Hex." I grab my brother as he passes by. I am pretty sure he was going to talk to one of the young women who have been eyeing him most of the afternoon, but they can wait. "How can we help him?"

Hex looks at Elliot and laughs. "He might be beyond help."

"I don't think he understands down time," Sander adds, coming over to join us. "Can't really blame him, with the life he's lived."

Elliot is only twenty-six. There is so much life still ahead of him, and if he cannot learn to relax, what will become of him? How will I be able to keep him in my employ when it only seems to cause him stress? He can keep me safe, but I cannot let him do it at the expense of his own life.

"Oh, this could be interesting," Hex says as a woman who looks to be close to my age approaches Elliot with a bouquet of wildflowers and a broad, dare I say flirtatious smile.

Despite her beauty, Elliot hardly gives her a glance, not even when she tucks a spring of purple sea lavender into the pocket of his shirt. He remains rigid, his eyes on the crowd. Not even a beautiful woman can tempt him to let down his guard?

He seemed to relax for a moment in the conference room last night in Windgaard. Somehow, I need to find a way to help him do so again. I thought my brothers would be able to help him, but he is clearly beyond their influence at this point. Or perhaps he was never susceptible in the first place. Elliot does seem to stick to a plan once he has made it, and his single goal is to keep me safe. Nothing else seems to matter.

It never occurred to me until now how much I demand of a protection agent. I have asked for his mind, his body, and his time, and his life is no longer his own. Even if he did take an interest in someone, that interest could never turn into anything but a fleeting flirtation because he will be needed at my side. Always. He will need to go wherever I go.

No wonder he carries so much stress.

"You know him better than I do," I say to my brothers, frowning as a child approaches Elliot now with an offering of something in her hands. It looks like a pastry on a serviette. Elliot wrinkles his nose and shakes his head. "What does he do for fun?"

"Fun?" Hex snickers. "He spars."

"Trains," Sander adds.

"If he isn't with the guards, he's studying with Gregor."

"The only time he ever sits still is when he's asleep, and even then..."

The child comes over to our side of the square, her steps careful as she watches the pastry in her hands so it does not fall. Elliot follows her with his eyes, which widen when he sees how far I have gotten from him, and though he takes a step, he freezes when I shoot him a warning look.

Once I am certain he will remain where he is, I crouch to match the height of the girl and smile at her. "That looks delicious."

"My mum made it," she tells me with a worried expression on her face. I can barely hear her over the music. "For the big, scary man."

I only just manage to hold back a laugh. "That's very nice of your mum."

"Do you want it, Princess? He told me no."

Cupping my hands beneath hers, I smile wider and shake my head. "No, but I think we can get the big, scary man to change his mind. Should we try?"

She looks nervous, but she nods. "Okay."

"What's your name?"

"Elsa."

"That is a lovely name. Come." Putting my hand on the girl's shoulder, I direct her back to where Elliot is standing.

He watches us warily, his eyes as much on Elsa as they are on me. Is he really so on edge that a tiny child frightens him?

"Elliot, this is Elsa. She says her mother made this pastry for you in particular."

"I don't want..." He stops when I glare at him, his jaw clenching tighter as if my censure caused him pain. Then he surprises me by sinking down to one knee and holding out his hand. "Thank you, Elsa."

The little girl places the pastry on his large palm, her expression expectant.

Something shifts in the big, scary soldier when he looks down at the pastry, then back at Elsa. Everything about him softens, and a smile breaks across his face as he leans an elbow on his knee. "This looks really good," he tells her, his voice impossibly gentle. He takes the purple flower from his pocket and holds it out to her. "Is this a good trade?"

Elsa slowly nods as her fingers curl around the blossoms.

Grinning, Elliot looks back down at the pastry in his hand. "Did you help your mom make this?"

"I made the filling," Elsa practically whispers.

"What did you put inside?"

"Gooseberries."

His eyebrows rise high in exaggerated surprise. "I don't think I've ever tried a gooseberry before."

"They're my second favorite," Elsa replies with a little more confidence than before.

Elliot grins. "What's your first favorite?"

"Blackberries, but we ate them already."

"Well, it's a good thing you did, because otherwise you would have made me a blackberry pastry, and I've already tried those." He takes a massive bite of the pastry, humming and expressing how good it is through his mouthful until Elsa starts giggling. Then he shoves the rest of the pastry into his mouth, and the little girl practically squeals with laughter.

"I can get you another!" she says and darts off.

Rising, Elliot fights to chew his mouthful as I fight to keep from laughing. I could not have expected that interaction, and I have no idea how to react. Elliot, on the other hand, grimaces and licks cream from his lips while he searches the crowd for wherever Elsa went.

"You have a little..." I reach up, wiping a bit of cream from the corner of his mouth before my propriety can remind me that that is hardly a professional action to take. Horrified by my indecorum, I freeze with my hand hovering between us and embarrassment scorching my cheeks.

Whatever shifted in our relationship last night, it should not have given me permission to be so brazen.

Elliot's eyes linger on the cream on my thumb for a long few seconds, then he holds the serviette toward me with a grunt. "Thanks."

Vitte, I have made everything awkward. Taking the cloth, I search for a way to take his attention off me. "What in the world was that?"

His eyes dart to the serviette in my hand. "What was what?"

I would rather we did not discuss my informal contact just now, so I explain, "If I didn't know better, I might have thought you were possessed by someone else a moment ago."

Understanding dawns on him, and he looks over the crowd again, finding Elsa across the square with a woman who must be her mother. Her mother smiles at us as she talks to Elsa. "You don't think I know how to act around kids?" He either finds that amusing or insulting, and I do not know which. "Why, because I'm a big, scary man?"

I gasp. "You heard me?"

Chuckling, he tilts his head to one side. "Read your lips. I'm assuming she called me that first."

"You were rather terrifying, I think."

"I wasn't trying to be." He narrows his eyes. "But answer the question."

Grinning, I shift so I am standing next to him and watching the crowd the same way he is. He does have a decent vantage point here, with a good view of the musicians and the people gathered around tables and chairs as they talk and share their food. "No, I did not think you knew how to act around kids. I thought you were in the Army for your entire adult life."

"I was."

I sense more to that answer, so I nudge his arm. "But?"

He sighs heavily. "But while I was a training officer on base, I lived with a buddy's family. He has two little girls." As his gaze grows distant, he rolls his shoulder, the same one he massaged last night. But whatever discomfort it might be giving him, it seems to disappear when Elsa returns with two more pastries. His smile comes back in full force as he drops down to the girl's level again.

"I brought you one too, Princess!" Elsa says with so much excitement that I laugh.

Crouching next to Elliot, I take my gift and thank the sweet girl for bringing it to me. I wish I had something I could give her in return, but all I've had to share today are promises for when I take the throne. "You had better run back to your mum before she worries," I tell her. "It was wonderful to meet you, Elsa."

She curtsies wobbly. "And you, Princess." She turns to leave but pauses, looking back at us. "My mum says you two are a beautiful couple," she says, then runs off, leaving Elliot and me on our own.

"Oh," I say on a breath, suddenly dizzy. "But we're not..." *We are not a couple.* That is what I should have said to the girl before she was too far, but her words caught me off guard. "Why would anyone think that about us?"

Elliot grunts and stands, helping me up with him. "Interesting," he mutters. His eyes narrow slightly as he gazes across the crowd like he did before, though he does not seem to be looking at anything in particular. I, on the other hand, am entirely focused on the warmth of his fingers still touching my elbow. Why has he not let go? "People are paying more attention to you than I thought."

Willing myself to ignore the contact between us, I look up at his face. "Then they should have realized that I have not been close to you for most of the afternoon."

The muscles in Elliot's jaw flex. "Yeah, that's not happening again. You're staying within arm's length from here on out."

"What do you suppose people will begin to say then?" I ask, inexplicably blushing at the thought of Elliot always within reach like this. "If someone already assumed we are a couple, then—"

"It's not true," Elliot interrupts, dropping his hand and looking at me, "so it doesn't..." His words trail off, leaving the last word on a breath. "...matter." For a moment, his eyes flit all over my face as if he is seeing it for the first time, and I burn hotter beneath his searching gaze. But then he ducks his head and chuckles. "It's only natural for your bodyguard to be close to you, don't you think?"

What little air is in my lungs slips out in an exhale, and my next breath takes an embarrassing amount of concentration. "Yes. Yes, of course you would be close, and it is foolish for anyone to think you are anything but my protector."

"Exactly."

And it is foolish for *me* to think there is something between us that is not there. He is my bodyguard and my friend. Nothing more. *I know this.* He obviously knows it too.

Setting my shoulders back, I force my thoughts to stay in reality. "I never would have guessed you had a way with children," I say calmly, "but it is nice to see you are more than a barbarian."

Elliot snorts a quick laugh. "You only called me that once, when I carried you out of Invem. Have you been thinking that about me this whole time?"

"Naturally," I lie as I think about how entirely *un*-barbaric he has been since that day. From the start, really. In truth, he has been so different from what I first thought him to be that it is becoming increasingly difficult to put him into any sort of box at all.

Elliot Reid is unique among men.

With lively music in the air and so many delicious smells and a cool breeze coming off the sea, the silence between us as we stand at the edge of the celebration grows comfortable, the way it should be between friends, and I begin relaxing fully into the moment. Elliot is right, and neither Elsa's mum's nor anyone else's speculation has anything to do with the truth.

Thankfully, for the first time all day, Elliot finally looks like *he* has relaxed as well, and more than ever I wish I could have given Elsa more than a smile and a few words. The little girl has no idea what she has given my bodyguard, far beyond a couple of pastries. A moment away from his worries was exactly what he needed.

"Coming here was never a political strategy, was it?" he asks after a while.

I grin. "Do you think I lied to Markham?"

Though he scoffs at my use of Grimstad's given name—or perhaps he is scoffing at my question in general—Elliot's tranquility remains as he watches the festivities. "I don't think you ever lie, Rapunzel."

Warmth blossoms in my chest with his comment. "I did not realize how nice it would be for someone to think that about me."

He turns to me, his eyes searching again. "Are you telling me it isn't true? You're a liar?" Despite his teasing tone, his expression is serious.

Lifting my chin, I shrug one shoulder. "I *am* a politician."

"You're a lot more than that, Freya. What you do doesn't make up all of who you are."

Silence settles between us once more, somehow louder than the chatter and music surrounding us. He is saying so much with his warm brown gaze, and I wish I could hear his unspoken thoughts. Does he truly believe I am more than a princess when I so often feel as if I have forgotten who I am underneath? I spoke that fear to him a few days ago, unsure if he really heard me because he instantly tried to argue.

What does Elliot see when he looks at me?

Swallowing, I keep my question to myself, too afraid of the answer. "The same is true for you, you know," I say quietly. "You are more than just a bodyguard, and I do not want you to get lost in your role and forget to live. You—Elliot—matter in this world."

Nothing about Elliot's demeanor or expression changes. He is frozen in time, eyes locked on mine while the world continues moving around us. I want him to believe me. I *need* him to believe, as much as I am coming to learn that *I* need *him* on this campaign with me. Another guard could protect my body, but Elliot seems to look after the rest of me as well. He cares so much that he has given his all for my sake.

Someone needs to look after him in return.

The music comes to an end, the musicians bowing amidst applause. Elliot blinks and drops his gaze as he claps, breaking the tension holding us together. A moment later, one of the violinists starts up a traditional Candoran love song, and the other musicians join in after a few measures. It is a lovely song with a calming rhythm, and it sparks a desire in me that is so strong I cannot ignore it, even knowing how it will skew outside perception even more.

"Dance with me."

Elliot's eyes snap to mine again. "What?"

I hold out a hand. "Dance with me."

"I heard you the first time." He studies my hand, brow furrowed like no one has ever asked him to dance before. Maybe that is true. Maybe Elliot Reid has lived a life deprived of all the good and beautiful things the world has to offer. Just as he has been teaching me to let go of my formalities, it seems I need to teach him to let go of his responsibilities every now and then.

Relax.

It will be good for us both.

I smile. "Please."

"I don't..." He shakes his head. "I don't know how."

Grabbing his right hand, I guide it to my back, then take his other hand and hold it aloft before sliding my left hand to his shoulder. "Let me show you how to dance like a Candoran." I take a step back, pulling him with me. "Let me help you be more than a bodyguard tonight."

For a man who claims not to know how to dance, he picks up the steps quickly as I guide him through a Candoran waltz. He gains confidence as we go, so different from the nobles and diplomats I have danced with over the years, a lot of whom tend to be so afraid of stepping on my toes that their eyes never leave our feet. Those who are confident enough to meet my eyes as we dance are often *too* confident, leaving me squirming under their gazes.

But Elliot has a way of making me feel nothing but safe as he takes the lead halfway through the song. He keeps half his attention on the people around us while the other half stays on me. He still looks like the same intimidating soldier, but now that I know there is a softer side of him, one who makes little children giggle, I can see deeper than I did before. See the man who would fly to the other side of the world to protect a stranger, even when she wants him to leave.

He is a good man. Better than I could have guessed.

The music shifts to a Candoran lullaby, softer than the song before, and Elliot pulls me closer to his body. His hand moves from the middle of my back up to my shoulder blade until I'm leaning into him, my head against his collarbone and our hands clasped between us. Wearing clothes he borrowed from a man in town, he smells like the ocean breeze and woodsmoke, and he is warm. So warm.

I could stay here in his embrace forever.

Chapter Seventeen

FREYA

If I lose this election, perhaps I will move here to Havenford and live out my days in the simplicity of this place. Elliot can come with me and forget he ever had any worries, and I will enjoy watching him laugh as he dances in a circle with a group of children and loses a stone throwing competition to a sixty-year-old shepherd named Rand. We both could be happy here, not as a princess and her bodyguard but as friends.

I could dance with Elliot every night and feel that overwhelming sense of safety he gives me when he holds me. I do not think anything could hurt me if I were in his arms, physically or otherwise.

"I'm losing my touch," Elliot says breathlessly, coming to where I sat on a low wall to watch him compete with the locals. His stone sailed across the beach as if it weighed nothing but still landed nearly a meter behind Rand's. With bright eyes and flushed cheeks, Elliot looks his age for the first time as he runs a hand through his windswept hair and grins. *Twenty-six.* He is so young. "Maybe you should hire Rand to be your bodyguard," he says and sits next to me, his arm bumping mine in his nearness.

His jest settles heavy in my heart like the stone he just threw, and my smile is forced. For how rough things started between us, I cannot imagine anyone else being at my side. "If I have a need for someone to throw stones, I know where to find him."

His expression softens. "Don't worry, Princess. I'm not going anywhere."

"That is a relief." My casual tone belies how glad I am for his reassurance, and I fix my eyes on the clouds in the horizon, gilded orange by the setting sun. Most of the people of Havenford have come down to the beach to enjoy the last of the sun's rays, but we are on our own here at the sand's edge. "Thank you, by the way."

He shifts to better face me, his leg pressing against mine in a way that feels both foreign and familiar. This easy contact between us is new, but after the way he held me when we danced, the connection now seems natural. "For what?"

"For letting me enjoy today."

Exhaling slowly, he rubs a hand on his thigh as if nervous. "You were right."

"Likely, yes, but what about?"

That gets a chuckle out of him. "I needed to relax. I got stuck in my head, and I'm no good to you if I can't even think straight." When I grin wide, he narrows his eyes. "But I expect you to keep your promise, Rapunzel. I'm in charge from here on out."

I snicker. "Of course." I always strive to keep my promises, but I never said I would make it easy for him. Going forward in my campaign, flexibility and adaptability will be my greatest allies. Elliot will simply have to plan accordingly because I will not know the best course of action until I am in it. I learned as much in Windgaard.

He growls a bit, his scowl deepening. "Why do I get the feeling you're plotting against me?"

"Likely because I am."

"Freya."

"Elliot." I lift my chin and grin at him with all the haughtiness I can summon.

He shakes his head, like he has no idea what to do with me. "You're a pain in the neck, you know that?" And yet he smiles, like he cannot contain his affection for me.

I did not realize how much I would treasure his good opinion, and his expression seems to give me a strength that will never wane. I rather like the way he is looking at me. Though Elsa's words about us being a couple echo in my head, I ignore them and instead tease, "I happen to think I am delightful, and my friends would agree."

"Your friends, the celebrities." He rolls his eyes.

"Have you forgotten that one of those celebrities is your cousin?"

"Don't remind me." But then his gaze catches on something behind me, and he grows tense, all of his mirth gone in an instant.

Turning, I search for what put him on edge and frown when I find Markham standing a few meters away with a hesitant expression. While I do think it is a good idea to be wary when it comes to Markham Grimstad, my opponent has done nothing to deserve Elliot's hatred.

"Your Highness," Markham says, bowing his head. "Could I have a word with you alone?"

"No," Elliot says at the same time I say, "Of course."

"Freya," Elliot growls, "you shouldn't—"

"The day is not over," I argue and slip from the wall to walk to Markham's side, my pace less demure than it should be in case Elliot tries to stop me. I reach Markham unhindered and turn back to Elliot in surprise.

He hasn't moved from his spot on the wall despite the furious expression on his face. "Stay within sight," he orders gruffly.

"Of course," Markham replies, and offers me his arm. True to his word, he leads me only far enough that Elliot will not be able to hear our conversation, stopping next to one of the stone houses abutting the beach. My curiosity is nearly unbearable, so I am glad when he starts speaking immediately. "I've been wanting to have this conversation since meeting you in Breckenholt, so I'm grateful you're willing to hear me out."

"Be grateful my bodyguard is in a good mood," I reply with a wry smile.

Markham returns the smile, though his eyes jump to Elliot with a flash of anxiety behind them. "Yes, well, it only makes sense that he wouldn't trust me, under the circumstances."

"The circumstances being that you are trying to usurp my birthright, yes."

He bites the inside of his lips and seems to fight a laugh. "You don't like to mince words, do you?"

"I believe a direct approach is always better."

"In that case, I have a proposal for you."

I tilt my head as my curiosity builds. While I was not fond of him after our first meeting, Markham has always intrigued me. His passion for Candora far exceeds that of most of his peers, and his ambition and perseverance are admirable. "What sort of proposal?"

"The literal sort."

His words settle over me like a heavy blanket, muffling the sounds of the surf and people playing games as I process what he just said to me. *The literal sort.* That could mean a few things, but it seems as if he is suggesting... "I am not sure I understand," I say slowly, as if the sluggishness of my speech might counteract the high velocity at which my brain is rolling through the possibilities. "Are you trying to say you are proposing—"

"Marriage, yes." Markham purses his lips together when I gasp. "I know this seems to be coming from nowhere, but—"

"Did you just propose *marriage* to the future queen of Candora?" Elliot asks, appearing at my side as if he teleported here. His voice is tight. Sharp. Like his expression. He must have read Markham's lips like he did with me earlier and leapt into action.

"Yes, I believe he did," I say breathlessly. I am suddenly dizzy, and the crash of waves and shouts of villagers become deafening beneath the sound of my heartbeat in my ears.

I cannot breathe, and I stare at Markham, hoping he will say something to contradict himself.

He does not. "I know it sounds absurd."

"You've got that right," Elliot growls, placing a steadying hand on my back.

"But give me a chance to explain."

"Please do," I mutter, forcing my lungs to fill. "As quickly and succinctly as possible."

For some reason, Markham seems to find my direction amusing, and his smile does nothing to help the panic slowly rising in my chest. "You and I are opponents, but we both want what's best for Candora. At the moment, we are dividing our people when we should be bringing them together. Candora's strength has always been in the unity of its people, but right now the classes are more divided than they have been in over a century. You and I could bridge that gap."

I swallow. "With...marriage?"

Markham nods, more animated now. "With you as the reigning monarch and me at your side as king, we could use our differences to our benefit. Address both sides of each issue. You will have the support of the noble class, and with my common background, the masses who have been left unheard will finally have a voice."

I hate to admit it, but he makes a good point. The House of Commons was created for the purpose of benefiting those who are not of the nobility, but any decisions they make go to the House of Lords and the ruling monarch, who ultimately decide the laws of the country. There have been many attempted reforms that have been overturned by the time they reach the top, in part because the lords and ladies making the decisions have little to no experience with circumstances different from their own and cannot understand why a change may be needed.

If Markham and I were to become a united front, there would be a direct line from the people to the monarchy.

"You're serious, Grim?" Elliot says, shifting forward. He's watching Markham warily, his jaw tight. "Is this some convoluted way to get yourself into power without having to rely on votes?"

Calm as ever, Markham speaks to me rather than answering Elliot. "I told you my stance on marriage, and I wouldn't propose the idea if I didn't think it would benefit us both, as well as the kingdom. Nor do I expect you to give me an answer tonight. I know this came as a surprise."

Surprise. As if a marriage proposal is akin to thinking there was one more biscuit in the bag but reaching in to find none. "Markham..." I touch shaking fingers to my forehead and take a deep breath.

"Think about it, Your Highness. And I mean truly give it some thought. If a union doesn't make sense for you politically, or if you think the people are better off with us as opponents, you can turn me down." As if to prove his point, he steps back, putting some space between us. "Take a few days, but the sooner you decide, the sooner we know how the election will proceed." With a quick bow of his head, he turns and heads into the village, fading into the shadows as the sun sinks below the horizon.

Elliot swears, echoing my own thoughts. "He's crazy."

"Is he?" I reply. A shiver runs through me, and I tuck my arms around myself to stave off the chill left by Markham's departure.

Muttering something about how a Havenford fisherman has his jacket, Elliot wraps an arm around my shoulders and pulls me against his side. As before, his body warms mine, but the heat does not reach my center. Uncertainty and insecurity sit like an icy barrier around my soul. I feel so ill equipped to process this development, and a voice in the back of my mind is telling me that Markham's proposal might very well be the only way I can have the future I have wanted my entire life.

"You're not considering him, are you?" Elliot asks sharply, as if I spoke my thoughts out loud.

I wince at his tone. "He is right, Elliot."

"He's nervous."

"He said he has thought about this from the start."

"He can say whatever he wants, but that doesn't make it true. If he's so convinced that marrying him is what's best for Candora, then why did he wait until you started your campaign? Why not weeks ago? *Months* ago? He doesn't have a chance of winning, and he knows it."

I wish I could be so certain. "Yes, I gained some ground in Windgaard yesterday," I say, "but one informal meet-and-greet on the street does not counteract years of disparity." Sighing, I step away from his hold so I can look him in the eyes. "You know as well as I do that he has the majority of the people on his side. I have been on the road for mere days and have only a week and a half to change the minds of an entire country."

"You don't know how people will vote," he argues. "The loudest voices are always the ones of dissent."

"That has no bearing on this!" I start to pace in the hope that it will calm my racing heart. "The nobility have always held more power than they ought, and there needs to be a change."

"I won't argue that," Elliot snaps back, "but that doesn't mean you should lie down at Grimstad's feet and roll over."

I shoot him a glare to match his scowl. "A political alliance is not a surrender, Mr. Reid."

"Giving into fear and throwing away everything you stand for isn't a selfless act!"

His words feel like a slap, and I march up to him, wishing I were taller so I could meet him eye to eye. "I am *not* afraid," I say through my teeth.

"You are, and that's okay." His anger fades as he stands there, mere inches from me but feeling so much farther when his expression loses all traces of emotion. A mask. "Grimstad blindsided you, not just with his proposal but with his candidacy in the first place. You've barely had any time to defend your worthiness for a throne that was always supposed to be yours, and no one can blame you for feeling like you're out of your depth. So you're scared. So what? Suck it up and keep moving forward."

"'Suck it up'," I whisper, furrowing my brow. "Have you forgotten that I am a princess, Mr. Reid?"

"Have you forgotten that you and I are friends now, *Your Highness*?" His mask slips, making way for frustration as he shakes his head and looks at the place Markham disappeared behind a house. "I'm sorry. I know I'm supposed to keep my opinions to myself. But I care about you too much to let you make a choice you're going to regret."

Several words bounce around in my head with equal force but completely differing sentiments. *Let you. Regret. I care about you.* As much as I want to remind Elliot of his place, he is right to worry about regret. But caring about me? It feels unthinkable, even after seeing the way he has run himself ragged trying to keep me safe.

I am a job to him. A stressor.

You and I are friends.

As a breeze carries his unfamiliar scent to my nose, I return to that moment in his arms when we danced. He did not feel like a friend then. He was something different.

Something dangerous.

You two are a beautiful couple.

"Elliot," I murmur, unsure what I can say.

"Oi! Elliot!" Hex's voice cuts through the air, startling me, and my brother lopes over to us and plants his hand on Elliot's shoulder. "I reckon you and I should see which of us can come the closest to Rand's stone throw, yeah?"

Elliot's gaze remains fixed on the houses behind me, as if he did not notice Hex at all.

Hex frowns. "Mate, what—"

"He's here," Elliot hisses, instantly jumping into action. Grabbing my arm, he pulls me behind his back at the same time he snatches his gun from its holster. "The lurker, ten o'clock."

Swearing, Hex whips his head around to look in the right direction and bursts into a run, straight for a figure who vanishes down a side street.

Fear washes over me, leaving me dizzy. "Lurker?" I gasp. "What—"

Elliot stuffs his fingers into his mouth and whistles so loudly that my ears ring, then he backs me up against the wall, arms on either side of my head as he shields me with his body. My eyes lock on the shiny metal of his gun near my ear, my thoughts jumbled, and I can't look away.

"Sir!" Multiple voices echo the word around us. Palace guards coming up from the beach?

"Elliot!" *Sander.*

"Possible hostile, south-southwest," Elliot growls, pulling my attention to him. "Five with me. The rest, support pursuit." He barely turns his head toward his men, keeping his sharp focus on me.

"Details," Sander demands as several guards rush off in the same direction as Hex.

Sliding his arm behind my back, Elliot pulls me forward, not giving me a chance to get my bearings before he's ushering me up a different street, back toward the inn. Half a dozen guards, my brother included, surround us as we go. "Same man," he says, the words clipped.

"As Breckenholt?" Sander asks.

I stumble on a cobblestone, but Elliot holds so tightly to me that I come nowhere close to falling. A blessing, I suppose, as I try to understand what is happening. The same man as who?

"He was half hidden, watching the princess."

Sander swears and runs a hand through his hair. "Hex?"

"Went after him."

"Good. What do you need from me?" I have never seen Sander this serious or focused, even as the less talkative twin, and he almost looks like a different person as he matches Elliot's long strides perfectly. My carefree brother has been replaced by an imposing soldier, ready to follow orders.

Slowing his steps, Elliot waits for the guard in front of us to do a quick sweep of an intersecting street before we resume our hurried pace. "I need you to find Grimstad."

"What?" The word slips off my tongue at the same time I try to come to a halt, though Elliot's arm makes stopping impossible. "Grimstad? Why would—"

"Keep moving, Princess," Elliot growls.

I gape at him, still fighting his hold. "You are giving me an order?"

"Sun's down. Your day's over, and you promised to obey. Don't make this harder than it needs to be."

Flashbacks of him carrying me over his shoulders in Invem fill my mind, and I relent, letting him continue guiding me up the street. "At least explain what is happening," I demand, breathless from our speed.

Elliot glances down at me, his jaw tight and indecision in his eyes. If it were up to him, I am certain he would tell me nothing, but at this point he knows better than to fight me in every instance. He chooses to concede this particular battle. "Remember the man I told you about? The one watching the hotel in Breckenholt?"

Barely. "You said he was in Kirkstead as well, yes?"

"Inside the church," Sander confirms.

So were a hundred other people. "You told me I did not need to worry about that man," I argue, which is the very reason I had all but forgotten about him.

"That was before he showed up here," Elliot says. "Sander." He nods to his left, and Sander slips down an alley and disappears. Presumably to find Markham.

As the streets grow darker, my fear and confusion dim as well, and each step away from the beach is like a step toward normalcy. My thoughts still, leaving me with only facts rather than unfounded fears. An unidentified Candoran man was in Breckenholt, watching my hotel. The same man witnessed my disaster of a Q&A. Here in Havenford, he was, as Elliot put it, 'half hidden' and 'watching' me.

That is not much to go on.

We are all silent until we reach the inn, where Elliot directs half of the guards to check the building and my room despite two unfortunate guards having been stationed here all day. The rest of us remain outside in the chill dusk air, and I cannot simply stand here and accept this course of events.

"Elliot?"

As his eyes sweep the empty street, my bodyguard acknowledges me with merely a grunt.

"Did he have a weapon?"

That catches his attention, and he looks at me with a furrowed brow. "What?"

I fold my arms. "This 'possible hostile.' Was he armed?"

"Freya."

"*Did you see a weapon,* Elliot?"

He grits his teeth. "No. But that doesn't mean—"

"It doesn't mean you need to jump to the worst conclusions, correct," I finish for him, anger rising in my throat. All of this madness for what could be nothing at all?

Elliot narrows his eyes. "Three sightings in four locations is a pattern."

"Markham has been at all four."

"And you know how I feel about Markham Grimstad," he snaps.

The two guards outside with us glance at each other with wide eyes, and I can only imagine their thoughts. *The princess is arguing with her bodyguard yet again.* It was foolish to think Elliot and I had come to trust each other enough to not get on the other's nerves so thoroughly, but before Markham proposed, things had felt different between us. Elliot had relaxed and let me see not the soldier but the man. He had trusted me to take command of the day, and we were both happier for it.

One possible threat, likely nothing dangerous at all, should not be enough to send us right back to the beginning.

"Leave Markham out of this," I say, keeping my voice at a calm, normal volume despite my frustration with the man in front of me. "What do you plan to do when Sander finds him?"

Elliot folds his arm, and the gun still clutched in his fingers catches the light from the inn's windows above us, putting me on edge. "I plan to get answers."

"If he does not have answers?"

"He will."

I glare at him. "Humor me."

Clenching his jaw, Elliot signals to the two guards, sending them to each corner of the narrow block and leaving us alone. "What are you doing?" he asks, his voice strained.

I lift my chin. "I am questioning your judgment, Mr. Reid."

"My—" He huffs, shaking his head. "This is *my job.*"

"And this is *my country,*" I counter, waving a hand around us. "I have spent my entire life in Candora, and while we are not a perfect country and have our share of problems, in my experience, Candorans are good to each other. No one would resort to threatening me if they did not have a legitimate reason."

He groans. "That is a naive and dangerous way to look at the world for someone planning to lead a country of flawed human beings, and it'll get you killed. People do selfish things. All the time."

"Yes," I agree, "but if you are going to expect every stranger you come across to be inherently evil instead of choosing to trust them, then how can I expect them to trust *me*?"

Holstering his gun, Elliot shakes his head and looks at me like I have no comprehension of what is happening around me. "Freya, this isn't—"

"I am not saying you are wrong about this lurker," I say, "but I am asking you to be less rash. To *think* before you act, Elliot!"

"How can I think when I can't focus on anything but *you*?"

As Elliot freezes, his eyes wide, my breath seems to turn to ice in my lungs. He looks as shocked by his admission as I am. Whether it was a secret that slipped out or a revelation to us both, I cannot say.

"What does that mean?" I whisper, once again thinking of the way Elsa's mum thought Elliot and I were romantically involved.

He shakes his head. "I don't know."

"Elliot."

He lifts a hand, refusing to look at me now. "You're right," he says in a measured tone, like each word requires a good deal of effort. I can almost see his mind trying to make sense of this moment as he stares at the cobblestones between us. "I didn't have enough information to assume the lurker was dangerous. But if I don't factor in every possible threat, I can't..." He looks up, his eyes stormy and his lungs heaving. "I *need* you to be safe, Freya. If I don't know that I've done everything in my power to make that happen, I'll never..."

Though deep down I know it is a bad idea, I cross the distance between us and place my palm on his cheek. His skin is warm and rough with stubble, and his eyes are fixed on mine, so full of emotions that I could not begin to comprehend everything he is feeling right now. He cares so much, and I wish I knew what haunts him. Why he carries so much fear.

"Okay," I say as gently as I can, as if using any force will frighten him away. "I will trust you, Elliot Reid, if you will promise to trust me in return. We need each other. Neither of us can do this alone."

Exhaling slowly, he nods and wraps his fingers around my wrist, holding my hand against his jaw. Those emotions behind his eyes are still in full view, nothing hidden, and I might get lost in his gaze trying to decipher them. "I trust you," he breathes, shifting infinitesimally closer. I feel each and every millimeter that disappears between us.

"You and I are still friends," I remind him, though the words do not seem to fit like they did only yesterday.

Elliot does not acknowledge my comment, nor does he move until the guards open the door to the inn and tell him that the space is clear. His hand falls, as does mine, and we both seem to be waiting for the other to decide what happens next. Which of us is truly in command?

Perhaps there is not an answer to that, just as there is no word I can use for the feeling in my heart that grows stronger with each second I look into Elliot's eyes.

Not one I can acknowledge.

CHAPTER EIGHTEEN

ELLIOT

I PRESS THE TOP of my phone to my forehead and take a deep breath. Then another. This isn't what I want to hear, and instinct tells me I should be out there finding this guy. But a stronger voice in my head disagrees.

If you are going to expect every stranger you come across to be inherently evil instead of choosing to trust them, then how can I expect them to trust me?

Freya's right.

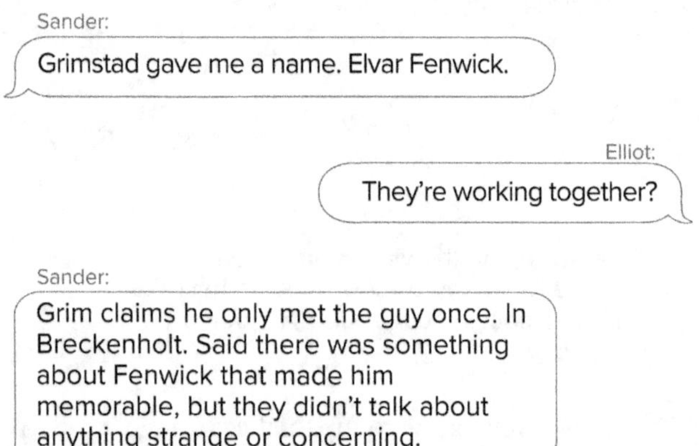

He doesn't have to worry. I can barely keep my eyes open. I was already running on fumes, and today has been a beast of a day.

Not all of it bad. For the first time in a long time, I was enjoying myself enough to forget the heaviness of my role that had gotten almost unbearable since the start of the campaign. I could breathe again.

Let me help you be more than a bodyguard tonight.

It's been hours since our dance, and I can still feel her in my arms.

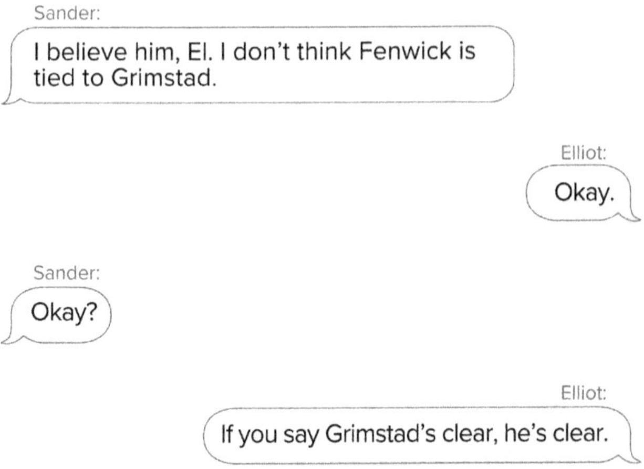

With you as the reigning monarch and me at your side as king, we could use our differences to our benefit.

I hate that everything he said made sense, but she can't really be thinking about saying yes, can she? Royals marry for political advantage all the time, but she's not just a royal. She's...so much more.

We have a name, and that's more than we had before. Enough to do some digging and see if the lurker is really a threat. Prove which one of us is right. Honestly, I hope it's her. Everything will be so much easier if I'm not constantly looking over my shoulder. If I can keep my focus on her.

I will trust you, Elliot Reid, if you will promise to trust me in return.

I trust her more than I should.

It's me I'm not sure I can trust. She's under my skin now, and for a moment I wondered if we...

But we can't. Can't even entertain the idea, for so many reasons.

My mum says you two are a beautiful couple.

That's a problem. I need to keep my head down. Avoid being alone with her. Stop wondering if she would let me hold her again without some sort of danger giving me an excuse to pull her close.

Bax:

> Rookie's officially out, Reid. You're in as soon as you say the word.

Wade:

> AKA Cap already talked to the men upstairs, and you're cleared to take your old spot.

North:

> Just gotta give up the pretty princess first.

Bax:

> We need you, Reid. Come back where you belong.

We need each other. Neither of us can do this alone.

I don't know how it changed, but somewhere between a tour bus and a seaside sunset, my priority shifted. It's not about filling my role to the best of my ability. It's about her. Making sure she's safe and confident and happy.

Happy. That won't come from marrying Markham Grimstad, a man she barely knows. If there was more time, she could decide if they would even fit together, but her sole focus is helping her country thrive by whatever means necessary. She'll do what she has to because that's who she is, and if accepting his proposal is the clearest way to accomplish her goals...

A political alliance is not a surrender.

But it's not a good idea, either.

Derek:

> Checking in to see how things are going with Freya.

Or I thought I was, but it hasn't been working. We were becoming friends, and then things took a turn I never expected them to take.

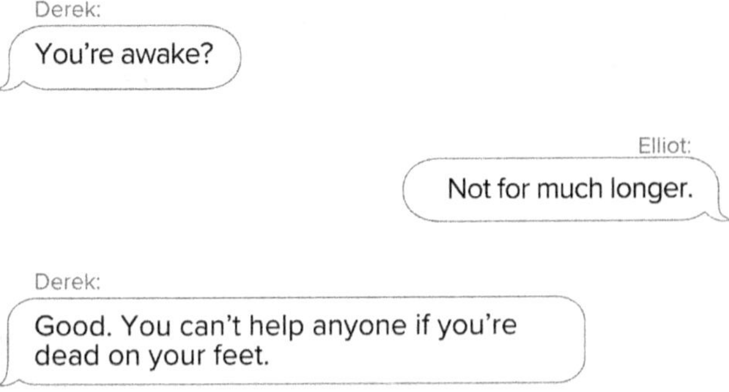

Sometimes I swear he can see me. Or he's in my head. Either way, he has spent his life studying people and reads me better than anyone, even from thousands of miles away. Since I told him about the struggles I went through after Griff died, he knows how easy it is for me to take on responsibility that shouldn't be mine to bear alone.

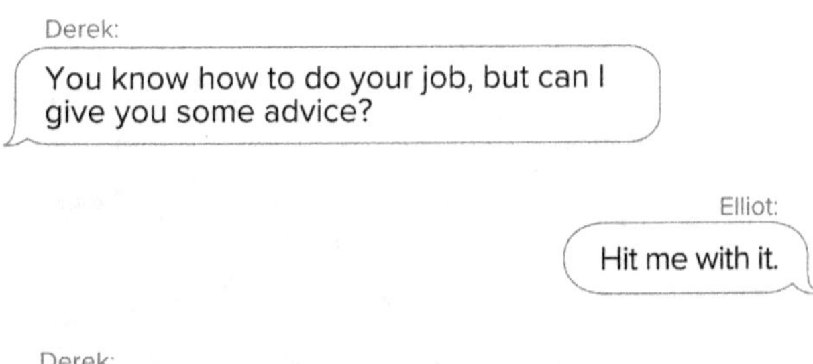

How does he always say the right thing? Since the day I met him, he has known exactly what I need to hear.

Freya's asleep in the next room over, and in a few hours she'll be ready to face her next challenge, most likely in a way I can't prepare for because she is always going to do things her way, like Derek said. That's what makes her great, and who am I to stop her? I've been trying too hard to control everything, forgetting that I'm not the one who's been preparing for a crown my whole life.

I know my place. I need to stay there instead of entertaining thoughts of *more* when that's not something I can have. If Freya can keep a cool head through surprise proposals and unknown threats, I can find a way to do the same, no matter what I'm up against. Trust my team. Trust *her*.

I need to do better.

Suck it up and keep moving forward.

For her.

Hollywood Hot Scoop

Royal Super Soldier's Identity Revealed!

As the Candoran election creeps closer, Princess Freya has been making the rounds through her home country in a desperate attempt to appeal to the regular crowd. We all know how well she does among the rich and famous, but it's clear she has no idea how to interact with normal people. Check out the slideshow below to see her donning an apron and pretending to cook, posing with a book at an orphanage, and nearly getting her hand bitten off by a sheep doing who knows what. Nice work, Your Highness, but I don't think staged do-gooding will get people to vote for you.

But here's what you really want to know: the name of Freya's super hunky bodyguard!

That's right, we have all the details! Turns out he's one of America's finest heroes (in all senses of the word, am I right, ladies?) and only recently retired from the US Special Forces. The last time I was this invested in a soldier was back when the scrumptious Seth Hastings traded his camo for cashmere and handed off his badge to take up a new career as a private bodyguard. But instead of protecting a metaphorical King of Art, like Hastings did, our new favorite soldier has an actual, real-life princess under his care!

Elliot Reid, 26, left his role as a Sergeant First Class and now holds the coveted title of Senior Protection Officer for Princess Freya Alverra. We've tracked down a partial list of some of his most impressive ops (see the link below), but we all know he's gotta be the G.O.A.T. if he's been entrusted with the princess's safety. Even just looking at this man of muscle, it's clear why he got the job. I'm sure we're all wishing we needed a bodyguard so we could get a man like him all up in our business!

And with the way Little Miss Princess looks at Elliot like he's the only man she needs in her life (see the rest of the photos in the slideshow below), I'm predicting some trouble brewing among the Glam Gang. Derek Riley is likely going to be replaced as Freya's leading man, so there's only one question we want to know: will the rest of the gang follow their fearless leader, or is Derek going to have to fight for custody of his friends? I don't know about you, but if I knew a princess/bodyguard duo like this, I wouldn't want to give them up.

Not even for the likes of Derek Riley.

The longer I look at Elliot, the more I think there might be someone to give Derek a run for his money as the sexiest man alive. Derek's reign as the king of our hearts might be ending as Freya's uncertain reign begins.

Stay tuned for more of Elliot Reid's backstory and how he ended up becoming one of the most important people in the world! XO

CHAPTER NINETEEN

FREYA

"For the last time, Mum, I am doing the best I can."

"Lady Falkheim was extremely disappointed by your lack of manners, Freya, and I do not understand why you felt the need to rudely leave her garden party after being there for less than two hours."

Pressing my phone to my chest for a moment, I sigh and settle against the back of my seat, exhaustion pulling my eyes closed. I knew I should not have answered my mother's call, but generally one does not ignore a queen. Even if the queen is one's overbearing mother. I suppose I should be grateful that she lasted more than a week before butting her nose into my campaign, but that does not make this conversation any less tiring.

I was already exhausted, made worse by the fact that I am stuck in a horse-drawn coach because Elliot thought it too dangerous for me to be on horseback through the mountain pass to get to the city of Skalridge.

The pass is too narrow and rugged for automobiles, so a portion of my entourage is taking the cars the long way around to meet us at Lynholm two days from now.

Everyone else is in a saddle.

Lifting my phone to my ear once more, I try for a controlled tone. "I left because the orphanage could only accommodate me during a set time frame. I intended to return to the party as soon as I was finished, but the rain ended Lady Falkheim's fête early."

Mum exhales sharply. "You cannot blame everything on the weather, Freya." I imagine her alone in her office, her fingers pinching the bridge of her nose. I know she is alone because she has me on speakerphone, and she would never allow anyone to overhear a conversation like this. "I thought your whole purpose of this trip was to interact with *all* of your people, and yet you have neglected nearly every nobleman and woman you have encountered."

This argument has been going on for almost half an hour, and at some point I should probably feign a bad connection and hang up. "They're going to vote for me either way," I mutter. Nothing about Markham's platform would be appealing to those already in possession of power and wealth, so I firmly believe the nobility will be on my side no matter what I do.

Unless, of course, I choose to accept Grimstad's proposal. Something tells me the noble class would not appreciate that political move.

"Mum," I say, louder, "I am doing everything I can to win the hearts of the Candoran people, and addressing the complaints of an entire county of farmers is a far more valuable use of my time than listening to Lord Mossley prattle on about his stamp collection."

Across from me, Elliot poorly stifles a snicker as he watches the mountainside roll by. He has been pretending not to listen to this conversation, but I would not be surprised if he has heard every word my mother has said. She has not been quiet this afternoon.

"Freya Isolde," Mum sighs. "While I am aware that you are your own person and will not follow in my footsteps exactly, you must take care not to make too many waves. Your position in the polls is precarious at best, and the more you deviate from tradition, the more you will be seen as a liability."

Elliot's eyebrows pull together—he can definitely hear Mum—and I have to bite my tongue to keep from saying something petulant to my mother. *You and I must be looking at different polls.*

As of this morning, popular opinion is trending in my favor after a continuous climb over the last four days. I am almost confident about the upcoming election, though I keep reminding myself that a good deal could change in a week.

When I have no response for my mother, she sighs heavily. "I had another reason for calling this morning."

"Oh?"

"I have seen...concerning...reports circulating over the last several days."

"Could you be more specific?"

She lowers her voice. "About you and Mr. Reid."

My stomach lurches as heat rises up my neck. Naturally, Elliot notices the change in my demeanor and sits up straighter, his eyes fixed on me. Whether Mum spoke quietly because she knows Elliot is in the coach with me or because it is a delicate topic, I do not think he heard what she said, or he would have more than worried curiosity furrowing his brow.

Shaking my head at him, I take a steadying breath. "What is it you have seen?" I ask Mum, though I already know the answer.

Hot Scoop is not the only one to have noticed a change in behavior between my bodyguard and me.

One opinion piece in particular stood out to me in yesterday's national paper, and I read it so many times that I could recite it from memory if asked.

Has Princess Freya found the one? I don't know about any-one else, but I think the princess has fallen in love with her new bodyguard. They're always looking at each other with INTENSITY. I get that he's supposed to protect her and all, but blimey, if I had a man looking at me like the world revolves around me, I would have stars in my eyes just like Freya does. Tell me I'm not alone in thinking we could have an American king pretty soon. I wouldn't even be mad.

"According to several sources," Mum says, "you and Mr. Reid have grown rather close."

There is no way to have this discussion without Elliot discerning what it is about, so I keep my eyes on him as I say, "Of course we have grown close. He is my bodyguard and goes wherever I go."

Elliot's eyebrows drop, his body growing tense to match mine and a question in his gaze.

Mum's voice grows sharper. "I have seen pictures, Freya."

Pictures will not have told her that Elliot and I have shared an unspo-ken agreement to avoid repeating anything that happened in Havenford. We have not argued. We have not danced together. We have hardly even spoken, and certainly not about anything vulnerable. Elliot has given me no reason to think he needs help relaxing, and I have done my best to give him no reason to physically handle me. Things between us have been more professional than ever.

That being said...

The more I watch this man, the more I am coming to see the small, beautiful things that make up Elliot Reid. He shows utmost respect to the men under his command, and my brothers have begun taking more initiative and showing more confidence each time Elliot puts his trust in them and their abilities. He has been following my lead but never hesitates to tweak my plans when dissatisfied with the level of security, always in a way that still aligns with my goals. When I am out in public and interacting with people on the street, he interacts with them too, slipping into Candoran like it is his first language whenever someone prefers it to English.

Sometimes it is all I can do to keep my attention on what I am doing rather than watching Elliot grow more and more comfortable in my world with each passing day.

I clear my throat, pulling myself back to the conversation and ignoring the...well, the *intensity* of Elliot's gaze. "You of all people should know that context is everything."

"*You* of all people should know that context is too easily removed," Mum counters. "The entire country thinks you have romantic feelings toward a member of your staff, and if I did not know better, some of these photos would have me believing it."

If *I* did not know better, I might admit that the country is more accurate in their assessment than I would like.

"Elliot has been nothing but professional from the moment he took up his post," I say, a bit too sharply.

Wincing, he tilts his head as if to say, *'Are you sure about that?'*

I wrinkle my nose. *'Havenford does not count,'* I mouth at him, biting my lip when he fights a smile. Besides, I would not say anything he did was *unprofessional*. He pushed against boundaries, but if anyone crossed a line, I did. I asked him to dance. I pushed him too far with the lurker. I touched his cheek and wondered, if only for a moment, if we could—

"Are you listening to me, Freya?" Mum asks loudly.

No, because every day it gets easier to get lost in thoughts of what can never be. "Sorry, Mum, the signal in the Skalridge pass is not as strong as it could be." Which is not a lie, though the slight rise in one of Elliot's eyebrows suggests he thinks otherwise.

"I asked if you are planning to snub Rensvik tonight as you have done with so many other nobles this week," Mum says with frustration.

I stifle a groan and clench my jaw. The Duke of Rensvik planned a dinner party for when I arrive in Skalridge, complete with a dozen other members of the nobility from the north end of the country. This county is the farthest from the capital that we can get, which means the nobles in the area all tend to lean toward more traditional views. It will likely be the worst evening of the campaign, and a part of me has been hoping some disaster befalls us on the way.

"I have every intention of attending, even if he will spend the entire time treating me as a child," I say stiffly.

"Intention does not equal action, Freya. If you continue to neglect your duties, not only as a future queen but as a current princess, then—"

"Do you have any other lectures for me this morning, Your Majesty?" I regret my words as soon as I speak them, but I am too tired to keep my emotions in check.

I regret my outburst less when Elliot's lips twist up into a smirk, his eyes bright with pride. Yes, our actions since Havenford have been entirely professional. No, the gossips are not wrong about the way he looks at me and I look at him.

How could I not admire him when he has let me choose my own path and supported me every step of the way?

"Do you always have to be this willful, Freya?" Mum asks wearily. "I am trying to help you."

She means well. Deep down, I know she loves me and wants me to succeed. But at what point in my life will she accept that I am an adult and capable of making my own choices? When I am forty? Sixty? "I don't need your help when it comes to my campaign," I say, matching her flat tone. "If I can't do *this* on my own, how am I supposed to rule a country on my own?"

"You will not always be on your own," she argues. "Someday, hopefully sooner than later, you will have someone at your side to support you, as I am supporting you now, and you must learn to accept advice from him, as he will be a king beside you."

I grit my teeth and wait for the censure that is coming.

"But that someone cannot be Elliot Reid. You know this, yes?"

Of course I do, but as I meet Elliot's gaze once again, my heart disagrees. His smile has faded, his expression turning more stony than amused, which means he heard my mother's gentle edict. I want nothing more than to tell her she is wrong, but I am certain Elliot knows as well as I do that our lives cannot intersect in that way. Not without consequences.

Not without changing laws and making a good many waves. Elliot is not nobility. He is not a politician. He is not even Candoran. Everything about him goes against the laws of my country.

"Mum."

"These photos say more than what you are willing to admit to yourself, but whatever you are feeling, Freya, it is fleeting. Do not get swept up in the exhilaration of a forbidden crush when it will only lead to heartbreak."

I take a deep breath and sit up as straight as I can to give my voice confidence, wishing I could be alone when I say this. But it needs to be said. "I understand your concern, but this is a non-issue. My priorities are first to win the election, then to find my footing as queen. If at some point I choose an attachment to someone, it will not be Elliot."

Oh, I did not like saying that.

With a stiff spine and my eyes on my lap, I do my best to stay strong as I say, "We are almost to Skalridge. Thank you for your suggestions. I will see you in Stonemere for the Celestial Ball in a few days, but I need to focus on my campaign. So, unless you have something urgent to discuss with me that is unrelated to the election, I likely will not answer your call."

"Freya."

"Goodbye, Mum." I hang up and drop my phone onto the seat next to me, far more exhausted than when the call began. Though I close my eyes and rest my head against the back of the seat, I can feel Elliot's gaze searing into me, and with nowhere to go, a conversation is inevitable. "I am sorry."

"Don't be."

"She is making assumptions without any information to substantiate—"

"Freya."

I open my eyes, calming at the sight of his gentle smile. He has been so different in the days since we left Havenford, solid and steady in a way I needed so badly. My mother thinks I need support, but I already have it. In every way except the one I do not let myself consider.

Elliot's smile twitches. "Are we ever going to talk about—"

"*No.*"

We both flinch at the harshness I put into the word.

Relaxing my shoulders, I swallow and try again. "I was not lying when I said I need to focus on the campaign, Elliot."

"Just when you said we were close to Skalridge." He smirks and leans his elbows on his knees, eliminating some of the space between us. "We probably still have five miles to go, at least."

"Do you have a map in your head?"

"Yeah."

Oh, he is serious? A snicker escapes me, and I relax for the first time since seeing my mother's number light up my screen. "You continue to amaze me, Elliot Reid."

"It's part of my training." He breathes in deep, a thoughtful look in his eyes. "You haven't told her about Grimstad," he mutters, flexing the fingers in his right hand before clasping his hands together. "Why?"

What a question. Markham and I have not crossed paths as often as I expected us to. Though we both visited Alderholt on the same day, I was busy with the farmers while Markham spent his time in town speaking to manufacturers. Our next two stops were opposites, so we only saw each other in passing on the road between the two towns. The lack of interaction has been a blessing and a curse when it comes to Markham's proposal.

On the one hand, he has not pressured me to make a decision. On the other, it is far too easy to ignore the prospect and pretend I do not have a choice to make.

"You know what my mother is like," I say, shaking my head. "Whether she approves of the idea or thinks it laughable, she would try to make the decision for me."

"You've gotten pretty good at making your own decisions, Freya." He purses his lips. "Have you made one about this?"

My chest tightens, and I cannot bear to look at him. It is difficult enough to accept that I am not allowed to feel something for Elliot; considering a lifetime commitment to a man I hardly know is even worse. I never planned for love in my life—it was something I would unlikely find as a future queen. Hoped for it? Yes. My parents' marriage was strategic, a princess and the son of an earl, but they were fortunate to forge a love together over time. I assumed my life would follow a similar trajectory.

But a union with Markham—strategic though it may be—carries a good deal of risk. He is not noble, so our marriage would be a stark shift from tradition. He is my political opponent, and choosing to align with him might be seen as weakness. While I may come to respect him, could I learn to love him? There is no way to know.

"No," I say, answering Elliot's question as I look up at him again. "No, I have not decided."

"You're running out of time," he reminds me.

"I am aware."

"Do you…" He grimaces. "Do you want to talk it through?"

The tightness in my chest grows more painful. "With you?"

He shrugs. "I'm the only one here."

Despite desperately wanting someone to help me figure out my best options, this is not a conversation I can have with Elliot Reid. "I am surprised you are here," I say to change the topic. I scoot forward in my seat, as if being closer might convince him to give me an honest response. "One of my brothers could have sat with me like they have all week."

He sits up, squirming a bit as he maintains a professional distance between us. "I thought I could give them a break."

"From me?" I snort a laugh. "How flattering."

Smiling, he shakes his head and seems to relax again. "You know that's not what I meant."

"What did you mean?"

"I'm giving them a break from me."

"Oh?"

He chuckles. "Turns out talking to you unlocked something in me, and since I've been keeping a professional distance from you, they're the next best thing for conversation." Twisting his lips, he tilts his head to the side and lifts his eyebrows, looking so expressive that I cannot help but smile. "For the record, I definitely prefer talking to you, Rapunzel."

He has not called me that in days, and the nickname feels like an embrace. "I've missed talking to you too," I whisper.

The space between us warms, quiet and comfortable. I have spent more time than normal speaking with my friends in California over text and video calls these last few days, but more than ever I have wanted to talk to the man sitting across from me. He unlocked something in me as well, and I have never felt that my friends would understand my fears of taking the throne. They are all so confident in their spheres and know exactly who they are.

Elliot, for all his skills and talents, was so afraid of making a mistake and getting me hurt that he started to fall apart by the time we reached Havenford. I can imagine no man more qualified than he is, and he still feared to fail.

If anyone can understand me, he can, and I hate that he has kept his distance. But we both know the limits of our relationship, and it is dangerous to be close to him.

"You should probably stop looking at me like that," he murmurs in a voice so low it is almost a growl.

Shivering, I refuse to look away, if only to have some control over this thing between us, whatever it is. "I am to be a queen, and I will look at you however I would like."

Though he shakes his head, his eyes twinkle with amusement. "You're trouble."

"Perhaps that is why Markham thought to run against me."

"He's running against you because he doesn't know you," Elliot argues. "If he knew the woman I know, he'd back down in an instant."

Blushing, I clasp my hands in my lap as I ask, "And who is the woman you know?" I am playing with fire, asking this question, but I need to know.

Exhaling slowly, Elliot leans forward once more. There is not as much space in the coach as in the town car, so as he rests his elbows on his knees, our faces are only a foot apart. "She's bold," he says to his hands, linked together a few inches away from my knees. "Confident. She thinks of everyone's needs but her own and is intelligent and clever, and every time she finds a new way to connect to her people, I am left more and more in awe of her." His eyes lift to meet mine, a fire burning in their brown depths. "She's going to be an amazing queen, and I'm going to stand by her proudly."

Vitte. I should not have asked, and I cannot stop from reaching out and putting my hand over his in gratitude.

Elliot's eyes drop to where our fingers touch, growing darker with each passing second. Does he feel the electric charge that I do? "Princess," he murmurs. A warning, but one I do not heed because he does not free his hands from mine.

Swallowing, I slowly slide my fingers between his hands to separate them and make it possible to hold his hand properly. "Do you truly think I will be a good queen?"

With something akin to frustration in his eyes, he shakes his head. "You know I do." Then he surprises me by lifting my hand to his lips and placing a gentle kiss on my knuckle. "I don't know why you keep doubting yourself."

I doubt myself because despite rising support for me in the polls, there are still many people around the kingdom holding rallies against me. Markham still has significant influence. Two of the palace guards have caught glimpses of Elvar Fenwick since leaving Havenford, and the lurker must have a reason for following me. With each sighting, I am less convinced that he is not as dangerous as Elliot first believed.

"Debate is tomorrow," Elliot says, speaking of an event Sander suggested when he spoke to Markham in Havenford.

Though I am grateful for the new topic of conversation, this one makes me as nervous as anything else. Markham agreed to the debate without hesitation, and while it will be a good way for each of us to showcase our platforms, it will also put me in front of the entire country.

Elliot must sense my fear of that publicity because he adds, "It'll be a good way to show the rest of Candora who you are, and they're going to love you."

Emotion sticks in my throat, so I can only whisper, "Do you really think so?"

Elliot swallows, lifting his eyes to mine. "How could they not?" he murmurs back.

We sit that way, hands clasped and gazes locked together, until the coach comes to a halt and a guard opens the door, announcing our arrival in the isolated city of Skalridge. Tonight, I will endure the dinner with the Duke of Rensvik, and tomorrow, I will debate with Markham.

Each day brings me closer to my future, whether I am ready for it or not.

At least I will have Elliot with me, no matter what.

Chapter Twenty

ELLIOT

I PROBABLY SHOULDN'T HAVE left the princess's side, but this was too good an opportunity to pass up. She has Hex and Sander with her, along with a dozen palace guards, and Rensvik seems like the kind of guy who has his own security. I have confidence that she'll be safe, especially if I learn something useful tonight.

"Sir, are you sure this is a good idea?"

Ignoring Rothesby, the guard I brought with me, I keep my eyes trained on the man walking ahead of us in the rain. Visibility is lower than I would like, so we need to keep on his tail. It'll be dark soon and even harder to follow him, so I'm going to take my chance while I've got it.

This is the first time one of us has seen Fenwick without him seeing us first.

"Wouldn't it be better to detain him rather than simply following him?"

Fenwick turns a corner, and I pick up my pace to avoid losing him. Thankfully, he's on a straight path again, but I maintain the smaller distance. It was a miracle that I saw Fenwick in the first place, catching sight of him down a side street while on the way to Rensvik's dinner. The twins were with Freya in the coach, so I leapt from my horse and grabbed Rothesby, ordering one of the other guards to inform the princess that I would be at the duke's estate shortly.

That might have been a lie, depending on what Fenwick decides to do tonight.

"I don't have any legal grounds to detain him," I say, pausing behind a stairway when Fenwick turns his head to one side and adjusts his hat. "I'd be committing treason if I captured him. That would cause a whole lot of trouble, not just for me but for the royal family as well."

Rothesby stumbles, making me wonder if he was a poor choice of companion tonight. I picked him because he was the closest, but I don't know much about him other than him being one of the best shots in the guard. He could be terrible under pressure, but it's too late now. "Oh," he chokes out. "That would be bad."

"Bad indeed," I agree. Which is a pity. According to the RIA, who has a painfully small amount of information about Elvar Fenwick considering they're an intelligence agency, Fenwick lives here in Skalridge. Were I anyone else, I would have already broken into his apartment and taken a look around. My time in the Special Forces was never easy, but right now I miss having sanctioned orders to break and enter into hostile environments.

Fenwick pauses at the next street corner, tugging his jacket tighter as he stands beneath a street light.

Ducking out of sight behind a well-placed shrub and dragging Rothesby with me, I peer through the leaves and try to figure out what his next move might be.

"He shouldn't be standing in the light," Rothesby mutters. "Not if he wants to stay hidden."

"Maybe he doesn't want to stay hidden," I mutter back. We're close enough to be heard if we're not careful.

"He's been hiding from us all week," Rothesby argues.

"But he doesn't know we're here."

"What is he waiting for?"

The answer to that question comes a moment later, when a large man under an umbrella appears from the cross street, stopping at Fenwick's side. Though the new arrival faces us, the umbrella blocks the light and hides his features in shadow. The two men talk, but through the rain their voices are only indiscernible rumbles. If I could only see their faces, I could get a read on what they're saying. At the very least, their emotions could give me a sense of the nature of their conversation.

Cursing under my breath, I search the street between me and the men to see if there's any way I could get closer, but if I move from this spot, the bigger guy will almost certainly see me. I need to find a way to—

A body rushes past me, and it takes me two full seconds to realize it's Rothesby moving down the sidewalk at a fast clip, his collar turned up and a newspaper over his head. He keeps his head ducked low, so when he runs straight into Fenwick and his buddy, it looks unintentional. Rothesby apologizes profusely, still with his head down, and grabs the newspaper from where he dropped it upon colliding with the two men. He picks up his jog again, turning the corner and disappearing.

I'm contemplating the best way to get Rothesby fired when a disgruntled voice cuts through the rain. "...exactly why we need a new Candora."

My breath catches in my throat, but the men's voices stay too low except for a word or two, nothing useful. They speak for another two minutes, then the big man crosses the street as Fenwick continues forward.

I'm about to follow the bigger guy when a voice right behind me says, "Did you catch any of that?"

Cursing, I fight the instinct to grab my gun. "Rothesby!" I gasp, swearing again. "Where did you…" My eyes catch on the alley we're standing next to, noting how it leads to the next street over.

"I found a place to hide around the corner." He frowns at me. "I thought, if the conversation wasn't friendly, they would get to the point quicker if interrupted. Sir, are you—"

"What did you hear?" I press a hand to my heart to will it to calm down. I never used to be this jumpy, and I'm glad only Rothesby saw my reaction. Hex and Sander would have all sorts of jokes for me if they witnessed that.

"Not a lot," Rothesby says, still looking at me with concern. "They mentioned the debate and how they expect Grimstad to put Princess Freya in her place once and for all."

Like that would ever happen. Grimstad is charismatic, yes, but Freya has this way with words that surprises me every time. She almost always says the right thing, even when under pressure, and sometimes it takes all my concentration to keep an eye on what's happening around her instead of getting sucked into whatever conversation she's having. Sander was genius when he suggested the debate because it's where Freya is going to shine the most.

"Did they say anything else?" I ask.

Rothesby shakes his head. "Not much I could understand."

"Did you get a look at the other guy?"

"He kept his face hidden."

Swearing, I look down the street, but both men have disappeared. Fenwick's apartment is somewhere in this direction, so there's a good chance he's headed home. We could go that way and hope he has his shutters open for us to see inside, but at this point I'm really grasping at straws. He might just be a zealous Grimstad supporter and has been following *him* this whole time instead of Freya. As for the other guy, he was heading for one of the busier streets in Skalridge, and we didn't see enough to be able to pick him out of a crowd.

"What do you want to do, sir?"

That's a loaded question. I want to know for certain if Fenwick is dangerous. I want to make sure Freya wins this election so she can stop worrying. I want another chance alone with her in the coach so I can do things differently and tell her how I feel about her, even if she refuses to talk about it.

I just spent four days watching her charm her people with nothing but her genuine self. I sat on the other side of a wall and listened to her talk to her friends about their problems instead of her own even though she's dealing with so much right now. I stood back and let her be the future queen because it was obvious that I was only getting in her way before.

What I want is to live in a world where I could actually be an option for her, but that's not going to happen.

"Sir?"

I clear my throat and stand up straight, really feeling the rain for the first time as it continues to fall in heavy sheets. We're both soaked to the bone, and at this elevation the night is going to get cold. "Let's go back to the hotel. You can have the rest of the night off after all this, and I'll go meet up with the others to get the princess home safely."

"With respect, sir, you shouldn't go alone. I'll join you."

I'm about to argue when I remember how he caught me off guard a minute ago. At least I've been sleeping lately, but I'm still on edge. It doesn't help that I'm no closer to having answers about Fenwick than I was four days ago, and every time I look at Freya, I wish things I shouldn't be wishing.

Giving Rothesby a nod and a soft "thank you," I lead the way back to the hotel so we can change into dry clothes and find a way to get to the duke's estate. As we walk, I mentally run through the security plans Gregor and I have been working on for tomorrow's debate. Local police from Skalridge will combine with the men I've brought with me, and the arena where the event is being held is on the small side, which makes it easier to control who comes in and out.

As long as we're diligent during the actual event, we've prepared as much as we can.

After we've reached the hotel, I'm pulling on a dry shirt after taking a quick shower when my phone buzzes on the bed. I tense, expecting an emergency from Carsten—the guard I put in charge tonight—but it's a text from one of my old squad members.

Wade:

> I know you're ignoring the group chat, but I wanted to check and see how you're doing today. I know it was harder on you than anyone.

I frown, not sure what he's talking about. What was harder? But then my eyes flick up to the date at the top of the screen, and my stomach drops as the realization hits. Griff died a year ago today. I've been so focused on Freya and her campaign that I haven't paid attention, and I can't decide if that makes me a terrible friend for forgetting or if it means I'm healing.

Sitting on the edge of the bed, I type out the first text I've sent to one of my brothers-in-arms in more than six months.

Elliot:

> I'm okay. I've been distracted and didn't realize the day.

Wade:

> That's good.

Wade is the quietest of the ODA, usually sitting back while louder voices like Bax or North command attention, but he always had my back, even when things got rough. We worked closely together, and he was the one who suggested I take a break and work on base for a while.

But he's also been one of the more vocal guys about me coming back to the team. I have no contractual obligations to the Army at this point because I made sure I fulfilled the required years of service before resigning, but from the sound of things, it wouldn't take much for me to reenlist and get back on my team.

Though I hate acknowledging it, I've had moments when I thought about starting the process. Mostly during those moments when Freya seems to be leaning toward accepting Grimstad's marriage proposal. I've found my rhythm with this post over the last few days, but the idea of being behind her while he gets to be at her side...

"She hasn't made a decision," I remind myself, but that doesn't mean much. There's a fifty percent chance that my job is about to become a lot more painful than it already is.

Choosing not to respond to Wade's last message, I instead send a text to Nora, Griff's wife, and tell her that I wish I could be there for her and the girls. I can't imagine how hard a day like today will be for them. To my surprise, she responds quickly.

Nora:

> Thanks, Elliot. It means a lot to know you're thinking about him too.

Guilt floods my belly, but I ignore it and focus on the picture she sends with her text. It's a selfie she took with her two daughters in front of Griff's headstone, and though she was clearly crying at some point, she's smiling right alongside her girls. I can't help but laugh at the messy state of the girls' hair, which was a pretty common occurrence when I lived with them, and a pang of sadness hits me. I thought I was ready to move on, but I miss those girls. It felt less like Griff was gone when I was around them because they were so much like their dad. Even with how little they got to see him before he died.

Nora:

> Melody can't stop telling her friends about how her Uncle Elliot takes care of a real-life princess.

Elliot:

> I bet they don't believe her.

Nora:

> Not even a little bit. But we're all proud of you for finding something good, Elliot.

I wonder if she's read any of the tabloids. Is she talking about the job, or is she talking about Freya?

Elliot:

> I should get back to work, but tell the girls hi for me.

Nora:

> Of course. Good luck with everything!

It's nearly impossible to look at Freya through a professional lens at this point, so I need all the luck I can get. I need to get her through this campaign so she can win the election—preferably sans Grimstad as her husband—and then I can work on getting over these feelings that keep growing. By law, Freya and I can never be anything but friends, and that's going to have to be enough.

Otherwise, someone else is going to have to look after her, and I'm not sure that's something I can allow.

Chapter Twenty-One

FREYA

Spending so much time around regular Candoran people has made it difficult to mingle with nobility when I am at my best. Currently, when I am worried about Elliot and whatever it was that pulled him away, I am finding it nearly impossible to tolerate the sheer snobbery in front of me, and my patience is almost at an end.

Which is unfortunate, considering I have endured less than an hour of this dinner party and still have many to go unless I wish to anger my mother more than I already have.

The idea is more tempting than it should be.

"Your Highness," the Duke of Rensvik says, his voice dripping with arrogance. "I am sure your meals have been lacking the last several days, so you can imagine how glad I am that you deigned to join us this evening."

By my count, this is the fourth time he has said something to this effect, and my answer has been the same each time. "On the contrary, Your Grace. I have enjoyed some of the best meals of my life while on this journey. Though, I will say this venison is delicious." The last time the duke brought up his "superior" offerings, I mentioned the crowberry sauce on the duck. Before that was the trout. With my luck, he will keep asking until I have complimented everything on the table.

The food truly is delicious, but the company has left much to be desired.

Most of it, anyway. My brothers have made the evening tolerable thus far by sharing withering looks with me whenever someone says something particularly arrogant or insulting, and as neither of them gives a fig about maintaining a solid relationship with any of the lords and ladies in attendance, they have uttered quite a few underhanded comments that have made me smile.

The brightest spot of the evening has, to my surprise, been the presence of Markham Grimstad.

When we arrived at the duke's estate, I was shocked beyond belief to see Markham standing alone in a corner of the drawing room. I only had time to ask him why he was here and get his response—"I was surprised to get an invitation, but His Grace insisted I come."—before I was pulled away into other conversations, but something about seeing him across the table from me has given me strength to endure the party thus far.

True, he is too far at the end of the table for me to speak to him during dinner without being incredibly rude to the other guests, but his presence is strangely calming.

Rensvik harrumphs and turns his conversation to the viscount sitting across from him, leaving me temporarily on my own. I would have liked to sit in the middle of the table, where I could engage more people in conversation, but I am certain the duke wanted to showcase the fact that the future queen attended his party when I missed so many other events.

I make eye contact with Markham at the foot of the table, and he smiles as he lifts his drink to me in a toast. As far as I can tell, no one has bothered to speak to him beyond basic niceties, but he does not seem to mind. In fact, he has looked rather amused all evening as he listens to the inane conversations happening around him. I wonder what he would say about it all if I were close enough to listen.

I know my *own* thoughts. The nobility used to care more about the people under their responsibility, and now they act as if they are important simply because of what they were born to, not because of their actions as leaders. How did we fall so far behind the rest of the modern world that power is only held by the wealthy?

As I look at the people who for most of my adult life have been my only contacts outside of foreign dignitaries and my small group of friends, I see nothing in them that connects me to them. Nothing but privilege that is not always deserved. It is a strange thought, to feel as though I am not one of them. Queen or not, I will always be their peer, trapped in an aristocratic lifestyle that has failed to change alongside the rest of the world.

Glancing at Markham again, I finally consider what would happen if I accepted his proposal. Instead of perpetuating the separation of the classes, we would be building a historic bridge. Members of the nobility have married outside their social class, but never has an Alverra ignored tradition.

Markham said I would become the reigning queen with him as a lesser king at my side, which is the only acceptable solution. Were he to keep his name on the ballot and be voted in as the ruling monarch, he would have a good deal more power than me, and I would be little more than an advisor. Surely he would prefer that option to the reverse, but when he proposed, he spoke of me as the true queen. So, he either becomes king at my side and influences change through me, or he becomes king by vote, and *everything* changes under his solitary rule.

Regardless of my choice, his chances of the throne are great. But not guaranteed.

Elliot asked him if his proposal was a way to easily win, and at the time he was the more popular choice. As sentiments have begun to change, will he still keep the offer open? I do not know him enough to know what his true desire is. I believe him when he says he wants what is best for Candora, but what is best for Markham Grimstad?

What is best for *me*?

If I decline his proposal, he might win the election, and I would be left with nothing. If I accept, the people will have no alternative on the ballot, and I cannot see them voting against me when Markham would be at my side.

Accepting his hand would almost certainly secure my position.

"What say you, Princess Freya?" Rensvik's booming voice pulls my attention back to my end of the table.

Elliot is not here to whisper in my ear what the duke has been talking about like he did in the session of Lords, and my stomach twists. Outside of traveling, I have not gone without my bodyguard for more than a few minutes all week, and I feel his absence more than ever in this moment. "Forgive me," I say curtly. "I wasn't listening."

Though he falters, Rensvik is quick to say, "I was commenting on this year's Royal Equestrian Festival."

Of course he was. It is an event that only members of the nobility can attend and is something I have long thought was a waste of money and resources. I love our equestrian roots and our slower way of life, but owning horses is becoming more and more uncommon and impractical, particularly in the cities where the majority of Candorans live. Even here in Skalridge, a city with no vehicles, most people are on foot.

"Ah," I say, sitting up straighter. "I'm afraid I've been distracted this evening, and my thoughts were on the needs of our people. Did you know only one in ten families even owns a horse? Those festival funds would be better utilized within public transportation rather than for the aristocracy's amusement."

The duke frowns. "You are suggesting we do away with the festival? Alongside the Celestial Ball, it is a favorite event."

I tilt my head to one side. The entire table has taken an interest in our conversation, and I can either hold my tongue or speak my mind. Mum would have me remain polite and save my debate for the next Parliament meeting.

But I am not my mum.

"So, you don't think a rail line to Skalridge would be beneficial for the people you have sworn to serve?" I ask coolly. "I wonder how much more your city would thrive with better access to the outside world."

"The people of Skalridge cherish a simpler way of life," Rensvik argues.

"The people of Skalridge have no other choice!" My voice rises louder than I meant it to, and while most of the table gawks at me, my brothers and Markham all fight smiles. Markham seems particularly pleased by my outburst.

I have already insulted most sensibilities tonight, so I might as well make it worse. "Mr. Grimstad," I say, keeping my volume above normal, "you have spent more time among the people than I have. What is your opinion on this?"

"Your Highness," Rensvik says, "perhaps this is not the place to—"

"Markham, if you will." I gesture to him.

Markham shifts uncomfortably in his seat, likely unprepared, but from the little I know about him, he will have something to say. He does not disappoint. "For the most part, Candorans do appreciate a slower pace, and one of the reasons people stay within the country is because we have an idyllic way of life, free from modern complexities."

"There, you see?" the duke says with an air of finality.

"That being said," Markham continues, "there is a difference between a way of life that's chosen and one that's forced. Not everyone values tradition over progress, and we have so many brilliant people in our country who will never have a chance to better the world because they're stuck in circumstances they can't change."

"Brilliantly said," Hex says, raising his glass as Sander does the same.

Several pairs of eyes turn to me, waiting for my rebuttal. If they are hoping for an argument, they are not going to get it from me.

"Mr. Grimstad and I differ on many things," I say, "but our people's desperate need for opportunity is not one of them. If you truly want my opinion on the Equestrian Festival, Your Grace, then you should know that it is a waste of money that could do much good elsewhere, and I recommend it be done away with."

It seems I have stunned the nobility into silence for the first time in their lives. Good. It is going to happen far more often once I sit on the throne.

But will Markham be at my side when I do?

I wish that were an easier question to answer.

The rest of the dinner passes quietly, with conversations few and far between. It seems no one wishes to start another debate, for which I am grateful, so any talk that breaks the silence keeps to unimportant topics such as the weather or the food. Rensvik spends most of the time glowering at his food and avoiding eye contact with me, and I can only imagine the conversation I will have with my mother as soon as she finds out.

In my defense, I came to the party. I have been here the entire time, and I have interacted with the nobles. Those were her requirements.

When dinner ends and the group adjourns to the drawing room, I am not surprised when Markham comes straight for me.

"Your Highness," he says with a bow.

I smile. "Freya, please."

Glancing around the room and finding my bodyguard absent, I am guessing, he returns my smile. "Is that because we're friends or because you've made a decision?"

Instead of the answer he wants to hear, I say, "It is because you are one of three people in this room who do not test my patience."

He chuckles. "Are you sure about that? Because I do need an answer. Soon. Ideally we could announce our engagement at the debate tomorrow, but if—"

"Announce your *what*?" Hex asks loudly from just behind me.

I shut my eyes and grimace. I had been doing so well at keeping the proposal a secret from everyone but Elliot. Until now, apparently. "Hex, please do not panic."

My brother wraps an arm around my shoulders, his hold so tight it is almost painful. "Tell me I heard you wrong, Grim," he growls. "Or do Sander and I need to have a private word with you? I like your politics, but that doesn't mean I like the idea of you marrying my sister."

"Forgive me," Grimstad says, quietly enough that I open my eyes to see the apology in his eyes. "I assumed you told them."

"It's true?" Hex hisses. I try to slip from beneath his arm, but he holds me tight. "Does Elliot know about this?"

"Yes," I whisper. "It is true, and he knows. Would you stop glaring at Markham? You are drawing too much attention."

"You are the future Queen of Candora," Hex all but spits. "You draw the attention on your own, especially if you're even thinking of tying yourself to this cretin."

"Hex," I snap. "Be kind."

"Not to him." Hex grits his teeth, sneering at the man in front of me. "Not if he's daft enough to suggest something so ridiculous."

"It is not ridiculous!" I argue, though I regret saying anything when Markham's eyebrows lift. I cannot have him assuming that is an answer to his proposal.

"When?" Hex demands.

By now, most in the room have caught on to my brother's tension, including Sander, and there are far too many eyes and ears trained on us for me to want to have this conversation. As Sander makes his way across the room, I gesture for Markham to follow, and I pinch Hex's side to get him to release me so I can walk.

Only when the four of us are alone in the corridor outside the drawing room do I speak again.

"Yes," I say with exasperation. "Markham proposed to me when we were in Havenford." Sander's eyes fly wide, and Hex starts to protest, but I hold up a finger. "No, I have not given him an answer."

"Why?" Sander asks, his eyes on Markham, and I am not certain who his question is for.

Markham chooses to respond before I can. "Because my campaign has divided the country, and I thought a union would help both sides."

"You could have chosen not to run in the first place," Sander says icily.

"I could have," Markham agrees. "But I firmly believe that Candora needs reform, and I didn't know for sure where your sister would stand." He looks at me and dips his head. "I'm sorry, Freya. There was no way to know what you—"

"She's 'Your Highness' to you," Hex says with another glare.

"I gave him permission to use my name," I reply, rolling my eyes.

"And Elliot knows?" Sander asks in disbelief. "He's okay with whatever this is?" He waves a hand between Markham and me.

Elliot and I may not have discussed the matter for long in the coach today, but I can guess his opinion. It likely has not changed from what it was initially. "Elliot does not approve," I admit.

"Of course he doesn't," Hex says. "Not when he's fall—"

Sander elbows him in the side. "Freya, are you considering it? Saying yes?"

I look at Markham, though a large part of me wants Hex to finish his sentence. "Yes, I am considering."

The smile Markham gives me in return is soft and should, in theory, bring some sort of peace to my admission, but it makes me nauseous. Markham is a good man. I believe that, even if there is much to learn about him. On paper, he could be the best match I could ever find. He is ambitious and strong-willed, and he has the Candorans' best interests at heart. No, he does not come from nobility, but that only adds to his appeal after that dinner I endured.

I need to give my regrets to the Duke of Rensvik for disrupting his party and, unfortunately, leaving early, because I cannot go back into that room full of nobles. Markham is right, and I need to decide sooner than later, but to do that I need time to think. Time to talk things through with people I trust.

I should have done this days ago.

Touching my hand to Markham's arm, I offer a small smile. "I need more time," I tell him. "But soon. I promise."

"Of course."

"Sander, could you make our excuses to the duke?"

Sander meets Hex's gaze, unenthused by the turn in the conversation, but he nods and slips back into the drawing room.

I take Hex's arm. "I need some air."

"I'm not surprised," he grumbles in reply and leads me outside to the courtyard of Rensvik's sprawling estate, leaving Markham on his own inside. I hope Markham stays for the duration of the party; he could benefit from more time with the noble class, just as I needed more time with the working class.

Though a few guards notice us and take a step toward me, I hold them back with a raised hand. As before, I wish Elliot were here. This is not a conversation I would like him to hear, but I could use his support.

Honestly, I think I might crave his support in everything I do at this point.

"I need a moment alone," I tell Hex.

He narrows his eyes. "Why?"

"Because I want to speak to my friends, and you do not need to be part of that conversation."

Mumbling under his breath, Hex moves several meters away and folds his arms, telling me that he will not go any farther. It will have to do.

Pulling my phone from my clutch, I open the group I have with my friends and start a video call, hardly caring who answers. I need advice, and I will take it from any of them.

The call connects, and I wait to see which of my friends picks up first.

To my surprise, it is Hank, a man I have not had much of a chance to talk to since he and Bonnie started dating six months ago. I have only met him a few times, but I have always liked him.

"Freya!" he says, his smile warm and bright. His gentle personality is a complete antithesis to the murder mysteries he writes, and I love the contradiction he presents. "How's the campaign going?"

Relaxing a bit, I return his smile with one of my own. Over the last few days, I have spoken with my friends more than I usually do, but Hank has only been on a call once, as he is on a deadline. I am grateful for his question and the fact that he cares, even if we have not known each other long. "Better than I expected, after the way it started."

"That's good to hear. Bonnie has been keeping up on all the *Hot Scoop* stories, and they don't seem to be causing any real problems for you. Hopefully things stay that way."

It is not *Hot Scoop* causing the problems, no. It is the tension that built so quickly between Elliot and me once we became friends. Tension that people have started to notice and is a large part of why it is so difficult to make my decision about Markham. I have known Elliot for only a couple of weeks longer than I have known Markham, but Markham does not make me feel what I feel with Elliot.

"No," I mutter, reminding myself of why I made this call. It was not to think about my bodyguard. "I suppose *Hot Scoop* does not have much power this far from its origin."

No one else has joined the call, and I wonder what the others are doing right now. It is the middle of the day in California, so they must all be busy. Derek is *always* busy, but I cannot always expect the others to answer spontaneous calls.

"So," Hank says, and his eyebrows lift enough to tell me he has realized I had a reason for calling.

I sigh and look behind me to make sure all of the guards except Hex are out of earshot. "So," I repeat. "I received a proposal recently."

"What kind of proposal?"

"The literal kind." A surprising smile lifts the corners of my mouth as I use Markham's own words. If it were not me in the situation, I might find it all rather humorous.

Hank's eyebrows rise higher. "Like, someone asked you to marry them?"

I twist my lips to the side. "Yes."

Eyes going wide, he sits up straighter. It looks like he is in the house he bought in Los Angeles a few months ago, and I wonder if I interrupted a writing session with this call. I am grateful he answered, if that is the case. "Wait, you're serious?"

I nod gravely. "Entirely."

"Who asked you? A crazy fan? Because that happens to Bonnie all the time, and they're never serious. Well, they *are* serious, but it's not like she would ever—"

"It was Markham Grimstad."

Hank blinks. "The man who's running against you?"

"The very one."

"Is he really that desperate to be king?"

I suppose that is a logical conclusion, if Hank and Elliot thought the same thing. "No, I think he is determined to bring balance to the Candoran people, and adding someone of his background and perspective to the monarchy could do that in a way no one has before. No ruler has married outside nobility since the beginning of Candora."

"Ah, got to love tradition."

Gripping my phone tighter, I nod and glance behind me to make sure Hex is still giving me privacy. His eyes are on me, but his expression is no more frustrated than it was before. I turn back to my phone. "Markham proposed because a union between us would eliminate the need for people to choose."

"What if they want to choose?" Hank asks.

That is a good point. "If we take that away, will they feel as though their chance for a voice is gone?" I wonder out loud.

He shrugs. "Maybe. You know your people better than I do."

"And Markham knows them even better than that. What if this is the best thing for Candora?"

"Do you want to marry the guy?"

It is my turn to shrug, and I wish I had more answers. But this is why I sought the help of my friends. "I want my country to thrive."

"That doesn't really answer the question, Freya."

"I know." I think of Elliot's response to my arguments when Markham first proposed. *Giving into fear and throwing away everything you stand for isn't a selfless act.* It *feels* selfless, sacrificing my chances for happiness for the sake of my people. But could Elliot be right? Would it simply be giving in to fear?

"What if you do one of those hypothetical situations that you do with Bonnie all the time?" Hank asks.

Since Bonnie fell for Hank, I have not had to walk her through possible future outcomes, but the reminder of our conversations makes me smile. We used to go through the worsts and bests of so many different things in her life. "That is a good idea."

"Say you agree to the marriage. What will that look like in terms of your positions?"

That one is easy. "Assuming a marriage means he would remove his name from the ballot, I would be the reigning queen and true monarch. Markham would be king at my side but have significantly less influence, particularly because he does not already have a title. I would have full power over international matters, and his duties would be tied to domestic affairs. Though, I would have veto power over any of his decisions."

Hank nods. "Sounds reasonable. Would you butt heads all the time on things?"

That one is not as easy to answer. "I do not think so. We may not always agree, but I think he and I could benefit from differing opinions in a lot of instances. I have already learned and grown so much since learning about his campaign."

"Makes sense, but there's always that chance that you'll argue more than you'll agree. You've told us about how different his platform is from yours."

"That is true." But I choose to believe Markham has an open mind, as I do.

Hank's smile turns sympathetic. "Here's the hard one."

I brace myself, wondering what he might say. What does Hank think is difficult?

Pursing his lips, he seems to take a moment to prepare me for his coming question. What he asks is not what I expect. "Would you start a family with him?"

The question hits me in the stomach, leaving me breathless and nauseous. "Oh."

Hank tilts his head to one side. "That's quite a reaction to that one."

"We would be married." I say that out loud more for my own benefit than for Hank's. In all my thoughts over the last few days, I never thought to consider anything beyond the legal ties. "And as the king and queen, we would be expected to continue the royal line or risk the monarchy falling to collapse." That is already one of the issues with my candidacy. I have no prospects and therefore have little chance of procuring an heir anytime soon. The very nature of our government is uncertain because I have spent too much of my young life focused on my career rather than my personal life.

Hank waits patiently for me to keep talking, his smile growing.

I press a hand to my stomach and close my eyes. "I do want children," I mutter as I truly think about what a marriage with Markham would entail beyond politics and publicity. My nausea builds until I feel dizzy. "I am not certain I would want children with him."

"With who?" That is not Hank.

I jump and open my eyes, realizing someone else has joined the call. *Liam.* "No one," I say quickly.

Liam narrows his eyes and pushes wet hair from his forehead. He is in his pool and likely just finished a swim, and he could not have picked a worse moment to jump into the conversation. "Peach, are you *pregnant?*"

"Who's pregnant?" a female voice asks right as Carissa appears on the screen, her blonde curls taking up most of the window as she situates herself on Cole's lap.

Mortification burns hot in my face as I desperately search for a way to steer the conversation away from—

"Freya is trying to decide if she's going to have some guy's baby," Liam says with all the confidence of a man who knows exactly what is going on, when his summary could not be farther from the truth.

"*What?*" Cole growls, tugging Carissa's phone closer to his face. "Freya, what's going on?"

I take a deep breath. "I—"

"Wait," Carissa says with a gasp, "did you and Elliot—"

"No!" I shriek as my embarrassment floods my entire body, leaving me feeling like I may combust. "No, we have not—"

"Freya!" The voice that shouts my name is so recognizable that relief washes over me as I turn to see Elliot running toward me from the outer gate. He comes to my side, a hand on my waist as he searches my face as if looking for whatever troubles me. "Are you okay?"

"Is that Elliot?" Carissa asks excitedly.

Elliot's eyes jump to the phone in my hand, and he frowns. "Oh."

"Was it him who knocked you up, Freya?" Liam asks, bringing his face close to the screen as if to get a better look at my bodyguard.

Cole swears. "What did you do to her, Reid?"

This is a nightmare. "Nothing!" I practically squeak. If I did not know that my friends would not let this conversation go, I would power my phone down right now and pray for a way to turn back time.

"Freya!" Cole says, almost pleading. "What the he—"

"Language," I say breathlessly.

Cole ignores me. "Reid, I don't care that you know Derek. If you even touched the princess, then I swear I'll—"

"Enough!" I shout, all too aware of everything around me. The guards stationed on the grounds are staring in my direction, Sander is now standing next to Hex, both of them looking murderous, and Elliot cannot seem to take his eyes off me despite the half-formed threats Cole threw at him. My poor bodyguard chose a terrible time to join me, but his warm hand on my side is the only thing keeping me upright at the moment.

I wonder if Elliot wants kids. Or even a relationship. He is so focused on his job that it seems silly to wonder. But after the way he interacted with Elsa and the other kids in Havenford, I can imagine him being an incredible father. He would look so masculine with a tiny baby held in his capable arms, and that child would want for nothing.

Taking a steadying breath, I fix my eyes on my phone and force those fantasies away. They can never come true. Not with me. "You are all making this harder," I say to the phone. "Except you, Hank. For the most part, you were helpful."

He smiles and pushes his glasses up his nose. "Keep going through those hypotheticals, and I think you'll get your answer."

Cole makes a growling sound deep in his throat. "Hypotheticals about having kids?"

"What?" Elliot says in alarm.

"Marriage," Hank corrects before I can find a believable lie.

Who am I kidding? My friends know me too well and would catch even the most well-thought out fib.

Cole scowls. "Marriage to whom?"

My eyes drift to Elliot on the screen, taking in the way his full attention is on me and not my phone. Even without making eye contact with him, I can feel his intense gaze warming me from the inside out. "I have always known my marriage, should it happen, would be political," I say, knowing it is not an answer to Cole's question. I have to fight to keep the disappointment out of my voice. Markham is a good man, yes, but I cannot picture him as a father, no matter how hard I try. I can barely imagine feeling any real affection toward him.

I know what is best for Candora, but at what cost?

"Freya," Elliot murmurs, leaning closer as if he senses the turmoil inside me. "What do you need?"

I need him not to ask questions like that when the answer is a moment in his arms. To let myself be held by him and pretend, like I did in Havenford, that I could live a different life, one in which the thing I want most no longer stands in the way of *who* I want most.

In a different life, I think I could be happy with Elliot.

"I really hope you're going to tell us what's going on," Liam says, resting his arms on the edge of his pool and dropping his chin onto them. "Just to be clear, you're *not* pregnant?"

I let out a weak chuckle. "Nowhere close."

"And you're not getting married?" Cole asks.

That one is harder to answer, but I try. "I have not agreed to a marriage, no." Elliot's hand tightens against my side, sending a shiver through me. "Does anyone else have any ridiculous questions?"

"Are any of the *Hot Scoop* stories true?" Carissa asks.

I look at Elliot. Elliot looks at me. Annoying as *Hollywood Hot Scoop* can be, the tabloid has not caused me as much trouble as the opinion piece in yesterday's paper did. Not only is my mother convinced I am making a mistake when it comes to my bodyguard, but the opinion piece put into words something both Elliot and I have successfully avoided addressing before today.

But the last *Hot Scoop* article I saw also mentioned trouble brewing with Derek, and that is something I *can* address without hurting Elliot. I wish Derek were here, but he has been filming the last few days and struggles to get on a group call on the best of days. I could really use his advice lately.

Standing straighter, I smile at my friends. "When it comes to my relationship with all of you—Derek, Bonnie, and Kasey included—I have no intention of severing our friendship. That gruesome tabloid can say what they want about us, but they will never get between us."

"It seems like that's their goal," Elliot mutters. He spoke so quietly that he may have been talking to himself, but as he is standing right next to me...

I look at him, raising my eyebrows. "Do you think?"

"We should get you back to the hotel," he replies, lowering his own eyebrows to contrast. "*Hot Scoop* is unimportant, and you'll want to be rested for the debate tomorrow."

"Oo, good luck with the debate!" Carissa says. "You're going to be awesome!"

I smile at her, wishing I had her confidence. "Thank you."

"And you're right," Cole adds, calmer than he was before. "No matter what, we're all sticking together." His eyebrows dip low, and his eyes flick from one part of the screen to the other, as if he might be looking from me to Elliot. "You know we have your back—princess, queen, or no royalty at all. Right?"

His words, echoed by the others, are a balm to my anxious heart, and I blink away tears that prick my eyes. "Of course. Thank you."

"I've got my eye on you, Reid," he adds.

Rolling my eyes, I say my goodbyes and take a moment to breathe. The election is not for another five days, but tomorrow is going to be more decisive than I want it to be. The televised debate will reach the entire country, and this is one of my last chances to prove to my people that I can lead them into a bright future.

No pressure at all.

I have prepared as much as I could—thanks to long conversations with my brothers while traveling between towns over the last few days—and I simply have to show up and do my best. Until then, I need to ensure my thoughts do not get trapped on Markham's proposal or Elliot's disappearance today or the idea that I am less certain about the life I want than I ever have been.

Chapter Twenty-Two

Elliot

There's a chance I've spent too much time around American politics because the debate has been less name-calling and arguing than I expected and more polite conversation and complimenting. In the hour they have been talking on the large stage that was set up in Skalridge's event center, Freya and Grimstad have praised each other's responses more times than I can count, building off the other's answers as they bring their own thoughts to the issues presented by the moderator.

It's been nice, seeing two influential political figures treat each other with such a high level of respect when they would have every right to be defensive and fight for their side.

It has also been one of the worst hours of my life, for no reason other than watching Freya mesh so well with Markham Grimstad is making it abundantly clear why he thought it would be a good idea to propose and why Freya didn't immediately shut him down.

These two would make an incredible pair and be even more incredible rulers.

"She's killing it," Sander says, his voice low because the audience has been so quiet and attentive that I'm pretty sure someone would hear him if he spoke any louder. "This is where she really shines. When she gets a chance to talk about what she knows and what she has planned, she's brilliant."

"She's brilliant all the time," I mutter.

The problem is that Grimstad is equally brilliant, and the more he talks, the more Freya warms up to him. I've got an uncomfortable pressure building behind my sternum, and if there weren't a few hundred people staring down the princess and posing (admittedly unlikely) threats, I would be anywhere but here.

Feeling something for my charge is bad enough, but being jealous of the guy who might actually be perfect for her? I've hit a new low.

"You alright, mate?" Sander asks, leaning closer.

I have no idea what my expression is doing, but it doesn't surprise me that he's asking. Nothing about this is alright, and there's only so much I can do to keep my feelings to myself.

We didn't talk after leaving the duke's estate, but I heard enough of Freya's conversation with her friends to get an idea about where her thoughts were. She's thinking about *kids* with Grimstad, which means she's considering his proposal more than I thought. I knew she couldn't shut him down without deliberation, but I thought...

I don't know what I thought. Candoran law doesn't want me to have her. The queen doesn't want me to have her. Even her friends warned me to stay away. All throughout the night, I kept telling myself that it's better to let her go, but every reason I found to quell my interest just made it grow so much more until I could no longer deny how I feel.

First time I fall for someone, and she's the one person I can't have.

"You're unnaturally tense," Sander says and bumps his arm into mine.

"Stop distracting me," I grunt and shift my eyes to the other side of the stage, where Hex and Rothesby have taken the other two posts. The rest of the guards are patrolling the audience or outside, along with most of the Skalridge police force who searched everyone as they came in. I've done everything I can to ensure nothing goes wrong with this debate, and since it's the only one happening and is being broadcast across the country, I don't think anyone—Fenwick included—would be stupid enough to try to disrupt things unless they have a death wish.

"We have one more question for the two of you before we adjourn for the day," the moderator says, and the energy of the crowd shifts from enthralled to restless, like all of the people here hadn't realized how long they were sitting quiet and still until someone pointed out the impending conclusion.

I shift my weight, scanning the audience for any signs of danger. I don't know why. Nothing has happened so far, and clearly my ideas about what might happen in this job are radical compared to the average Candoran crime rate. Fenwick shouldn't be able to get in if the guards and the police are doing their jobs right, and the rest of the audience seem to be fans of both Grimstad and Freya.

"In ten years," the moderator says, "what will Candora look like under your leadership? To go with that, how will the average Candoran's life be better?"

"Would you like to take this one first, Your Highness?" Grimstad says, gesturing toward her.

She smiles sweetly. "No, I think you've earned the right to be heard."

Look at her, sounding more and more like an Average Joe. Polite as ever, though.

Movement across the stage pulls my gaze to Hex, whose eyes are fixed on something in the audience as his hand works its way toward the gun he carries. I follow his hard gaze, but it's hard to tell where he's looking. I wish we had earpieces.

"There," Sander says, locking his eyes on someone near the center of the auditorium. He must have also seen his twin's attention shift.

Using both their sightlines, I find what they're staring at: *Fenwick*.

Resisting the urge to pull my gun, I tune out Grimstad's response and put my whole focus into Fenwick. He's hiding his eyes beneath a hat, but that shouldn't have been enough to get him into the arena. He's sitting so still that I have to assume he's going to try something. Everyone else is nodding along to whatever Grimstad is saying or looking at their phones, but Fenwick hasn't moved an inch.

"What should we do?" Sander asks under his breath. "I can—"

"No." Though I speak to Sander, I look straight at Hex and only speak again when he looks at me, since he reads lips almost as well as I do. "The two of you will be the first ones out if something happens. You're not putting yourselves in danger."

Hex frowns and shakes his head.

I glare at him. "That's an order, Your Highness. As a prince of Candora, your life is valuable. Understand?"

Sander grunts, which had better be an agreement, and though Hex looks like he wants to keep arguing, he nudges Rothesby and tells him that Fenwick is in the audience. That's about all we can do from up here, and I'm kicking myself again for not thinking ahead when it comes to communicating with the rest of the team. I have no way to alert anyone else without Fenwick realizing we know he's here, and that could trigger him to act.

How did he get in?

I curse under my breath as the audience applauds. Freya starts her closing arguments as soon as they quiet down, and that's when Fenwick moves.

Not a lot. Just a shift of his shoulders, but with how still he's been over the last couple of minutes, that bit of movement is enough to send a jolt of adrenaline through me. My hand itches to grab my gun and be ready for whatever comes, but I'm currently on a stage in front of the entire country. I can't go around flashing a weapon when there's no visible threat.

I hate this. I hate that I can't do anything but stand here and hope I'm being paranoid again. Hope Fenwick is a loyal supporter of Grimstad and here for the debate like everyone else.

But that would be too convenient.

"El," Sander says at the same time the audience starts clapping for Freya. Grimstad stands, holding out his hand to help Freya from her chair.

Fenwick stands as well, a hand reaching into his jacket as his glare comes into view with his lifted chin.

"Everyone down!" I dart forward but not fast enough. The gunshot echoes in the arena, and Freya and Grimstad topple over Freya's seat. "No!" My shout is drowned out by screams in the crowd, and I leap over Grimstad's abandoned chair and find both candidates on the floor. My heart skips a few beats while I search for injuries.

She's unharmed.

Grimstad isn't.

"Markham!" Freya cries, scrambling over to him and grabbing his bleeding arm. "Why did you jump in front of me?"

"Get her out of here, Reid," he growls, ignoring her completely and keeping his eyes on me. "Go!"

He doesn't have to tell me twice. Tucking my arm around Freya's back, I lift her up and make a break for the wing of the stage, doing my best to keep my body between her and the screaming crowd.

The second gunshot is a whole lot louder than the first.

Chapter Twenty-Three

FREYA

I have been afraid before, but never like this.

"Elliot!" I gasp.

He does not stop moving, which means I cannot stop moving. With the second gunshot, we stumbled to a back hallway that is far too small for us to be running through, but that has not hindered my bodyguard or decreased his speed. He is right next to me, an arm around my waist as he hurries me toward the nearest exit.

But I need to go back.

People are in danger. Someone has a weapon, and someone else may have gotten hurt, and I cannot run when I need to ensure everyone is—

"Freya!" Elliot growls, pushing me faster. "Keep moving!"

We reach the doors, and Elliot bursts through them without first making sure the coast is clear. That is unlike him.

The guard stationed at the door swears loudly before realizing who we are, and then his eyes go wide. "Sir?"

"Armed assailants inside," Elliot says with all the gruffness of a seasoned soldier. "One confirmed casualty. I don't know who else might have—"

"I need to go back!" I say with all the force I can muster. Which is not much. My limbs have begun to shake, threatening to collapse beneath me. "More people may be hurt."

Elliot clenches his jaw. "No."

"Yes!"

"Elliot!" Sander barrels through the door we came through, his eyes wild. "It's chaos in there. You need to get her out of here now!" I have never seen him afraid like this, and terror shoots through me. Where is Hex?

I step forward. "What's going—"

"Unlatch the horse!" Elliot orders the guard. He grabs my arm in a vise-grip and pulls me toward the waiting coach without yielding.

The instant the horse is freed from the coach, Elliot lifts me onto its back despite the lack of a saddle, and with the help of the guard, he climbs up beside me and urges the horse forward.

"This horse is not meant for riding," I say as people start filling the street, escaping the arena behind us. It is an unimportant thing to note, even though the animal is far too large for me to comfortably sit astride. I feel as if reality is playing out on a screen in front of me and I am detached from my body. The real problems are too big for me to process. I still try.

Markham was injured. Someone tried to shoot me. My brothers are still in danger. Elliot has tucked an arm around me and kicked the horse into a canter, heading for one of the passes, toward our next stop where the vehicles will be waiting.

The city falls behind us in a blur.

We have been riding for hours or minutes. I do not know. My heart is aching and my mind spinning, and Elliot holds so tight to me that breathing is difficult. Instead of the city, nothing but trees surround us now, and Elliot has slowed the horse to a walk and moved us into the forest rather than on the open road.

As we continue to ride away from the arena and the people who need me, I ask a question despite knowing the answer. "Can we go back?"

Elliot grunts and shifts behind me. "It's not safe."

But a dense forest is acceptable? "We should not have left, Elliot. We should not have run when we could have helped."

"You could have been killed," he argues, loosening his hold on me. "If Grimstad hadn't..." He grunts again.

He sounds angry. Is it really so difficult to admit that Markham might be a good man? "That is why I have to go back! He was hurt!"

"He'll be fine. He was only..." He takes a breath, his lungs expanding against my back in a stuttered sort of motion. "The bullet only grazed him."

The horse comes to a halt in a small clearing, though I have no idea why Elliot would not keep moving if he thinks it is too dangerous to go back to Skalridge. If he intends to go to our next stop, we need to move quickly to arrive before night sets in. But I will not go quietly.

Now that we have stopped riding and the adrenaline is leaving my system, I can think more clearly. Fear is making way for irritation and curiosity. "Elliot, we need to go back. I need to know who would do such a terrible thing and put people at risk like that."

"Fenwick." His voice comes out breathy against my neck. "I think he's...some sort of radical." Elliot's hands slip from my waist and the reins, and the next thing I know he's on the ground, landing in a heap in the underbrush.

"Elliot!" I grab the reins as the horse shuffles nervously, and I guide him several feet away before he accidentally tramples the man lying motionless in the dirt. Then I slide from the horse's back, landing hard but upright, and dart back to Elliot.

His entire right side beneath his jacket is covered in blood.

Swearing, I drop to my knees next to him and grab the handkerchief I put in my pocket this morning. It will not do much, but I have to stem the flow somehow. But first I need to find the wound, and he is not conscious to tell me where it is.

Choosing the bloodiest part of Elliot's side, just below his ribcage, I ball up the cloth and press it against his body.

Elliot lets out a growl of pain that makes me jump back, my heart beating so swiftly that I fear it may stop. "What was that?" he snarls, curling in on himself. "Are you trying to kill me faster?"

I can only gape at him, even though I should probably be grateful that he is still very much alive. "What?"

He glares at me. "That hurt."

He cannot be serious. "I am trying to keep you alive! You have lost so much blood already!"

"I haven't lost anything. I know exactly where it is." He gestures to his middle and shuts his eyes tight.

I sit back on my heels, clenching the bloody handkerchief in my fingers. "You are hilarious."

"I like to think so."

If he is alert enough to make jokes, surely he is not in any true danger. Although, he did fall off the horse—not a sign of good health.

"Elliot, you were shot."

He opens one eye to look at me. "Oddly enough, I'm aware of that."

"Why did you not say?" And how did I not notice?

Groaning, he slowly rolls to his back again and stretches out, one hand pressed to his hip. "It's not that bad. I was more concerned about getting you away from the city. Give me that." Taking the cloth from me, he struggles out of his jacket, then unhooks his shoulder holster.

When he starts unbuttoning his blood-stained shirt, I realize I have sat motionless for longer than I should, and I grab his trembling hands to stop him. "Let me."

His eyes glow gold in the afternoon sunlight when he looks at me, and there is as much surprise in his expression as there is pain. "You don't have to—"

"That bullet would have hit me if you had not been protecting me. Let me help you, Elliot."

With his eyebrows pulling low, he seems to struggle with relinquishing control as he slowly pulls his hands from mine and lets them fall to the ground at his sides. "I need to know if the bullet is still in there."

If by 'in there' he means in the muscle beneath his ribcage... Swallowing, I finish unbuttoning his shirt and push the soaked fabric aside, revealing the source of the blood. I have not spent much time around other people's blood, and my stomach twists as I take the handkerchief and use it to soak up what I can and give myself a better view. At first, I try to keep my hands clean, but that is useless because I have to press the cloth to his wound to try to stem the flow.

"There is too much blood," I whisper, hating that I am not strong enough to remain confident. Instead of a cool head and a plan, I have nothing but tears blurring my vision. Elliot was injured because of me. His pain is my fault.

"Hey." Elliot curls cold fingers around my wrist, and when I meet his gaze, he lifts one corner of his mouth up in a smile. "I'm okay, Princess."

"You're clearly not."

He chuckles, then winces. "No, probably not okay. But I'll live. Unless the bullet is still inside me, in which case things are going to get more complicated."

"I can't see—"

"Let me..." Grunting, he twists his torso until he reveals the side of his back. "It came in back there, right?"

Again, I have to wipe the blood away, and now my fingers are coated in it. There is more blood at his back than I would like, and I think he should not be lying the way he is if we are to stop the bleeding. But I need to answer his question. "I...I think so."

Falling back down, he nods and shuts his eyes. "Two holes. Good sign."

"Nothing about this is good, Elliot."

That gets another pained chuckle out of him. "And here I thought I was the paranoid one."

"You were right." I shake my head as my mind again runs through what happened after the debate. Though I do not know what Fenwick hoped to gain by attempting to destroy the monarchy, Elliot has been right about him from the beginning. "Is that why you disappeared yesterday? Because you suspected something like this would happen?"

Elliot nods slowly, his brow furrowed as he studies me. There is a darkness in his eyes that worries me. "I saw Fenwick in the city and followed him. I didn't learn anything useful, and I should have stuck with him until I did. I could have prevented this."

If anyone could have prevented this, it was me. If I had only listened to Elliot and trusted his instincts at the start instead of holding him back, perhaps no one would have gotten hurt. Or if I had accepted that I alone am not good for Candora and let Markham announce our engagement at the debate. Or—

"I need you to make sure my shirt is in one piece, Rapunzel."

I meet Elliot's golden gaze once more. "What? Your shirt? I think it is beyond saving, even if you wash it."

His laugh quickly turns into a groan as he places his hand over mine where I have been holding the handkerchief to his skin. "Stop making me laugh. No. If there's a piece missing, it could have been left inside me, and I'm not eager to deal with the infection that would come with that."

"Assuming you live long enough for one to set in," I mutter. "You are too big, Elliot. I need you to roll over."

"Yes, ma'am."

It takes both of us to get him on his left side—he is losing strength—but that gives me the leverage to guide his arm out of the sleeve and leave his torso mostly bare aside from the dog tags he always wears. Every movement makes him paler than before, but when I announce that the back of his shirt has a slice but no missing fabric, he seems to relax for the first time since we stopped riding. But he is far from out of danger.

"Elliot, you need a physician."

"Probably," he agrees.

"I am not a physician."

"No?" He looks up at me and smirks. "Seems like a missed opportunity, with how smart you are. Then again..." To my horror, he sits up, his whole body shaking until he is upright and holding himself up with one hand. "You'll be too busy being a queen to ever have the time to practice."

While I can appreciate the compliment, I am more worried about the way he looks like he may pass out at any moment. "Elliot, what are you doing?"

He slides out of the other shirtsleeve. "We can't stay here."

"But you—"

"I've had worse." Taking up his shirt, he rolls it from top to bottom and starts wrapping the sleeves around his torso as if to tie it like a bandage.

I roll my eyes and grab it from him. "You have missed the wound, Sergeant." Shifting the fabric so it better covers both sides of his wound, I tie the shirt in a firm knot as I continue to speak. "Whatever you have endured before, it has no bearing on your current situation. You are not fit to go anywhere until we can find you medical assistance."

He lifts his eyebrows and looks around. "Where are we going to find that?"

Scowling, I adjust the shirt if only to give me something to do other than stare at the sheer amount of muscle on the man in front of me. Now that I am slightly less worried about him bleeding out, I cannot seem to look away. This is not the first time I have seen him without a shirt, but I was not this close before. Nor did I have feelings for him then. This is not the time to admire him, and yet...

"I am aware that our circumstances are not ideal," I say as my eyes start trailing over his tattoos. I did not notice the wings before, painted on either side of a ridged scar on his shoulder, and I reach out to run my fingers over them.

Elliot tenses at my touch and looks down at his shoulder.

"What do they mean?" I ask in a whisper.

His hand slowly rises to wrap around the dog tags sitting against his chest, covering the name Joshua Griffin. "They're in honor of a fallen brother-in-arms. He took fire that should have been mine and saved my life."

Oh. He said that so easily. So calmly. If that had been me, I do not think I would ever feel anything but guilty. I feel guilty enough for my current situation, and Elliot is still alive.

My thoughts must be on my face because Elliot gently touches my cheek as he says, "It was the worst thing I've ever gone through and the reason I resigned. His death wasn't directly my fault, but... It should have been me who died."

Tears prick my eyes. "I'm glad it wasn't," I whisper, hating every word. I should not be grateful for something like that. I should never be glad that someone lost his life. But the thought of Elliot not being here with me... A sob breaks from me as so many emotions come rushing to the surface, everything I have been feeling for days but refused to release.

Guilt, fear, inadequacy, loneliness, affection. It all spills from me in a watery mess of tears.

Elliot tucks his arm around me and pulls me into his chest.

I let out a cry that is almost a laugh. "Oh, this is ridiculous!" I complain.

He tightens his hold. "What?"

"You are bleeding, probably dying, and I am the one falling apart!" Sniffling, I try to sit up straight again, but he will not let me. "Elliot, I am to be a queen!"

"I hope so."

"I cannot sit here blubbering like a child when you need me to be strong."

"I don't need that, Freya." His hand moves to my hair, fingers working their way into the style my attendant wove it into and sending a shiver through me. "All I need is for you to be safe. And I'm glad too."

This time when I pull back, he gives me enough room to meet his eyes. "Why?"

Lips quirking up, he leans forward until his forehead touches mine. "Because I don't know if I can let anyone else protect you. Even if I've done a terrible job of it so far. I need..." He exhales and slumps forward, and I have to press my arm against his chest to hold him up.

"You need help," I finish for him. "Can you stand?" If I can get him on the horse, I can try to find someone who can help. While most people in this area live within the valley of Skalridge, there are some in the mountains. If there is no one close, I will take him back to the city and hope he lasts that long.

Grunting, Elliot takes a few deep breaths before he shifts his legs, ready to try to stand. "I'll be fine," he says.

It is clearly a lie. While he manages to stand with my assistance, his first step nearly sends him back down to the ground. He has lost too much blood, and I fear he will not have the strength to survive long enough to find help. Even then, I will never get him on the horse on my own.

"What do I do?" I ask as I tuck myself under his arm, hoping to hold his significant weight without dropping him.

Elliot hums. "Give me a minute."

"I worry you do not *have* a minute."

The smile he gives me is so much like the roguish smirks he gave me on the day we met that I cannot help but smile back at him. "It almost sounds like you care, Rapunzel."

Of course I care. I have wanted to tell him so many times, but it took a bullet for me to admit it out loud. "Elliot, I—"

"If—" he groans "—*when* I pass out, promise me you won't go wandering around looking for help."

My smile immediately shifts to a scowl. "I will promise no such thing."

"Freya, please." He closes his eyes, leaning more heavily into me. "I need to know you'll be safe. Find somewhere to hide and wait for...the palace guards...to find you."

"How will the—"

"Tracker." He moans, breaths shallow. "In your hair."

I gasp. "What?"

Before he can explain—assuming he would choose to in the first place—he loses consciousness, and it takes everything in me to slow his fall. I end up in a heap on top of him as he crashes to the ground, my tears threatening to break loose again. The forest around me begins to darken as the sun dips behind the mountains.

"Elliot," I whisper, knowing he will not respond as I press my palm to his cheek. I want him to tell me what to do. I *need* him to be okay. "Please don't leave me."

CHAPTER TWENTY-FOUR

ELLIOT

That's the last time I let myself get shot.

It's the pain that wakes me, a deep, throbbing ache that makes me feel like half my torso's been blown away. Every breath I take is laced with fire, and I wish I could black out again just to give me some more time to build up my strength.

But I can't do that.

"Freya." The word scratches from my throat as I try to get my eyes to open. I hope I wasn't out long, but if I was, she'd better have listened to me and stayed put. "Freya!"

"Easy, lad."

My eyes fly open at the sound of a gruff male voice, and the instant I see a grizzled man in front of me, I lunge at him. Or, I try. I barely move at all before the pain in my side nearly makes me pass out again.

"Where's the princess?" I growl through the pain. I reach for my gun, only to remember I left it in the dirt in the woods. "Where the hell is she?"

The man chuckles and dips a rag in a bowl of water. "Of course you would choose to wake the one moment she is not in the room."

Room. Though I desperately need to know Freya is safe, I let my eyes take in my surroundings for the first time. Everything is dim, lit only by a crackling fireplace, but I can make out enough to know we're in some sort of cabin. A very *small* cabin, one that is in such a state of disrepair that I wonder if anyone has been here in a while.

"Where—" I snarl when the man presses his cloth to my side and sends a wave of piercing pain through my body. Gritting my teeth, I grab his wrist before he can try again. "Touch me again, and I'll kill you, old man. *Where is the princess?*"

"Vitte, Elliot," a soft and familiar voice says, "that is no way to act when you are a guest."

My eyes jump to the other end of the cabin, where Freya is stepping through a door and into the firelight. Relief washes over me, and I'm so glad to see her in one piece that I don't even care that my eyes are filling with tears. She's okay. She's smiling. *She's okay.* "Freya," I whisper right as the man touches my wound again and drags a groan out of me. I turn a glare to him and his mane of gray hair. "Try that again. I dare you."

Freya comes over to us and shakes her head at me, annoyance clear in her eyes as she settles in a chair next to the old man. "For how often you seem to have been injured, you are quite the baby when it comes to pain, aren't you?" Then she takes my hand, and her touch dulls the agonizing sensation left by the man's cloth scratching over my tattered skin. "Wulfric is helping you, so please try not to threaten him again."

I meet Wulfric's eyes, hating how amused he looks at my expense. But I'm in bad shape, and if Freya trusts him, I'm going to have to do the same. "Fine," I grumble and grit my teeth as he brings the cloth toward me again. He keeps his touches gentle, but the pain is still nearly unbearable. To distract myself, I turn my focus to Freya. "Your hair is down."

She glances at the blonde locks tumbling over her shoulders. "Yes, well, it was coming out of its coiffure, and I worried I would lose whatever tracker you put in there if I did not put everything in a safe place. It is the jeweled pin, I am guessing?" She picks it up from a little table and holds it in the light, where the blue jewels sparkle in the firelight.

I nod, grateful that she would think to secure it rather than letting it get lost in the woods. "I should have told you it was there."

Smiling, she places the pin back on the table and wraps her hand around the one already holding mine. "I would have removed it if you had. I would have felt like a child. But I am grateful for your foresight."

I can't have been out long if the rest of the guards haven't found us yet, but I also have no idea where we are or how difficult it might be for them to get to us. The mountains around Skalridge are steep and dangerous, and that tracker will only be so useful.

Wulfric hits an especially sore spot, and I grunt, shutting my eyes against the pain. "But not enough foresight to prevent this." I'm just glad I managed to be between Freya and whoever shot me, and we're lucky the bullet didn't hit her when it passed through me. "Fenwick wasn't working alone."

"I believe so," Freya agrees. "I had some time to think over things before Wulfric found us."

I look at the old man again, and he meets my gaze for only a moment before returning his attention to my wound. There's something wild about him, with his bushy beard and worn clothes, but his blue eyes are kind. "Who are you?" I ask. I should thank him for his help first, but I'm not ready to trust this guy yet.

While Freya scoffs, probably guessing my thought process, Wulfric gives me a yellow-toothed smile. He replaces his bowl and cloth with a needle and thread and looks at me once more. "Wulfric Tjoren."

"Can we trust you, Wulfric Tjoren?"

Instead of saying yes, he chuckles and threads the needle with squinted eyes. "Do you have a choice?" he asks in Candoran.

That's a terrible response, and if I wasn't half dead on a rock-hard bed, I would grab Freya and get out of here. But he's right, and I don't have much of a choice right now. "No," I say in English, too tired to translate for myself. "But if you do anything to hurt the princess, I will—"

He pokes the needle into my skin, drawing a growl out of me. "I am not a royalist, Elliot," he says with a matter-of-fact tone, still speaking Candoran. "Neither am I otherwise. I exist in my own sphere and mind my own business. When I come across someone who needs my help, I help."

"And we are grateful," Freya says, matching his choice of language and giving the man a warm smile. "He already stitched up your back," she tells me in English. "So you're halfway there."

I'm not sure if I'm worried that talking will distract Wulfric and his obnoxiously thick needle or if I'm still trying to decide if I believe him, but either way, I keep quiet as he works. I also keep my eyes on Freya, who looks right back at me and seems to have all sorts of thoughts going through her head while the only sounds in the room are the crackling of the fire and the snip of scissors in between each stitch.

Eventually, the silence becomes too much, and I reach up with my free hand, running some of Freya's hair through my fingers. "I like your hair down." It's such a dumb thing to say under the circumstances, but I don't care. I'm eager for any distraction from the rough sensation of non-medical-grade thread sliding through my skin. Plus, I really do like her hair. She looks more alive with it down. Real.

Freya rewards my comment with a warm smile. "My mess of hair? Thank you. It drives me quite mad when it is loose and free like this, but I can never bring myself to cut it and make it more manageable."

"You hide behind it." That sounds like an accusation, but I'm desperate to know if it's true. She so rarely lets it down.

She dips her head and nods. "If I look like a princess on the outside, maybe people will believe I am a princess on the inside as well. The most humorous part of that is the fact that I have no idea how to do anything with it on my own." She sighs and looks up at me, pink blossoming on her cheeks. "You must think me pathetic, always relying on other people."

"Never."

"Before this campaign, I relied on my mother's direction. She has been a wise and benevolent queen, and I thought I knew the sort of ruler I wanted to be. Presenting myself the same way she does made sense." She smooths her fingers over a wrinkle in the blanket beneath me and smiles sadly. "But when left to stand on my own, I am never as polished as she wants me to be, and I feel less than her." With that, she wraps her fingers around a chunk of her hair, as if it's revealing all her shortcomings.

"I can teach you." The words are out of my mouth before I can think about what I'm saying, and I wince. This is going to lead somewhere I'm not sure I want it to go. "Not... I think you're exactly the sort of ruler you should be, polished or not. I mean I can teach you how to do your hair." I grimace. "If you want. I don't know much, but I can do a few different braids and things. Enough to help you feel confident in yourself, at least."

She cocks her head, a bit of uncertainty entering her expression. "How?"

I already told her about Griff dying. This can't be any worse. "You know that friend who took the fire for me?" I touch the dog tags sitting cool against my chest, and her eyes follow the movement. "He had a family back home. A wife and two little girls."

Recognition sparks in her eyes. "The family you stayed with when you were on the base?"

I nod. "After Griff died, his wife, Nora, wasn't doing well. She was having a hard time looking after herself, let alone the girls. And I was…" I grimace, hating that I'm about to admit this to someone other than Derek. Telling him was bad enough, and I don't want Freya to think less of me. But I already almost let her get shot at—twice—so maybe her opinion is pretty low as it is. "I was struggling in the field," I say quietly. "Making mistakes. Losing Griff messed me up, and it did the same to Nora. So when it got to a point where I was too much of a liability to my team, I left my ODA and took up a position on the base so I could help *someone*, and Nora invited me to stay with them instead of getting my own apartment.

"Griff was my best friend, so Nora and the girls already felt like family. Being around them kept me from getting lost in the guilt. I couldn't focus on the loss in my life when I was busy helping get the girls ready for school on the days Nora couldn't find the energy to get out of bed."

Those days were a long time ago, but the pain and guilt haven't fully gone away.

"Why did you leave them?" Freya asks, slowly releasing her hold on her hair.

I shrug one shoulder. "They didn't need me anymore. And I was getting restless. My contract with the Army was ending, so I needed to choose if I was staying or going, and my newfound cousin told me about this job that he thought would be good for me." Chuckling, I glance down the halfway stitched wound in my side. "I guess Derek can't always be right."

It's only when Freya reaches forward and brushes a tear from my cheek that I realize I started crying at some point, and her nearness surprises me. I thought for sure I'd scared her off by now. "Do you miss that family?" she asks, ignoring my poor attempt at a joke.

I gape at her for a second, trying to figure out why she would be looking at me with so much emotion in her eyes. Almost like she's about to start crying with me. "Some—" I hiss in pain as Wulfric pokes me. Cursing under my breath, I give him a proper glare that doesn't seem to faze him at all before I turn back to Freya. "Sometimes. The girls are a handful, but they're cute. And way more emotionally savvy than they should be. They crawled into my bed the night after I found out my dad had died, trying to cheer me up, and that almost broke me. Not because of my own hurt but because they were too young to understand death as well as they do."

I've never felt like I deserved that kind of love they showed me that night, but I will always be grateful for it. Those girls were so strong. Still are. They'll be okay despite what they've been through, and I wish I could be more like them.

Freya's eyes are on our hands now, and I can practically see her thoughts racing behind them. "Elliot," she says in a quiet voice. "Do you want a family?"

"Yes." Even I'm surprised by my quick response, so when Freya's eyes jump to mine, I shrug and try to explain. "Even when my dad was alive, I was alone most of my life. I have Derek now, I guess, but I've always wanted more." I've been talking way too much, so I ask, "What about you?" before I remember the conversation she had with her friends last night. About having kids with Grimstad.

Her gaze turns sad. So sad that my breath hitches, my stomach twisting into knots as I try not to think about what that misery might mean. "Yes," she whispers, her eyes filling with tears. "Yes, I do. But..."

Even though it causes a lot of pain because I have to lean, I reach over and brush my thumb across her cheek. "Tell me." I have never wanted something less.

She sniffs and tries to smile. "I also want to do what is best for my country."

A pit settles in my stomach, heavy and uncomfortable. "What are you saying?"

Wulfric coughs and picks up his bowl, glancing between us. "More water," he mumbles before shuffling to the door and disappearing, leaving us alone.

"Freya." I need to be eye level with her, so I take a deep breath and push through the pain of sitting up and facing her despite the worried glare she gives me. I take both of her hands, but she doesn't respond to my touch as she drops her gaze.

"Markham is right," she says, each word hitting me straight in the chest. "An alliance between us would solve so many problems that Candora is facing."

She can't marry him. I don't *want* her to marry him. But it's not like she can marry *me*, so what right do I have to say anything against the match? "He could give you a family," I say instead of begging her to turn him down.

Freya looks at me, her lips twisting up in a sad smile. "Maybe, but that is not what I want. Not with him."

I lean closer. I can't help it. The way she's looking at me, I almost wonder if... "Is there anyone you *do* want that with?" I shouldn't ask that. It's none of my business. There's only one answer I'll like, and she'll never say—

"Elliot." Freya squeezes my hands. Leans in. Looks at me like I have all the answers.

And I'm pretty sure I'm about to make the worst mistake of my life.

Chapter Twenty-Five

Freya

"Freya." Elliot speaks in a whisper, his eyes roaming my face and lingering on my lips. He wants this as much as I do, but there is hesitation in his eyes.

I understand why. We need to talk about this and what it would mean, but right now I do not want to talk. I want to know how it would feel to kiss the soldier who has become a fixture of my life in only a few weeks.

Freeing one of my hands, I lift it to his cheek, then slide my fingers through the short hair on the side of his head. I am being bolder than I ever have been, but before Wulfric found us, I thought I was going to lose this man. That is not a pain I wish to endure. I do not know what I would do without him.

Elliot's eyebrows pull together, but he doesn't shy away from my touch. He leans into it, closing his eyes. "What are you doing, Rapunzel?" His fingers find my hair near my collarbone and wrap around the locks, making me smile despite my nerves.

I move closer until our noses almost touch. "I am answering your question."

He shakes his head, but the movement brings him close enough that his nose brushes mine, and I can nearly taste him. "We shouldn't do this."

"I have lived my entire life dictated by shoulds and should nots," I whisper. "Let me have this moment for myself."

He drops his forehead to mine and takes a shaky breath. "Freya."

"Will you kiss me, Elliot? Please? Just this once." If he resists me again, I will accept his choice, no matter how much I want otherwise. At least I will know that he is not willing to—

Elliot's hand slides to the back of my neck, cutting off my thoughts as he pulls me across the last bit of distance between us and presses his lips to mine. While this is not my first kiss, I do not think a few stolen kisses from fellow dignitaries at events in my young adult years really gave me a good grasp of how my body would respond to someone I am attracted to. Those long-ago kisses were secret and exciting, but they did not spark a fire to life in my chest and drown out the world around me.

But as Elliot kisses me, his lips warm and soft, I become all too aware that this is unlike anything I have experienced before now.

He pulls back, breathless, and brushes his thumb across my cheek. "Frey—"

I cut him off, pulling him close again and taking my turn, asking him for more.

He obliges. As he parts my lips, deepening the kiss, something shifts between us, like the ground falls away and sends us into a freefall. I press a hand to his smooth chest as the kiss intensifies and grows more heated, my other hand gripping his hair. I am desperate to be nearer to him, so when Elliot's large hands wrap around my waist and tug me toward him, it is only logical for me to move to his lap.

I am halfway to him when he curses and pulls back, glaring down at the angry red wound on his torso as his face drains of what little color it had.

"Oh!" I cry, immediately moving back to my chair. "Elliot, I am so sorry!"

Groaning, he slowly lowers himself onto his back, wincing when he rests on the stitches there. "Not your fault," he grunts, shutting his eyes. I can only imagine the pain he is in—for a moment, I forgot about the bullet holes.

"I should not have done that," I whisper, covering my mouth with my hand. My lips feel swollen, tingling with the remnants of Elliot's kiss. I may never recover, and all I want is to do it again.

His expression twists even more than it already was. "I told you it was a bad idea."

Though he cannot see me, I glare at him anyway. "Kissing you was a bad idea only because you are injured, not because it should not have happened."

That gets him to look at me again. "Freya, I'm your *bodyguard*."

"I am aware."

"We can't..." He grits his teeth and shakes his head.

Taking a slow breath, I wait a moment to let his pain recede. But if he thinks we are going to kiss like that and pretend nothing happened, he is wrong. I have spent the last several days ignoring the tension between us, but I cannot do it anymore. "Elliot," I say firmly, "there is a connection between us that goes beyond tabloid speculation and internet gossip. You cannot argue that."

His scowl seems only half-hearted as he looks at me, but his jaw is so tight that he says nothing.

So I continue. "I am well aware that a relationship would be complicated at best."

He huffs a small laugh.

"I have never met anyone who infuriates me the way you do, and I am certain I drive you half mad most days."

He grunts.

"There are few people who would want us to be together."

"Is there a point to this?" he asks in a grumble.

I grin. "There is a point to everything I say, Elliot." When he smiles back at me, my heart swells with affection for this man. There is every reason I should not—cannot—entertain ideas of being with him, but those reasons fade with each second we gaze into each other's eyes.

"You and I," I say, taking his hand and lacing my fingers through his. "We are not an obvious pairing. But surely you can admit that we are good for each other." I look down at the haphazard stitches holding his skin together. "For the most part," I add with a wince.

"This would have happened even if I wasn't falling for you, Princess."

My eyes jump back to his. "You're...?"

"Falling? Yeah." He looks downright angry about it, though I feel as if the ground has disappeared from beneath me once again. "Do you have any idea how frustrating that is? This wasn't supposed to happen." He gestures between us. "*We're* not supposed to happen."

Despite his words, I smile wider and bring his hand to my lips to brush a kiss against his knuckles. "If I have learned anything from my friends and their stories, love always comes in the most unexpected of ways. You and I are no different."

It is only when his face goes slack that I realize what I said. *Love.* I could take it back, explain that I did not mean things the way they sounded, but I do not. I let my words fill the space between us and settle in my chest. I love my friends as I love my family, but the way I feel about Elliot is different. That should scare me, but I am more afraid of keeping these feelings to myself and never giving them a chance to blossom.

"Your friends," Elliot says after a long while, "the celebrities?" He quirks his lips up in a smile that warms me to the core. "You know you can't base anything on their lives, right?"

"I can when I am a princess," I argue.

"But I'm not." He winces, his smile shifting to amusement. "You know what I mean. I'm not royal."

"I know."

"Even if I wasn't your bodyguard, I'm not Candoran. I can't..." He has thought about a future together like I have? He shakes his head and sighs. "Laws aside, I'm not royalty material."

"You are not," I agree. "But I think you could be."

Groaning, he adjusts himself on the bed, tilting to the side to lessen the pressure on his stitches. "You don't know that, Rapunzel. I'm just a kid from Montana with a lot of weird and specific skills that don't really translate to anything outside of the Special Forces."

I snicker and stand because he looks wildly uncomfortable, and the least I can do after he took a bullet for me is help him relax. "You are remarkable with languages," I tell him as I help him roll over to his left side, leaving both sides of his wound exposed and untouched. Despite his beautifully muscled body, he must be cold after losing so much blood, so I take a blanket and drape it over him. "You have a natural inclination toward reading body language and facial expressions." He is turned toward the wall now, and I would like to see his face while we talk, so I settle on the bed, my back against the wall and his head on my lap. He fights me but doesn't resist for long, resting the full weight of his head on my leg. "You are far more intelligent when it comes to politics than you pretend to be."

He looks up at me with his eyebrows low but his eyes soft. Like he wants to argue against everything I am saying but does not want me to stop talking. He looks so tired—of course he is tired—and he should really sleep while he can. I do not know how long it will take for someone to come for us, but he needs his strength.

"You keep a cool head when it matters," I tell him and start running my fingers through his hair, smiling when his eyes immediately slide closed. "You make connections with people. And you are selfless, and strong, and kind, and more than once I have wondered what it would be like to have you by my side, not as my protector but as my equal."

I am not usually this open with people, particularly when it comes to my heart, but Elliot makes it easy. He has proven time and time again that I can trust him. That he has my best interest at heart, and not just because he is paid for that. It is who he is.

"I'm no good for you," he mumbles, half asleep now.

I snicker. "Who says so?"

"Your mom. The internet. Everyone."

"Not me. I think you and I could be something great, Elliot Reid. *You* could be great, if you would only give yourself a chance."

He hums but says nothing, and soon his breathing slows and deepens. I continue running my fingers through his hair, thinking through the things I said to him. I meant every word, but his qualifications, great though they are, will only go so far. A man like him marrying a queen, assuming that is the direction our lives take us, is not unheard of in other parts of the world, but Candora is steeped in tradition. I cannot know if my people would accept him if we found a way around the laws preventing it in the first place.

Am I willing to take that risk?

Wulfric comes back inside a few minutes after Elliot falls asleep, his gentle eyes taking in the pair of us. When he first came across me in the forest, his wild look frightened me, but he has been nothing but kind. The way Candorans have been for centuries. I wonder what he would think of a queen marrying someone like Elliot.

"You are not a royalist, Wulfric," I say to him, keeping my voice low to not wake the man asleep in my lap. Using Wulfric's own words will hopefully make him receptive to my coming question. "Do you think the monarchy needs to change?"

Setting a bucket of water on his rickety table, he shrugs. "Politics don't have much effect out here."

"Would it bother you? If a queen married someone like him?" I nod down to Elliot, smiling at the way he looks so peaceful. He was in so much pain before, even unconscious, but now I no longer fear for his life. He will take time to recover, but I am certain he will survive.

Filling a cup with some of the water, Wulfric grunts before handing it over to me. "Depends on your reasons, I suppose. Are you trying to stir up trouble?"

I smirk at him. "I have never been known to stir up trouble, as fun as that sounds." No, if I were to begin a relationship with Elliot, I would do it fully knowing the consequences of my choice. Prepared to pay for them, whatever the price may be.

As it stands, Candoran law prevents a monarch from marrying a non-citizen in order to protect the country from foreign influence. Gaining Candoran citizenship takes time, and as proven by today's near-catastrophe, the longer I remain single and childless, the more vulnerable the throne will be, so time is not on my side. If I had met Elliot years ago, before my mother ever announced her retirement, we might have had a chance to convince the people to love him as I am coming to.

But that is not reality.

Perhaps marrying Grimstad is not as selfless as I first thought, but it is impossible to see a relationship with Elliot as anything *but* selfish. Are these my choices? Give up my own happiness for the sake of my people, or betray my people for the sake of my happiness? Why must it be one or the other?

Still stroking Elliot's hair, I look down at the soldier and imagine this being my life. Not the gunshot wound or holing up in a rundown cabin in the woods, obviously. But having Elliot close to me. Kissing him. Trusting him with my thoughts and my heart.

Building a family with him.

My body warms at the thought, but guilt builds too. I was born to privilege, and with that comes responsibility. I have made many promises throughout my campaign, things I truly believe in, and I would never forgive myself if I did not follow through.

"Can someone like me be allowed to choose love?" I am not really asking Wulfric. No Candoran monarch has ever married this far beneath them, and even choosing Markham would go against tradition. But at least he is Candoran. And known by the people.

In reality, neither Markham nor Elliot are beneath me. Not where it matters. They are good men, with so much potential, and they should have every opportunity for a life of greatness. Markham will find that no matter what I choose; he has the ambition and the confidence to get whatever he wants. But Elliot? *Just a kid from Montana.* He is so much more than that, even if he cannot see it himself. He is not Candoran and has no title, but I fear he will soon have my entire heart.

If only that could be enough.

Chapter Twenty-Six

Elliot

"If someone hadn't already tried it, I would kill you, Elliot."

I know Sander is serious, but I can't help but smirk at him as he paces the length of Wulfric's cabin. I've been awake for less than ten minutes, jarred from a deep sleep by the arrival of a veritable army of palace guards and police, as well as two anxiety-ridden princes. But my mind is still fuzzy, my body is exhausted, and I don't have it in me to match the man's energy.

Besides, my head is full of dreams about Freya's lips and the way she kisses with confidence and authority, turning it into a competition in the best way. I'm not in the mood to be threatened when I would much rather take Hex's place on the other side of the cabin, with Freya in his arms and her head on his shoulder.

"Relax," I mumble, wishing I could have slept for more than an hour or two. "I'm fine."

Sander stops mid-stride and narrows his eyes at me. "You have a hole in the middle of your body. You are not fine."

I look down at the fresh bandage placed on my torso by a Skalridge doctor who came with the entourage. He wasn't thrilled by Wulfric's rudimentary stitches but declared them passable enough until I can get to a hospital. "Technically, it's on my right—"

"You should have told me, El." Sander's voice breaks for the first time since I met the guy, and he slowly sinks into a chair like his strength has left him. I've never seen him like this. "You could have died, and I would have lost one of my best friends."

Okay, I can be serious for a second. Though I'm tempted to stay on the bed and never move again, I sit up and wait until he looks at me. "As long as I'm in this job, there's always going to be that danger, San. I've been through worse, trust me."

"Because that makes me feel better," he grumbles back.

"I didn't tell you I was wounded because I needed you to stay safe. You're more important than me."

He doesn't like that, his miserable expression shifting into a scowl that drops the temperature of the room. He mutters something in Candoran, too quick and low for me to understand him, but I doubt it's anything good.

My eyes flit over to Freya for the millionth time since the twins arrived with their little army, all of whom have been kind enough to stay outside and watch the perimeter while Wulfric shouts at them to not tromp all over his bellflowers. The princess, tucked in the safety of her brother's hold, has her eyes closed and looks like she could be asleep if not for the little smile on her lips.

Lips that I want to taste again.

She was still on the bed with me when Hex and Sander stormed inside in what I assume was a poorly planned rescue, and despite the chaos around us, she spent a long few seconds looking down at me, her fingers brushing my face with a featherlight touch that left me shivering.

As if she feels my gaze, Freya opens her eyes and smiles weakly at me. My body reacts to that smile with a longing that I won't be able to ignore as easily as I did before. Not now that I know the feel of her hands in my hair and on my skin. Now that I know how she tastes.

"Tell me everything you know," I say to Sander, my voice strained. I need a distraction before I march over to the princess and pull her into my arms.

Sander glances between me and his sister with his eyes full of suspicion, but it's not like he doesn't already know how I feel about Freya. There's a reason I sat with Freya during the ride to Skalridge to give the twins a break from me; Sander and Hex have been subjected to my frustration with the situation more than they likely wanted. I couldn't admit anything about my feelings to Freya, so I admitted it all to them, hoping they would have advice.

They didn't. Mostly they teased me about liking their uptight and significantly older sister.

But I think Sander is finally realizing how serious my feelings really are as he studies me. "Fenwick had someone on the inside who let him in before we ever got to the arena," he says as he sits on the chair next to the bed. "According to his own words after the guards detained him, 'The royals have had their turn, and it's time for a new age of Candora.'"

I wrinkle my nose. "Now I know why I had such a bad feeling about the guy." As I speak, my wounds throb, and I grunt and press a hand to my ribcage to try to distract from the pain. I could have taken something other than basic painkillers, but anything stronger would have dulled my senses more than they already are. I'm regretting that decision right now, even if the drugs haven't had a chance to kick in yet. "What about the other shooter?" I ask. "The one who got me."

Sander growls low in his throat and glares at the bandage on my waist. "Disgruntled blueback. He let Fenwick inside."

I lift my eyebrows as a swear slips from my tongue. "A cop?" I should be grateful that he didn't hit anything important. "I thought Candorans were all about a peaceful existence."

"From the little we know, he was hit with hard times and denied government assistance, and he blames the monarchy for his family going hungry." Sander shakes his head. "He never should have been neglected like that."

"That doesn't mean assassinating the princess is a good idea." I frown at him and the way he almost looks guilty. "His choices are not your fault, Sander."

"But his circumstances are because of *my family's* choices," he retorts.

"What could *you* have done? You've never wanted the throne."

"But that doesn't make me any less of a prince," he snaps, then shrinks in on himself and bows his head, clasping his hands at the back of his neck. "What am I even doing with my life?" he mutters, more to himself than to me.

In the two months I've known the twins, Hex and Sander have both seemed perfectly content. They're incredibly smart and the best fighters I've ever seen, but I figured they were happy to live more regular lives as palace guards instead of using their talents for better things. Sander is clearly in crisis right now, and I don't know how to help him because I have no idea what he wants. I wonder if *he* knows.

Sighing, he sits up straight and fixes a calm expression on his face that almost looks believable. "Rothesby recognized the blueback as the man you saw last night when you were tailing Fenwick. He and three other guards are taking both shooters to Invem."

"Good." I'm disappointed I won't get to interrogate either of them until we get back to the capital, but it's for the best. I doubt I could handle that conversation calmly.

"Rothesby also thinks there were others at the debate, but they got spooked and ran when the first two attempts failed. He and Hex went after a few suspicious men in the mayhem but couldn't catch them."

I glare at Hex across the room, but the prince isn't looking at me. Probably on purpose, since I ordered him to run if things went south. Not dive into the fray. Rothesby, on the other hand, deserves a raise. "At least most of them were cowards," I grumble, though I hate the idea of more people out there with enough anger to threaten a princess. It's not like I can do anything about it in my current state, so I change the subject. "What about Grimstad?"

Sander glances at his sister, making my stomach twist. I really don't like the way she's connected to Grimstad in his mind. "From what I've heard, the wound was mostly superficial," he mutters, "but Mum convinced him to head straight to Stonemere for some recovery time before the Celestial Ball instead of finishing his campaign."

I swear under my breath. I'd forgotten all about the ball, a big annual celebration among the nobility that sounds like the worst night of my life. That includes being stitched up by a dull needle without anything to numb the pain. At least tonight I got a kiss out of it.

That won't happen at a royal ball. Or maybe ever again.

"Grim took a bullet for the princess," I mutter, as if I need a reminder of why he's a better choice for Freya. She may have said that she doesn't want to have a family with the guy, but that doesn't mean she won't marry him if it makes the most sense for her country. Last night was a fluke, a moment of passion that I shouldn't have allowed, no matter how much I wanted it.

"So did you," Sander replies, looking from me to Freya. "Did...did something happen between you two?"

"Me and Grim? No, he—"

"You know what I'm asking, El."

Yeah, I do, but I can't admit that I crossed a line. Not even to him. He and Hex are my closest friends here in Candora, but they're still princes. Their life is not my life, and it never can be.

So I lie. "Aside from her putting my life in the hands of a questionable Candoran hermit? No."

Even though it's a bad idea, I look at Freya, reading her lips as she tells Hex that she was so afraid and didn't know what to do. I failed her. I've been a terrible bodyguard from the start, and the only reason she's still alive is because of Grimstad. Not me. From the beginning, I've made everything harder for her.

Grunting, I stand and head outside, realizing too late that it's freezing tonight and I'm not wearing a shirt. But if I go back inside, Sander will keep trying to talk to me. Or Hex will accuse me of letting Freya down by not preventing the shooting in the first place. I need a moment to myself, so I ignore the palace guards who try to ask about my wound or what happened after we left the arena, passing all of them until I end up at the edge of a small pond.

The rhythmic croaking of frogs fills the air, and mist hangs heavy over the water as the moon reflects in the pond. As crickets chirp to each other, I can see why Wulfric would choose to live here. It's peaceful. Calm. Something I've rarely experienced in my life.

Most of the calm in my life has come from Freya.

"Are you hoping to catch your death?" a soft voice says behind me.

I don't turn around, even if my heart kicks up a notch at the sound of Freya's worry-laden words. "Nah. I'm pretty good at surviving."

"It is freezing out here, Elliot." Before I can respond, she tucks a blanket over my shoulders. "I refused to lose you in the forest, and I will not do so now."

Lose me. She can never *have* me. "You shouldn't be out here, Rapunzel," I mutter, pulling the blanket tighter around me. It *is* cold, and I lost enough blood that my body isn't doing a great job of keeping me warm.

Freya comes to my side, her arm pressed to mine. Behind her, two guards stand with their backs to us and at a far enough distance that they're unlikely to hear our conversation. If I were anyone else, I doubt they would take their eyes off the princess after what happened today, but I'm grateful for the privacy they're giving us for now.

Freya leans a little more heavily against me. "I do believe I am not obligated to take any order from you unless my safety is at stake."

"You wouldn't listen even if it was."

"How are you feeling?"

Sighing, I turn to face her, planning to tell her I'm perfectly fine and we should get ready to leave. But at the sight of her hair spilling over her shoulders in the moonlight, my heart throbs in my chest and leaves my resolve feeling slippery. I don't want to leave this place. Leaving means riding the rest of the way through the pass, which sounds exhausting and painful, and facing reality as soon as we get to the town on the other side where the royal vehicles are waiting for us.

I would so much rather stay in this little guard-surrounded bubble and pretend we're alone again, like we were before.

"Sit down," I say, adjusting the blanket to free my arms.

Freya frowns. "What?"

Pointing at a log near her feet, I repeat my command with raised eyebrows. "Please," I add when she gapes at me.

"I will remind you about orders." But she does sit, wrapping her arms around her knees. She's wearing a jacket that was probably supplied to her by one of the guards, but I don't miss the shiver that runs through her.

Slipping the blanket from my shoulders, I drape it around her and speak over her when she tries to protest. "Take it, Freya. I need my hands free for this."

"For what, exactly?"

Instead of answering, I slide my fingers into her hair and start pulling it away from her face. It's been a few months since I last braided the girls' hair, and neither of them had quite this much. But Freya needs someone to help her tame her waves, and Runa isn't here. I wasn't much help to the princess after leaving the arena, but I can be useful now.

"It is still hard to believe you are as skilled with hair as you are with everything else," Freya murmurs as I take pieces of her hair on one side of her part to do a Dutch braid.

"No one said I was skilled."

The frogs continue their song as I work, helping fill the silence between us. I don't mind that we aren't talking. Freya's hair is not only long but thick, and it's taking all of my concentration to weave it into something that will last longer than a few minutes without any pins to hold it in place. I'm hoping for a functional braid crown, something to last until we meet up with the rest of the staff.

Freya sits with the blanket tucked around her, her arms hugging her legs, and she looks like a regular human this way instead of a princess who never lets anything get to her. I wish I could see her face and have a chance at guessing what she might be thinking about, but since my whole focus is on the back of her head, I start replaying some of the things she said last night.

She was full of compliments, and frankly I might have dreamed up half of them in my wounded delirium, but I was still conscious for one thing in particular: *You could be royal material.*

Freya isn't one to lie. But does she really think I could be...enough?

My fingers grow still on her scalp, and Freya tilts her head back to look at me. "Elliot?"

Unable to resist, I brush a finger along her temple, then resume my braiding, working more quickly now that I've finished braiding across the front of her head. I just need to work the rest of her hair into the braid I've already done and hope that it stays in place. "I said a lot of things last night," I mutter. "Things I probably wouldn't have said if I hadn't been shot."

"So did I. Do you regret anything?"

"It's hard to regret being honest." And I will never regret that kiss. I shouldn't have done it, but her request felt enough like an order that my body overtook my brain and obeyed. If not for the holes in my side, I'm not sure I would have *stopped* kissing her once I started.

Finished with the last of the braid, I tuck the end into the crown and settle on the log, facing the opposite direction from the princess but pressed up against her side. "Do you? Regret anything, I mean."

After admiring my handiwork by tilting her head from one side to the other and patting the front of the crown with her hand, she takes one end of the blanket and holds it out to me. It's an awkward way to share, facing the wrong way, but I'll take the warmth however I can get it.

"I cannot regret saying what I feel," she says, her voice as soft as the breeze around us. "And you..." Her hand lifts to my chest, cold fingers splaying across my skin. "You make me question everything I thought I knew, Elliot Reid."

"That sounds like a terrible thing to do." Kissing her would be equally terrible, but that doesn't mean I'm not tempted. Close as we are and relatively on our own, now could be my only chance to taste her again.

Freya smiles. "Or the best thing." Is she talking about making her question things or kissing? "I always thought I knew what I wanted."

"But?" As a chill shudders through me when the breeze picks up, I lean closer to her, as much for warmth as from simple desire.

She lowers her forehead onto my bare shoulder and sighs. "But I did not realize there were other choices I could make." She shivers.

Cursing under my breath, I ignore the pain in my side as I straddle the log, and then I pull her close, tucking her legs over mine and wrapping my arms around her beneath the blanket. "You should really go inside," I murmur, not meaning a word of it as I pull her into my chest. I'm keeping her warm. That's it.

Freya nuzzles closer. "This is far better."

I curse again as desire rolls through me. It's a good thing her face is in my neck, or I would already be kissing her. "Saying things like that is going to get me into trouble, Princess," I growl.

"I *am* a princess, yes. I can say whatever I would like."

"And I'm a bodyguard who should really keep his mouth shut instead of saying..." The words stick in my throat. Probably for the best. I was vulnerable enough as it was before I fell asleep, and the later the night gets, the more exposed I feel.

But Freya lifts her head, her bright blue eyes boring into mine. "Saying what, Elliot?"

I shake my head. It shouldn't be this hard, but it is. "I'm not the kind of guy who regularly shares his feelings, Rapunzel."

"It may come as a shock, but neither am I." Chuckling, she reaches up and brushes her fingers along my jaw. "You and Derek are more similar than you may realize, keeping things to yourself the way you do, but you are safe here, Elliot. With me. I will never treat your feelings lightly."

"Being a king sounds terrifying." The admission slips from my tongue so easily, but it's a big one. With a lot of implications I can't take back now that they're out there, like the fact that I have considered *marriage* with this woman even though that's completely insane.

Not to mention impossible.

With her hand still touching my face, Freya bites her lip—taunting me—before she says, "Can I let you in on a secret?"

I nod, my eyes locked on her mouth.

"Being a queen sounds terrifying too."

"What?" Thoroughly distracted, I meet her gaze and find her eyes welling up with tears. The sight sends a sharp pain straight to my chest. I'm already embracing her, so I rub my hand up and down her arm in the hope that I can give her some kind of comfort. "But you've always wanted—"

"To be queen," she finishes with a tiny nod. "Since I was a little girl, I have wanted nothing else so badly. I knew it would be difficult, but it never frightened me. Until recently."

I curse, increasing the speed of my rubbing. "You were shot at. That would scare anyone."

"Yes, but I was not talking about that. There will always be risks, but I am surrounded by the best of men who will do everything they can to keep me safe. What frightens me is you."

My hand freezes. "Me?"

"Yes." Her fingers run along my jaw one more time before sliding down my neck to my chest, lower and lower until she hovers over the gauze taped to my side. "I worried I had lost you, Elliot, and I pictured a world where you did not exist anymore. A world where I became queen and married a stranger and lived out my days in bare contentment, lacking anything resembling happiness.

"I am afraid that if I take the throne, that mediocrity I imagined will be my future because, beyond the laws making it impossible, I can never *ask* you to take up the mantle with me. I can never force you into a life you are not prepared for."

I can't resist anymore. Tilting her chin up with my finger, I press my lips to hers and close my eyes, losing myself in the sensation of the kiss. This woman is so *good*. Everything she does is to the benefit of everyone but herself, and I am in awe of her.

And I can't get enough of kissing her.

Even though I hold back, contenting myself with a closed-mouth kiss unlike the one last night, it still sets my heart racing. I lean more into Freya, but it's not long before my wound starts to ache sharply. Groaning, I pull back and curse my body for interrupting yet again.

Freya smiles and presses her hand to my chest once more, and the skin beneath her palm seems to burn. "It is for the best that I cannot kiss you the way I wish to, Elliot Reid."

"Nope. That's never a good thing." It's really annoying that my body endured everything I put it through in the Special Forces, but one tiny bullet can get in the way of what I really want. "Freya, I..." I don't even know what I want to say as I gaze into her eyes. There are too many questions when it comes to a romance between us, and I don't even know if I would be a good partner let alone a good monarch. But I want to be more than what I am, if only because that's what she sees in me. I've never felt this way. About anyone.

I desperately want to be the man she thinks I can be.

Someone clears their throat, and I look up to find Hex standing a few feet away, his eyes discerning as he studies the way we're cuddled together. He looks worried. Even sad. He knows as well as we do that this can't end well.

"Mum wants to talk to you," he says to Freya. His eyes jump to me. "And Gregor is on the line for you, El."

"Mum already knows I am perfectly safe thanks to Elliot," Freya says without any indication that she plans to move anytime soon.

I, however, know I need to talk to the head of security sooner than later, which means reality is coming whether I want it to or not. "You need to talk to your mom," I murmur, touching my forehead to her temple because I don't have the energy to resist.

She sighs. "Duty calls."

"And you." I narrow my eyes at Hex. "You were supposed to get out of the arena."

Hex doesn't look nearly as repentant as he should. "Technically I did."

"Going after suspects."

He shrugs. "I got a good look at a couple of them."

"Then you can pass that information to the RIA."

He wrinkles his nose, his distaste for the agency coming through his nonchalance. "Why?"

"Because an intelligence agency is exactly the department who should investigate dissent against the crown. Not a prince."

With a hefty sigh, Hex rolls his eyes and grabs his phone. "You're right, but I am only doing this because no one else saw the blokes' faces. If this makes the RIA even more persistent about me joining them, I'm blaming you." He looks at Freya, some of his frustration softening. "Sander's on the phone with Mum." Then at me again. "Carsten has Gregor on the line."

Waiting until he wanders back toward Wulfric's cabin before I say anything, I slowly loosen my hold on the princess. "I guess we have to get back to reality."

"I am terrified of what my mother is going to say."

"I'm equally afraid of Gregor. I can only imagine the messages on my phone right now. It's somewhere in the woods with my gun." I'll need to send one of the guards to find both things.

Freya snickers. "Poor Runa was holding on to mine, and I am certain Derek has heard of what happened at the debate and has tried to reach me many times. My friends are probably as panicked as my mother."

"On the plus side, I doubt anyone will be talking about our stolen glances for a while."

With bright eyes, Freya surprises me with a quick kiss against my lips before she stands, leaving the blanket with me. "Or stolen kisses," she says with a smirk. "Can you imagine what the internet will do when they find out?"

When. Not *if.* It takes me a lot longer than I'd like to get to my feet as my body protests the movement, and Freya is already halfway to the cabin before I find the strength to start walking. But she looks back at me and smiles so warmly that I completely forget about the pain.

All I can think about is a future full of stolen kisses and shared blankets.

There's no way this is going to end well.

Chapter Twenty-Seven

FREYA

THERE IS A GOOD chance I am dreaming right now rather than sitting at the breakfast table at the royal family home in Stonemere. Why? Because I am certain I just heard the butler announce the arrival of Derek Riley.

Stifling a yawn, I shake my head a bit as if that might wake me up. "Forgive me," I say to the butler. "I believe I heard you wrong. *Who* is in the parlor?"

"Mr. Derek Riley, Your Highness."

I wish I had not risen so early, beating both my brothers to breakfast. It is not that I do not believe what the butler is telling me, but I do not understand, and they could explain it to me. "Why?" I ask out loud. But as soon as I do, I finally process what he said, and excitement bursts to life in my chest. "Wait, he's here? In Candora?"

The butler's lips twitch, though he is far too professional to actually smile. "Yes, Your Highness. He said not to rush you and that he is happy to wait."

I am already on my feet, eager to see my friend. He was not supposed to arrive for two more days, just in time for the election. With two palace guards trailing behind me, I hurry across the house to the family parlor. Sure enough, Derek is standing at one of the windows, looking out over Stonemere Lake. I am surprised to see him alone; most often when he travels lately, his bodyguard, Hunter, is right by his side. But that does not make me any less glad to see him.

"Derek!" I barely give him time to turn around before I pounce on him, leaping into his arms like a baby koala the same way Liam always does. "What are you doing here?"

His laugh is strained. "You knew I was coming." The tension is in his voice as well, though I can tell he is trying to hide it.

Sliding to my feet and stepping back, I scrutinize my friend. He is wearing sweats and a baseball hat pulled over his dark hair, and while this is an uncommon look for him in regular life, it is fairly normal attire for when he travels, especially if he charters a private flight. His face is scruffy with the beginnings of a dark beard, but that is nothing new. Unless his current role requires him to be clean shaven, he usually sports some level of facial hair.

It is his eyes that worry me. They are tired beyond the normal weariness that comes from flying to the other side of the world.

"What is the matter?" I ask, frowning at him.

I see the instant he realizes he was not properly masking. His eyes light up, facial muscles tightening his expression to one of careful nonchalance. In the place of my oldest friend now stands Hollywood's most popular actor.

"Nothing's the matter with me," he says lightly. "I'm more worried about you. How are you holding up?"

As soon as I was reunited with my phone, I spent hours on a video call with my friends, assuring them that I was unharmed and safe. Derek was on that call, and though he was quiet, I was certain he believed me when I said I had no lasting damage from what happened at the debate.

I narrow my eyes. "Do not lie to me, Derek Riley."

His chuckle sounds so natural that had I not seen the weariness and tension in his eyes a moment ago, I would believe him. "The election is in two days, Peach. You're allowed to be stressed."

"You came early because you thought I would be stressed?" It is a very Derek thing to do, but he already planned to come on Election Day, when the rest of my friends are coming to support me, and Derek's schedule is always so tight.

I find it difficult to believe he happened to have an extra couple of days open when he is in the middle of filming.

"I like your hair down like this," he says, ignoring my question. "You don't wear it loose very often."

To be frank, I was hoping I could convince Elliot to braid it again. Not because Runa is incapable of doing my hair but because Elliot and I have not been alone for even a moment since we left Wulfric's two days ago. I woke early this morning, eager to see him, but was disappointed to find a couple of palace guards outside my door rather than my bodyguard. They told me Elliot had been ordered by Gregor to rest.

While I agree that Elliot has not taken adequate time to heal, I do not like when he is not near. I miss his touch. He has kept a respectable distance the last couple of days—with so much attention on me right now, that has been necessary—but there is an ache in my chest that I did not realize could build so quickly. We have had no time alone and therefore no time to talk about...everything.

"Derek," I say as forcefully as I can. Gesturing to the nearest sofa, I wait until he sits beside me. "Why are you really here?"

His jaw tightens, telling me I was right to think there is more at play. Pulling the hat from his head, he runs his hand through his dark hair in a way that makes him look anxious.

Derek Riley is *never* anxious.

"What is it?" I ask tersely.

He sighs. "I heard about the conversation you had with the gang the night before the debate. About Grimstad."

Discomfort pools in my chest, leaving me overwarm. "Hank told you." He was the only one who got the name of my potential betrothed.

"No, he didn't, but I'm more worried about why *you* didn't tell me." A hard edge enters his eyes, something I do not see in him often. Leaning forward, he grabs hold of my hand. "Freya, I know you. I know you're going to be struggling with this decision, especially when you and Elliot..." He bites his tongue.

I narrow my eyes. "When Elliot and I what, Derek?"

"Like I said. I know you."

What he does *not* say is that he knows how I feel about my bodyguard, but I can see it in his eyes. Derek is more diligent about reading the tabloids than any of us, and he would have seen not only *Hot Scoop*'s claims but any stories in Candoran newspapers as well. More than likely, he read the opinion piece that I have yet to get out of my head, and he saw all the pictures.

"Talk to me, Freya." He sounds desperate in a way, and I wonder if the last *Hot Scoop* story I read bothered him more than it should have. The one that talked about how he and I are sure to be at odds now that I have Elliot in my life. It is a good thing *Hot Scoop* does not know that Elliot and Derek are cousins and not simply connected through me, or I am certain things would have gotten far more complicated.

I have avoided the internet since leaving Skalridge, but perhaps people have said more. Enough to get under Derek's skin.

"What would you like me to say?" I ask, dropping my eyes to our clasped hands. "Markham Grimstad proposed marriage, and I should have given him an answer days ago, but everything has been so..." There is not even a proper word to describe the state of my life.

Derek's voice drops half an octave. "Are you considering him?"

"Of course I am." I know better than to lie.

"Why?" Because it is Derek sitting across from me, he is not asking because he thinks I have lost my mind. He genuinely wants to know my reasons so he can understand.

Didn't I want this only days ago? A chance to talk to my oldest friend about a situation I can barely think about because every time I do it hurts? But I wanted that before someone tried to take my life. Before Elliot kissed me. Before I thought I might lose a man who means more to me than anyone ever has before.

Before I felt like I was being torn in half.

Everything is so much bigger now.

As tears sting my eyes, I take a shaky breath. "It is best for Candora," I whisper. "Aligning with Grimstad gives both sides of my country a voice in a way they've never had before, and I do not have the knowledge to know what the majority of my people need. Not the way he does. More than that, I have wanted to be queen my whole life, and I am terrified that uniting with Grimstad is the only way that will happen."

"Okay," Derek says, calmer now. He reaches up and brushes a tear from my cheek, at the same time lifting my head so I meet his eyes. "Those are all good reasons, Freya. Except that last one."

I laugh mournfully. "You are far too optimistic for your own good, Derek Riley."

He snickers. "You know that's not true. I'm being realistic. I've seen the polls as well as you have, and you pulled to the lead in a matter of days."

"That was before the debate," I argue glumly. "Before the assassination attempt. What do the polls say now?"

He frowns. "I don't know, actually. I haven't had a chance to get online for a couple of days. Janie's been rearranging things so I could get here sooner."

Derek's most recent assistant is very good at what she does, but sometimes I wonder if he relies on her more than he should. "You could have come when you were supposed to."

The flat look he gives me brings a bit of light to my heavy heart. "Freya," he chides, "you needed someone to talk to, and Elliot wasn't going to cut it. I couldn't leave you stuck here with only your brothers for company while you deal with all of this."

"My brothers have actually been really great," I say with a brief smile.

Derek lifts an eyebrow. "The rogue and the spy? That's surprising."

Which one is which?

"Anyway." He squeezes my hand, giving me a stern look. "Tell me why you would choose *not* to marry Grimstad." He says the word 'marry' like it tastes bitter, which is strange coming from him. Those who truly know Derek know that he wants a life partner more than anyone. But maybe that is why he thinks accepting Grimstad's offer may not be a good decision. To Derek, marriage is not something to take lightly.

I have never taken anything more seriously.

"Well," I say with a bit more snap in my tone than I intend, "you already know one of my biggest reasons to decline."

His mouth twists into a smirk that reminds me so much of Elliot that it almost hurts to see. At what point did things switch to Elliot being more familiar than Derek? "Yeah, I do," he says. "Grimstad's a politician."

I whack his shoulder. "*I* am a politician, Derek!"

"Exactly. I know how frustrating you people can be."

"I don't know why *Hot Scoop* thinks you're so perfect when you are nothing but annoying."

Something dark flashes across Derek's eyes, but his smile does not falter, so maybe I imagined it. "Annoying? That's nice of you to say to the guy who's here to help you make a decision."

"You have not hidden your opinion on the subject," I grumble. "You don't want me to marry him."

"No, I don't, but it's not my choice to make." His smile fades to something more serious, and he shifts in his seat to face me. "Freya, why have you really not given Grimstad an answer yet?"

I would rather not voice it out loud. "You already know."

"Why?"

"Derek."

"I need you to say it."

"Because I am falling in love with Elliot." I exhale, any strength I might have had leaving with my breath. "Is that what you wanted to hear?"

Derek purses his lips in sympathy. "I wanted you to be honest with yourself. But..." He grimaces.

I sigh. "You rarely hold your tongue with me, Derek. Don't do it now."

"He's been a good influence on you, hasn't he?"

"Why do you say that like it's a bad thing? He is your family, Derek."

"I didn't expect him to..." Shaking his head, he drops my hand and gets to his feet, moving to the window so his back is to me. "I thought if he took the position, it would be good for both of you, but you weren't supposed to fall for each other."

"'Supposed to'?" I repeat, frowning at him. "Derek, you could not have predicted our feelings."

"Exactly the problem," he mutters. "Now you're in a mess I don't know how to get you out of."

I stand, not sure if I am angry or confused or simply frustrated by the way he tries to control everything. He has seen enough life to know that that is not how things work. Elliot figured it out, so why can't Derek?

"Listen to me, Derek Riley Reid," I say firmly.

He spins around, his blue eyes wide and his mouth open, in what might be the first time I have caught him off guard. "What? How did you...?"

I roll my eyes. "Elliot *Reid* is your cousin on your father's side, and you despise lying, so the name Riley had to come from somewhere."

His hand moves to his hair again in the same anxious movement as before. "Right."

Moving slowly, I step toward him until we are only a foot apart, and he looks down at me like a cornered animal. I have never seen Derek so uncertain, so I hope he will listen to me as I say, "Nothing in my life right now is your fault."

"But—"

"I am talking, Derek." Glaring, I hold up a hand as he clenches his mouth shut. "*Nothing* is your fault. Yes, I have *Hot Scoop*'s interest because I am your friend. Yes, you introduced Elliot into my life. But you do not write the tabloids. You did not cause my heart to want him. That, unfortunately, was all Elliot, though I can hardly fault him for being the best of men."

The air slides from Derek's lungs in a slow exhale, and he dips his chin, lacking his usual calm confidence. "So, are your feelings for my cousin your only good reason to turn down Grimstad?" he asks quietly.

"I never said it was a good reason," I say, just as soft. "Elliot and I can never be anything more than what we are now."

He looks up. "Why not?"

"Candora forbids it."

He opens his mouth, likely with a hundred questions, but his phone takes his attention as he pulls it from his pocket. He quickly reads whatever message he received, then taps on something, his brow furrowing deeper with every passing second as his eyes jump across the screen. Just as I am about to ask him if everything is okay, he turns an alarming shade of white.

"Derek!" I grab his arm, but he doesn't take his eyes from his phone.

"Where's Elliot?"

"Why?"

"Where is he, Freya?"

A jolt of fear shoots through me at the urgency in his voice, and I step back once. "What is happening, Derek?"

Finally looking up, he stares at me for a long few seconds like I might have the answer to a question he doesn't want to ask. "Freya," he all but begs.

"He is supposed to be resting, though whether he has listened remains to be seen."

My words seem to pull Derek from whatever he was lost in, shifting his expression from fear to confusion. "Resting?" he repeats, almost instantly turning to panic as he curses under his breath. "Freya, was Elliot..." He curses again, this time losing the hat entirely as he runs a hand through his hair. "Why did no one tell me he was wounded?"

I can't decide if he is overreacting or if something is seriously wrong, but more than anything I hate that Derek has shut me out. "Because the two of you are cut from the same cloth," I grumble. *Too proud to be vulnerable.*

Derek's eyes flash with fire. "What do you mean?"

Why does he seem afraid of my answer? I take a step closer, narrowing my eyes when he takes a step back. "Because your cousin is very much like you," I say slowly. "Derek, what—"

"Have you read this?" he asks, holding up his phone.

I recognize *Hot Scoop*'s website, but the headline is unfamiliar. "I haven't been on the internet any more than you have because I am not keen to relive the debate. Should I have read it?"

"No!" Derek coughs. Takes a breath. Resets to his usual calm self. I do not believe his acting for a second, and I am getting tired of him thinking he can hide from me. Something is wrong, and I need to know what it is. "They were pretty tame, all things considered," he says with false nonchalance, "but you should focus on the election instead of paying attention to tabloid writers who don't know what they're talking about."

Well now I *have* to see what they said about me. Pulling my phone from my pocket, I begin looking up the tabloid, but Derek grabs my phone out of my hands. "Hey!"

He holds my phone over his head, and the man is so tall that I do not even try to reach it. "It's a bad idea, Peach."

"Derek Riley, you give me my phone this instant!" Out of the corner of my eye, I see the palace guards step forward to come to my aid, but I hold up a hand to stop them. Derek is being incredibly frustrating, but he is no danger to me.

Unfortunately, I probably should let them intervene because it is clear Derek has no intention of returning my phone. "Will you trust me?" he asks, a hint of desperation in his voice. "No good is going to come from reading *Hot Scoop* articles."

"I'd like to think I am beyond being affected by that nonsense."

"It's not you I'm worried about." Derek frowns, finally letting his face relax. It seems he was already acting when I first arrived because he looks far more tired now than he did when I walked into the room. He looks positively worn down in a way I have never seen him before.

My stomach twists. With the election to worry about and the proposal from Markham to decide on and a bone-deep need to be close to Elliot whenever possible, I am at my maximum. But something is bothering

Derek, and Derek Riley is not the sort of person who lets himself be bothered. If he cannot fix something on his own, he usually knows someone who can fix it for him.

What has frightened him so thoroughly?

"Derek, what is going on?" I whisper.

He swallows and looks at my phone in his hand like it might hold the answers. Or maybe it holds the problem. "I really need to talk to Elliot, Freya. *Please.*"

Derek was already acting strange, but this is something worse. I have *never* seen my friend like this, not in the seven years we have been friends. "Okay." I take his hand, waiting until he looks at me before I say, "Whatever this is, I am here for you, Derek. Just as you are always here for all of us. We can fix it."

"Thanks, Peach, but I don't think there's anything to fix. Not yet, anyway."

"What does that mean?"

Sighing, he squeezes my hand and pulls me in for a tight embrace. "I'll tell you when I can. I promise."

I wish Cole were here. Or Liam or Bonnie. Cole has known Derek longer than anyone, and he can always get Derek to let his guard down. Liam is so lovable that it is impossible to keep secrets from him, and Bonnie has spent the most time with Derek because of the relationship they feigned a while back. I thought *I* had a strong enough relationship with Derek for him to tell me his woes and worries, but apparently I was wrong.

All I can do now is help him as best I can and hope he is just having an off day.

Still holding Derek's hand, I lead him out into the corridor and toward the family wing, since Elliot has been staying in the room next to mine, and we are both quiet as we walk. That is not unusual for us, but the tension between us is. I dislike it immensely.

When we come across Hex and a woman I do not recognize, I am more than grateful for the momentary reprieve. "Hex!" I say with as much enthusiasm as I can muster. "You remember Derek, yes?" Thank goodness I encountered the brother who dislikes Derek the least.

Still, Hex's expression hardens as soon as he makes eye contact with my friend, and he glances at the woman beside him as if calculating how he wants to act around her. "Sure," he mutters and holds his head high. "I remember he has a hard time bowing to royalty."

I whack my hand across Derek's chest right as he starts bending down. "Don't do that, Derek. Hex, do not be a pain. Derek is a friend."

"Of yours," Hex replies.

Did I mix up my brothers and mistake Sander for Hex? I thought Hex liked Derek, at least a little bit. "Derek, I am so sorry. He should not be—"

"I think it's my fault, Your Highness," the woman says, dipping her head toward me. "I'm afraid I've put your brother in a bad mood."

Hex grunts in response. "This is Astrid Storme," he tells me without looking at the woman.

"*Agent* Storme," she corrects, snickering at the way Hex is behaving like a petulant child. "RIA."

Oh, she is an intelligence agent? But she looks so...nice. Sweet. There is a sharpness in her gaze, but if I had not been told, I would never have guessed her occupation. "It is lovely to meet you."

"I would like to speak to you when you have a free moment, Your Highness," Agent Storme says. "About what happened in Skalridge. As the palace guards suspected, we're finding evidence that there were more than two people involved in the attempt on your life, and any details you can give me would be most appreciated."

"For the record," Hex says roughly, "I've told her everything about that afternoon, but she is refusing to go back to Invem until she talks to everyone involved." With the way he glares at her, I am certain he has been trying all morning to rid himself of the RIA operative.

I should spare my brother, after all he has done for me these last few weeks. I am not keen to leave Derek with whatever is troubling him, but maybe Elliot will be able to help him where I cannot. Assuming Derek even lets him.

Putting on a smile, I slip my hand from Derek's and say, "I would be happy to speak with you now, if you are free, Agent Storme." I turn to Derek. "Elliot's room is the third from the left. He may be asleep, but—"

"He's on the roof, actually," Hex says with the eagerness of someone much younger than his actual age. Apparently I made the right move for his sake, and he looks far happier than he did a moment ago. "I'll take you, Riley."

Derek hesitates, looking from me to Agent Storme with a calculating look, and I wonder if he is considering asking if he can join in on the conversation. But he was not at the debate, and I need him to deal with whatever is bothering him before it becomes a problem. The Celestial Ball is tonight, and if I decide to accept Markham's hand, we will have to announce the engagement at the ball. I cannot give Derek the attention he needs when that choice is looming over me.

"Go," I tell him, then gesture for Agent Storme to follow me down the hall and back to the parlor.

All the while wishing I could be in a cabin in the woods with no troubles and no other company than a willful bodyguard with warm brown eyes.

Hollywood Hot Scoop

Hot Debate, Hotter Heroes, and a Royal Near-Miss!

Never fear, Scoopers! Princess Freya is safe and sound! In a press conference yesterday, our favorite princess confirmed there was an assassination attempt at Wednesday's debate but that she walked away from the skirmish unharmed. There's been no statement about who the shooter was, but we can all concur that Freya was the primary target based on the footage below. (Viewer discretion advised.)

Not going to lie, we haven't been talking enough about Freya's opponent, Markham Grimstad, who not only took a bullet for the princess but is also a fine piece of man candy and proof that Candorans are built different. If I had a rival here in Los Angeles, he wouldn't be jumping in front of me and risking his life while looking sexy doing it. Part of me wishes I could vote for the guy just so I can get his face on a five-dollar bill.

But I digress. I know you're all wondering why Sergeant Reid wasn't the one saving the day when Freya's life was in jeopardy, and don't worry your pretty little heads. Reid was there (see him leap into action at minute 0:47), and our sources say there's a high chance he was injured just like Grimstad. We've compared footage from before and after the debate, and our handsome hero isn't looking as hearty as he was before. Alverra security has kept quiet on the subject, but I'm convinced Elliot took a hit and is putting on a brave face.

Or maybe keeping the love of his life safe is taking its toll. Impressive as Elliot Reid is, he isn't perfect. He's certainly not his older brother.

That's right! Super Soldier has a big bro, and I am positively bursting from keeping this secret because it's going to Blow. Your. Mind. Talent and looks clearly run in the family, but that is a story for another day.

Make sure you hit that subscribe button because this family tie is going to be the juiciest scoop we've ever had! XO

CHAPTER TWENTY-EIGHT

ELLIOT

Two more days. I have two days before Freya is voted queen and everything changes. She'd probably be the first to tell me that she will still be the same person, no matter which crown she wears, but deep in my gut I know things will change. A princess has to be cognizant of her country's well-being, but a queen can think of nothing else. She'll be even more of a target than she is now, which means my job will be harder, which means I'll be spending more energy keeping her safe and won't have as many chances to be alone with her.

No dances in Havenford. No late nights in mountain cabins.

I want to keep Freya safe. More than anything. But to do that I have to give up our potential. A princess dating her protection agent is bad enough. A queen marrying her bodyguard is...

Impossible. At this point, I should know that. But with all this time being around her without really being *with* her, I've had plenty of time to wonder about what my future with her could look like if things were different.

But I've also had to come to some conclusions about what I'm willing to do—or not do—if it means I can make sure she's safe and happy for the rest of her life.

Maybe I—

"Elliot."

My gun's in my hand and pointed at Derek's chest a full two seconds before I register that it's him standing several paces behind me and holding his hands in the air. Cursing, I lower the weapon but keep a hold on it. Just in case. In case of what, I don't know, but I think I have a right to be on edge after everything.

"Derek," I breathe, willing my heart to calm. "What are you doing here?"

He looks...off. Tired. In the few times I've interacted with this guy, he's always been polished and put together, to the point where it gets annoying to know someone can be as perfect as he seems to be. But right now he looks worn down and anxious, and that is not making me want to put away my gun.

He clears his throat and looks around. It's a good view from up here, at the top of a turret overlooking the large lake that spans the area behind the house. The skies are clear and the sun is shining strong, promising perfect weather later. Staff members dart about the grounds and in and out of the house, prepping everything for tonight's ball.

I've been leaning against the wall and watching everything from my vantage point for the last hour. Gregor ordered me to rest, but he didn't say *where* I had to be. I can sit up here as easily as I could have sat in my room, and this way I have an idea of what's going on around the estate.

"I wanted to check on Freya after what happened," Derek says finally, taking a hesitant step toward me. "And check on you."

It's been a while since we last talked. Havenford? A lot has happened in that time, and I can only imagine what he's heard through the grapevine. Did he hear something he shouldn't have and fly all the way to Candora two days early to tell me to back off like his other friends did?

Good news for him, I suppose—I never stood a chance anyway. Freya isn't even queen yet and I've barely spoken a word to her. I can't imagine that scenario will get any better when she takes the throne, so I should prepare to always be with her but never *with* her.

The problem is... I'm not sure I can actually do that if things go in a certain direction; Grimstad still has an actual chance with her. He arrived at the house before us, and I've only seen him once, arm in a sling and missing his usual calm swagger as he joined the royal family for dinner on our first night here. The queen profusely thanked him for protecting her daughter, and he sat in silence. I expected him to throw out false humility and tell her that anyone would have done what he did, but he kept his mouth shut and his head down.

I think the shooting spooked him.

While Freya hasn't spent much time around Grimstad, too busy talking to reporters and placating members of the House of Lords who are panicking about the assassination attempt and worried they'll be next, she hasn't given any indication that she plans to turn his proposal down. I've barely been able to sleep because of it, which is probably why Gregor ordered me to take it easy today. It's a good thing he didn't see how bad I got before Havenford, or he might have taken me off my post.

That would have been better for everyone involved.

"Freya's fine," I say, finally responding to Derek's comment.

"I know. I just saw her." He's showing next to no emotion, which only emphasizes the weary set of his shoulders. "I'm pretty sure she can get through anything without batting an eye."

He's not wrong, but I've seen Freya's confidence waver more than once. She puts on a brave face. Acts the part of a princess. But she's still human.

"I'm fine too," I add and narrow my eyes when Derek's features twitch, his mask slipping the slightest bit. "Why are you really here, Derek?"

He folds his arms, then changes his mind and tucks his hands into the pocket of his sweatshirt. It's weird to see him dressed so casually, but it's not like I know my cousin all that well. Maybe he dresses like this all the time and I'm just used to seeing him in pictures or video clips. Regardless, he's nervous.

That makes *me* nervous.

I didn't think Derek Riley *got* nervous, and I've kind of hated him for it until right this moment. Turns out I preferred him when he seemed to have an answer to everything.

"Did you read the latest *Hollywood Hot Scoop* article?" he asks eventually.

I huff out a laugh. "Nope. And I don't plan to."

"You probably should."

"Why?"

Instead of answering, he holds out his phone. No, it's *Freya's* phone, and while I want to ask why he has it, I'm more interested in the headline glaring up at me from the bright screen.

"I don't really need to read about the shooting, Derek. I was there." But I skim the article anyway, glossing over the fairly factual story until my eyes catch on my name. "How do they know I was injured?" I mutter, rubbing my jaw as I keep reading. I was very clear about not letting that be part of any press releases, and I thought I was hiding it well. But I—

My heart comes to a stuttering halt in my chest when I land on the words 'older brother.' But then my brain catches up, and I let out a laugh that feels as forced as Derek's current indifference. "They're really reaching now, aren't they?" I say. When Derek says nothing, I look up.

My stomach twists.

He looks like he just got *punched* in the stomach.

I may not have known him for long, but he's good at what he does and can usually hide his real feelings. I also know he's incredibly well-informed. He wouldn't react so strongly unless...

Swallowing, I scan the article again, and I'm starting to realize why he looks so beaten down. Beaten down is the wrong phrase, but he sure looks like someone delivered a heavy blow with this tease.

"Derek," I say slowly. Not really sure if I can say anything else. But I have to. "Are they talking about you?" Because that's the only reason I can figure he would be here, standing at the top of a tower and staring at me the same way he did when we first met. Like he can't believe I exist. "But we're cousins." I tuck Freya's phone into my pocket and shake my head. "That would be enough of a twist to reveal, so why would they..."

"*Hot Scoop* always operates with a grain of truth," Derek says, his voice rough and almost too quiet to hear. "The people behind the site are vile and manipulative, but they're not stupid enough to make wild claims without something to back them up. Especially when it comes to me. They wouldn't say something like this if it wasn't..."

I clench my jaw as my thoughts race through my head, leaving me dizzy. "There's no way."

He doesn't look as convinced as I want to be.

I shake my head as my heart starts pounding in my chest. "No. No, because if we're brothers, then either my dad isn't my dad, or your mom..." I stop when he meets my gaze with a nauseous expression. "Your mom," I repeat as he grits his teeth. "She would have had to..."

Derek sinks onto a stone bench and stuffs his hands into his hair. "Sleep with her brother-in-law when I was six? Yeah." He says it like he knows it for sure happened.

I'm going to be sick. "But Dad would never..."

"Mom would. I wouldn't be surprised if she manipulated him into doing it. She's good at that."

Mom. If this is true, that would mean his mom is my... I collapse onto the bench next to him as my mind starts spinning. Dad never talked about my mom. *Never.* The only thing he told me was that she left and never looked back and that we were better off without her. She wasn't even listed on my birth certificate, like she knew from the start she wasn't going to be in my life.

"Did you know?" I whisper. Is that why Derek came to my dad's funeral? Because we're half-brothers?

But he swallows and slowly shakes his head. "No. I knew she..." He swallows again. "I knew she cheated, but my dad took me and left her only a couple of months later, after I...after he found out. We wouldn't have known if she was..."

"Pregnant," I finish, clasping my hands around the back of my neck. I don't like this. I don't like this at all, and I feel like I'm going to pass out. "If this is true, it's no wonder your dad hates mine. If he really..."

"Yeah." He sounds breathy, like he's as lightheaded as I am. "I suspected, when we met. The timing of things... But I had no way to know for sure."

I swear under my breath. He's been sitting on this for almost a year? I don't blame him for keeping it to himself, but this is kind of a big deal. "What do we do?"

"Find out if it's true, first of all. Then we figure out how *Hot Scoop* learned about it."

I look up when Derek's voice grows stronger. He looks *pissed* as he starts typing on his phone, and if ever I thought he was just a spoiled celebrity, I'm not thinking that now. He looks like a guy who can get things done, and that calms my panic enough for me to let my thoughts settle a bit.

The brother thing might not be true. It might be a tabloid making a desperate attempt for attention, and that's fine because we're still cousins no matter what happens. And if it *is* true? Then that means I have an older brother. One who protects people.

Like I do.

This doesn't have to all be on him.

Taking a deep breath, I sit up straight. "What can I do?"

Derek doesn't look up from his phone. "I've got it."

"Derek."

He pauses at my sharp tone, eyes rising to meet mine.

"What can I do?" I ask again. "This doesn't affect just you, and we're in this together."

He seems confused. Like no one has ever stepped up when he's facing a problem. That's not true—he has multiple people in his employ—but has anyone who isn't on his payroll ever helped him? Maybe he hasn't *let* them help. Besides, I meant it. If what *Hot Scoop* said is real, this isn't just about him.

I might have a *brother*.

"Let me help," I say when he still doesn't respond.

Sighing, he glances at his phone before shaking his head. "Thanks, but this will be easier on my own. I need you to look after Freya. Keep her away from the internet until we figure this stuff out."

At least he said *we*, but I don't like that he's shutting me out. "You might be able to push your friends away, but you can't do that with me. If any of this is true, then you know I can be every bit as stubborn as you."

Derek might be my brother. I'm still struggling to process that, and I'm pretty sure he is too. But he's had his suspicions for almost a year, so why am I the one keeping a cool head now? If anyone deserves to freak out, it's me.

On the wild chance that *Hot Scoop* isn't completely blowing smoke, I have a mom. One I can actually find because she's a half-brother away from me.

She also abandoned me, so there's that too.

I haven't wanted to find her before; would I really want to find her now? Derek hasn't talked about his mom before today, and I'm getting the sense he's not exactly close with the woman. I wonder if he's even spoken to her since he and his dad went off on their own.

Right before I was born.

As my mind starts spiraling into existential crisis mode—so much for a cool head—my phone buzzes in my pocket, and I pull it out to check if it's Gregor or one of the twins. Only, it's Freya's phone that buzzed, and now I'm staring at a text from Markham Grimstad, who wants to go on a walk with the princess.

Swearing, I resist the urge to chuck the phone off the tower and instead stuff it back into my pocket.

Derek, who returned his attention to his phone while I got lost in thought, frowns at me. "Something wrong?"

"Everything's wrong," I grumble back. "I got shot three days ago, you might be the brother I've always wanted, and the woman I love is being pursued by a guy who's perfect for her."

For the first time since he showed up on the roof, Derek smiles. "Should I be insulted that you lumped me in with those other two things?"

Groaning, I run a hand down my face. "*That's* the thing you focus on? The wrong part is not knowing if it's true."

"Hmm." He glances at his phone again, but whatever he was doing doesn't seem as important now as he locks his phone and gives me his full attention. "You're really in love with her?" He asks that question carefully, but I'm not sensing any of the malice that I expected after the way Freya's other friends treated me. Neither does he sound happy, but I'll take what I can get.

I shrug. "Sure feels like it, but this is a first for me. You've been in love before; what does it feel like?"

He chuckles and stretches out his legs, relaxing as well as he can on a stone bench. "What makes you think I've been in love?"

Is he serious? I gesture a hand over him, hoping that's answer enough. "You're Derek Riley. Three quarters of the world's population is in love with you, so I figured you'd returned the favor once or twice."

He lifts an eyebrow. "Three quarters?"

"I mean, there have to be at least *some* people out there who don't find you attractive."

"You realize that if we really are brothers, *Hot Scoop* was insinuating you're as attractive as me, right? *Almost*," he adds with a smirk.

What in the world is this conversation coming to? I can't help but laugh as the ridiculousness of what we're saying to each other sinks in. "I'm pretty sure that ego of yours comes from your dad's side of the family, Riley."

He kicks his foot into mine. "That's your side too, Reid."

Oh. Right. That's true regardless of whether the *Hot Scoop* claim is accurate.

This is crazy.

"Okay," I say with a tired sigh and slump against the wall. Gregor was right when he said I should rest. "I'll let you handle this tabloid crap this one time because right now I'm barely handling my one job."

"You're doing fine, El."

"Someone tried to shoot her."

"They missed."

"Because Grimstad got in the way."

Derek nudges his elbow into my ribs, and I'm so glad my wound is on my other side, or he would have nearly hit it dead on. "So did you. You took a bullet for one of my best friends, Elliot, which in my eyes means you're the right person for the job. Though, maybe don't make a habit of it?"

I chuckle. "I've been shot at enough times that I can say I'm used to it, but that doesn't mean I like it. I'm hoping no one else is stupid enough to try to hurt the best thing to ever happen to Candora."

Pressing his lips together, he stands and leans on the wall overlooking the lake. "Do you think she'll win the election?"

"I don't know," I answer honestly, joining him in taking in the view. "I think she had a solid chance, but what happened at the debate could push people in either direction. Freya survived an assassination attempt, but her opponent is the one who saved her."

He's also waiting for her to make a decision about his proposal, and I don't know her mind enough to make a bet on what she'll choose. The odds aren't in my favor, in any sense.

"What's your opinion on this Grimstad guy?" Derek asks. "You really think he's perfect for Freya?"

I can feel his eyes on me, but I keep my gaze on the view, taking in the clouds reflecting on the smooth water of the lake and the green of the rolling hills beyond. Stonemere is a good-sized city, nestled at the bottom of a hill behind us, but it isn't Invem or Windgaard. It's quieter in this part of the country, tucked away on the west coast without any other towns nearby.

I wouldn't mind living in a place like this.

"I tried so hard to hate Grimstad," I mutter, ducking my head. "It drives me nuts that he's decent. More than decent. He's a solid choice, politically and otherwise."

"But he isn't you."

"Doesn't matter. If she becomes queen, I'm not an option anyway."

Derek hums but says nothing, leaving me to my thoughts.

I can stomach the idea of being around Freya without being able to love her the way I want to, as long as she's safe and happy. But if she chooses Grimstad, how can I stay? Stand behind her while he stands at her side, his hand in hers. His lips on her lips. Him giving her an heir...

I might throw up.

"Elliot."

"Hmm?"

"You look like you're spiraling."

"Pretty much."

"Talk to me."

Sighing, I run a hand through my hair but pause when I remember Derek did the same thing a minute ago. *Brothers.* Is it any wonder why I'm falling apart? This is too much. "I don't know what to do, and I hate that. I'm supposed to be the one with the plan. And the backup to the backup plan. But this? I don't... If she were anyone else, I would tell her to marry the guy. Secure her throne however she has to because she's the best person for the job but the people might not know that."

"But she's Freya," Derek says.

I nod. "The thought of her marrying him is killing me." That's putting it lightly. "I can't give her an alternative, so I can't ask her to say no. But I want her to."

"What will you do if she accepts him?"

My phone feels heavy in my pocket, almost as heavy as Freya's phone on the other side with its looming message from Grimstad. I got another batch of texts from my old team this morning. Half of them congratulated me on helping prevent an assassination. The other half told me it meant it was time for me to come home. If I don't take the chance now, the Army will fill the open spot with someone else, and I don't think I can learn to vibe with another ODA if I go back later.

It's now or never.

"I'm not meant for a quiet life," I mutter, mostly to myself. "And I can't watch her fall in love with someone else."

My future depends on Freya and the decision she makes tonight. I'll be in agony either way, but at least one path will mean I get to see her.

"Hey." Derek nudges his shoulder into mine. "Whatever happens, I'm here for you. So are my friends, if you need them."

I raise an eyebrow at him. "Your friends, the celebrities?"

The joke doesn't get quite the same reaction from Derek as it does from Freya. He rolls his eyes rather than laughing. "I'm a celebrity too, you know."

Faking a gasp, I run my eyes over the casual clothes he's wearing as if trying to see something that isn't there. "You? Really? I find that hard to believe."

With another eye roll, he pulls his phone from his pocket and starts for the stairs. "Tell that to the three quarters of the world who are in love with me. I should go make some phone calls before the ball and get to the bottom of this *Hot Scoop* mess. Keep your phone on you in case I need you."

"Hey." I stop him before he gets to the door to the spiral staircase, but suddenly I'm nervous to say what's on my tongue. "Uh. My life is kind of imploding right now, but I'm glad I have you in my family. In whatever way."

He smiles, some of the underlying stress melting from his features. There's still plenty of it left. "Me too."

I'm jumping to conclusions, but I can't tell if he's saying he's equally glad we're family or if he's telling me his life is also imploding. I'll have to ask him later. Right now, I need to work up the motivation to tell Freya that Grimstad wants to talk to her, even though I'd rather keep them away from each other as long as I can.

More than anything, I want to be nearby when she talks to him. Just in case.

Someone has to look after her heart if things go wrong, and it might as well be me until I have to leave.

It's my job, after all.

Chapter Twenty-Nine

When I finally get my first glimpse of Elliot coming toward me from the other end of the corridor, it feels like the world suddenly comes into focus. Even more so when he smiles, like everything was shifted a few millimeters until that smile put it all right again. He is alone, and though I wonder where Derek is, I can hardly concentrate on anything but the fact that, while escorting me in my search for Elliot, my two guards stopped on the other side of the doors to the family wing to speak to Gregor.

Which means I am also very much alone.

I see the moment Elliot realizes this too, and his eyes darken as he picks up his pace to cut the distance between us. His smile turns roguish as he gets closer, and his lips form my name without making a sound.

I am not as silent, breathing out his name with relief because I no longer have a weight on my chest now that he is here.

When he reaches me, Elliot's hand finds my waist and pulls me close, his forehead pressed to mine, and he seems to breathe me in before he murmurs, "Hey, Rapunzel."

"I do not recall giving you the morning off, Mr. Reid."

His other hand presses to the other side of my waist, enveloping me and pulling me even closer. "Mm, I was following orders."

"Not mine."

"What are you going to do about it?"

Feeling reckless, I tilt my head back and let my eyes rest on his lips. "I can think of a few things."

"Freya, is that you?"

I jump back at the sound of my mother's voice coming through the ajar door on my right, my heart pounding like it always did when I was caught doing something I should not as a child. I had not noticed where in the family wing Elliot and I reached each other, but *of course* it was directly in front of my parents' sitting room.

"Yes, Mum," I squeak, wincing at the guilt in my voice, then glaring when Elliot lifts an eyebrow, as if I am the only one in the wrong. Tempted to smack him in the chest, I clear the guilt from my throat and say, "I was just speaking with Agent Storme."

"Ah, is she still here?"

My eyes lock onto Elliot's hand, which slowly inches closer to mine, and I narrow my eyes. "She agreed to stay for the ball tonight." Elliot's pinky brushes mine, electric with the contact, and I drop my voice to whisper, "You are too bold, Mr. Reid."

He smirks as his fingers lace with mine. "So I've been told."

"Come inside a moment," Mum says, breaking us apart once more. Though her voice is stern, that is normal for her and does not necessarily mean she is angry. "You as well, Mr. Reid."

With a long, worried look at Elliot, who frowns, I set my shoulders back and push open the door, stepping inside with my head held high and Elliot a few paces behind me.

Both my parents are in the sitting room, each in their usual spots on the loveseat, Dad with a cup of tea and Mum with a tablet. The sight is so familiar that it almost calms me. *Almost.* The uncompromising furrow in Mum's brow does not promise a cheery conversation, and even Dad looks a bit worried.

Swallowing, I do my best not to look like a child as I sit on a chaise opposite them. "You wish to talk?"

Mum's eyes shift to Elliot behind me. "I hope you were able to rest this morning, Mr. Reid."

"Some, Your Majesty."

"Not enough," Dad says with a soft chuckle.

"I won't disagree," Elliot replies. "Derek Riley arrived at Stonemere this morning with some news from home, so my body has been at rest, but unfortunately my mind hasn't."

I twist to look at him and note the set of his jaw and hard lines around his eyes that were not there out in the hall. "What news?" I ask, knowing it likely has to do with whatever put Derek on edge.

Though he keeps his expression neutral, Elliot cannot hide the rise in tension in his body when his eyes jump to me for only a moment. "Nothing related to you or your campaign, Your Highness."

"If you need the day," Mum says, softening in a way she rarely softens with me, "Gregor can handle security during tonight's ball."

Elliot smiles. "With all due respect, ma'am, I'm determined to stay by the princess's side whenever possible until everything with the election is settled." He looks at me again, but so briefly that I cannot read what his eyes seem to be saying.

He did not say until the *election* is settled. He is talking about everything else. Is he saying he will not take another break until my life is a little more calm, or does he not intend to stay by my side beyond that? I hate that I do not know and cannot ask. Not here.

"Yes, well, that is precisely why I called you in here, Freya." Mum sets her tablet on the table in front of her and laces her fingers together on her lap, sitting up taller, and I brace for another lecture about being too close to my bodyguard. "I wonder when you were going to tell me that Markham Grimstad offered for your hand in marriage? Before or after you made the announcement?"

For a moment, I can hear nothing but a ringing in my ears, and I am certain I heard her wrong. But I know that look in her eyes, a mixture of anger and disappointment that leaves a sting that lingers long after she has left a room. I can barely breathe, but I have enough air to whisper, "How did you find out?"

She sighs. "So, it is true?"

Should I have told her as soon as Markham proposed? Yes. Not only is she my queen, but she is my mother. An offer of marriage, particularly on the eve of an election that will change the course of my life, is not something to hide. But I did. As far as I know, there are only five people—my friends excluded—who even know about the proposal, so I ask again. "How?"

"One of the staff heard you and Derek talking this morning," Dad says, offering a sympathetic smile. "I thought you would remember that the walls have ears, dear."

There were two palace guards in the room with me. Was it one of them who opened his big mouth? I suppose it hardly matters because my father is right, and I should have been more careful.

Feeling even more like a child than when I walked in here, I drop my head. "I was going to tell you."

"When?" Mum says, her tone sharp. "As you were marching to the courthouse?"

"I haven't accepted him yet," I snap back.

"For heaven's sake, why not?"

I lift my head to stare at her, once again certain that I heard her wrong. "What?"

Mum sighs more heavily this time, glancing at Dad as if to gain strength from the sight of him alone. When that fails, she reaches for his hand and holds it tight. "What are the terms of his proposal?"

"I..." I am too confused by her last question to answer this one.

Mum looks behind me.

"He offered to step back," Elliot says, hesitation in his words. "To let Freya become the elected monarch. As her husband, he gives the people a common voice without disrupting the nature of Candora's government."

"I have not accepted him," I say again. Why is Elliot speaking as if I have?

"Which could be seen as foolish on your part," Mum says, shaking her head at me. "Markham Grimstad has given you a way to ensure your victory, and you are questioning it?"

"Questioning a marriage to a man I do not know?" I reply. "Yes! Of course!"

"You are a *princess*, Freya. You have always known your duty." Her eyes slide to Elliot again, and her brow furrows, as if she is only now remembering the conversation we had over the phone a few days ago. "What is your opinion of this, Mr. Reid?"

Do not ask him that, I silently beg her. *Do not answer that*, I beg *him*.

No matter what he says, someone is not going to like the answer.

Though I do not look at him, I can almost feel Elliot's discomfort. "This really isn't my place," he says gruffly.

"I am asking you anyway," Mum replies. "You were clearly there when Grimstad proposed, and you have spent the last two weeks at my daughter's side. Since she cannot tell me why she is hesitating, perhaps you can."

"I won't speak for her, Your Majesty."

Thank you.

"But politically, a union makes the most sense. Grimstad's reasoning was that the country is divided, and he's not wrong. Especially now. If the princess wanted to secure her place on the throne, this would be the best way to do it."

"*The princess* has her own opinions," I say, and the words taste like ice. I refuse to look back at my bodyguard after thinking he would be on my side.

Now I understand why Derek was so certain I could not discuss the matter with Elliot. What I do *not* understand is how Elliot's opinion changed so thoroughly. When Grimstad first proposed, Elliot was so against the idea that he shouted at me in the streets of Havenford. After the moments we shared in Wulfric's cabin—even out in the corridor only a minute ago—I never would have thought Elliot would encourage me to take Grimstad's hand.

I know as well as he does that the law prevents him from being an option, but... My heart seems to turn to stone in my chest as that thought becomes clear in my mind, perhaps for the first time. *Elliot was never going to be a choice I could make.* No matter how much I want him, I can never have him.

He knows this.

Maybe this is his way of letting me go. Telling me that the battle to be together is not one worth fighting.

"We know this is a big decision," Dad says, and his gentle voice settles like a warm blanket around me. "You are a lot older than we were when we were married, so the decision must feel even bigger. But a political marriage is not always so bad, and you could do far worse than Markham Grimstad. Look at how things turned out for your mother and me. We knew nothing about each other before our betrothal, and yet love grew between us."

With my heart aching over a loss I did not realize I would experience today, I glance between my parents and smile despite everything. The way they look at each other... Even my stern and stoic mother softens when she meets her husband's eyes. "Dad, you are the gentlest man in existence and have the kindest heart. How could she not love you? Markham may be kind, but he is not like you."

"And you are not like me," Mum says, turning from Dad to look at me. She has said that before, and it always felt like an insult, no matter how many times I claimed the same thing. But today, with her words soft and her gaze warmer than I have ever seen it, it almost feels like...praise. "Freya," she says, "You and I have had our differences, and I have likely been harder on you than I should have."

A laugh escapes me in a quick exhale. "Likely?"

To my surprise, she actually smiles in return. "Without question," she amends. "You have always been so eager for the throne, and I wanted to help you be the best version of yourself. But what I thought was the right path is different from the path you have forged for yourself. I have pushed you. Too often. You know my opinion, but I will not push you in this decision. I will support whatever you choose." She sits forward, her eyes turning sad. "But you must know that time is running out. With the election in two days, you need—"

"I will make the announcement tonight." Strange, how my own voice sounds foreign to me. "All of you are right, and an alliance with Grimstad is best for everyone." Standing, I ignore the surprised looks on my parents' faces and turn to Elliot, though I cannot bring myself to meet his gaze. I keep my eyes on the place where the bullet tore through him, as if that is easier to face than whatever look might be in his eyes. "Mr. Reid, if you could escort me to where Markham is staying, he and I can have a conversation before the ball."

"Actually, I need a word with Mr. Reid in private," Mum says.

Elliot slips his hand into his pocket and withdraws my phone. "You'll probably find him in the gardens," he says, holding the device out to me. He sounds wrong too, like he is speaking through a mask.

When I take my phone, his fingers brush mine and leave my hand tingling with the same electricity from before, and I wonder how long it will take before I feel that connection with Markham instead. "Thank you," I say weakly.

"There will be plenty of guards to keep an eye on you wherever you go."

"Thank you," I say again. I don't know what else I *can* say. I look up enough to see him dip his chin in response, and then I slip from the room before my emotions catch up to me.

I am making the right decision. I know I am. But that does not mean it is not going to hurt.

CHAPTER THIRTY

ELLIOT

Even after she's gone, I can't stop staring at the door that shut behind her, blocking her from view.

That conversation couldn't have gone any worse if I'd tried.

"Elliot."

I reluctantly tear my eyes from the door to face Queen Ingrid, who smiles sadly at me, like she can see right through my armor to my raw heart underneath.

"How are you? Really?"

"Healing," I reply. While that's true physically, it's going to be a long time before I can feel good about convincing Freya to choose Grimstad. That was never my plan, but the words kept spilling from my mouth. It's not like I really expected her to make a different decision. I just...hoped.

"We have not had a chance to properly thank you for keeping our little girl safe.," Stellan says, and tears form in his eyes.

"You protected her with your life," Ingrid adds. "As you promised. For that we owe you so much."

I drop my chin. "You don't owe me anything. I was doing my job."

"We all know she is more than a job to you, Elliot."

Though afraid of what I'll find, I lift my gaze to Ingrid and feel something in me settle when I look at her. For the first time, she seems to have let her guard down and is fully letting me see the emotions she always keeps hidden, and her expression is one I've never seen directed at me. It's...motherly.

I was prepared to defend myself and refute any accusations that I crossed a line with Freya, one I shouldn't have even come close to. But this? I don't know what to do with this.

Ingrid tilts her head. "I wondered, after all the pictures, but I knew for sure when you spoke well of the union with Grimstad. You love her." It's not a question.

I shake my head anyway. "I can't love her."

"Why not?" Stellan asks.

Staring at him, I pull my eyebrows low. "I'm an American."

"Unfortunately," Ingrid says with a small smile. "But Americans have feelings, yes?"

"Feelings don't overwrite laws."

The queen's eyes travel over me. "I did not expect you to think so small, Elliot."

I don't know what she means by that, but I have another argument ready. "She picked Grimstad."

"Did she?" Stellan looks at his wife thoughtfully.

"Yes," I practically growl. "She did."

"She gave in too easily," Ingrid says.

"Easily?" I scoff, staring at the pair of them like I'm seeing them for the first time. They may be a king and queen, but they're really just flawed human beings like everyone else. "You think any of that was *easy* for her? She's only had time to think about the proposal for a *week*, on top of figuring out a campaign she wasn't prepared for, all to try to earn the one thing she's wanted her whole life, and then someone goes and shoots at her and reminds her that until she has an heir, the entire way of life for her country is at risk unless one of your sons sacrifices his life the way she did, which she would never expect them to do because she's the most selfless person I've ever known."

Suddenly her voice is in my head, words spoken in a whisper that made me feel more alive than I had in over a year when she first spoke them. *Let me have this moment for myself.* Seconds before she asked me to kiss her. The one time she was selfish, and she went above and beyond, stealing my heart from my chest and refusing to give it back.

"Freya's not going to change her mind," I say when neither monarch responds to my rant. Surely they know that.

My phone buzzes, and I slip it from my pocket to see a text from Derek, asking if I can meet him at the outer gates. Either he found something or he has a plan, and the distraction will be nice. Maybe I've lost the love of my life, but there's a good chance I'm gaining a brother through all of this.

Sighing, I return my focus to Ingrid and Stellan. "She made her choice. Now I have to make mine."

Chapter Thirty-One

Freya

I CAN ADMIT THAT I enjoy a good party now and then, and the Celestial Ball was always a favorite of mine when I was a girl. As a celebration of Candora's formation, when the many warring clans met together under the midnight sky and agreed to peace under the rule of the first Alverra king, this ball has been a tribute to our history since the beginning. A way to look back at our past written in the stars and see how far we have come.

But tonight feels different.

I have been greeting guests and dodging questions for the last hour, and I finally have a moment to myself thanks to my mother pulling the Duke of Rensvik into a conversation after he cornered me to talk about the Equine Festival again. I think she could see my patience ready to snap, and I am grateful to her for rescuing me.

She has been very...sweet...to me since our conversation this morning. Enough so that I am more suspicious than relieved, like she knows something I do not. I thought she would be happy with my decision—marrying Markham is what she would have done in my situation—but every time our gazes meet, there seems to be a sort of sadness behind her eyes. She is making me nervous, even though she assured me everything was ready for me to announce my intentions with Markham.

Playing with the crescent-shaped silver cuff on my wrist, I use my brief reprieve to look out over the ballroom. Whoever planned this year's event, they have certainly outshone years past, and there is so much to admire. My gaze starts at the top, drawn to the canopy of twinkling lights strung overhead, but it is the sparkling chandelier that always takes center stage. It was designed to mimic the night sky and its constellations, and I spent hours as a young girl trying to map them all, mesmerized by the way each crystal catches the light.

Deep blue banners emblazoned with the Candoran and Alverra crests and a smattering of silver-threaded stars line the walls, and all of the windows and doors on the east side of the room are open to the night. A small orchestra in the corner plays Candora's more traditional ballroom songs, while nobles and politicians and notable figures mingle and dance in their finery. The air is heavy with the fragrance of roses and hyacinth and the fresh scent of the lake beyond the terrace. Something else too. It smells like the end of summer.

The end of my world as I know it.

The Celestial Ball marks a time of remembrance and tradition, but it also heralds growth and change. Change for the better, I hope.

I fiddle with my cuff again. I made the right choice.

"Are you calculating if you can run?" A nudge at my elbow pulls my eyes to my brother next to me. He is looking at me with an amused smile, and while the twins in tuxes are nearly impossible to tell apart, I am certain this is Sander.

I smooth my hand along my sparkling midnight-blue gown, hoping to hide my nerves. "Not unless you think I need to. Mum already rescued me from Rensvik."

We both look over at our mother, whose unbreakable exterior is beginning to crack as the duke regales her with talk of who knows what. She should have brought Dad with her when she glided across the ballroom to get to me; he can sit and listen to practically anyone while remaining unfailingly polite.

Sander's eyes drift to the two guards standing a few meters behind me. "No Elliot tonight?"

"No." Despite what he told my mother this morning about staying by my side, I have not seen Elliot since I left him with my parents, and I am worried. Rothesby, one of my guards for the day, said Elliot has been dealing with a problem and not to worry, but his reassurance did little to comfort me.

"Where is Hex?" I ask to keep my thoughts from getting stuck on my bodyguard. "I have barely seen him tonight." In truth, I have barely seen anyone aside from the endless stream of nobles hoping to add their voices to the chorus of well-wishes and scandalized fear mongering. I have been quite occupied. For the most part, that has been intentional.

It is harder to be nervous when I have no time to think.

Sander grunts and nods to the middle of those dancing a traditional Candoran country dance. "Agent Storme is here tonight, so I would imagine he's hiding from her."

"Is there some history there that I don't know about?"

"We were in school together."

"Oh."

Unlike me, who had private tutors until I went to university, Hex and Sander chose to go to secondary school and then to a highly rated college in Invem after their exams at sixteen. But they did not go to university, so if they were in school with the RIA agent I spoke to this morning, it would have been when they were teenagers. I was in Paris then and not as close to my brothers as I am now, so I can only imagine the terrors they were back then.

"My condolences to her," I say with as straight a face as I can muster.

Sander chuckles. "She can hold her own, which is why Hex is hiding."

"She is still trying to convince him to join the RIA?"

"Yes, but he won't do it."

I turn to my brother, tilting my head. "Why is he so against it?" That is a question I should ask Hex, and I have, but his answer changes every time. Sander will know the real reason.

Clenching his jaw, he watches the dancers for a long moment as if debating with himself. "Because he doesn't think he's good enough," he says eventually.

My mouth falls open. "What? *Hex*?"

He shrugs and drops his gaze to his feet. "Too wild to be a proper prince, too royal to be a proper palace guard. Never good enough. The RIA would be no different for him."

"But that is—"

"It's hard to feel worthy when you know they let you win the fight. When no one ever looks at you and sees a king."

Oh. I press a hand over my heart as I see a part of my brother I have never seen before. He is not talking about Hex anymore. "Do...do you want to be a king, Sander?"

He snorts a laugh and shakes his head, looking out over the ballroom again. "Not in a million years." His eyes start to trail someone, and I follow his gaze to find Agent Storme in the sea of blue. "But no one ever wondered if I *could*."

Apparently there are a lot of things I have missed about my brothers. Maybe, when this is all over, I can find time to figure out who they really are beneath the carefree facades. I wish I could do that *now*, but I have a country to inform about my engagement.

"So, you chose him?" Sander says, clearly ready to turn the conversation away from himself. He nods to our right, where Markham is deep in discussion with a few members of Lords.

As surprised as I am to see the nobles talking to Markham so readily, I am not in the least surprised that I feel nothing when my future husband looks up at me and smiles.

I force a smile in return. "I accepted his proposal, yes."

"That's not what I asked." Sander turns to face me, eyebrows low. "You chose Grimstad over Elliot."

The hole that has been forming in my chest all day grows a little bigger. "Elliot was never a choice."

"He was always a choice. From the very start."

Scoffing, I grab handfuls of my gown, as if holding the silky blue fabric might steady me. "I tried to send him away at the start."

Sander rolls his eyes. "You and I both know he would have been gone on day one if you'd really wanted it. You're Freya Alverra, and you can make anything happen." His attention catches on something over my head, and he narrows his eyes. "Why is the actor here?"

I turn to see Derek standing at the edge of the ballroom in a tuxedo, looking for all the world as if he belongs here as he surveys the room. Gone are the exhaustion and anxiety from before, leaving behind an untouchable Hollywood superstar. "Derek is my friend," I say, suddenly desperate to know what he and Elliot learned today. Did they fix the problem, or is that what Elliot has been 'dealing with'? Derek would not be this calm if it was still an issue.

"A man who lies about who he is is not a friend you should keep," Sander all but growls. "He's not the perfect man you think he is, Freya." Before I can respond, he stalks in Derek's direction, presumably to say something similar to Derek's face.

I should try to stop him, but I let him go to avoid making a scene. I know that Derek is not perfect, no matter what he lets the world see, but lying? Putting up a front to protect oneself is not the same as intentional deceit, and Derek has his reasons for keeping so many shields up all the time. Perhaps someday he will tell me what those reasons are, but I know better than anyone that he has to share on his own terms.

Thankfully, Sander is waylaid by Agent Storme before he ever reaches Derek, and as the pair of them speak and head in the opposite direction, I use the opportunity to walk toward my friend, hopefully to get at least one answer today that does not make me feel worse.

I make it three whole steps before Hex intercepts me, and though his eyes are on Agent Storme's retreating back, I feel the full brunt of his sharp words. "How could you do it?"

Will I not get any peace today? Taking a steadying breath, I wait until my frustration settles. "Do what, Hendrick?"

Only when he seems certain he has avoided the RIA agent does he shift his glare to me. "Send Elliot away. If you're not willing to admit that you're in love with him yet, that's fine, but—"

"Wait." Putting my hand on his arm, I have to fight through a wave of dizziness that washed over me as soon as he said Elliot's name. "What do you mean, send him away? I didn't send him anywhere!" The last time I saw Elliot was in my parents' sitting room, and... "No." I grip his arm tighter as I realize why my mother seems so concerned whenever she looks at me. "Mum sacked him? But he didn't do anything wrong! Why would she fire him if he was the best protector I have ever had? If she found out about the kiss we shared, then I should take the blame. I'm the one who asked him to—"

"Mum?" Hex wrinkles his nose at me, but the longer he looks at me, the more he seems to be putting together pieces of a puzzle I cannot see. "No, Freya," he says, gentler now. "You picked Grimstad and broke Elliot's heart, so now's he going back to the Special Forces because he's a bloody hero and can't learn to keep himself out of danger."

"Back to the Special Forces?" I whisper, panic rising in my throat. "But he can't leave."

"He can, and I don't blame him if he does." Hex frowns at me. "Did you really expect him to stay at your side and watch you devote yourself to another man? Elliot's a solid bloke, but no one is that perfect." He looks behind me and groans. "Except *he* must be if you chose *him* for the rest of your life."

Completely overwhelmed, I spin around right as Markham reaches my side and cups my elbow with his palm, looking at me with concern.

"Freya, are you alright?"

I am far from alright, but I can barely process my thoughts let alone explain my panic to Markham. I *did* expect Elliot to stay by my side, selfish as that is. After he all but told me I should make the choice I did, I thought we could find a new normal and move forward as friends.

I thought I could learn to shift my affection from him to Markham.

With the way my heart pounds now at the mere thought of Elliot leaving, that change will not be so easy.

"Freya," Markham says again, moving his hand from my elbow to the small of my back. "You're pale."

I look at Hex, who clenches his jaw and looks down. Disappointed.

"Freya," my mother says behind me, choosing the worst possible moment to interrupt. "It is nearly time to make your announcement."

Already? My eyes dart around the room. Looking for an escape? No. I made this choice. It is what Candora needs.

"Let's give her a moment, Your Majesty," Markham says, pressing his hand harder into my back. For support, I assume, but I feel crowded and want to shrink away from his touch.

I find Derek in the same place he was before. His gaze is already on me, worry in his eyes, and he steps toward me, ready to come tell me what to do. But a hand lands on his shoulder, holding him in place as someone...

"Elliot," I whisper. *He's here.*

Elliot holds Derek back as he comes into view with his eyes focused on me. Everything around him seems to fade, leaving my full attention fixed on where he stands. His tux matches Derek's, but something about his bearing makes him look more impressive than his cousin, and I cannot help but compare the two of them as they stand next to each other.

When I first learned of their family connection, I could see the similarities, but this is the first time I have seen them side by side. Derek, with his dark hair and blue eyes, has a more striking appearance, while Elliot's lighter hair and brown eyes give him a softer feel. But they have the same jawline, and their noses look almost identical. As Derek leans closer to Elliot to mutter something in his ear, they get the same wrinkle between their eyebrows.

"Vitte," Hex says, "they're practically the same person." He must be seeing what I am.

"Hendrick," Mum scolds, "that language is unbecoming of a Prince of Candora." But her fingers are on her jaw as she also studies the two men.

"Who is that with Reid?" Markham asks. "A brother?"

"Derek Riley," I say with a frown. "Elliot's...cousin."

Both Derek and Elliot notice my frown and step forward, pausing to look at each other before Derek nods and urges Elliot onward.

I do not take a breath until Elliot reaches our little gathering, stopping on Hex's other side so I am surrounded by the four of them. If I felt crowded before, now I am entirely trapped.

"Your Highness," Elliot says and bows to me.

Has he ever bowed to me? His head, perhaps, but never a formal bow like this. It feels wrong to see him bent at the waist, a fist over his heart.

"Where have you been?" I ask, the words coming out shaky.

As he stands, Elliot's eyes shift from Hex to Markham to my mother in quick succession, then land on me. His expression shows me very little of what he is feeling, but Hex called him heartbroken. If that were true, surely he would not look so indifferent. "Forgive me, Your Highness. I had something unavoidable come up, but I'm here now."

Stop calling me that. Those are the words I want to say, but they stick in my throat. Along with others. *I don't want you to leave.*

But I cannot ask him to stay. Maybe Hex was wrong about the state of Elliot's heart, but he was right about this. If I am choosing Markham, I need to let Elliot go.

"We are glad to have you with us for however long we can, Elliot," Mum says, then puts her hand on my shoulder. "As I was saying, Freya, if you are going to make your announcement, now is the time. Before we release the lanterns."

"Yes." Forcing my eyes from Elliot, I take a slow breath and turn to the man at my side. "You still want this?" I ask Markham.

Though his injured arm is in a sling, a reminder of him throwing his body between mine and a bullet, Markham stands tall and strong. He will be good for Candora. "I want this if you want this," he says, moving his hand from my back to offer his arm to hold.

As I slip my arm through his, my fingers start to tremble. It is only because this is a big decision, and there is no way to know how the people of Candora will react. Not because I am making a mistake. Uniting like this will take away their chance to choose their leader, but everyone will have a voice. That is what matters.

Unable to find *my* voice, I nod at my mother.

A familiar disappointment wrinkles the corners of her eyes, but she nods in return and leads the way to the stage. She will give her toast to a prosperous year, as she does every year at the Celestial Ball, and then I will stand before my country with Markham at my side.

Announce our engagement.

Secure my future as queen.

Arm in arm, Markham and I stand to the side as my mother steps up to the microphone with my father behind her. I have watched her make this speech time after time, and she has never been anything but poised and regal, a true queen through and through. Tonight, however, her shoulders lack their usual rigidity. Her always smooth forehead is lined with uncertainty. Despite the attention of hundreds of people, she looks over at me, then at Markham. The sadness in her eyes deepens as her gaze travels to something behind us.

I turn just in time to see a flash of pain on Elliot's face before his mask slips back into place, leaving him emotionless once more. He is looking at the queen, not at me, but he must feel my stare because his eyes meet mine, and I get another glimpse of his pain.

It mirrors mine.

"As you all know," Mum says finally, "I have decided to step down as Candora's queen, a decision I did not make lightly. Our country has a rich history of peace and prosperity, in part because Candorans have always valued our heritage and traditions passed through the ages. As my ancestors have done before me, I have been honored to uphold those traditions through an ever-changing world.

"But my time is over. Today we celebrate a day when our leaders united for a single cause, and many became one. When Osric Alverra took on the mantle of the first Candoran king, some saw his action as a quest for power over the clans, but I believe it was the opposite. Osric gave everything to ensure his people would thrive and be happy. As a Queen of Candora, I have shared Osric's sacrifice and given years of my life to this country. I willingly gave my time, my energy, and my very soul to this country, and I have only had one regret."

She looks over at me again, and her eyes glisten with tears that she will not let fall because Ingrid Alverra is too strong to cry. I, on the other hand, tear up instantly at the sight of her pain. Mum has never talked of regrets, and though she is speaking to an entire country, deep down I know she is mostly speaking to me. Whatever she wants me to hear, it must be important, so I stand frozen. Waiting.

"I regret not having more time with my family," she says without the strength of her earlier words, and yet each one pierces my heart. "I love Candora more than I can say, and I would give my life a hundred times over to protect my people. But so many times, I wish I had had the courage to set aside my duty to be with those I love most.

"Candora is full of people who love hard and treat each other with kindness, and that inherent goodness has made me proud to be your queen. But somehow, while wearing the Candoran crown, I forgot what it means to truly be Candoran. More than a nationality, to be Candoran is to be true to your heart. To listen, learn, and love fully instead of letting fear hold you back. To remember that you will always have a whole country to stand with you and offer support when you need it most."

I don't know when I make the decision to leave. Somewhere in the middle, I think, when she speaks of duty and love. At first, I move slowly, ignoring Markham's whispered question as I slip from his arm and through the crowd to the nearest door, one taking me outside to the terrace that overlooks the lake. Mum's words wash over me from the speakers overhead as I go, every line settling deep inside me and fueling my need to escape, and the instant I step beyond the stone walls, I can no longer hold back.

I run.

CHAPTER THIRTY-TWO

FREYA

CROSSING THE TERRACE AS quickly as I can, I run to the stairs, down to the ground level and past guards who call after me but do not follow. Not when shouted orders to stay at their posts follow me instead.

I should have known Elliot would come after me, but when I reach the edge of the lake and stumble to a halt to face him, the sight of him bathed in moonlight still makes my heart pound in my chest. Seeing Markham at his side disarms me almost as forcefully. Fighting to draw air into my lungs, I look from one man to the other and silently beg one of them to choose for me. To tell me what to do because I have never been so torn.

With a long, meaningful look between him and Markham, Elliot is the first to move, ducking his head and stepping back until he is out of earshot. Then he turns, keeping me in his periphery but showing me that he will not read any of this conversation on my lips. I almost wish he would, but I am grateful for the privacy nonetheless.

Markham looks more unsure than I have ever seen him, his brow furrowed and his eyes on the soil at his feet, and the man who always knows what to say remains silent.

Which means, in Elliot's words, I have to 'suck it up and keep moving forward.'

I take a shaky breath, not knowing what to say. "How is your arm?"

Markham glances at his sling, then at me, and a small smile plays on his mouth. "Could be worse."

"I am sorry you ever had to take that bullet for me."

"I would do it again in a heartbeat." Ducking his head again, he scuffs the toe of his shoe in the dirt. "I've always firmly believed that the mark of a good leader is someone willing to sacrifice their wants and needs for the good of others."

Tears well in my eyes again, and I blink them away. "I agree with you."

He lifts his head, fixing me with a look of so much raw emotion that I could hardly put a name to it. Sadness and love and fear and admiration all rolled into something beautiful and heartbreaking. "But not like this." He gestures between us, and each breath he takes seems to tuck away more and more of that emotion leaving him vulnerable until he is the man I first met. Nothing but calm confidence that reminds me so much of Derek. "Freya, I can't let you do this."

I barely breathe as I stand there in the moonlight. "I made my choice, Markham. I gave you a promise."

"Then let me be the one to break it. This is not a sacrifice I can allow when you and I both know you don't want to be married to me."

"You are a good man," I say, needing him to know that. "And you would be a good husband."

"I think so too." He smiles, then shakes his head. "But not yours. Your heart belongs to someone else, Freya, and I won't get in the way of that."

"You are making this too easy," I complain. Not that I want him to make it difficult, but do I really deserve his kindness after everything?

Chuckling, he steps forward and presses a kiss to my forehead, leaving me feeling entirely inadequate because he has never been anything but *good*. "Friends?"

I brush a tear from my cheek, wishing I had been stronger. "Of course." Though he turns to go back inside, I call his name to stop him. "No matter what happens in the election, Candora needs you."

With a smile and a soft, "Maybe," he continues on his way to the stairs, offering Elliot a small nod and a few muttered words as he passes.

Elliot and I both watch him go, and when Markham disappears, Elliot turns to me with his eyes full of questions. He looks the part of a soldier right now, his arms clasped behind his back and his shoulders taut, and I wonder if a part of him *wants* to go back to the Army. His brothers-in-arms are there—his family—and I have often thought his talents are wasted on looking after a stubborn princess like me. He carries pain from the loss of his friend, but I have caused him pain here too.

Wrapping my arms around myself as the night air cools my skin, I search for something to say. This is harder than it was with Markham, and I don't know how this conversation is going to end.

"What happened with you and Derek?" I ask, and though my voice is too quiet for him to hear me from this distance, he seems to read my question easily enough.

A smile lifts the corner of his mouth, catching me off guard. With a quick glance at the empty grounds, he comes toward me. Each step makes my heart beat faster and leaves me desperate to tell him how things ended with Markham.

He speaks before I can, stopping at least a meter away from me. Farther than I would like. "*Hot Scoop* posted a story this morning and hinted that I might not be as alone as I thought when it comes to my family."

"*Hot Scoop* hints at a lot of things." More confused than anything, I step forward to close some of the space between us. He doesn't stop me, so I take another step. "Besides, you are not alone. Your cousin is right inside." I wave toward the house.

Elliot catches my hand mid-wave, and he seems to relax as he curls his fingers around mine. "According to *Hot Scoop*, I have a brother."

Though my stomach twists, I remind myself of all the lies the silly tabloid has claimed to be true. "Oh?"

His smile grows. "According to the blood test Derek and I took earlier today, *Hot Scoop* is right. Well, half right."

"I don't understand," I admit, in part because his smile is becoming rather distracting. "You have a half-brother? But who..." The rest of what he said hits me all at once, and my jaw drops. "Derek? But how did *Hot Scoop*—"

"I'm happy to tell you everything, Rapunzel." His voice drops lower, almost into a growl, as he tugs me closer and says, "But do you really want to talk about Derek right now?"

A shiver runs through me from the way he's looking at me. "No," I say, breathless. "No, we have much more important things to discuss." Movement on the terrace catches my eye, and I realize everyone is coming outside to release the ceremonial lanterns into the sky. Any of them could look down to the lake and see us, and that is the last thing I want. Gripping Elliot's hand, I start pulling him down the shoreline toward one of my favorite places in Stonemere. "But not here."

CHAPTER THIRTY-THREE

ELLIOT

I have no idea where we're going, but it's really hard to care when Freya keeps a tight hold on my hand as she leads the way down a moonlit gravel path that follows the lakeshore. While I'm doing my best not to get my hopes up until I have solid evidence that things are going the way I hope, Grimstad's parting words to me as he walked by held a lot of implications.

"Take care of her."

I'm her bodyguard, so he could have been telling me to do my job. But Grimstad knows he doesn't need to tell me that; I have a bullet wound to match his, proving I'm pretty committed to my post.

When we reach a thicket of trees on the far edge of the grounds, Freya takes a sharp right toward the lake, nearly pulling me off balance from the sudden change in direction. I can't see much as the moon disappears through the leaves, but my feet hit wood only moments before the trees open up to reveal a long dock stretching out over the water.

Dropping my hand, Freya stops at the dock's edge, and a quick glance back tells me the trees are dense enough to block us from view of the house. Another good sign, but I still refuse to jump to conclusions.

I was so certain that Freya would step onto that stage inside and confidently tell the world that she was making the mistake of marrying a man she didn't love. I was wrong about her not changing her mind, and if I'm wrong about this too, I'm not sure I'll make it out the other side.

Until she says the words, I have to operate under the assumption that nothing has changed.

But now that we've stopped moving—now that we're alone—I can't take my eyes off the princess. From the first moment I saw her at the start of the ball, she was breathtaking, and I spent a long time watching her from a security lookout while I worked up the courage to be in the same room as her. Derek called me a coward—I nearly punched him in the nose for that—and went down to enjoy the ball, and I stood there in awe of this woman.

Seeing her inside and from a distance was nothing compared to now.

She's always beautiful, but right now, her shimmery blue dress hugs her curves and makes her look taller. In the moonlight, her skin is porcelain, her hair a creamy white, and the tiara on her head glitters like stars. When she turns to face me, her cheeks are flushed with color and leave me breathless.

"Hex said you're leaving," she whispers as her eyes rove over me, sparking a trail of heat in their wake.

If she had looked at me like this before I put in my notice, I never would have been able to say the words. I swallow. "I was."

"Was?" Her gaze is so hopeful that my heart feels like it's going to beat out of my chest.

Forcing a breath, I slide my hands into my pockets to keep them from doing things they shouldn't. "That kind of depends on what you said to Grimstad back there."

Freya smiles. "I told him I would not break my promise."

That's why I didn't let myself hope. "I see."

"*He* called off the engagement."

So, she would have gone through with it if he hadn't stepped back. That...hurts. Blowing out a breath, I try for a cheery tone as I say, "Okay, he's a good enough guy that he's allowed to be picky, but pretty much anyone is going to be a step down from a princess, so I don't know why he would—"

"He knew my heart already belonged to someone and could never be his."

My body freezes, and I stare at her while I try to come up with any meaning for what she just said other than the one I want. Anything that might give me a reason to doubt. I've got nothing, unless she's about to tell me that she's been in love with Derek this whole time, in which case she might as well take my heart out of my chest and stomp on it a few times.

With another breathtaking smile, Freya steps close and brushes her fingertips along my jaw with a painfully light touch, and it's all I can do not to wrap her up in my arms. I still don't know where this is going, and Freya taught me to take my time. Think things through before I act. "You are beautiful, Elliot Reid."

A curse slips off my tongue, and I take a step back, away from her reach, so I can breathe. Think. "You're not marrying Grimstad," I say because I'm not sure I believe it.

She shakes her head. "It would not have been fair to either of us."

"'Either of us,' meaning...?" I hold my breath and wait.

Freya's eyes seem to glitter in the moonlight, just like her crown. "You and me, Elliot."

I swear again and run a hand through my hair. I'm on the verge of hyperventilating and struggle to get any words out. "So, you're not... I mean, you're..." Drop me in freezing waters in enemy territory and make me swim a mile in full gear? No problem. Ask me to figure out the feelings of the woman I love? Impossible.

Chuckling, she touches the jewels strung around her neck. "I am unattached. Well, I suppose that isn't necessarily true, given I am very much attached to you, but technically speaking, you and I haven't discussed the particulars of what we are, so it's hard to say if—"

"Stop talking."

She blinks, caught off guard by my rough command, and lifts a delicate eyebrow. "Did I say something wrong? I was only saying—"

"Stop."

She narrows her eyes. "How quickly you forget that I do not take orders from—"

"*Freya.*" On that exasperated word, I lunge forward and grab her, pressing my lips to hers because it's probably the only way to shut her up.

Completely empty of self-control, I kiss Freya with everything I've got, wrapping my arm around her waist and pulling her against my body. Her hands slide into my hair, tugging a growl out of me, and I do everything I can to get her closer. My hand is on her back, at her neck, in her hair, tangling in the thick tresses and getting stuck but I don't care.

I thought I was falling for her, but this doesn't feel like falling.

I've hit the bottom so hard that I may never recover.

A thunderous explosion booms overhead, and Freya pulls back, leaving me bereft without her mouth on mine. The large gold firework reflects in her eyes when she looks up, and I am completely awestruck. I've never seen a more beautiful sight.

"I'm in love with you," I say, struggling to find the air to get the words out as more fireworks join the first.

Freya's gaze drops back to me, her expression turning unreadable. Is she afraid? Sad? Nervous? I can't tell.

I tuck a loose bit of hair behind her ear. Her hair is a mess, but I can fix it later. "I'm sorry for saying that." Then I shake my head, berating myself. "No, I'm not sorry. I love you. I know things are complicated, but I—"

She slams into me, knocking me back a step as her lips lock with mine again, and then she's deepening the kiss and pulling herself flush against my body. She kisses with a wild passion, and I can barely keep up, and it's the best thing I've ever experienced. It's better than that first moment when you jump from a plane at twenty thousand feet in the dead of night, and you don't know how far the ground is below you but you don't care because there's nothing like the exhilaration of the freefall. I feel weightless but with my feet firmly on solid ground, and her kiss is more familiar than anything I've known.

I never want her to stop.

She pulls away—of course she does—but keeps her arms around my neck and her fingers in the hair at the base of my skull as she looks at me. "I think we're beyond complicated, Elliot," she admits. I don't hear her through the fireworks, but I read the words on her swollen lips. "I don't know what comes next."

Wrapping her in a tight hug, I speak in her ear so she'll hear me. "It doesn't matter. You're going to be a queen. I can't predict the future, but I do know right now."

The sounds of the fireworks fade, leaving the world in a tenuous silence I'm almost afraid to break. But I have more to say, so I gently push Freya back so I can look her in the eyes. "No matter what happens in two days, I will stand by your side, Freya. Wherever you go, whoever you become, I will always protect you. Your body." I run my hand down her arm. "Your heart." I touch a finger to the soft skin just below her collar bone. "Your mind." I press my forehead to hers and close my eyes. "No matter what."

"So, you are not leaving?"

I chuckle. "Assuming there's a grace period for resignations, no. I don't think I could have left anyway, even if you did marry Grimstad." I could have gone to the farthest reaches of the earth, and my heart still would have stayed behind in Candora.

"Elliot." Freya waits until I open my eyes, then she smiles, gliding her fingers across my face, from my temple to my cheek, my nose to my jaw. The touch is as featherlight as the last time and completely maddening, and I never want her to stop. Then her fingers find my lips, and I'm done for. "I don't think I would have *let* you leave. You are stubborn, but I am worse."

Cursing under my breath, I tuck my hand behind her neck and drag her mouth back to mine. Who needs oxygen when there is kissing to be done? I could get lost in the taste of her.

Freya breaks the kiss far too soon and plants her hand over my mouth before I can try to keep it going. "Elliot, are you sure you know what you're getting into? I'm not—"

Grabbing her wrist, I tug her hand down and steal a quick kiss. Then another. And then I kiss her long and slow until I think my body might burst from the tension of it, and only then do I pull away.

"Freya Isolde Marit Alverra, I know exactly who you are."

"Vitte," she breathes and grabs me, exploring my mouth with her own like there's something she's looking for. Her next words are spoken against my lips like a prayer. "Elliot Parker Reid, your tongue is dangerous around my name."

I grin. "Only then?"

"*Foren skaar og himlen!*" Freya follows her Candoran exclamation with another kiss that is almost enough to completely mute my thoughts.

But I have enough mental capacity left to translate: *For heaven's sake and the skies*. I can't hold back my laugh, even when Freya is doing her best to keep me distracted.

My laughter finally breaks us apart, and I get my first good look at the princess since I first kissed her. Her dress looks mostly unrumpled, tight as it is, but everything else about her, from her makeup to her hair, makes it extremely obvious that she was kissed senseless.

Biting my lip, I reach up and gently free the tiara from her head, the first step to making her look presentable again. Freya wraps her fingers around my wrist to pause my movements, and together we look down at the jeweled silver crown I'm holding between us. The air around us, a moment ago charged with heat and passion and warm words, starts to cool, but not in a bad way.

It's more like we're sinking back into reality, and there's one piece of the future that we should probably talk about before this thing between us goes any further. Like before, Freya has made her choice. I need to make mine.

Chapter Thirty-Four

Freya

How is a girl supposed to recover from kissing Elliot Reid? I feel as if my head is no longer attached to my body, and if I let go of his arm, I will float away and vanish in a flash of sodium and potassium, my own little firework.

Elliot lifts my tiara with the hand I am not holding captive and balances it on his own head, and I nearly die of asphyxiation at the sight. "Come here," he says, gently taking me by the arms and turning me around so my back is to him. Then his hands are in my hair, removing pin after pin and letting my waves fall down my back.

Inexplicably, I start to cry, an unfortunate reaction that is made worse when my eyes catch on the dozens of lanterns coming into view overhead and in the water's reflection. Softly glowing with flickering light, they float from the house and slowly sink toward the lake, surrounding us in the most beautiful sight I have ever seen. I have come to this ball each year for much of my life, but never have I felt this way, like nothing will ever go wrong again.

It is all because of the man behind me.

Once he has removed all the pins, his fingers start working their way across my scalp in a soothing motion, and my breaths come in tremors as my tears fall more freely. I feel so cherished. Cared for. *Loved.*

A sob breaks free, and I can no longer hide my overwhelming emotion.

"Hey, whoa." Elliot wraps his arms around me and pulls me into his chest. Instantly I feel entirely warm and safe and never want to leave. "What's wrong, Rapunzel?"

My tears are replaced by a soft laugh when I realize I am standing in a moment so like the one experienced by a fictional princess from an animated movie. All we are missing is a boat, but a dock will have to do. "Rapunzel," I whisper. "How fitting."

His embrace tightens. "Why are you crying?"

"Because I am happy."

"Maybe it's the American male in me talking, but I'm pretty sure tears are usually a sad thing."

I lean my head back, resting it against his solid body. He presses a kiss to my temple, and I close my eyes before the moment overwhelms me again. "You are wearing a crown." I know it is to keep my tiara safe, but I cannot help but imagine...

He chuckles, and I feel his laughter in my back. "It's not really my color, but I can see why you like to wear it."

"I hate wearing it," I argue. "I feel pretentious."

"As long as I won't be alone in that, I'll be happy."

Gasping, I spin in his arms, nearly knocking the tiara off his head. He grabs it to hold it in place, and again I am so struck by the sight of him looking so royal that for a moment I cannot find my words. "Elliot, what are you saying?"

He smiles despite my obvious distress. "I already said it. I go where you go."

"And if I become queen?"

"Then I'll figure out how this royalty thing works, assuming you still like me in a decade after I get citizenship." He is so calm about it. Children pretend all the time to be kings and queens, but when they grow up they realize that it is not the life of leisure they thought when they were young. Elliot already admitted his fear of being a king, and he has not spent his life preparing for the pressure like I have.

My tears start up again. "Elliot, I cannot ask you to—"

"You didn't ask. I'm choosing." He brushes a finger along my cheek. "I'm choosing you no matter how crazy your life might get."

"Why?" I gasp and drop my face into his chest to hide. "Don't answer that. What a terrible question!"

His fingers find their way back into my hair, taking up a slow rhythm against my scalp once more. Runa touches my hair all the time, but no one has ever played with it like this. No one has ever held me like this before. My friends are surprisingly affectionate for how private they are, but this is nothing like the way they embrace me.

"Maybe it's crazy, but I love you, Freya, and I want to have a front row seat when you rise to greatness in a few days. Whether it's as your bodyguard or something more, I want to be there for you. Is that okay?"

"Okay?" I whisper back. "No one has ever... I... You would really be a king?"

His lips press against the top of my head, and I open my eyes to watch the last of the lanterns drift away or fizzle out when they hit the water. The night is coming to an end.

"I'm not saying I'd be good at it," Elliot says, his voice softer now to match the quieting world around us. "And I'm not saying it doesn't still terrify me. But I've dodged sniper fire for three hours straight and climbed a hundred-foot cliff with a fractured ankle. How much worse could running a country be? Besides." He kisses my temple, then my cheek, my jaw, and starts up a trail from the shell of my ear down my neck, leaving me in shivers as I tilt my head back to give him better access. "I'd be standing beside a pretty incredible queen."

He sounds so confident. Then again, Elliot usually sounds confident. Intelligent as he is, there is still so much he does not know about being royalty. That says nothing about how the Candoran people might react to an American king in the first place, regardless of the limited power he would actually hold. Elliot can say he will do whatever it takes to be with me, but can he really mean that without knowing exactly what we are facing?

Perhaps it does not matter. It will likely be years before we can marry, and so much could change in that time. We will have to take this one day at a time. "Elliot?"

"Hmm?" His kisses stop, though he lingers with his lips against my skin.

Running my hand through his hair and gently pushing his head back so we can look at each other, I offer up a weak smile and touch my hand to his cheek. "Thank you. For tonight. This has been the best night of my life."

His expression hardens the slightest bit. "But?" he fills in for me.

I shake my head. "No. You gave me something beautiful. Thank you." Leaning up, I press my lips to his and memorize the taste of him. "But I should get back before my mother worries I have been taken captive and sends the entire palace guard after me."

He chuckles. "There it is." He takes my hand and steps back, his eyes roving over me. "I should probably fix your hair first so your mother doesn't think I've done anything too scandalous."

Matching his smile, I reach up and brush my fingers through *his* hair to try to tame the mess I made of it. "More than likely she has already come to some scandalous conclusions, but yes. That is a good idea."

"You don't think she's going to fire me for seducing a princess?"

"Would it change your mind about me if she did?"

Shaking his head, Elliot gives me a huge grin that lights up his entire face, and then he runs his fingers through my hair.

For the second time, the big, tattoo-covered soldier weaves my blonde waves into a neat crown across my head. He settles my tiara behind the braid, pinning it in place. Then he kisses me one more time before leading me back to the terrace and ending the most magical evening I have ever experienced.

Chapter Thirty-Five

ELLIOT

Turns out there's a giant upside to being a personal protection agent that I didn't consider when I first took the gig: no one questions you when you need a moment alone with your charge. With Freya stressing out about the election for the last day and a half, we have needed *many* moments alone.

I haven't let her have access to anything or anyone outside the castle in Invem, which has benefited us both. She has no way to find out what people are saying about the election or where polls are sitting, and I have an easy way to stop her from spiraling or hunting down her phone. The best part is she can't complain if she's busy kissing me.

I'm quickly learning about the many secret passages and hidden alcoves around the castle. I found a few in the month before I officially became Freya's bodyguard, but the princess knows this place inside and out and has been teaching me all sorts of things. For instance, there's a passageway from the upstairs library to the kitchen, and Freya used to stay up reading until late in the night and sneak down to steal food while she read. And there's a tapestry in the great hall with an empty space behind it; Freya used to hide in there during state dinners when she was a child so she could listen in on the discussions.

She has more of a rebellious streak than I ever thought possible, and I love it.

As for *my* stress levels, when Freya showed me some of the tunnels, I couldn't stop thinking I was living in the house where the game of Clue is set, and I've started stashing weapons around the palace. Just in case. But overall, I've been...happy. Calm.

Granted, we've been back in the capital since yesterday, and Gregor is so thorough in his job as head of security that I have yet to find any flaws in the security measures he's put in place, so there aren't a lot of reasons for me to be worried right now.

All that aside, I finally feel like I've found my place in this new life of mine. My job has its perks and is something I could be content doing for a long time, and I meant it when I said I would stand by Freya no matter what tonight's election brings. At this point, I'm almost desperately in love with her, and as long as I'm with her, I don't care about the *how*. Still, we've talked a lot over the last couple of days—in between all of the making out—and no matter how we feel about each other, a romantic relationship is going to be complicated at best.

So much of it depends on the results of tonight's election.

"So, what are your options?" Derek asks me. He's spent the last two days holed up in an office doing who knows what for work, which has been good and bad. It's given me more time alone with Freya, which in turn has kept my mind off the bombshell *Hot Scoop* still hasn't dropped, but we haven't had much of a chance to talk. Still, Derek has this way of making things seem possible, and with Freya in the other room with the rest of her friends who recently arrived, I'm glad to have someone to talk through my future with her.

I run a hand through my hair, glancing at the closed door separating us from the others. Though Carissa and Cole arrived this morning, they're currently out exploring Invem to try to beat jet-lag. I talked to Cole enough to know he still doesn't trust me, and he offered some pretty colorful threats in case I ever let Freya down. The others got here late last night and were too tired and travel-worn to really interact with anyone, so I still haven't met them. Eventually I'll get to know all of them, but we—me, Freya, and even Derek—all agreed that I should keep my distance for now. Derek still needs to tell them about how he and I are related, and Freya thinks she needs to ease her friends into the idea of her dating her bodyguard.

Basically, everything is on pause until after the election results come in.

"A few things," I say to answer Derek's question. I want to start pacing, but I keep myself planted in the chair across from the couch where Derek is sitting.

He looks way more like the celebrity he is than he did when he first got to Candora, but I don't think he's handling this *Hot Scoop* thing as well as he wants me to think. He's been avoiding his friends as much as I have, which doesn't make any sense to me. Out of anyone, he should be able to trust them with the messy parts of his life, but instead, he's out here with me.

Not that I'm complaining.

Derek sits forward, elbows on his knees and something lurking behind his eyes, like he's desperate for a problem he can fix. "Hit me with them."

I start with the simplest option. "I can live in Candora for the next five years and apply for a Residency Charter, and if that gets approved, then we could enter a probational marriage that would be legitimized in two years, assuming things go smoothly."

He frowns. "Seven years is…not ideal."

I'd wait my whole life if it meant I could support Freya in all aspects of her life. Which leads me to option two. "Alternatively, I'm not interested in power, and I don't have to put a label on things. So, if not being a king and not being her husband in legal terms is the only way I can be with her, I have no problem with that."

"I'm sensing a 'but,'" Derek says, lifting an eyebrow.

I nod. "But there's already a lot of anxiety throughout Candora when it comes to Freya being unmarried and heirless. Leaving her legally available like that could make her vulnerable to external pressure from other countries or a desperate Candoran hoping to leverage political power. Freya isn't the sort of person to submit to anyone, but…"

"But you don't like the idea of putting her in that position in the first place," Derek finishes for me, rubbing the back of his neck as he ponders. "I'm guessing there's a third option?"

Technically there are four, but as the fourth option only exists if Freya loses the election, I'm not particularly fond of it. Sure, that would simplify things, but Freya wants to be queen more than anything. She's had her doubts about what she wants for her future, but she'll be miserable if she loses. I know she will.

"The third option is appealing to Parliament to grant me special citizenship," I say with a sigh. This is the option I'm gunning for, but it has its own challenges. "The House of Lords is the harder sell. Most of the nobility is mired in tradition, and I pose a huge threat to their way of life and the status quo."

"Freya poses a threat to that too," Derek points out.

"Yeah, but they're either blind or not willing to admit that. Blaming any issues on the American brute is a lot more appealing than talking bad about your queen." They'll probably blame me anyway, but at least if they give me citizenship, I can remind them that they chose to let me in.

Derek hums thoughtfully. "What about the House of Commons?"

"I think they'll stand behind me, though I can't say that for sure. Weirdly, Grimstad seems to like me, and as Speaker of the House, he has enough influence that he'll be able to flip some votes if he needs to."

"But?"

I groan and swallow the frustration rising in my throat. "But Lords has full veto power over anything the House of Commons votes in."

"So, you either wait more than half a decade, risk bringing war or political subterfuge to Freya's reign, or you get cock-blocked by a bunch of old snobs," Derek sums up, a sympathetic grimace on his face.

Clenching my jaw, I nod and hope he has some magic solution for me. This sort of problem is what I'm supposed to be good at solving, but I don't know what to do. I hate it.

When Derek sits forward, I'm so sure he found the loophole that what he actually says falls flat on the floor between us: "Freya's going to be queen."

I blink. Narrow my eyes. Take a breath. "Yeah, that's not really new information, Riley."

He scoffs. "I'm no expert on Candoran government processes, but Freya can propose a constitutional change to better balance the power between the houses."

"Maybe, but any executive orders she makes are sent to the Houses for vote."

"But she only needs a sixty percent vote from Lords if she already has Commons behind her. Any Lord with an ounce of interest in his constituents knows it's a bad idea to go against a queen the people chose. Birthright or not, nobility still has to answer to public opinion or risk losing their seat."

I stare at him, trying to figure out how a Hollywood heartthrob can refer to the Candoran First Charter like it's common knowledge. Clearly there's a lot more to my brother than I realized.

"You think the nobility are going to vote to limit their own power?" I ask, curious to hear what he'll say.

He shrugs. "I think they've never had a monarch willing to challenge them. Like Queen Ingrid said, Candorans are inherently good people—and not many Lords will risk looking corrupt when the crown and Commons are aligned."

He might be on to something. "Historically, Commons has always sided with the people, and Lords with the crown," I murmur. "So opposing Freya would actually be breaking tradition."

Derek grins. "Exactly."

"But Freya can't make any executive orders until six months into her term."

"Six months is way better than seven years, El." He tilts his head to one side as he studies me. "I'll feel a lot better about your supposed devotion to one of my best friends once you've been together longer than a few days."

He's playing the older brother role surprisingly well given the shock we both got from the news about our shared parent. But I'm more interested in his solution than his worry about my relationship. A decent number of people would dislike the idea of a new queen changing the constitution so thoroughly, but I'm going to guess a lot of the common class would see it as a change toward modernity. As I observed during Freya's campaign tour, that's what Candora needs.

"Freya was right," I mutter as I start running through the possibilities of Derek's suggestion. What a balance of power could do to help not just our situation, but Candora as a whole.

He lifts an eyebrow. "About what?"

"You really do have a solution to everything."

As he rolls his eyes, I make my way to the door to Freya's sitting room and knock gently before stepping inside. My eyes scan the room until I find Freya on the couch between two dark-haired women, and only after she smiles at me do I pay attention to her friends.

The woman on Freya's right is Bonnie. I've seen her in a few movies, and Freya told me during one of our many recent conversations that Bonnie and Derek used to be an item, but their relationship was strictly for publicity. I don't know much about her, but Bonnie doesn't suit a guy like Derek. He needs someone pushy enough to force him to lower his mask now and then.

The woman on Freya's left is young—probably early twenties—but there's something in the way she studies me while I study her that makes me think she's not the sort of person anyone should mess with. Kasey, I think. Freya said that Kasey is an incredibly talented screenwriter and will have a movie coming out soon, so she fits right in with the actors.

Liam, a musician I'm familiar with because my old comrade Bax is a major fan, is sound asleep on the opposite couch, his feet over the arm and his head on the lap of another man who is either annoyed by the situation or amused as he writes something in a notebook. I can't actually tell because his expression is soft and muted, except when he smiles at Bonnie.

That must be Hank, Bonnie's fiancé. I owe him one for asking Freya about having kids with Grimstad because that might have been the first time she really thought about what *she* wanted instead of what was best for Candora.

Namely, having kids with *me* instead.

"Was there something you needed, Mr. Reid?" Freya asks, a knowing glint in her eyes.

I keep my expression neutral despite some of the things running through my imagination right now. "I'm sorry for the interruption, Your Highness, but you're needed for a moment in the Perseid Hall."

My made-up name for a non-existent room in the castle seems to throw her for a second, but then she smiles and rises to her feet. "I will return shortly," she tells her friends. They all look too jet-lagged to respond, and Hank is the only one who watches her move to the door.

His gaze catches on mine, and he smiles and nods. Like he's giving me permission.

I nod back, wondering how much he knows, then shut the door behind us.

Derek takes one look at the two of us and groans, rolling his eyes. "Are you both fifteen?"

"Meaning what?" I ask as I take Freya's hand, lacing our fingers together.

"You look like you're about to sneak under the bleachers during a pep rally."

Freya furrows her brow, confused, but I snort out a laugh. "No one actually goes to pep rallies, Derek. You only went to, what? Two years of high school before Hollywood found you?"

He grits his teeth, and it seems to pain him when he admits, "Year and a half." It's a miracle he turned out as normal as he did when he has spent half his life as a celebrity.

I grin. "No one's high school experience is like the movies. But..." Turning to Freya, I quickly kiss her temple before tugging her toward the door to the corridor. "I'll gladly give you a crash course on janitor closets, Princess."

"Poll results will start being reported in an hour!" Derek calls after us.

I have to let go of Freya's hand when we leave the room so we can walk at a normal, unsuspicious pace, which is unfortunate because the princess immediately starts wringing her hands. Derek deserves a punch in the jaw for reminding her about the ongoing election when she seemed to be handling her nerves before now. As we pass a few guards in search of somewhere private, I have to lock my hands behind my back to keep from touching her.

"Don't think about it," I tell her as gently as I can.

"Ha!" She runs her hands down the front of her blouse. "Do not think about the most important day of my life? Yes, that is great advice, El. I will do that."

"It's going to be okay."

"You don't know that."

Maybe not, but I know Freya. She did everything she could under the circumstances. If Grimstad had decided to run sooner, she would have had a better chance to show the people who she really is and interact with more of them, but he didn't.

Which is why I am determined to distract her.

I have no idea which room I pull Freya into, only that it isn't one we're likely to be interrupted in. The staff have been instructed to keep away from the family wing as much as possible, and Freya's family have mostly kept to themselves the last couple of days. Hex has been avoiding Agent Storme, who seems to have a score to settle with the prince, and Sander has been avoiding Hex for reasons I haven't taken the time to figure out, and the king and queen have been spending whatever time they can on their own and seem to be more than ready to hand over their roles to someone new so they can take a breath.

It's just the princess and me, alone in what I quickly realize is the royal castle equivalent of a janitor's closet.

Chuckling, I take in all the cleaning supplies. For a closet, the room is almost bigger than the bedroom I had as a kid. "What are the odds?" I mutter.

Unfortunately, Freya doesn't see the humor in the situation, her shoulders taut with anxiety as she starts pacing the space in front of me. She's going to make herself dizzy if she keeps it up, and I hate seeing her like this. "Elliot," she breathes, like a plea. "What if—"

"You have two choices right now, Rapunzel." My eyes jump to her hair like they always do when I call her that. I'm pretty sure Runa is ready to retire after the many times I've ruined her hairstyles and replaced them with one of mine over the last couple of days, and my fingers are itching to get tangled up in the intricate style she gave Freya for the press conference set to begin as soon as the election results start pouring in. The style is better than anything I can do, but there are few things I like as much as I like Freya's hair when it's loose.

Freya exhales loudly through her nose, bringing my attention back to her face and the frustration written there. Her cheeks are pink, like she knows what I was imagining, and I have to resist a smirk. "What are my choices, Mr. Reid?"

"Pulling out the big guns and calling me by my last name, huh?" I mutter, stepping toward her so quickly that she instinctively backs away. She runs into a shelf of towels, and I plant my hands on either side of her, boxing her in. "One." I say the word in a growl, loving the way she shivers at the sound. "We can talk about all the things that might happen in the next two hours." I lean in and brush my nose along her jaw. "We can talk it all through so you can brace yourself for the worst, knowing your closest friends are here to support you in whatever happens and nothing is going to change how I feel about you." I touch a kiss beneath her ear as her pulse at her neck picks up speed. "We can talk about what will happen when you become queen because that's the more likely outcome, and we can keep trying to find a way for us to be together in whatever way you want."

I'm pretty sure Derek found the solution, but it still has its risks and will require planning and consideration. I can tell Freya about it later, when she's not so worried about the much less distant future.

Freya's breath stutters in her lungs as her hands rise to my chest and set my own heart racing. "What is the second option?"

Pulling back, I give her a wicked grin. "Two, I kiss you so thoroughly that you forget all about the election."

"I like option two," she breathes and pulls my mouth down to meet hers in a hungry, desperate kiss that steals my breath.

Yeah, I like this option better too.

CHAPTER THIRTY-SIX

FREYA

Apparently, kissing a man only works as a distraction when one is actively doing it. After spending more time than we should have in the custodial supply room, during which my attention was thoroughly and sufficiently diverted, Elliot hastily put my hair in a French braid and promised to send for Runa to truly fix it before the press conference. He led me back to where my friends are waiting to walk with me into the conference room, but now that I am here and staring at the closed door separating me from some of the people I love most, I am worried I may never find the courage to step inside and then to the room beyond. The moment I join my friends is the moment I can no longer hide from reality, and all of my fears have come rushing back a hundredfold.

"Talk to me, Rapunzel." Elliot slips his hand into mine, and though I feel his gaze on me, I cannot bear to look at him.

He has been so good for me the last couple of days, and I can no longer envision a world in which he is not right beside me. But the future—our future—is so uncertain. Regardless of the election's outcome, being with him is going to be difficult. Not impossible, but it feels that way.

If Grimstad wins and takes the throne, my entire life will change. I will not need a bodyguard, and Elliot will need a new occupation. He is not the sort of person who can stand still, and neither am I, but finding somewhere we can both thrive would be a daunting task.

If I become queen, everything about our relationship becomes more complicated than ever. We can endure whatever comes, but it is difficult to think I am worth all the trouble.

I do not deserve the man beside me, but I have never been more grateful to have someone's love and support.

Turning to face Elliot, I brush my fingertips along his jaw like I have done so many times now. "I love you." The words taste sweet on my tongue and remind me of the taste of *him*.

His lips twitch in a momentary smile, but more than anything he looks relieved. At peace. *Happy*. "I love you," he repeats back to me, and then his smile grows, like he is recovering from the shock of my admission. I've implied the sentiment but haven't said those specific words before now. Tilting his head toward the door in front of us, he looks at me in a way that seems to say, *Ready for this?*

Can anyone be ready for a whole country to choose their fate?

Taking a deep breath and exhaling slowly, I nod once and reluctantly release Elliot's hand. I will tell my friends about him when all of this is over. When I know which direction our lives together are going to go.

I step through the door when Elliot opens it for me, and Derek is the first one I see. He takes one look at me and opens his arms, and I fall into his embrace like I am starved for affection. We have not had many chances to talk, but I am glad he is here. It is hard to feel like anything can go wrong when Derek Riley is around.

When any of my friends are around, really. I smile at the rest of my friends, ready to hug them all in turn and thank them for coming across the world to support me. But Cole is not here, and the group feels incomplete.

"Cole and Carissa got back to the castle later than planned, but they'll be here any minute," Derek says to me as he lets go and steps back to stand next to Elliot. He must have seen my worry, and I'm grateful he understood without me asking. "How are you feeling, Peach?"

That is when I fall apart.

As if the question knocked loose the last solid piece of the dam holding my emotions in check, it all comes flooding out in a rush of panic and hysteria. I am barely aware of anything around me as my body starts moving of its own accord, trying to escape the fear and anxiety by pacing the room. Somewhere through the chaos, Bonnie tells me everything will be okay and Liam yawns through some sort of reassurance that I neither understand nor believe. Derek is telling me to relax and breathe but I am about to combust or unravel or turn to stone. All of them at once.

"Peach!" Cole's voice breaks through the chaos, his soothing tone muting some of the wild thoughts running through my head. But only some. "You need to calm down."

"Already tried that," Derek says.

I fear no one will be able to help me.

"I'm not going anywhere near that." The amused remark a moment later comes from Elliot, and I turn to him in consternation.

He is likely doing what he can to interrupt my panic by shocking me out of it, but I do *not* appreciate his tone. "You are on thin ice, Mr. Reid," I snap at him.

But he only smiles and lifts a glass of champagne that feels like a premature celebration. Who even poured it? He probably did it for himself. *Presumptive American.* "Good thing I know how to float," he says, looking far too kissable as he smirks at me.

I groan. I do not need kisses, as much as I would enjoy them. I need something to get my mind off the fact that there is only a small corridor between me and Markham and a whole slew of reporters who are waiting to see which one of us will be giving a speech. I did not even prepare a speech. My gut told me that, were I to win, it would be because of my authenticity, and my speech should reflect that, but now I am realizing how utterly foolish that was as my friends break into soft conversation around me, likely talking about how I have lost my mind.

I need someone to give me something else to think about, and it seems Elliot is not willing to take that responsibility until his role in my life is no longer a secret. Bonnie and Kasey tried earlier, but they are too sweet and kept asking me how I was handling it all. Liam, as much as I love him, does not handle time zone changes well and looks as if he is halfway asleep again, and Hank is more of a listener than a talker. The only people who haven't given it a try are—

"Coleman!" I shout, turning to him. Cole and Carissa both jump in surprise. "I need a distraction." Fixing my gaze on Cole, I silently beg him to understand how desperately I need him right now. His old football team has had some drama lately; maybe that will be distracting enough. "Tell me about the Badgers. Someone won't let me on the internet"—I glare at Elliot, who simply chuckles and sips his champagne—"but I have heard that that sports reporter released a story about your corrupted team."

This should be good news, as the corruption is the reason Cole left football for rugby, but Cole does not look happy. He looks confused. "Did you just say '*won't*?" he asks, and some of my panic is instantly replaced with irritation. "Like, an actual contraction?"

This is not the time to discuss my shifting speech patterns. "Distraction!" Oh, but I do not want to yell at him when he is like a brother to me, so I force a breath and remind myself that I am a princess and should act like one. "Please."

I struggle to concentrate as he tells me about how there is a whole investigation starting up in the NFL revolving around illegal betting rings and game manipulation because Cole finally spoke out about why he left the sport, but he looks so relieved. And happy. I think a lot of his recent peace has come from the woman beside him, and I finally understand how Carissa changed him so much.

I would not have made it this far without Elliot.

My eyes drift his way, and he offers a small but warm smile that settles deep in my soul and soothes some of the fear inside me. He was right when he said my friends will support me no matter what happens in the next hour, because I would support my friends no matter what happened to them. Tabloids, libel, corruption, or elections cannot harm the bonds we have forged together. Nothing can separate us.

"Your Highness," Elliot says after glancing down at his phone. He meets my gaze again, his expression tight. "It's almost time."

I might be sick. "Do I have to?"

"No," Derek replies, "but I doubt the people will be very happy if you're not on camera when you find out you won the election."

"Camera!" The word squeaks out of me as awareness hits me hard. Elliot never got a chance to send for Runa, and in my panic I destroyed the haphazard braid holding my hair back. It is a wild mess around my shoulders now, and I am about to beg Elliot to fix it when Bonnie and Carissa hurry to my side and start wrangling my waves.

I keep my eyes on Elliot as they work, wishing he were the one running his fingers through my hair but grateful that my friends are here to help. *I love you*, I mouth to him.

You are perfection, he mouths back. I do not have his lip reading skills, but he makes it easy to understand his words because they are written all over his face.

I lift an eyebrow. *That was never in question.*

I can't wait to see how it feels to kiss a queen.

Whether that is actually what he said, my face heats so hot that I worry everyone will be able to read my thoughts. This man... *I can't wait to see how it feels to kiss a king*, I mouth back.

Elliot grins, but beside him, Derek groans and palms his face.

Apparently he can read lips too. What, is this a more common skill than I realized?

"It is not my fault you cannot mind your own business," I tell Derek in Candoran.

He rolls his eyes, which prompts Elliot to say, "You are the one who pushed us together," in Candoran as well, and the shapes of the sounds are more beautiful on his lips than they should be. I am impressed by how much he has picked up in the couple of months he has been here but not surprised. Elliot is a man of many talents, particularly when it comes to his tongue.

Oh, I need to keep my thoughts away from his tongue unless I wish to melt into the floor.

Glancing at the rest of our friends, who all do their best not to look interested in whatever the three of us are saying, Derek seems to think through his words carefully. As always, his Candoran is almost flawless as he says, "I knew you would be good for each other, but I never expected this."

Neither did I, Derek.

Bonnie and Carissa finish tucking a final braid around the bun at the back of my head, looking rather pleased with themselves for finally finding a way to help me. I hug them both, and then I have no more excuses to delay my entrance into the conference room.

"You can do this," I tell myself, wishing I sounded more confident; right now, I am a terrible motivator. "You..." The panic is returning, leaving me dizzy. "You can..."

Suddenly Elliot is at my side, a fiery look in his eyes. He is the only thing I can see. "If you don't go out there," he says slowly, "I will *make* you go out there. I'm not letting you miss out on your future just because you're scared." His eyes are saying so much more, but he does not give me a chance to try to interpret because he bends down and moves in, as if he is about to throw me over his shoulder like he did in Invem.

I applaud myself for only flinching a little and recognizing that he would not do something so cruel. Losing the election would be mortifying; being carried into the room over my bodyguard's shoulder would be a thousand times worse. Ignoring his tiny smirk, I stand as regal as I can. "That will not be necessary at the moment, Mr. Reid." But he may need to carry me *out* of the conference room when all this is over. I might not survive the evening.

That look is still in Elliot's eyes, and I know now what he is trying to tell me. *No matter what, I go where you go.*

My shoulders relax.

Everything will be okay.

CHAPTER THIRTY-SEVEN

FREYA

Everyone in the room stands when I enter. It is something I am used to, particularly when it comes to the press, but as I stride across the room, I feel out of place. Not because I chose to forgo a tiara today or because my hair is not as polished as it usually is when I face the world.

But seeing a room full of people bowing to me as if I am better than them makes it very clear that I do not deserve the life I was given. I feel entirely inadequate.

My parents, adorned in crowns, sit at the front of the room, proud and confident and so sure of their place in life. I always thought I was just like them, but after the last few weeks, I am not certain of anything when it comes to who I am and where I should be. Now I understand why my brothers have always seemed to float through life, though they are good at looking as regal as our parents as they stand behind Mum and Dad.

Markham is in the middle of a formal bow when I reach the podium where the winner will give his or her speech, and I gently touch his uninjured arm. "Please," I beg him, shaking my head when he looks up at me in confusion. "Of all people, you should never bow to anyone."

As my friends find seats on the front row, Elliot takes his place behind me on the stage, his expression as stoic as it was the first time I met him. But he cannot hide the pride from his eyes as he slowly scans the room. I feel his approval down to my toes.

Markham stands up straight. We have not spoken since the ball, and I wonder what he is thinking as he studies me. I have never been able to read him well, but at the moment I can hardly put a word to anything in his expression. "Your Highness."

"Please," I say again. "No matter the result tonight, you and I are still friends."

"Yes," he agrees, finally allowing a small smile. He offers me a handshake, and when I take it without hesitation, soft whispers start up among the press.

The reporters' impatience buzzes through the room; most of them have likely been watching the results on their phones as they come in. But per my instructions, there is nothing in the room that indicates how the election might turn out. Markham and I will know nothing until the final counts are in and the Candoran press secretary enters the room to announce who will be taking the throne.

Elliot's instructions were to keep me away from this conference room until only moments before the announcement is to be made, and Elliot does not have the capability of going against his word any more than I do.

As I move to stand next to my parents to wait for Secretary Ashlund to appear, a soft word from Markham pulls me to a stop again. "Freya?"

"Yes?"

His eyebrows pull low, his jaw tight, and I wonder if he regrets speaking my name when it takes him a long time to say anything. "I, er, I'm sorry. For running against you. I didn't think you understood what our people needed, and I thought this was the best way to help. You'll make a great queen."

Oh. Two weeks ago, I would have loved to hear him admit that, but now? "Markham, you do not need to apologize for anything you have done. Whichever of us wins, I—"

"I withdrew my candidacy yesterday."

Those words, spoken so quietly that no one in the audience would have heard him, feel like a slap to the face. "Withdrew?" I whisper. "What do you mean?"

"I took my name off the ballot."

"What?"

Markham shakes his head, looking for all the world like he has made irreparable mistakes in his life but is doing his best to fix them anyway. "You were always the better choice, Freya. If I had made the time to get to know you sooner, I would have seen that long before I ever got this far. I can still make an impact in Commons."

But... My mind is spinning again, but the thoughts whirling through it now are different from anything before this moment. If he is telling the truth—and I think he is—that means I have already won. Unless the unheard of happens and at least eighty-five percent of the people voted against my reign in favor of a complete revision of the government, I will be queen.

But I will not have been chosen.

"I won by default?" I ask, unable to hide the horror in my words. This would not have bothered me a month ago, but how can I be content knowing my people lost their chance to choose? The freedom to choose was one of the main reasons I couldn't bring myself to marry Markham.

That, and my love for the man standing behind me.

Markham's eyes are full of pity and apology and a good deal of confusion, but he seems to have lost his words as he stares at me. Out of the corner of my eye, I can see my mother and father frowning in my direction, likely wondering why I look like I have been given the most terrible news. Hex and Sander are in conversation with each other, their postures tense but their expressions thoughtful, and they must have gleaned enough from watching us to know what has happened.

Elliot steps forward so he's close enough to speak to me but not so close that anyone will think he is stepping beyond the bounds of his position. I wish he would come closer, but I know why he cannot. "Actually, you didn't," he says carefully. When I meet his gaze, he lifts his eyebrows slightly. "Markham's name was on the ballot, just like yours."

Markham shakes his head, looking as confused as I feel. "No, I definitely removed it."

"Okay, yes, you did. But I put it back on."

"That's not possible. How did you know I even—"

"Frankly, I still don't trust you." But Elliot smirks in a way that belies his words. "I wondered if you would do something like this, so I had one of the palace guards keep an eye on you."

Markham frowns. "But you have no authority to change the ballot."

"You're right." Elliot shrugs. "The queen put your name back, at my suggestion."

"Why?"

It was Markham who asked the question, but Elliot looks at me when he says, "Because the people deserve to choose."

In the first sign of aggression I have ever seen from him, Markham growls and looks like he is considering throwing his fist into Elliot's nose. "I don't want to be king, American."

Elliot does not waver. "You won't be, Grim."

"How can you be sure?" I whisper.

The look he gives me feels like a hug, so full of warmth and support that his thoughts are tangible between us. "Because you are the best person for Candora, and your people know that. Trust me."

I trust this man more than I trust anyone, especially myself, but he cannot know what is going to happen. As much as I want to be the queen the people choose, I would rather automatically take the position than leave my country scrambling to adapt. What if Markham wins the vote but declines? I do not know what would happen, whether I would be given the crown as the next best choice or if we would fall into a state of disorder that I have worked so hard to avoid.

"Elliot," I hiss, "why would you—"

The back door opens, and the whole room turns to watch Secretary Ashlund step into the room, a locked tablet in his hand.

I grab Elliot's hand just before my body freezes up and leaves me unable to move.

Ashlund climbs the stairs onto the stage, pausing at the top and taking in the scene before him. Me, holding my bodyguard's hand for dear life. Markham, holding his injured arm with a green tint to his skin. My mum, hands clasped together and pressed to her mouth.

Ashlund is a quiet man in his late forties who keeps to himself until he's in front of a camera. At that point, he flips on a switch and becomes confident and well-spoken and able to answer any question thrown at him. But what he sees tonight seems to knock him off balance, and his first step forward falters until he remembers himself and stands tall at the podium.

"Good evening," he says into the microphone as the cameras flash.

Elliot squeezes my hand, then tugs his fingers free and steps back to his place.

I still feel like my body has turned to ice, but I manage to shift and stand at Markham's side, facing the press.

"On behalf of Her Majesty, Queen Ingrid," Ashlund says, "I wish to thank the citizens of Candora for their participation in this unprecedented election and the continued upholding of the democracy of our nation. As you are all aware, we are here to announce the next Candoran Monarch to succeed Queen Ingrid Alverra, who has chosen to step down from her rule. Her Majesty recorded her Abdication Address in private this morning and therefore will not be speaking to us tonight, but the address will be available online and broadcast tomorrow at noon."

She did? I glance at my mother, whose eyes are on her lap now as she softly cries. I knew it would be difficult for her to step down, but I wonder if this transition will be harder than I realized. Particularly if she gave her speech in private, when she has never been one to shy away from the public. Perhaps, like with my brothers, I have a lot to learn about my mother as well.

"As of six o'clock on the evening of September twenty-first in the three hundred and forty-seventh year of Candora, all votes have been counted and verified." My head starts buzzing. "I would like to remind the people of Candora that should they feel an appeal is necessary contrary to the results of this election, they must file their complaint with their local leadership no later than September twenty-fourth at nine a.m." Oh, I had forgotten about the appeals. "I also remind the press that any information published that goes against the election result ruling as set forth by the combined House of Lords and House of Commons election committees is considered in contempt of the law and will be punished according to the law set forth in the Candoran First Charter and Constitution."

Will he not get to the point? I make eye contact with my friends, finding strength and comfort in their support. Liam gives me two thumbs up and a cheesy grin that coaxes a laugh out of me, and Cole exaggerates taking a breath, silently urging me to do the same. Derek smiles his ever-confident smile, telling me he will always be there for his friends.

I will be okay. No matter what happens.

"After a thorough and secure counting process, I am honored to officially announce that Freya Isolde Marit Alverra has won the ninth Candoran royal election with seventy-four percent of the vote, securing more than 400,000 votes."

Ashlund keeps talking, going off about The Crown's dedication to stability and prosperity and when the coronation will take place barring an appeals process, but I barely hear him.

I won.

I am going to be queen.

Every ounce of my energy is being used to hold myself together. I want to laugh, cry, sink into a heap on the floor and stay there for days because *I won*. I can hardly believe it.

But I am not imagining things because Liam and Carissa both jump up and start cheering before Hank and Kasey drag them back into their seats. Cole and Bonnie are smiling and crying at once and have never looked prouder. Derek's expression is muted compared to the others, but I don't think he is hiding anything. He is simply happy. Maybe a bit relieved.

My brothers have reined in their enthusiasm and are grinning in their place behind our parents, but I am certain they will be climbing through the secret passage to my bedroom tonight to celebrate with me. Catching their eyes, I try to convey my gratitude for their support, especially during the last few weeks, but I can only look at them so long before tears spring to my eyes.

Dad and Mum are in each other's arms. She is sobbing, and I hope they are happy tears, but they likely have a bittersweet edge. Dad is smiling at me as he pats Mum's arm, and while he has never enjoyed politics, he is proud of the choices I have made to get here.

And Elliot...

I'm afraid to turn to look at him, but I don't have to. I can feel his love, even from feet away, and if I close my eyes, I can imagine his arms around me as he speaks soft words of approval in my ear. *He knew.* He knew I would win, and he knew that I would never fully believe I was right for the position if it was given to me by default. I refuse to think what might have happened had he not been brought into my life when he was.

All of this is because of him.

I love you, I say in my head, hoping he can somehow hear me.

I love you.

I love you.

I can almost swear I hear him saying it right back.

EPILOGUE

ELLIOT

Eight months later

"You know I like you, Rothesby, but I think we've reached a point where I have to draw the line." I take a deep breath, baffled by the words about to come out of my mouth. "No, I don't need you to come into the stall with me."

Rothesby gapes at me. "But sir—"

"No." I hold up a hand. It was already weird that he followed me into the bathroom; joining me in the stall is too much.

Now I get why Freya was so annoyed with me my first week on the job, and I would go and apologize to her right now if I didn't think she would lord that over me for the rest of our lives. I never followed her into the bathroom, but I didn't give her any privacy beyond that.

Rothesby has made himself one of my favorites from the palace guards, but he's really starting to get on my nerves today.

"Here's what we're going to do," I say, folding my arms and giving the guy my most intimidating stare-down. "I'll let you check the stalls and make sure there's no one in here with us." There isn't. I've been watching the bathroom door all morning, keeping track of who has been in and out for the last two hours, and the place has been empty for the last fifteen minutes. "Then you're going to go *out* into the hall and keep guard outside until I'm done. Okay?"

He grimaces, hands curling into fists. "Sir, I really don't think—"

"Come on, man. Work with me here."

The thing is, I don't even need to go. I just need a chance to breathe. A single moment to myself.

It's depressing that the only place I could think to find some peace was in a bathroom.

Glancing at the door behind him, Rothesby seems to debate his options. He could stand his ground, which he usually does and is one of the reasons I like him, or he could give me this one compromise. He sighs, and then he stomps to the nearest stall and shoves the door open, hints of petulance in each of his actions.

Maybe I shouldn't have picked a guy so much like me to be my bodyguard.

Once he's checked all three stalls twice over and searched every corner of the facility for anything nefarious, Rothesby reluctantly heads out into the hall, warning me that he will come back in fifteen minutes if I'm not done by then.

He must have a lot of fiber in his diet if he thinks that's enough time for some people.

Now that I'm finally alone, I can breathe a bit easier, but I don't think anything is going to get rid of the knot in my chest that has been slowly but steadily growing for the last eight months. It's a constant reminder that I'm nowhere near good enough to be in the position that I'm in, and one of these days someone is going to figure that out and do something about it.

I can take care of myself—Rothesby would likely disagree—but I could never live with myself if someone else was put in danger because I made a mistake. I can't go through another Griff situation.

After using the toilet—I guess I did have to go—I splash my face with cold water and study my reflection. I look exhausted, but that's understandable given how chaotic the last twenty-four hours have been. I also look like I've aged a decade in the last half a year, and I can't fathom how Derek manages to keep his glowy, youthful look when he's under almost as much pressure as I am.

My perfect older brother is a pain in the neck sometimes, but I'm glad to have him in my life.

I've lost track of the number of times I've forgotten about the time difference and called Derek in the middle of the night, desperate for him to talk me off the ledge when I'm convinced I've made a huge mistake by going down the path I have. He always answers, and he always has some magical solution to anything I'm facing. I don't know how he does it.

Especially because there's something he's not telling me. I don't know what it is, but it's slowly eating at him to the point where I've been genuinely worried about him. Eventually he's going to crack if he doesn't let someone else help him with it. So far, he refuses to admit anything's wrong, no matter how hard I push, which is pretty par for the course with him. But I hate that I can't get past his shields.

If I can't even help my brother, how am I supposed to help an entire country?

My watch buzzes, and I tug my sleeve up to look at the message even though I won't be able to respond because Rothesby has my phone. The curse of not having any pockets at the moment.

Bax:

> So now that Reid is a motherfreaking king, does that mean we get diplomatic immunity in Candora?

I chuckle, bracing for the texts that will follow. Wherever my old ODA is right now, they must have either just woken up or not had internet access until now. I've been a king for a whole three hours now.

Wade:

> Are you planning on needing immunity, Bax?

Schulz:

> Will anyone be surprised if he does?

North:

> Seriously, Reid, you have to tell me your secret! King of a whole country!

Doyle:

> I'm still trying to figure out how he convinced a princess to even give him the time of day.

Roche:

> Just because you can't get a girl to talk to you doesn't mean the rest of us ever had a problem.

Voss:

> Are you forgetting that Reid never went out with us? Who knew he even had game?

Berg:

> Yeah, I thought he was nothing but business and hogging the coffee.

Bax:

> Still bitter that you didn't come back to the team, Reid.

I silence my watch before any more messages come in, suddenly feeling better. I'm still going to panic every time I remember the shiny crown sitting on my head—this thing is ostentatious to the max—but I have to remember that I'm human. Like any king or queen that has come before me, I'm never going to be perfect.

Sounds like my old brothers-in-arms won't be afraid to remind me of that.

There's a soft knock on the door, and I groan. "Rothesby, there's no way that was fifteen minutes."

But when the door opens, the face on the other side makes all of my frustration and nerves disappear in the space of a breath. "Are you hiding?" Freya asks, slipping inside the bathroom and looking around as she approaches.

Her dress swishes around her, sparkling in the overbright lights. The gown is monstrous and frankly ridiculous, but the shimmery gold of the fabric complements my navy-blue doublet and gold-adorned cape. We look like we stepped out of a painting from the eighteenth century, and I vowed early this morning that I will never wear knee-high boots again after today. But I also get to wear a sword at my hip with no one questioning me, so the outfit's not a total wash.

The instant this coronation party is over, I'm dumping all of this nonsense—it's overkill of the worst kind—but I'll never forget the way Freya looked at me this morning when she first saw me in my royal clothes. It was the kind of look that made me suggest skipping the coronation and staying in bed together instead.

Granted, I've suggested that alternative every morning since our wedding last week, so she's come to expect it. We won't get a proper honeymoon for another two weeks, but at least we were able to spend the last week on our own in Stonemere.

"Hiding?" I repeat, moving forward until my legs push into the vast expanse of her dress. I press a hand to her waist and pull her in close. "A royal never cowers."

"Did Hex tell you that? Because I caught him hiding behind a statue this morning when he thought Astrid was with me, so he has no room to talk."

Laughing, I press a kiss to her forehead and linger there, trying to soak up some of her strength. I'm grateful for a topic of conversation that doesn't involve my newly crowned status. "He's still avoiding her?"

She snickers. "Like a sailor dodging sirens."

"I'm still convinced Astrid only agreed to be your temporary bodyguard because it gives her easy access to your brother."

Agent Storme—Astrid—was heading up the investigation into anti-royalists until a month ago when Parliament voted to grant me special citizenship. While I don't love knowing she isn't at the forefront of that task force anymore, given the amount of evidence she and her team have been digging up about a whole underground ring of potential threats, I'm glad someone competent is looking after my new wife.

Wife. I love that word.

Freya sighs, tucking herself into my chest and relaxing in my hold. "I only wish she would stay. I like her."

I chuckle and take hold of her hand, lacing our fingers together against my chest. "But you also like half a dozen of the new guard recruits, and some of them show a lot of promise."

"Yes, because they are women."

Her matter-of-fact tone makes me laugh again, and I am so glad that she came to find me. I wasn't hiding from her, but she is almost always surrounded by nobility at these events, and now that I'm both her husband and king, I was surrounded too. Freya's a lot better at faking civility with guys like the Duke of Rensvik than I am.

I would have much rather been on the other side of the room, where Hex and Sander were chatting and laughing with members of the House of Commons. That group is way less pretentious and the reason I can stand here with my wife in the first place.

Freya's first executive act after reaching the six-month threshold of sitting on the throne was allowing women to join the palace guard, much to the delight of many female Candorans (and many of the current guards).

Her second proposal went toward fixing centuries of imbalance: introducing a Prime Minister, elected solely from the House of Commons, to oversee both Houses and work directly with the crown. Along with this reform, she proposed that the two Houses have equal voting weight. Any stalemates would be broken by the Prime Minister's vote, while ultimate authority rested with the reigning monarch, who retained two votes.

I'm still not sure how she convinced the House of Lords to pass that one, but as of two weeks ago, Markham Grimstad is the new Prime Minister and bound to thrive in his new role, and Freya has a better chance of passing any reforms she thinks will benefit the people on both sides. Candora is changing.

Changing for the better.

I can't wait to see what Freya does next.

"Will you tell me why you were hiding?" Freya asks, pulling her fingers free of mine so she can tickle her fingertips across my palm.

A shiver runs through me, a rush of desire that I try to ignore. "Can I say it's because your mom has been giving me tips for being royalty all morning?"

"You can say it, but it doesn't make it true."

I hum and lock my fingers between hers again before she distracts me too much. She's right; I love how much Ingrid is trying to help me figure out this new role after she all but convinced Freya to choose me. "Maybe I'm tired of Lady Falkheim poking me in the eye with that horrific feather in her hat."

Freya snorts out a laugh. "The vulture feather? It is atrocious! But no, I do not accept that excuse."

"I want to keep you all to myself." That one's true, but it won't hold up as an excuse. I just want to say it.

She leans back, standing straight again as she narrows her eyes at me. "Elliot Reid Alverra, tell me why you are nervous, or I will go back out there and let Rensvik know that you are eager to work with him directly on all projects going forward."

"Vitte, Rapunzel, you don't play." I wrinkle my nose, knowing if I don't come clean, she'll follow through with her threat. I don't plan on getting too deep into the politics too soon, but Rensvik would hold me to Freya's promise, no matter how long I wait to jump in. It's not worth the risk. "Fine. I'm terrified."

Freya tilts her head. "Of what?"

"Of messing up." I brush my thumb across her jaw, marveling at her natural beauty. "Of doing something to hurt Candora. Of not being the man you need me to be."

"Elliot." Smiling softly, she presses her hand to my cheek.

This isn't a new conversation, so I know what she'll say. She'll tell me that everyone is allowed to make mistakes as long as they own up to them and rectify them the best they can. She'll tell me that she loves me no matter how many imperfections. She'll tell me that I have time to learn.

She doesn't tell me any of those things. "You think too highly of yourself."

I blink. "What?"

With a shrug, she steps out of my hold and starts wandering the bathroom like it's an art gallery, even though there's not much to see. It's a *bathroom*. Sure, it's a bathroom inside the biggest cathedral in Invem, but that doesn't make it a marvel. "Exactly as I told you," she says with an air of casualness. "You think too highly of yourself."

"I think you're missing the point here, Rapunzel. I'm having the opposite problem."

"No." She turns to me, head held high, shoulders back, eyes focused and intense. "You think you are so powerful and influential that anything you do can affect an entire country."

"I..." I stop. Frown. "No, that's not..."

She lifts her eyebrows. "Tell me I am wrong."

"I don't..." I exhale all at once. It's not quite a laugh, but it's not a scoff either. I don't know what I'm feeling, but confusion is a big part of it. More than anything, she's right. "Wow."

Grinning now, Freya comes close and wraps her arms around my shoulders. "My husband, you are an incredible man with a brilliant mind and a good heart. But no one, not even me, is capable of failure of such magnitude that it cannot be fixed. As long as you are doing your best, you have so many allies to hold you up when you inevitably fail."

"This is one of the many reasons I love you," I mutter, pressing my forehead to hers as her words settle over me. She's right, like she always is. "You don't regret marrying a kid from Montana?"

She shakes her head. "Never."

"And you don't think the people will stage a coup now that there's a weak link on the throne?"

"We are not a chain, Elliot. We are our own selves, united and bound by love and loyalty. Besides, I'm the true royal here. You mostly exist as decoration." She rises up on her toes, her lips brushing mine.

I snicker and lean back. "I love you, but I am not kissing you in the men's toilet, Rapunzel. Especially after you just called me a decoration."

"Suit yourself." She turns to leave.

"Wait!" Grabbing her by the waist, I tug her against my body and capture her mouth, smiling when I taste champagne on her tongue. She only drinks when she's nervous, and I'm glad to see it's not just me.

She's all talk, this one.

But I love how she accepts her shortcomings and is always willing to face her fears and stand for what she thinks is right. She's going to do great things, and I am so lucky that I get to be at her side when she does. Neither of us knows what the next few decades will bring and where our lives might take us, but I know one thing for sure.

Wherever she goes, I go. To the end.

Not ready to say goodbye to Freya and Elliot? Get a free bonus epilogue at **https://BookHip.com/SFTLWBT**, or scan the code below!

Simple Love Stories (Sweet Love Stories)
Simplicity
Growing Young
Bittersweet Brews
In Front of Me
As Long as You Love Me
Dear Dalia
Let Go

Terms of Inheritance (Sweet Romance)
Forever You and Me
Holding On to Everything
A World without You
Love, Strictly Speaking

Historical Romances
The Thief and the Noble
A Twist of Christmas (part of The Holly and the Ivy anthology)
What Dreams May Come
This above All
Never Doubt I Love

ABOUT THE AUTHOR

Dana LeCheminant writes sweet romantic comedies, heartwarming contemporary love stories, and swoony historical romances—with a twist. Known for putting a fresh spin on beloved tropes, she lets her characters lead the way, believing they always know their stories best. Her books are full of banter, emotion, and connection—all of the swoon without any spice. When she's not dreaming up her next twisty trope or emotional arc, she's hiking the remote Utah backcountry or cruising down rivers in search of new inspiration. Dana has been telling stories since before she could spell and has no plans to stop anytime soon.

Dana loves connecting with her readers!
You can find her on social media (**@authordanalecheminant**) and on her website, **lecheminantbooks.com**.